In the Land of Porcelain

In the Land of Porcelain

a novel of City Buddha-Mind walking,
love,
and breaking free

by

Karen Lynn Allen

Cabbages and Kings Press

San Francisco, CA

A different version of this novel was previously published as Pearl City
Control Theory.

Published by:
Cabbages and Kings Press
San Francisco, California

ISBN 978-0-9671784-4-8 (print)
ISBN 978-0-9671784-5-5 (ebook)
Libary of Congress Control Number: 2023919950

www.karenlynnallenbooks.com

*Note: This is a work of fiction. Names, characters, and incidents are the
product of the author's imagination or are used fictitiously. Any resemblance
of the characters to actual persons, living or dead, is entirely coincidental.*

Cover art: Figurine of dancer Loie Fuller (1862 - 1928), by porcelain
designer Karl Theodor Eicher (1868-1946)

For Peter, Spencer,
Veronica, and Abigail

And for all the courageous women,
past and present,
who made and who make
the Domestic Violence
Intervention Program in Iowa City
possible.

Chapter One

I started walking, what I call City Buddha-Mind walking, the summer before Mark left for Georgetown. The day Mark left I woke up early, his arm heavy across me. I rolled out from under it, threw on some clothes, and slipped outside into the fragile San Francisco dawn.

City Buddha-Mind walking always took a few blocks to get going, to drop into the rhythm, to absorb the mood of the light and weather. Stepping out the door, I'd plan my course, visualize the terrain, and then head towards a good-sized hill to get my blood moving. Somewhere near the top I would find my pace for the day; I'd hit my stride. And then I could think. Or even better, not think. Just perceive

San Francisco has amazing light. Mark said he never thought my love affair with the city would last so long: for someone who prided herself in being practical and logical, couldn't I see that a city was just concrete and asphalt and throngs of people hassled from living so close together? But on a clear day the sunlight in San Francisco dazzles, etching color and form with a clarity so keen it stings the retina. Then, as afternoon darkens to evening, clouds roll in and tuck the city in under an opalescent blanket of pearl. For better or worse, I knew I belonged on this troubled tip of peninsula and nowhere else.

That summer before Mark left, our impending separation circled our heads like a buzzard. In August it descended with a swoop and found me on the crest of Liberty Street hugging my arms against the morning chill. The air was misty, the sky a lilac rose, the porcelain city spread in front of me. He's really going, I told myself. With a sharp plunge the process of flesh eating and bone pecking had begun.

"Come here," Mark said to me from rumpled sheets when I slipped back into our bedroom.

Mark had dark brown hair that curled in waves, broad shoulders, a defined jaw. The kind of guy that looks good even unshaven and half awake. He stretched out a hand to me and I went. After all, it would be a while before we had the chance again.

"Thank you for your patience, ladies and gentlemen. We will begin boarding Flight 642 to Washington in a few moments. Please remain seated until . . ."

Everyone in the crowded waiting area sprang to their feet clutching boarding passes like lottery tickets. Mark and I stayed where we were.

"So this is it," I said. "You're going 3000 miles away."

"Only for a while," Mark answered, trying to reassure me. But the fact was, he was excited. Eager. His whole future lay ahead of him. And me? Well, my future lay ahead of me too.

"Ladies and gentlemen, we will board by row. Please remain seated until . . ."

A queue half a block long coiled through the waiting area.

Mark and I weren't naive about what lay ahead. We recognized living apart would be difficult, even inconvenient, but Mark would study industriously, I would concentrate on my career, and we would crisscross the skies to see each other almost every month. Three years of law school would pass by in a flash. BCDR, my sister, Amanda, called it. Bi-coastal, dual rental. All sorts of couples were doing it these days.

"You could still come with me," Mark suggested. "You'd find a job in a week."

I'd just been promoted; I didn't want to move. "You could still go to law school here," I mumbled back.

"Airports are crummy places to say good-bye."

I handed Mark a copy of *One Hundred Years of Solitude* to read on the plane.

"Ladies and gentlemen, please. Only rows 36 through 42 should . . ."

Passengers trickled by like water through a clogged drain. Mark put his arms around me; I kept mine folded against the front of his chest. "Don't look so sad, Sara. It'll be okay. You'll see."

But I didn't see. I looked down at the ring on my left hand and idly circled it around my finger with my thumb. Was I crazy to be taking this kind of risk? There's no risk, I told myself.

"You'll wear a groove in your finger if you keep twisting your ring like that."

I leaned my head in, he leaned his against mine, and we stood, foreheads touching and silent amid the hubbub.

Amanda grandly tells our relatives she lives in San Francisco for its ambiance. Whenever I climb to the top of Liberty Street, the city at my feet, I always feel exhilarated, as if I've arrived at an apex of the world. With my pulse pounding from exertion, I gaze and gaze at the view, and as I do, I feel my heart crack and expand, just a little, like it does whenever I see someone I love from a distance.

"Last call for flight 642. I repeat, last . . ."

Mark and I stood close in the now deserted waiting area. "Time to go," he said.

I stretched out my hand in the gesture of an offer. "I love you."

Mark took my hand, told me he loved me too, and then inexorable forces of the universe sucked him away, yanking our orbits loose from each other.

So this is it, I thought despondently.

Mark walked jauntily down the ramp like an explorer off to jungles of deepest green.

Thinking back on that summer, I recognize I started walking to practice being without Mark. I'd go out for only an hour, take in a few hills, look over the city, and tell myself Washington was flat, really flat. I convinced myself interesting topography was essential to my sanity. Maybe it was. I'd return to find Mark reading the newspaper on the couch beneath his favorite poster of John Reed shaking hands with Emma Goldman. I'd tell myself I was lucky to be loved by someone so attractive, so intelligent, so passionate about justice and fairness. Then I'd say something like, "Why did we get married if we can't even agree on where to live?"

"Sara, Sara, Sara," he'd say and read on just a little further which always irritated me. I was important enough to stop mid-sentence for. Then Mark would sigh, put the paper down, and I'd forlornly curl up next to him on the couch.

No doubt it was easier in the past when the wife followed her husband wherever he went, or waited at home, no questions asked, but I knew compliance of that sort would be more unacceptable than my insecurity. Over the millennium of time, men have gone hunting, gone exploring, gone to war. At least graduate school was a relatively safe activity. Clearly Mark was going on a journey he needed. It took me much longer to realize I'd set off on a journey of my own.

Journeys. Everyone, including Mark, thought I stayed behind for my job, but it wasn't just for that. It was for San Francisco and independence and self-definition and topography, though I will say, getting promoted at the tender age of twenty-seven had taken me four years of determined effort, and just when I got it, boom, Mark wanted to move. I worked for a corporation called Appleton-Smith. Perhaps you've heard of it. They make everything under the sun, from laundry soap to snack crackers. My promotion had made me the manager of a group of people whose reason for being was to manufacture hand cream. Very large quantities of it. We made high quality, department store kind of stuff in nice containers with fancy labels. Scented, sometimes unscented, with glycerin or vitamin E or aloe added in, depending on what would sell. We didn't decide what sold, marketing and sales did. They said make it, we made it. My job was to get the materials, people, and machinery together as efficiently and inexpensively as possible while meeting quality standards. I had a business degree, but this job took the patience of a playground supervisor and the shrewdness of Talleyrand during the Reign of Terror. Some knowledge of logistics, machine maintenance, budgeting, and concise memo writing also came in handy. Really, the most important prerequisite for business is common sense, but as Voltaire said in an age with its own kinds of CEOs, padded expense accounts, and strained labor-management relations, common sense is not so common.

And so Mark left and I was miserable, but I did what I had to do and coped. Mark, in contrast, was immediately delighted with the challenges of law school. He joined an environmental student group, and his conversation began to narrow to events in Washington. I told him I was glad for him, and truly, I was. If Mark doesn't have a cause to immerse himself in, he's lost. During those first long weeks of September, I focused on my job; in the evenings, I plowed through novels like a caffeine junkie knocks back lattes. It was a simple existence, little to look forward to or regret, and I accepted that this was the price I had to pay for staying in San Francisco. There was, however, a minor factor that I didn't count on, one small principle of the universe that would eventually rip the pickets off my fenced-in life. Nature (as anyone in first-year physics will tell you) always abhors a vacuum.

One morning a month after Mark left, I was doing the usual: settling down into the turbulence of a bumpy Monday at work. Glancing at my watch, I was startled to see it was only ten o'clock. Already I'd returned six phone calls, dealt with a late glycerin truck, and consoled an employee sobbing in my office because his wife had left him over the weekend. Now I gazed out my large office window that looked onto the factory floor and listened to the muffled clatter of machinery seeping through the glass. On a good day the din roared like the ocean; today it sputtered like a dyspeptic lawn mower. I closed my eyes and wondered for the five hundredth time why I hadn't moved to Washington with Mark.

My eyes opened with a start. A man in an expensive charcoal gray suit stood quietly in my office doorway watching me.

"Are you Sara Whitfield?" he asked. "I believe I have an appointment to meet with you."

I quickly rose to my feet. "Yes, I'm Sara." Paul, my boss, had mentioned in passing we'd have a consultant coming this week from Merrisocks Gospout, a prestige consulting firm in the city. Foolish me, I'd assumed I'd be given pertinent details, like when and why, in due time.

"I'm Aaron Lambert," the consultant said, shaking my hand. As I hesitated, not sure whether to bluff or confess ignorance, Aaron calmly snapped opened his briefcase. "Accounting and purchasing procedures. That's why I'm here. Don't worry you're the third person I've met with this morning and the other two didn't know either." I winced. I hated for Appleton-Smith to look so disorganized to an outsider. What must he think of us? "Your company appears to like surprises," he commented dryly. "It must make this a festive place to work."

Not highly, that's what he thinks of us. Wonderful, I thought. Not only do I get a mystery consultant in my office before my second cup of coffee, I get an annoyed one. "Sorry. I wish I were more prepared. How can I help you?"

"Appleton-Smith's last audit showed problems with employees following purchasing procedures. What you and I need to do is go over your department records from the last year and trace a few equipment purchases."

I stifled a groan. No wonder Paul hadn't given me more warning —I would've been tempted to call in sick. Many people in my department purchased many things; I now hoped it'd all been done according to the snarled web of procedures our purchasing department loved to create. I looked at him, this consultant. In his thirties, black hair, intelligent eyes that probably didn't miss much, not as tall as Mark, maybe five ten. His gray suit was more than expensive, it was elegant, and he wore a subdued, but absolutely beautiful violet-blue silk tie. He looked used to higher stakes assignments: I wondered what he was doing auditing us. As Aaron settled back into his chair, he made a few notes and began to look less annoyed. I, on the other hand, began to feel as if the Spanish Inquisition had descended on me to extract a confession of guilt.

Aaron glanced up. "You look like I'm here to pull your teeth. Cheer up. This may be dull, but it won't be that bad."

Well, dullness I could take. After all, lately it'd been my constant companion. I had to dig out reams of computer reports, and then Aaron and I sat across from each other as we sorted through them.

"Are you an expert on accounting and purchasing procedures?" I asked.

"Not in the least," Aaron answered affably enough.

"Why did they bring you in then?"

"I think my main qualification is that I don't work for Appleton-Smith, which in theory makes me an unbiased observer."

"Oh," I said. "Are you?"

"Unbiased?" He sounded amused. "Enough for something this routine. Do you have a printout of orders from June and July?"

I flipped through a large stack to find it.

"How long have you worked for Appleton-Smith?" Aaron asked as he jotted down an account code.

"Four years."

"You're married?" he said conversationally.

I glanced at a picture of Mark propped in a frame on my desk and then at Aaron's left hand. No ring. "Yes. Are you?"

"No. Do you and your husband live on the Peninsula?"

"We live in the city, or at least I do. My husband's in Washington DC, going to law school."

Aaron pulled a calculator out of his briefcase. "A long-distance marriage. That must be challenging."

"I'm surviving. Whenever I'm bored, I just browse through old purchasing records and the hours fly by."

The corners of Aaron's mouth tugged into a smile. "A scintillating hobby. Is purchase order 45901 on your sheet?"

Scintillating, indeed. More like mind-numbing and coma-inducing. But he had a sense of humor, an encouraging sign. A friendly auditor is always preferable to a grumpy one.

"Three's too many," an angry voice boomed from out of the blue.

I looked up with dismay. "Joe—"

"One. Tell her we're doing one."

"Excuse me," I said to Aaron before hustling Joe, the production supervisor, out of my office and into the hall. I knew what he was upset about. "Joe, Althea wouldn't have scheduled the changeovers if they weren't necessary, you know that. She needs them to lower our inventories."

Joe was a Korean War veteran twice my age who'd run the mechanical side of the department for years. He tended to bark out orders like a Marine and wore a bristly crew cut so short I wasn't quite sure what color his hair was. He leaned forward now, pointing a stubby finger at my face. I steeled myself for the onslaught.

"What do they do in college these days—everyone sit around thinking how to screw up my packing lines? Changing over this much is like cutting off our legs when we're trying to run. I don't give a flying frog's hiney about inventories. I refuse, do you hear me? Refuse." With that he folded his thick arms over his barrel chest. Though Joe and I were roughly the same height, he had a good sixty pounds on me, and from time to time I'd seen him arm-wrestle some of the guys in the break room. Given the chance, he would've snapped my arm to the table like a straw.

I didn't like being yelled at, but I needed his cooperation, and he knew it. "Inventories cost money, Joe. It's money tied up that you can't do anything else with. Most other companies have been working to lower inventories for years."

"Things didn't used to be this way. We used to run one scent of hand cream for two weeks straight, and the lines ran smooth as silk."

"Joe, it's 1992, not 1962. You used to only have two scents and one size of tube. Now we've got bottles, tubes, and eight scents."

"Not doing it," he said, pointing again. "Not three. Make that woman understand."

"Maybe you could talk with Althea yourself. She could show you how she—"

"You talk with her. And tell her she gets one. No more."

I took a deep breath. I didn't want to do this, but I had to. "Let's compromise. How about two changeovers this week?"

"You got it." Joe sauntered down the hall pleased.

I irritably ran my hand through my hair that was chin length, brown, and quite straight. Now Althea would be upset. There must be some other way to deal with Joe, I thought. Until I found it, this stonewalling would go on and on.

"Sorry," I said to Aaron, slipping back in my chair after giving Althea the bad news, not that I'd needed to. She'd heard the whole conversation from her office. As had Aaron, no doubt. "Sometimes I feel more like a referee than manager around here."

"No problem," he replied. We both got back to our numbers.

Near noon, I was getting hungry and glanced at my watch. Aaron put down the stack of forms he held. "This'll take at least another hour. Can I take you to lunch?"

"Sorry?" I said, surprised.

"Lunch. You're a client. It's a common practice."

I was used to eating alone, reading a book over a sandwich at a deli. Well, Amanda had been encouraging me to be more social, and besides, he might be interesting to talk to. I said yes and suggested a Chinese restaurant close by.

"What do you think of Appleton-Smith?" I asked after we ordered.

Aaron poured us both tea. "The truth? A standard company making standard mistakes."

I blinked in surprise. Surely we were a little better than standard?

"Sorry if that's blunt," he said, noting my reaction. "Your particular department seems to be doing well."

"How do you know? You've been analyzing purchase orders the last two hours."

"Your lines didn't stop running during those two hours, the equipment's clean and well-tended, your employees pay attention to their work, and you have Deming's Fourteen Points on your wall. All good signs."

I couldn't help but be pleased by his words. "Thanks," I said.

"It wasn't meant as a compliment, just an observation."

"Then thanks for noticing."

He paused, evaluating me. "You don't get much positive feedback at work, do you?"

I shrugged. Not since Jack retired, I thought, but it wasn't worth going into. I eyed Aaron speculatively as our food was served, impressed he knew about Deming's Fourteen Points. I was curious about what made him tick. "Most consultants I know do nothing but work," I observed, picking up my chopsticks.

"The job can be demanding," he agreed.

"Outside work, what do you do?"

Aaron looked me over a second. "Outside work, I write poetry."

"A poet," I said, tilting my head to one side. "In a business suit?"

"It pays the bills. Business does, I mean, not poetry."

A poet, I thought, has come to Appleton-Smith. How extraordinary. "I don't read much poetry," I said. "I suppose I should."

"These days more people seem to be writing poetry than reading it," he said without rancor. "Maybe it's a dying genre."

"I read a lot of novels," I offered.

"Novels," he repeated. "What kind?"

"Oh, classics mostly. I majored in business in college, and now I've got a lot to catch up on. I tend to hop around between centuries. If I were more disciplined, I guess I'd do it properly, start with *Robinson Crusoe* and move forward."

"Literature's not like accounting. A random order will probably help." Aaron appeared amused as he sipped his tea. "Do you like your job?" he asked. "You seem to be doing well: you have a lot of responsibility."

"It's why I didn't go to Washington." I looked across the room at a scene of Chinese pilgrims traversing a bridge under a cloud of cherry blossoms. Perhaps I looked wistful because his next question surprised me.

"You have regrets?"

"Oh, no. I mean, Mark just left, and I'm living with my sister, and we keep each other company. I once read a book where someone criticized Americans for not having time for an interior life. Now I've got time for it." As I readjusted my chopsticks in my fingers, it occurred to me that I shouldn't let the conversation get any more personal. Curiosity, however, overwhelmed etiquette. "What about you?" I asked. "Any relationships, girlfriends?"

"A long distance one" he answered with a smile. "Familiar story."

"So we have something in common. What's her name?"

"Elizabeth. We're engaged, actually."

"Congratulations," I said. "Where does she live?"

"Boston. She's studying at Harvard Divinity School to be a minister."

"That's unusual. Good for her."

"Yes, she's remarkable."

Definitely in love, I thought. How nice. I always liked it when men spoke highly of the woman in their life. "And you don't mind being alone?" I couldn't resist asking.

Aaron looked up from his chopsticks. "I suppose I'm used to it." He drank some more tea, his eyes curious as he scrutinized me. His expression reminded me of the way people at the Museum of Modern Art look when they like a piece well enough to struggle with it, though I didn't think I'd been that oblique. How black his lashes are, I thought, and his eyes were an interesting blue. Sapphire? You're staring, Sara. I glanced back over at the pilgrims.

After lunch we didn't find any major deviations and finished up the audit. I told him which aspects of our purchasing procedures were insane (in my opinion) and suggested improvements. When Aaron went on to the Shampoo and Foaming Baths department, I gave a sigh of relief at having passed the inquisition. Why had he asked me to lunch? Well, maybe for consultants it was bad form to eat a sandwich solo at a deli. He'd been intriguing to talk to anyway.

I met with Althea later that afternoon. She was a tall black woman in her early thirties who looked less than cheerful as she sat down in my office. I wondered what Althea's life was like outside of work. I knew she had a husband and a three-year-old daughter, that she sang in her church choir, and that was about it. I didn't imagine it was easy to be black and work at Appleton-Smith, there were so few African Americans working here.

We discussed her project to get smaller quantities of tubes more frequently from our supplier so we could cut our tube inventories. I asked if she needed any help.

"I could use you not changing the schedule when Joe yells," Althea said, brushing a piece of lint off the sleeve of her deep purple sweater. "With all the fuss he makes, you'd think I was scheduling him for a root canal. I thought he had a project to reduce changeover time."

"He does," I said with a sigh, "but he's convinced the lines run better on longer runs. I wish engineering would deliver the new parts like they promised. That should make things easier."

"Hmm." She sounded as if she agreed with me, but she was also frowning.

"Althea, do you like working here?"

Althea's face turned blank and impassive, like a cat ready to ignore a scolding. "It's a job."

"You're doing good work; keep pushing, okay? If it gets too ugly, come talk to me. Let me know how I can help."

"Sara, you need to figure out what'll get those bozos to change. You do your work, I'll do mine."

"You sound angry."

"Maybe I am. You're the boss, stop caving in. Do what you know is right."

We were both silent, not exactly looking at each other. "Anything else?"

"Nope. That's all the glad tidings for today."

She rose. This meeting with her wasn't going any better than my run-in with Joe.

"Althea—" She turned. I paused, grasping for some bridge, some connection. "I—I like the color of your sweater."

"Thanks," she answered deadpan.

Sara, how utterly, utterly inadequate. My eyes followed Althea's elegant, straight back as she left the room, and then I put my head down in my arms. Immediately I popped back up. I could be seen through my office window, and I knew appearing on the verge of despair wouldn't help me any. I wanted to support Althea and to get Joe to change, but there were times I felt powerless to accomplish either. The guys running the lines were on Joe's side. If I pushed Joe too hard, he could create mishaps that would ensure no hand cream got produced for weeks, and it'd be my head on the block. The old plant manager, Jack, had warned when he promoted me that I'd have to dance carefully on this job, but he'd assured me I could do it. How I wish Jack hadn't retired and moved to Arizona.

What would Deming say? Good old Edwards Deming, the first business quality guru, ignored by his own country in the wake of World War II and made a hero by the Japanese instead. As Aaron had noted, on the wall above my desk I'd hung a poster of Deming's Fourteen Points. Point number nine now stood out accusingly: "Break down barriers between departments." The barrier between Joe and Althea should be an easy one to conquer, a little baby step when I had so far to go.

"For heaven's sake, quit with the moping," Amanda said after I'd wandered listlessly around the apartment that evening. Amanda, my older sister, was much less responsible and more cheerfully manic than I could ever be. When we were little, we created some costumes and tricks and put on a circus for our parents. Amanda had Dad shine a flashlight on her as she introduced us as "Serious Sara, Amazing Amanda," a pronouncement I resented but accepted as truth. Now I was living with her, ILOM, itinerant lodger of the moment. I was by no means the first to have the honor.

"Your sympathy is touching," I said. "Next time, send a card."

"Look, I'm plenty sympathetic, but you've got to quit wasting your energy feeling bad. Either move to Washington or get busy living."

"I'm in transition. I've got to refigure out my life."

"So get a hobby. Take a class. Volunteer somewhere. Sara, look at you; you're turning into a hermit. Next thing you know, you'll stop taking showers."

"My personal hygiene is not at risk," I said crisply. "Having no social life isn't a crime. It's what I feel like. I feel withdrawn. Like a turtle." I could picture two little eyes staring out from the shadow of its shell.

Amanda went into the kitchen and came back out. "Here's the phone book, here's the newspaper. There's plenty to do in a city like this. Give yourself some structured activities, or you'll end up doing nothing but reading."

I took the phone book and newspaper and plopped them on the coffee table. I wanted understanding, not solutions. "I'll do it when I feel like it," I said, getting up off the couch.

"Where are you going?"

"To my room."

"You're going to read," she accused.

"Yep. Solzhenitsyn. *Gulag Archipelago*." I left the room.

On Wednesday of the same week, Aaron stopped by my office. I hadn't seen him since Monday, and immediately I feared he'd found a miscoded purchase order and I'd have to spend the rest of the day on a treadmill of numbers. It was quite the opposite. He apologized for the short notice, but he had tickets to the symphony the next evening, and would I be interested? I tapped my pen against my lower lip. Well, he was interesting, well-mannered, and quite betrothed. The symphony sounded appealing—I did need to get out more—but would Mark get upset? Aaron stood waiting for my response. I decided that I'd call Mark and tell him. If he had a fit, I could always cancel. I told Aaron yes, and we agreed on a restaurant where we'd meet for dinner. It was all casual and painless, nothing like the clumsy awkwardness of dating.

"I've got a date," I told Mark that night on the phone.

"Oh?"

"Just kidding. I'm going to the symphony with a guy I met at work. He's practically married to some woman in Boston. We'll commiserate about our long-distance phone bills."

"Sounds kind of dull. You should go see that new Noam Chomsky documentary instead. I'm sure it's playing somewhere in the city. Hey, did you hear what they're proposing as the latest safeguard against oil spills? It's such a joke."

"No, tell me."

He certainly took it well, I thought later as I hung up. I went over to the living room window and gazed at fog blotting out the lights of the Financial District. I'd always coveted this view from Amanda's apartment, and now it was mine, too, for a while. Suddenly I wished with all my heart that I could turn and find Mark stretched out on the couch, reading the paper with his reassuring frown of concentration. But it was a ridiculous wish. I could see in the window's reflection that the couch was empty. What could you see from Mark's apartment? I'd find out in two weeks when I flew out to Washington to visit him.

Restlessly I picked up the newspaper still lying on the coffee table where I'd dropped it days ago. Maybe Amanda had a point. I turned to the section that listed organizations looking for volunteers and saw that a shelter for battered women wanted someone to teach how to budget and how to balance a checkbook. I could do that. I called the number and left my name on an answering machine.

A few minutes later Amanda bounded in the front door, home late from her job at an art supply store. She was humming to herself in a pleasant sort of way. Over the past decade Amanda had changed her hair color more often than some people change their sheets, but lately she'd settled on a deep brownish red, permed and cut in a short bob.

"You're in a good mood," I said.

She hung up her coat and headed to the kitchen. "Yes, indeedy."

I followed behind. "Why so chipper?"

"I've got a date for Friday night."

"My, my. Who's the lucky guy?"

"You haven't met him." Amanda peered into the freezer. "He's a doctor." She whisked a frozen dinner out, stabbed the plastic wrapping in a couple of places with a knife and popped it in the microwave.

I frowned. "I thought you didn't like doctors." In college she'd gone out with a medical student who'd argued constantly, was too busy to see her, forgot her birthday, and then called every day for two months after she gave him the boot. She'd had no trouble being merciless.

"I don't. But this one's different."

"Statistically improbable. How'd you meet him?"

"He came in the store, and we started talking."

"Amanda, doctors don't buy art supplies."

"This one does. His wife's an artist—monoprints, I guess."

"He's married?"

"Yep." Amanda pulled her dinner from the beeping microwave. "A lot of people are these days."

"Oh, Amanda. It's sleazy, it's worm-like. It's so, so . . . Genine." Genine was our father's second wife, former girlfriend.

Amanda peeled the plastic off her chicken enchilada, yipping as steam burnt her fingers. "So I'm Miss Scum of the Earth. I've been called worse. And it's nothing at all like Genine, thank you very much."

"You have an affair, he dumps you—then what? You'll get hurt."

"I'm a big girl. If I get hurt, it won't be the first time."

I sighed. "I care about you."

"Yeah, I know." She put down her plate and hugged me. "I appreciate it, but it won't do any good."

"Amanda—" I paused, undecided whether to tell her about the symphony. If I did, she'd give me as much grief as I'd just given her.

"Sara. What?" She faced me, eyebrows raised, hands on her hips.

"Forget it. I'm going to bed."

"You going to go read?"

"I feel like walking, actually, but it's dark and I don't want to go alone."

"I'll go with you," she offered. "For a short one."

We went just to the top of the hill, the wind whipping our breath away. The bank of clouds had blown away, uncovering the lights of the Bay Bridge and the East Bay as well as the spangled downtown skyline.

"What a magnificent city," Amanda said.

"You can't see any of the problems from up here," I said dourly. "No homeless, no crime, no potholes, no AIDS."

"Sometimes illusions are a nice break."

At that moment I felt content to be living in San Francisco with my sister. We went home and I read until eleven, lying in a bed still more compressed and hollowed on Mark's side than mine.

Chapter Two

Thursday morning started off inauspiciously with traffic more snarled than Amanda's hair when she teased it into a bouffant. I ended up ten minutes late to work and irate at the entire human race for not telecommuting so I could drive unimpeded. As I hurried past the packing lines to my office, I noticed the unusual sound of my own footsteps. I stopped and saw a few workers chatting with each other as they wiped down equipment that should've been spitting out eighty tubes of hand cream a minute. The rest of the department looked like a manufacturing ghost town in a post-industrial western. It did not cheer me up.

"A motor went out in the making system," Joe said when I asked him what was going on. "No spare in the storeroom and can't get one from the parts place until two. We got trucks waiting on the loading dock, too."

"Why not until two?"

Joe leaned against my doorway with his thick arms folded across his chest. "That's the best they can do. First they told me it wouldn't be here until tomorrow, but I sweet-talked them into today."

"Every hour we're down is a thousand dollars down the drain," I said, irritated. "Where's this parts place anyway?"

"Oakland."

"Well, we're not talking South Dakota here. Can't someone go get it?"

"Against company policy," Joe said. "You're not supposed to drive your own car on company business on account of insurance."

"Then take the company car. Let's get going."

"Only the plant manager drives that car. Right, I'm supposed to say, 'Hey, Paul, buddy, toss me the keys.' What else do you want me to do today, stick my finger in a light socket?"

Joe appeared to relish his role as prophet of doom. I called Madge, the plant manager's secretary, and asked to use the car. She told me Paul was on a conference call with Chicago and couldn't be disturbed. "Look," I said, "I'll tell him about it later—I'm sure he won't mind. Do you have the keys? Great." I hung up and turned to Joe. "Go."

Joe gave me a nonchalant salute. "Yes, ma'am. I'll send Jim. Won't be me getting in trouble. I'm just following orders."

Joe must've sent Jim off with some urgency because Jim returned with the part in under an hour, and the making system was up and running again by ten-thirty. The incident irked me because I didn't like endless small crises, having to put out one fire and then sniff around for the smoke of the next. Now I'd have to investigate why our preventive maintenance program hadn't caught the motor before it failed, and I had no doubt I'd be impressed by the creativity of the excuses. One of my favorite lines from T.S. Eliot is, "Streets that follow like a tedious argument of insidious intent." Lots of tedious streets in my line of work. At the risk of mixing my metaphor beyond recovery, I wanted to build a mass transit system but was constantly interrupted to fix potholes. Did Deming put up with this kind of stuff in Japan? It didn't matter, I told myself. Deming's first point was constancy of purpose. If great manufacturing was my goal, I had to keep my eyes on the prize.

For lunch I went to my favorite deli to eat my standard avocado and cucumber sandwich. Having decided recently to tackle Tolstoy, my mind now wandered in and among the indolent lives of the Russian aristocracy. Motors did not break down in that world, I reflected. Trains might run over people, but you didn't read about passengers waiting endlessly on the platform due to a broken engine. Better to die of a broken heart than of sheer exasperation, though, on second thought, perhaps the two weren't so far apart. Broken hearts just had the advantage of making better copy.

That afternoon I had my bimonthly meeting with Paul, the plant manager, and I apprehensively headed to his office. The week before I'd been in an ornery mood and disagreed with Paul, in front of his boss no less, severely annoying him. I was usually careful about that sort of thing, never embarrass your boss being a preeminent rule of survival, but Mark hadn't been home when I called the night before, Joe had been on my case about something, and the hard disk on my computer had crashed. The fact that I'd been right and his boss had agreed with me had made it even worse. I doubted whether Paul had forgiven me yet.

When headquarters transferred Paul Everett to our plant after Jack retired, all of us immediately recognized him as a fast tracker. He didn't know much about manufacturing, but once you were above a certain rung on the corporate ladder ambition became the only necessary qualification, and Paul had this in spades. In his late thirties, he lived in Hillsborough, belonged to the country club there, and played golf often. Above his corporate regulation white shirt and red tie, his face was always as tanned as a movie star's.

I knocked on Paul's door and let myself into his recently redecorated office. Beige walls had morphed into a muted celadon-teal, abstract prints now hung over an aqua sofa, and new office botany rounded out the decor. As I made my way towards a 19th century escritoire that served as Paul's desk, my steps left footprints in a plush carpet. I wondered if vacuuming between meetings was included in Madge's job description.

"Hello Sara," Paul said, laying his copy of Forbes aside. "How did the audit with the guy from Merrisocks go?"

Something about Paul's offhand tone made me wary. "Fine," I said.

"Good, good. Terrible nuisance, the whole thing, but Chicago's cracking down on procedural deviations. No point having rules if people don't follow them. Of course, I wasn't worried about your department: I know you run a tight ship. So, Sara, I want to ask you, where does Creams and Lotions stand in reducing inventories?"

The question startled me as he and I had talked this over several times before. Well, repetition is the key to learning, I told myself. I quickly listed off our goals and then told him about Althea's work with our tube supplier and the quick changeover project Joe was reluctantly implementing.

"Great." Paul smiled, showing his even white teeth. "Think you could give a presentation on what you just told me to Bob Enders? He'll be out here in a few weeks, and he's really into this short run and lower inventory thing." Bob was the vice-president for manufacturing, Paul's boss's boss.

"Could we involve Althea and Joe too?" I wanted Althea and Joe to get credit for the work they were doing, as well as for them to realize I wasn't the only one in the company interested in inventories.

"No, let's have just you do it this time. I'm hearing lower inventories is going to be the next big thing, and it looks like we'll be riding the crest—at least we're out there ahead of the other plants."

"That's good, I guess. I don't think we're much ahead of the competition though."

Paul leaned back, crossed one leg over the other and folded his hands around his bent knee. "The other plants are our competition, in a sense anyway."

I said nothing, a polite smile on my face. I'd already learned that disagreeing with Paul on this point wasn't productive, discretion being the better part of not wasting one's time.

"How's Althea doing?" Paul said, appearing to jot notes on a pad of paper.

"Pretty well. There are some issues between her and Joe that need smoothing out."

"Hmm." Paul tugged his black sock higher up his leg. "It's important Althea's happy here. Appleton-Smith's affirmative action numbers aren't as good as they should be, and Chicago expects our plant to be higher than average because we're out here in California. We need to make up for all our Midwest plants. Those Midwest plants are really bad, let me tell you. Can't get a minority to stay."

"Of course, it's more than a question of numbers," I countered. "Althea's doing a great job ordering materials and scheduling—"

"Great. Glad to hear it. So we don't have to worry about her quitting or anything. Super."

As I trudged back to my own office that was lavishly furnished with linoleum tile, a gray metal bookcase and matching desk, I jammed my hands in the pockets of my blazer. I hate this place, I thought. Why did I ever think this job was worth staying for? It's just today, the other half of my brain counseled me. Even if sometimes Paul's a jerk, most of the time he leaves you alone. At least he didn't chastise me for using the company car. He must've forgiven my indiscretion in front of his boss the previous week.

That evening I was late getting away from work, I didn't have time to go home to change, and then I couldn't park anywhere near the restaurant where I was supposed to meet Aaron. To make up time, I practically jogged all the way from where I finally found a space and felt a disheveled mess when I reached the restaurant. I longed for a nice relaxing jaunt up a hill. The restaurant was small, and Aaron was waiting for me outside. His suit looked so precise and formal, especially compared to the wrinkled wad of linen my own had become. He noticed me and smiled.

"Sorry I'm late," I said breathlessly. "It's been kind of a bad day."

"You're not very late. Let's hope the evening will be better." Aaron looked right then as if everything in the world consistently amused him, and I envied his equanimity in the face of the chaos of daily life.

All the waiters in the restaurant were dressed in black, wore ponytails, and glided around in Chinese cotton-soled shoes. A pony-tailed host guided us ethereally to our table.

"Why was your day bad?" Aaron said as we sat down. "More irritating consultants asking you annoying questions?"

I stretched my palms flat on the cool marble table between us. "I'll take an irritating consultant over an irritating boss any day. Besides, you weren't irritating; you were very patient. If I'd been you, I would've started hitting people over the head with clipboards. And I didn't see you around today—is the audit over?"

"I finished my report this afternoon. I included some of your recommendations, by the way. There may be a follow-up study on cost allocations, but I won't be doing it."

"Why, you're tired of being dazzled by the blinding efficiency of Appleton-Smith?" I was curious which of my recommendations he'd included but pleased he'd agreed with me on at least some of them.

Aaron laughed. "On a monotony scale of one to ten, I give accounting and purchasing procedures a twelve and a half. The person who was supposed to do Appleton-Smith had a death in her family; I told her I'd cover for her. She'll probably do your cost allocation project."

"Sounds like we were an inconvenient detour for you."

He shrugged. "Detours aren't always bad. You never know what the unexpected holds."

As muted jazz drifted through the restaurant, the world of work began to ebb, and a semblance of serenity took its place. Our table was illumined by a candle nestled in a bowl of cat's eye marbles, its dancing light flickering on us both. The evening drew on a luxurious cast, and stray thoughts of Russian aristocrats passed through my mind. Lives led without bosses, broken machinery, and squabbling employees. Reality check. They didn't have to work because they lived off other people's work—good for nothing, as my father would say. "Be responsible and productive" had been one of his mottos for Amanda and me as we grew up, not that it'd had much effect on my rebel sister.

I have to make money to live, I reminded myself. I would hate being dependent on Mark, to have to ask him like my mother asked my father for an allowance to buy clothes and groceries. Besides, sometimes my job wasn't so bad. Sometimes things would click, and the particular project I'd be working on would actually happen. Then I'd have made a step toward Deming's vision, and however briefly, I'd feel good, satisfied even. Unfortunately, I only got two or three of those moments a year. I'd willingly have traded pay raises for more.

Aaron looked up from his menu, prompting me to open my own. Who was this Aaron Lambert, I wondered? Amanda would've had him pegged in the first five minutes.

As we ate, I discovered Aaron's parents still lived in Boston and that his sister worked for a magazine in Manhattan. I heard about a posh boarding school and summer cottages on the beach, a privileged upbringing that Aaron readily admitted and didn't take too seriously.

"What are you doing out here in San Francisco?" I asked. "Boston or New York would be more likely, wouldn't they?"

Aaron refilled my wine glass and his own. "San Francisco's not so improbable. Like most everyone here, I'm living my own quiet rebellion. San Francisco's a good place for it."

"Rebellion? But you're not the Haight-Ashbury type—you're the model son type."

Aaron raised his eyebrows. "Model son?"

"Let's see, you generally wore clean shirts to school, you graduated with honors, you brought your dates home by the time their fathers said, and to this day you call your mother on her birthday."

"If I didn't call," Aaron responded with a laugh, "the repercussions would be severe and unpleasant. That's more enlightened self-interest than anything else. And as I remember, I brought my dates home at all sorts of hours without their fathers being involved. How about you? You hardly strike me as someone with a history of delinquency."

"Me, I was an angel daughter. I never disobeyed. But we're talking about you. So you're claiming you're not now and never were a model son?"

"So model, I got kicked out of school when I was sixteen."

"Really?" I leaned forward with interest. "What for—selling drugs, smuggling weapons into class?"

"Nothing so criminal, sorry to disappoint you. I used to sneak off campus at night and walk around for hours to get away and think. I'd get caught and reprimanded and then do it again until finally they suspended me. I don't suppose I blame them. They couldn't have had all of us wandering around like moody little Hamlets—they'd have gotten complaints from the neighbors."

"A fairly minor infraction, though. In my high school we had a guy who was an arsonist. What happened?"

"They wanted me to guarantee in writing I'd follow the rules, which I refused to do, so they sent me home where I sulked and threw darts in the basement. It's when I got started with poetry, actually. After a couple weeks of my mother ready to murder me, my father convinced me that being obstinate about something so small was pointless when my future was at stake. I wrote my letter, got back in, and had to study like hell to catch up." Aaron smiled wryly. "I give my father a lot of credit, he was very patient. Looking back, though, sometimes I wish he hadn't been so persuasive."

"Where would you be today if he hadn't? Living in a hut on some beach in Brazil writing poetry?"

Aaron laughed. "That's a good question. No, no Brazilian beaches, I don't think."

Aaron's dissatisfaction with his privileged upbringing surprised me. I was a public-school kid all the way. In college I'd envied those like him who didn't need loans, who hadn't had to work at part-time jobs, whose parents wrote out the tuition check without the constant complaining I'd heard from my father. As if it'd been my fault he'd had to pay alimony. "Instead, here you are, very successful," I said.

"By some standards. Not all of them mine."

We were silent in the spell of the flickering candle. "And what about Elizabeth?" I asked, wanting to remind myself of his fiancée's existence. "Will she come out here to join your rebellion when she finishes, or will you go back to Boston?"

He looked down at his wine glass. "It's a question we haven't answered yet. We still have some time."

"When's the wedding?"

"June. After Elizabeth graduates."

Aaron dexterously turned the conversation back to Appleton-Smith, asking how long I'd been in my job, what positions I'd held before my promotion, what my goals were for my department. Since I could talk about my ideas for better manufacturing until the cows came home, he let me rattle on about Deming and even seemed to understand why reducing inventories might be a good idea.

"Do you have a mentor at work?" he asked as our plates were cleared.

I shook my head. "Not since Jack, our old plant manager, retired, anyway."

"How about at your corporate headquarters—is anyone there sponsoring you, looking out for you?"

I raised my eyebrows. "I've only been to the place twice for training sessions. I hardly know anyone there."

Aaron nodded thoughtfully and asked a figure in black for the bill. We argued briefly over who would pay it. When I insisted that I should since he'd paid for the symphony tickets, Aaron handed me the check with his air of equanimity intact.

A light fog had spread through the street, and the night felt damp as we made our way four blocks to the symphony hall. We walked quietly, separately. Something moved in a doorway as we passed by, startling me. Shadow turned into a grizzled man squatted on a doorstep, wrapped in a tattered sleeping bag, his life possessions in a grocery cart beside him. I edged closer to Aaron, and he glanced at me, both of us silent as we walked.

We turned a corner, and suddenly, ahead of us, brilliant light streamed from the huge, curved windows of the symphony hall. I could see those already inside climbing the main staircase, their hands supported by gleaming brass banisters. As voices drifted down to us from the third-floor outdoor terrace, I thought about shadow and light and what they both hid. The people up on the terrace couldn't see the homeless in the doorways acridly smelling of urine, though perhaps they, too, passed them as they came here, turning away from the pain as I did. Guilt doesn't fix anything, I told myself. All my guilt and a dollar would've bought that man back there maybe a cup of coffee, maybe half a bottle of Thunderbird. I should be doing more.

Aaron and I found our seats and glanced at our programs as dissonant elements of the symphony tuned up. The formality of dinner had been more comfortable. I felt self-conscious now side-by-side, a few inches apart. The guest pianist and the conductor appeared, the audience applauded, and moments later the violins of Tchaikovsky flowed through the auditorium, serene and expansive like a grand European river. I glanced at Aaron. He was watching the stage, his elbow on an armrest, the fingers of one hand supporting the side of his head. There was a permanent crease on his face next to his mouth, and it crossed my mind what it would be like to sleep with him.

Sara. No. Absolutely not, I admonished myself, not a little shocked.

Forget about him and concentrate, the sane side of my brain ordered as the music swirled and cascaded around me. Ah, those decadent, indolent, nineteenth century Russians. With a sigh I settled back into the richness of it.

After the concert ended, Aaron walked me back to the side street where I'd parked my car. It was almost eerily quiet. Mark's probably asleep right now, I thought—he was a very sound sleeper. Although I knew Mark lived nowhere near the Capitol Building, somehow I visualized his apartment right across the street from it. It felt right to picture him asleep in the glow of the white dome, dreaming of congressional subcommittees. Alone. Of course he was alone. As I paused on the sidewalk next to my car, keys in hand, the chill fingers of a breeze seeped through my jacket. I shivered and folded my arms.

"The symphony was wonderful," I said to Aaron. "Listening to Tchaikovsky made me think of what it must've been like to live in St. Petersburg before the revolution—you know, the Winter Palace, dinners at midnight, streets filled with snow and sleighs."

Aaron wasn't wearing a coat over his suit, but he didn't seem cold. "Like most aristocracies, it was no doubt nice for a few and bad for the many. But I'm not being considerate. Realism's never appropriate after an evening of Tchaikovsky. I'm glad you enjoyed the symphony, Sara, and I'm glad you were free tonight. And thank you for dinner," he added politely. "May I offer some advice?"

I shrugged in surprise. "Sure."

"Don't let the supervisor who works for you undermine your authority."

"What do you mean?"

"If you want him to do three changeovers, he should do three changeovers."

"You're saying I should never compromise?"

"You need to get him to buy into the objective, not botch the implementation. Get him to agree with you and your scheduler on a level of changeovers for the next three months. That may involve some compromise. After that, hold him to it. Don't let him sabotage it."

I looked down at the car keys in my hand. "I need Joe. I have to stay on his good side."

"I realize that. But you can't let him bully you. Otherwise, he might as well be the department manager."

I frowned, trying to absorb what he was saying, although Jack, my old boss, had told me something similar before. The thing was, Jack had backed me up with Joe when I started the job. Things between Joe and me had worsened when Paul arrived.

"I should be going," Aaron said.

"Uh, me, too."

As we stood there, both ready to leave, I knew San Francisco was a big enough town that I might never see him again. Well, it was better that way. Though he might know a lot about corporations, I was married, he was engaged, and if I were his fiancée, I wouldn't want him inviting random women to the symphony. Still, I wondered again which of my purchasing procedure improvements he'd thought highly enough of to recommend.

I got in my car and edged out of what had become an extremely tight parallel parking spot, backing up and creeping forward three times before I could clear the car ahead of me. When I pulled out into the street and looked around, he'd gone.

I felt oddly empty driving home until I remembered that in two weeks I'd be on a plane to Washington. It would be wonderful to see Mark, to have him hold me, to hear he loved me. My thoughts at the symphony disconcerted me. It'd been a long time since I'd let myself even momentarily think sexually of someone other than Mark. I'd have to concentrate harder or start running colder water in my morning showers. I preferred concentration.

"Hullo," Amanda called from the living room as I came in the door. I flopped down on the couch next to her, pulled off my shoes, and put my feet up on the coffee table. Dressed in a hot pink T-shirt and spandex yoga pants, Amanda was carefully giving herself a pedicure. She pointed the remote control at the TV and turned the volume down. "You're just getting in now?"

"I went to the symphony. I needed Tchaikovsky after a day like today."

"Really? Did you go by yourself?"

"No, a guy I met at work had tickets and asked me to go."

"Why'd he ask you?" she said turning towards me while taking care not to disturb the cotton balls between her toes.

"How would I know? Maybe everyone else had already turned him down."

"Well, you tear my head off about Robert but think it's perfectly natural for people to ask you out."

"Robert?"

"The adulterous doctor I'm seeing tomorrow night. I'm sure you remember."

I yawned and rubbed my feet. "Aaron's practically married to this woman who's studying to be a minister in Boston. He just wanted somebody to go the symphony with. Mark knows all about it."

"I see your conscience is clear." Amanda smiled. "Far be it from me to criticize. You're having a miserable time of it, and you deserve all the fun you can get. So his name's Aaron. Will you be seeing more of him?"

"I doubt it," I said. Of course not. Lucky Elizabeth—Aaron was obviously head over heels. I leaned my head back against the top of the couch and looked up at the ceiling. There'd been a time when Mark had been head over heels for me. Ancient history now, but no one stays madly in love their entire married life.

"Doubt's a sign of a healthy mind," Amanda quipped. She put the cap back on the polish and looked over at me again. "Geez, Sara, you look beat. You've been working too hard. You want a cup of tea? Actually, I'm kind of paralyzed here till this dries. Could you be a doll and make a cup for both of us?" I pried myself off the couch. "Speaking of beating," she said as I neared the door, "you got a call from the Domestic Violence Shelter. I wrote it down by the phone. Meg somebody. She said you can call her at home any time until eleven. You going to volunteer there, or did you want them to take you in?"

I called and set up a time to meet with Meg on Saturday. Meg was a volunteer who coordinated the other volunteers at the shelter. She would give me an orientation and get me started counseling women on their finances. After I hung up, I looked in the phone book for the address of the shelter, curious where it was located. Only the phone number was listed so I had to call Meg back.

"Sorry," she told me. "I shouldn't expect people to be mind readers." The shelter turned out to be in the Mission district, a fifteen-minute walk from where I lived.

"Why isn't the address in the phone book? How do women know where to find you?"

"They have to call first. It's safer not to advertise the shelter location—we have enough men skulking around the place as it is."

Why would men be skulking around there, I wondered. The city was getting more crime-ridden every day. The government should give people living in cities tax credits as a kind of civilian combat pay.

Saturday morning I knocked on the door of the shelter and waited quite a while for a response. "I'm looking for Meg?" I said uncertainly when the door opened at last. I was given directions to a room down the hall. Meg, a tall, large woman with short blond hair and dangling earrings in the shape of parrots, introduced herself.

"Why do you want to volunteer here?" she asked right off.

I shrugged my shoulders, a little embarrassed. "My husband just started law school in Washington, and I have extra time, so I thought I'd branch out and volunteer."

"Are you a survivor?"

"Excuse me?"

"A domestic abuse survivor?"

"No. Not that I know of."

"Not that you know of."

"No. No domestic abuse."

"I'm a survivor," Meg said. "A lot of us who volunteer are, that's why I asked. If you really want to help other women, it helps to be clear on your own motivation. Survivors especially. You're probably thinking I'm nosy. I am, but don't take it personally. So your husband's not abusive, you've never been in an abusive relationship, you've got some spare time, and you want to help. Why here?"

"I have a background in business, and I thought I could do what you're looking for. Was I wrong?"

She smiled. "Probably not. As I said, it's nothing personal. I'll give you a tour of the shelter, some training on power and control theory, and then get you going with the financial counseling."

"What's power and control theory?"

"Intro to Domestic Violence—the basics of how men try to control women. Even though you'll be counseling about budgets and checkbooks, you should have some background in the types of abuse and the psychology behind them."

"Why do you say men controlling women? Isn't some of the abuse women hitting men?"

Meg nodded patiently. She'd obviously heard the question before. "Power and control issues can go both ways, and there's abuse even in gay and lesbian relationships. But the majority of the physical abuse is by men against women, and it's women who usually end up in emergency rooms with black eyes and broken bones. Unpleasant, but there it is. I'll give you the house tour now. Get ready for sensory overload."

I felt chastised. I knew I was ignorant about domestic violence: the idea of people hitting each other was completely alien to me. As we walked through the house we saw women and children in the living room watching Saturday morning cartoons, women drinking coffee at a table in the kitchen, toys scattered, and children playing and roaming in every imaginable corner of the rest of the house, with half a dozen climbing on a play structure in the small backyard.

"We have fifteen women today and thirty children," Meg said. "The house feels crowded right now, but around noon some volunteers will come to take a bunch of kids to the park."

"How long do people stay here?"

"Two to three weeks usually. Women with kids can have a hard time finding housing, so sometimes they might stay a couple months."

"You said there are guys skulking around here," I said. "I never thought this was that bad of a neighborhood."

"It's not the neighborhood, the neighborhood's very supportive. It's usually women's husbands or boyfriends. They find out they're here and come to get them. Power and control. A woman in an abusive relationship is most likely to get killed when she tries to leave. In the Bay Area, one woman dies at the hands of her husband or boyfriend every month."

"What do you do when it happens?"

"Call the police. Get a no contact order from the court. It's nice having the law on your side. That and we put bulletproof windows in last year. The men usually back off."

"It sounds frightening."

Meg paused. "I hate to say you get used to it, but you do. The police are generally helpful, and we're saving lives. Are you still interested? None of the staff or volunteers have ever been attacked."

Was she trying to intimidate me? "I'll be here next Saturday morning at ten," I said.

So I began teaching women the mysteries of personal budgeting and balancing a checkbook. I bought some inexpensive calculators and showed women how to use them for basic math. The major problem was that their incomes were usually well below their expenses. I couldn't solve this for them, but I could give them a better understanding of what their expenses really were and help them put together a spending plan. A few weeks into it I added a serious talk about credit cards. Some of the women were clueless; others listened and caught on. As I explained what the columns in the checkbook were for, I'd look into a woman's face, sometimes still bruised and puffy, sometimes teeth missing, and wonder if I faced her situation—violent husband, kids, bad or no job, no money—would I be able to get myself out? There were so many forces locking them in place.

"He's not always so bad," one woman told me who was thinking of going back, even though she'd ended up with a concussion the previous week. Her husband had shoved her down some stairs. He hadn't liked the length of her skirt. "He wouldn't get so mad if he didn't love me," she went on. "I talked to him last night. He begged me to come home, said he'd never do it again. Course, he's said that before. But the thing is, I'm married to him. I was always taught you make your bed, you lie in it."

I didn't know what to say. Meg would need to talk to her. Women leave an average of seven times before they finally leave for good, Meg told me. I'd walk home, shaking my head. The volunteering cut into my walking, but I still managed many miles a week and made significant progress with Tolstoy. At work I sat Althea down with Joe, and the three of us, after much haggling, agreed to ten changeovers a month for the next three months.

Two weeks into all this, I headed out to Washington for a long weekend with Mark. The flight was full, and I was seated next to a pugnacious two-year-old whom I placated as best I could with pretzels. When we finally landed at Washington National, I was ready to burst off the plane. At the top of the jetway I scanned the crowd and saw Mark off to one side, tall and broad shouldered in jeans and a gray sweatshirt. His hair was a little overgrown, and the stubble on his handsome jaw was noticeable as he glanced at each passenger, looking for me. I had an impulse to run to him but was blocked by my toddler seat companion who was further torturing his mother with a temper tantrum. She managed to drag him aside; a moment later I was flinging my carry-on bag to the ground and hugging Mark.

"Nice to see you," I said to his sweatshirt. I looked up, we smiled at each other, and I felt a crazy momentary shyness.

"Wonderful to see you," Mark said, squeezing me close again.

People streamed around us like a river around two boulders in its bed. We walked to the Metro stop holding hands and talking of Mark's newfound desire to go into environmental law. Sitting on the train with my feet resting on my bag, I leaned my head on Mark's shoulder, listened to his critique of the Secretary of the Interior, and sighed contentedly. I belonged; things were right. Mark loved me, and everything would work out. Three years weren't so long.

When we reached Mark's apartment in the basement of a three-story brownstone, we immediately began making love. "I've missed you," he whispered as we shed clothes all over his shoebox of a studio. His face was scratchy against mine but having him stop kissing me was the last thing I wanted as we stood next to his single bed, his arms tightly around me, my hands pressing against the tops of his bare shoulders as the tension built.

I broke away and pulled him down to me on the bed. "Six weeks is a long time," I said.

"Way too long to be without you," Mark said.

I closed my eyes, relaxing and concentrating on his hands and mouth that oddly felt both foreign and familiar. I hadn't realized how much I'd missed lying close to him, the feel of his skin, the mass and weight of his body. I'd put it all out of my mind to avoid the pain of wanting and not having. The man I now wrapped my arms around was both my husband and a stranger—not a bad combination, as far as sex went anyway.

We made dinner at his apartment and as we ate discussed plans for the weekend. "I need to study some," Mark said. "The law school had more students accept this year than they wanted, so they're trying to flush us out with the workload. You'd think they were paying us, instead of us paying them. Maybe you could go to some museums tomorrow. The Museum of Arts and Industry has a good exhibit on the history of work—they even quote Engels at one point, although their class analysis of the Industrial Revolution is way pathetic. Probably they didn't want to offend anyone in Congress so their funding wouldn't get cut. As if anyone in Congress would even accidentally step foot inside the Museum of Arts and Industry."

I've done plenty of wandering around by myself lately, that's the last thing I want to do, I thought. But I knew it was important to Mark to do well in his classes. He'd be happier once he'd established himself this semester, and I should be understanding. Art museums sounded appealing: I'd had enough of work at work.

"Okay, you study, and I'll hit the museums, but Sunday we'll do something together, right? Maybe we could rent a car and go see Monticello or Mount Vernon."

"Tell you what, let's go to Alexandria. You'll like it, and we can take the Metro there. How does Ethiopian food sound for tomorrow night?"

I shrugged. "Fine."

"A couple of my friends live in Adams Morgan where the Ethiopian places are—we could all go to dinner together."

"Mark, I kind of just wanted to be with you."

"They really want to meet you. You'll like them. Be a little social for once."

I stood up to clear the dishes to the sink in his minuscule kitchen. East coast or west, some things didn't change, I thought— Mark's tendency to be obliviously inconsiderate one of them. No, I told myself, don't get mad. He wants to show you his new world, his new friends. To make you a part of his life here. Control your temper. Be nice.

"I'm a very social person," I said, discounting my recent hermitic lifestyle.

"Right," Mark laughed. "It's settled then?" He caught my arm and pulled me to him. "Come here, my little socialite."

It rained the next day, and I walked from Mark's apartment to the East Wing of the National Gallery under Mark's enormous black umbrella. The Metro would've been more practical, but it felt bracingly good to be outside breathing fresh air and avoiding puddles. As I strolled through the exhibits at the East Wing, however, I yawned sleepily. Sharing a single bed with Mark had been a challenge. I must've woken up every time he turned over. Still, it'd been wonderful to have him next to me all night, worth the lost sleep.

After lunch I crossed the soggy Mall to the Freer Gallery to see Whistler's Peacock Room. I'd read about it ages ago, and when I found it tucked away in a corner of the museum, I wasn't disappointed. Commissioned to decorate some long-ago millionaire's dining room, Whistler had gotten carried away and painted gold peacocks all over the room's dark turquoise walls. The golden birds pranced and preened, even glittered if you caught the light the right way. Above the fireplace hung a full-length portrait of a young European woman, *The Princess from the Land of Porcelain*. She held a fan in one of her languorous hands while her wild dark hair cascaded over her draped rose kimono. Gilded shelving on each wall displayed an opulent collection of porcelain from all over Asia and the Middle East. Overall, the effect was remarkable, but Whistler had quarreled bitterly with his patron, and after finishing his creation he never saw the Peacock Room again.

This room would suit Aaron, I thought. So formal and restrained, but when you looked closely, fanciful and exuberant in detail. Would I really describe Aaron that way? Maybe not, but there was something submerged in him, glittering even, though hard to get to. Oh, this was absurd, I told myself. I was the one being fanciful, bordering on hallucinatory. I sighed and went to collect my damp umbrella from the coat check.

At the Ethiopian restaurant, I met three other first-year law students Mark had invited: Hal, Doug, and Patricia. The three men immediately dove into a discussion involving a well-known professor and a controversial case. The conversation soon sank into legal references beyond my ability to follow. I was surprised that much jargon could be learned in just six weeks. I turned to Patricia, an elegant woman with long blond hair. As we talked I learned she was divorced, had a six-year-old son named Benji, and that law school was the cornerstone of her plan to reconstruct her life. This information took a while to elicit, as Patricia seemed disinclined to talk much about anything. Occasionally she'd jangle the five or six silver bracelets on her arm. I didn't think her distance was due to shyness. She didn't appear unhappy or annoyed, just reserved. Inscrutable.

When Mark brought up our plan to go to Alexandria the next day, Patricia mentioned that she and Benji hadn't been there but intended to go eventually. Blithely, without the slightest hesitation, Mark invited her to come with us. I couldn't believe the words were coming out of his mouth.

"No," Patricia said, "I'm sure you don't want a six-year-old slowing you down."

"Kids get tired easy," I agreed.

"These kinds of places are just made for kids," Mark said. "You enjoy it more when you see it through their eyes." When did Mark develop such an enthusiasm for children, I wondered with alarm.

Glancing at me, Patricia smiled faintly. "You two don't have that much time together. I won't impose—"

"It's no imposition," Mark assured her. "We'd love it, wouldn't we, Sara?"

An intense wave of discomfort washed over me as everyone turned to hear my response. I hated being polite, but I hated being rude even more. I should get on a plane back home tonight, I thought. Tomorrow Mark and Patricia and Benji could take the Metro to another planet for all I cared, I'd be walking up a hill on the other side of the continent.

I managed a tightly gracious, "Yes, please come with us. Mark, I'm feeling tired—must be jet lag. Could we go home now?"

"It's settled then. Let's meet tomorrow at ten."

Patricia shrugged slightly, and her smile seemed sad. No doubt going to Alexandria with us was the last thing she wanted to do as well.

During the cab ride home, I sat apart from Mark in the back seat slumped down, my arms folded across my chest. "How can you be so inconsiderate? You promised me we'd be together tomorrow. I spend the whole day walking around museums by myself, and then you practically force Patricia to come with us."

"I didn't force her. For crying out loud, Sara, can you think about someone besides yourself for a minute? Patricia's a single parent. The father's in Atlanta, and she and Benji don't get out much. I'm surprised at you. Usually you're more sensitive."

The cab driver signaled and turned a corner. He appeared to ignore our argument completely. It was beneath his attention and probably should've been beneath ours. In the backs of cabs across Washington that day the fates of nations had no doubt been determined, and here Mark and I were gridlocked in trivialities. Still, just because it was trivial was no reason to give in. "I go home Tuesday. I can't believe you think I'm selfish for wanting to spend one day alone with you."

"I said insensitive, not selfish." He tried to put his arm around me, but I shrugged it away and turned to the window.

"Fine," I said. "You go play surrogate father in Alexandria. I'll insensitively go back to San Francisco."

Mark gave a deep sigh; I concentrated on looking out the window. When we got back to the apartment, I started to pack.

"What are you doing?" Mark said.

"What does it look like? I'll take a red eye home. I hope the movie's good."

"This is ridiculous."

"It certainly is," I said, cramming my sneakers into my bag. "It's ridiculous I spent the money and took the time off work to come out here since your new friends are evidently more important than I am."

"Look, I'll call Patricia and cancel. Will that make you happy?"

"Yes."

"Okay." Mark got the phone book out, and instantaneously I began to feel guilty. His giving in had been a calculated risk on his part, I was sure. He was just waiting for my conscience to kick in. I sat down on the bed and watched as he pushed buttons on the phone.

"Mark—" He looked at me, eyebrows raised. "I'm sorry," I said. Mark hung up the receiver and sat down next to me. "I love you," he said, his arm around me. "Of course I want to spend time with you."

"But we've been apart so long, and this one measly weekend is supposed to last until Thanksgiving, and now I hardly get to see you. I've missed you so much. I need more than this."

"You're seeing me right now, aren't you? It's been hard for me, too, excruciating sometimes. It's made me realize just how important you are to me. Look, I'll call Patricia. I'll go with her and Benji another weekend."

"It's okay," I said. "We can all go to Alexandria together." Mark hugged me with one arm. My smile was weak and twisted, a far cry from satisfied, but I turned my face towards his shoulder for comfort. I looked up. "Maybe we could go to a movie together tomorrow night? Just you and me?"

He kissed me, one of his hands on my neck. "How about Monday afternoon? Monday afternoon we'll do whatever you want."

"What's wrong with tomorrow night?"

"I've got a case Monday morning that I've got to study for, but you have a book, don't you? You could come to the library with me and read."

I wasn't supposed to need Tolstoy if I had Mark. I felt tired down to my bones, too tired to keep fighting. Monday afternoon.

"I suppose," I said and got a kiss on the cheek and very nearly a pat on the head. Mark went into the bathroom to brush his teeth while I sat staring at old water-stained wallpaper wondering what was the difference between compromise and never getting what you wanted.

The weather turned, and Sunday was a clear, warm fall day. Benji proved to be somewhat hyperactive, and Patricia was kept busy deterring him from darting out into the street or grabbing things in the shops we browsed through. We wound up the afternoon strolling along the riverfront licking ice cream cones. All the running around had finally worn Benji out, and he had a hard time eating his chocolate ice cream faster than it could melt over his white t-shirt. By the time he finished, he looked like the "before" child in a laundry bleach ad. That Patricia could remain patient and spotless throughout the ordeal amazed me. After Benji's hands and face were wiped off, Mark put him on his shoulders and walked down the block to show Benji whatever sights we hadn't already seen.

Patricia and I stayed on the bench where we were, watching the river. The sun still felt warm, and as it lowered in the sky, it cast long shadows into the golden air. Patricia turned towards me. "Thanks for letting us come with you. Benji likes Mark, and he doesn't get to do things like this very often."

"It's been a nice day, hasn't it? I'm glad you could come with us," I said, partly to be polite, partly because I could afford to be, knew I should be, generous. At least I'd enjoyed the last few hours after I'd finally conquered my irritation and let the day go as it would.

"I know you and Mark wanted to be together," Patricia said. "It wasn't an easy decision, was it?"

"To be honest, no. But . . ." I raised a hand in the air, palm up. The trees had just begun to turn color with dapples of yellow amid the green leaves. The breeze was full of autumn and river, and the water gently lapped against the bank. "It's been a fine day," I finished. A redemption, of a sort, had occurred. We sat on the bench in the sunlight in silence until Mark returned carrying a sleeping Benji.

Chapter Three

Amanda picked me up from the airport in a foul mood because Robert the adulterous doctor had stood her up the night before. As we sped north on the freeway, I reached my hand out the car window to feel the air that smelled of dry grass and eucalyptus. "Visualize Tofu," said a bumper sticker on a Saab ahead of us. What does that mean, I thought, besides the fact that I'm definitely back in California. However surreal and bizarre, I preferred California's unapologetic craziness to the subtler, repressed neuroses of my country's capital. Of course, my irritation with Mark had something to do with that.

"Goddamn bastard," Amanda said. "Violin concert. The kid's five years old, what's he doing playing the violin? What a bastard. Couldn't call me. I mean, he has a car phone he's so proud of—how could he use that as an excuse?"

"So drop him, Amanda."

"Your sympathy overwhelms me. Do you like my sunglasses? Got them at a flea market last weekend." She handed me a pair of cat's-eye frames that were studded along the top with rhinestones. "The man's a dirt bag. I always pick dirt bags. Sara, what's wrong with me?"

I put on her sunglasses, folded my arms, and slouched in my seat. "You always pick dirt bags."

"You're right. How was Washington?"

"Mark studied. I saw museums."

"You don't look too thrilled. You know, he calls me sometimes after his wife goes to sleep. I'm an idiot, that's what I am. How can I care about a man who thinks the height of creativity is having a personalized license plate? I'm thirty, what am I doing with my life?"

Amanda swung around a car that was sluggishly obeying the speed limit. "Watch out," I said. "If you get us smashed into pulp, it won't matter if the guy's a dirt bag. If you're that upset, let me drive."

"I'm fine. It's my car. And don't get attached to those glasses; they only work with red hair." I handed the glasses back to her and then clenched my armrest as she swerved into yet another lane. She turned towards me to continue the conversation. "So Mark studied the whole time. Typical. You know, I wondered if you were going to come back at all. I thought maybe you'd call me to send your stuff."

"If I moved there, I probably wouldn't see him any more than I do now. He's really into school. Law is his life."

"Poor Sara. You look tragic, but Mark's always been self-centered. You might as well accept it. Men rarely change: look at Dad, he's a paragon of consistency. He treats Genine the same way he treated Mom, she just puts up with it better."

"If they don't change, why are you still going out with this skankhead doctor?"

"I'm not. I'm dropping him this instant."

"Good."

"I don't suppose you're going to give up on Mark."

"No, because I love him. And luckily he's married to me, not someone else."

Amanda shook her head. "What we do for love. It's such a silly game."

As we climbed the stairs to our apartment, a delivery guy dropped off a dozen roses with a message saying, "Forgive me, Robert."

"What a sleaze bag," I said.

"What a sweet, sweet man," Amanda said before heading to the kitchen for a vase. Being a paragon of consistency was not something my sister would ever find herself accused of.

I tossed my suitcase on my bed and wandered restlessly around the apartment, an extension of Amanda's personality that had taken her years to perfect. In my room she'd had roommates over the years, so she hadn't done much with it. The rest she'd transformed into, as she called it, acceptable space. In the living room she'd painted two walls midnight blue, the other two a deep rust red, and hung up her collection of African masks. After our father moved to San Diego, Amanda took him to an African arts imports store there. After none too subtly making her preferences known, she'd received a mask in the mail every Christmas and birthday since. My father always gave me scarves as presents. I had a drawer full of ones I never wore.

Amanda's apartment was surreal in more than just a figurative sense. Surrealists were one of her great passions. In the hallway she'd hung a set of black-and-white Man Ray photographs from the Twenties and Thirties. Klee and Miró posters adorned the intensely magenta walls of her bedroom, and a framed photo of Dali and his curlicue mustache stood on her nightstand. She offered to let me paint my room whatever color I wanted, but the off-white was fine. When I moved in, I hung up a Klimt calendar over my desk and was happy with my space. After all, it was only temporary.

Now I irritably sorted through my mail and stumbled over a pile of dirty clothes. This wasn't doing me any good. Time for some City Buddha-Mind walking.

Cast Amanda and Mark from your mind and consider the unity of all creation, I instructed myself determinedly as I crested the first hill. At the top I could see a slow-motion avalanche of fog cascading over Twin Peaks that would soon engulf my neighborhood. Though cities weren't the most inspiring places to contemplate nature, its forces were inescapable even here. Mesmerized, I watched the gray clouds billow and tumble while the three spires of Sutro Tower sailed above like the masts of a ghost ship. Ah, San Francisco. No, I didn't regret staying at all.

On my way home, I passed by our neighborhood bookstore and on impulse headed in. The precise notes of a Haydn quartet greeted me while burning incense in the air reminded me of a high church mass. Since I was far from finishing Tolstoy, I didn't immediately understand what had brought me through the door, and I browsed indifferently through the floor-to-ceiling shelves crammed with books until I found a section labeled "Bay Area Poets." The jumble of slim colorful paperbacks included two thin volumes by Aaron Lambert. I was surprised by my surprise. Had I doubted him so strongly? I ran a finger down the spine of one of the books, drew it towards me, and read a few lines, but the words ricocheted inside my head with little meaning. On the back cover there was no picture of the author, only a short biographical note indicating he lived in San Francisco.

Behind the cash register, a man with a black goatee and a small gold ring through one nostril was engrossed in a newspaper. It seemed frivolous buying the book, but if I put it on the shelf in my room, no one would know it was there. Safe enough. Maybe I'd start a collection of San Francisco poetry—extend my horizons. If one small book could push me this far outside my comfort zone, my horizons had ample room for expansion.

"Have you read much of him?" the man asked me as I handed him money.

"Not really."

"He reads sometimes, you know. At Brittle Books on Clement."

"Does he? Thanks." I stuffed the book and its little sack in my coat pocket before climbing the hill home. In my room I slipped the narrow paperback between *Mrs. Dalloway* and *The Ambassadors*. If I squinted, I could hardly see it. The paper sack smelled faintly of incense as I crinkled it up and tossed it into the trash.

At work the next day the changeover parts from engineering finally arrived. Joe promptly informed me they weren't going to work.

"Why is that?" I asked, looking up from my computer as I attempted to finish a report Paul had told me that morning he wanted by noon.

"Pieces don't line up worth squat. Holes aren't in the right places. And they're so flimsy, you could cut them apart with toenail clippers." Joe had brought one in to show me, and now he stood turning it over in his heavy, worn hands. He shook his head, apparently regretting so much time and money had gone into creating such an inferior object. "Bunch of junk."

I took the piece from him. It did look flimsy, its unpolished metal dully reflecting the fluorescent light overhead. "Joe, can you show me where the parts fit on the line?"

Only one piece didn't actually line up, and that was because it was missing an entire set of holes. I convinced Joe to have one of the mechanics drill the holes in our shop. The parts did seem less solid than our current ones, but they were also lighter and easier to lift. We decided to keep individual maintenance records on the new parts to see if they wore out more quickly.

"And Joe," I said, "can you time our next changeover with the new parts?"

"Why?"

"Just to see how much difference they make."

That request turned out to be a strategic error. The new parts apparently only reduced changeover times from three hours to two hours and fifty minutes. The shorter the changeover, the less productivity lost: my goal was to get them under thirty minutes. "That's okay," I said brightly. "I'm sure they'll take some getting used to. Let's graph it and measure our progress." I made a large graph on white paper with heavy black lines and put it up by the packing lines. By the end of the week, changeover times had dipped under two hours.

"Super job," I told everyone at our weekly meeting of the whole department. "Get our changeover time under an hour and we'll celebrate with pizza for everyone."

Managing to appear proud and annoyed at the same time, Joe rubbed his fuzzy crew cut head. "Anyone got any brilliant ideas on how to cut changeover times in half—again?" He glanced over at me, trying to convey that they'd already accomplished one miracle, how come I was asking for another? I smiled encouragingly. The department came up with a list of thirty ideas in less than ten minutes, a testament to the motivating powers of free pizza.

Saturday morning I was getting ready to go to the domestic violence shelter when Amanda called out that the phone was for me.

Our phone—black, to suit Amanda's taste—resided in a shallow niche in the hallway. As I picked it up, I gazed absently at a Man

Ray photo of a woman's nude back that'd been positioned and marked with scrolls to resemble a violin. The violin woman, I called her. I'd already racked up hours staring at the pearl grey curves of her back while listening to Mark's treatises on the environment.

"Hello?" I said. It was Aaron.

Feeling an urgent need for privacy, I pulled the phone to my room with the cord stretching just far enough for me to shut my door. Aaron asked how I'd been, and I gave him a general account of my trip to Washington. I certainly wasn't going to tell him about my problems with Mark, although maybe he'd be sympathetic. Maybe when he visited Elizabeth he was surrounded by people who droned on about the convolutions of the Trinity.

"How are things at work?" he asked.

"Okay. You were right about the cost accounting. Our accounting manager flipped out, but he'll get over it." So why are you calling me, I thought. And what will I say when you tell me?

"Sara, I was wondering if you'd like to see an exhibit of Frida Kahlo's paintings with me at the Mexican Museum at Fort Mason. It's small but I've heard it's good."

I was pleased but confused. Did he want somebody to accompany him to cultural events, and since I was married, I was non-threatening to his fiancée?

"When were you thinking of going?" I said.

"Tomorrow morning. I know it's last minute. I didn't give you much notice for the symphony either, did I? If you're interested, we could have breakfast beforehand."

I wanted to say yes so badly it gave me pause. Seconds ticked by.

"Sara, are you still there?"

I had to broach the subject. "What does, um, Elizabeth think about you inviting women to museums?"

"Why, what does—what's your husband's name?"

"Mark."

"Does Mark not approve of museums?" Amusement had crept into Aaron's voice.

"He likes museums just fine," I replied.

"Broad-minded of him."

This is ridiculous, Sara, decide. "What time?"

"How about we meet at Greens restaurant at ten?"

It was just breakfast and a museum, I told myself. At least Aaron was offering to go with me to a museum, not send me there on my own. I shrugged on my coat and headed to the shelter.

When I got there, two women had signed up to meet with me, but the first was nowhere to be seen. "She went shopping," someone said. I'd been stood up, not for the first time there. The second one, a short black woman with large shoulders and a no-nonsense attitude, was ready to go. Her name was Karla.

"I want you to tell me," she said right off.

"You want me to tell you what?"

"How to be like you."

"Like me? I'm not a psychological kind of counselor, Karla. I'm not qualified."

"I don't care about that psycho crap. You got nice clothes. You don't got no man beating you. Tell me how."

I sighed, looking at her. What to do, what to say. "You're not me, Karla. What's right for me might not be right for you."

She waved her hand to brush away my cobwebs. "Sara, cut the crap. Tell me."

Her skin was darker than Althea's, and her hair was pulled tightly flat along her head into a minuscule ponytail. Her eyes were large, and, I felt, accusing. "You need a job," I said.

"Yeah. I got one."

"Where?"

"Burger King."

She had two kids, no benefits at her job, and $200 in savings. "You have a place to live?" I asked.

"No. Well, I did in Oakland, but my ex is there, and I'm not going back. I live here now. My kids, things are going to be different for them."

I sighed again. Karla stared at me unblinking. She wanted me to transform her life. I wanted to shrink back from her so obvious need.

"You need a better job," I said.

"Yeah."

"What do you like to do?"

"Doesn't matter. I'll do whatever pays."

"What are you good at?"

She puckered her lips. "Numbers. I make change real well."

Before Burger King, she'd worked at a hardware store. We went through some basic math. She knew it.

"If you like numbers, how about bookkeeping? It could lead to other things."

"Yes," she said with certainty.

"Okay, let me think. I need to talk to Meg and maybe make some phone calls. Let's get back together Monday."

"How about tomorrow?"

"I can't tomorrow. Monday."

She frowned, her forehead creasing. "That's it? Can't we do more today?"

I looked at her a moment. "All right, let's go."

We went to a used bookstore and found a worn textbook called *Introduction to Accounting* that had exercises at the end of each chapter and only cost three dollars. "Read the first chapter and answer the questions. First do it by hand and then check your answers with this." I gave her a calculator and showed her how to use it.

She was finally satisfied I'd given her enough to do. I wondered if she'd be able to concentrate on it at all between her kids, her job, and her chaotic living situation.

Back at the shelter, I found Meg and asked if there were training programs Karla could attend.

"Two or three, but they all have six-month waiting lists. We can call to get her on them."

"Six months," I said, disappointed. "Maybe she could take a class at City College. The new semester starts in January. And then we could look into getting her an entry-level accounts payable job, or something like that."

"You really want to help her."

"I think she could do it."

"Good," Meg said, but she seemed to have misgivings.

"Why are you hesitant?" I asked.

"Help Karla, don't rescue her. Do you understand the difference?"
I paused. "Maybe not."

"Think about it."

I walked home with my hands in my pockets feeling down. I thought Meg didn't like me, didn't trust me, or something worse. Maybe I was over-enthusiastic about Karla, but surely that was better than not caring. I'd stop by City College on my way home Monday and pick up the course catalog for the next semester.

That evening I talked with Mark on the phone. He'd taken Benji to see a turtle movie and had been disappointed. Given the serious problems kids Benji's age were going to inherit, pizza, karate, and sarcasm were grossly inadequate for the task at hand. He'd tried to explain to Benji about racism, the national debt, and the hole in the ozone layer, but the kid didn't have a trace of political consciousness developed yet.

"I gave up and bought him an ice cream cone," he said.

"Don't despair, Mark, I'm sure he'll pick it up eventually, when he's about twenty. Let him enjoy his life in the meantime. Did Patricia go to the movie, too?"

"No, she needed to study. She's very intense about doing well this year."

"Mark," I said and paused, wondering if I should tell him about the Mexican museum.

"Mmm?"

"I, um, love you."

"Love you, too, Sara. Gotta go hit the books for a couple more hours. This next case is a killer."

I woke up early the next morning, well before my alarm, and walked for an hour to Fort Mason. Low fog gave me a feeling of walking underwater, and a damp urban smell curled up from the city sewers. The city was hushed with little traffic. Although I tried to clear my thoughts for the higher vistas of Buddha-Mind walking, Joe and Karla kept popping up, and even Patricia occupied a few blocks.

About halfway there I saw a mother holding two dark-haired little girls by the hand, one older than the other, probably headed to church. The girls were identically dressed in ruffled, navy blue dresses with white polka dots, their hair tied with floppy white bows. They looked like little dolls, but I remembered how much Amanda and I had despised being dressed alike. We had polka dot outfits, too. Ours were turquoise stretch pants with white polka dots and white tops with turquoise polka dots. I remember my mother insisting we wear them one Sunday when we went to visit our grandparents. I must've been four and Amanda seven years old. Amanda screamed and moaned; I complied. On the way there, we sat in the backseat of the car punching each other on our identically clad thighs until our father told us to cut it out or he'd stop the car and leave us by the side of the road. After that we contented ourselves with the silent but entertaining who-can-make-the-most-repulsive-gargoyle-face game.

It was that evening, after we came home, that has always stood out in my mind. My parents were arguing in the kitchen and dinner was late. Amanda and I lay stomach down next to each other on a shiny red vinyl beanbag chair about two feet from the TV set. We were watching *Bewitched*, our necks craned up, our turquoise legs pointing pigeon-toed into the floor. As the fighting grew louder, Amanda turned up the volume. When the sound of dishes breaking could be heard over Endora's cackles, Amanda turned up the volume even more. Finally, my father came out and sank heavily into his armchair the rest of us were forbidden to sit in. I looked at him. I thought he was so handsome.

"Come here, princess," he said.

Amanda looked sideways at me as I got up. I was his favorite. I went and sat in his lap and leaned back against him, my small hand on top of his on the armrest. Amanda ignored us as if we didn't exist.

"Turn it down, Amanda," my father said.

After Amanda adjusted the sound, I could hear my mother in the kitchen furiously chopping vegetables and sniffing every once in a while. I watched Samantha twitch her nose and make a copy of Darrin, much to his dismay. I wanted to be a witch so I could wiggle my nose and turn into a fairy princess in a magic land where nobody could go except me. Well, maybe I'd let Amanda in to be my servant, but there'd be absolutely no yelling or dish breaking.

Dinner was ready at last. My mother's eyes were red, her hair needed combing, and I remember thinking, she's so stupid. As a teenager I spent endless hours consoling my mother, but at age four, I had no compassion. He would always win; didn't she know that? Why did she bother to argue and make our dinner late?

When Amanda turned eight, she refused to be dressed like me any longer, and I was relieved.

I climbed up and over Pacific Heights, descended through the trendy shops and restaurants of Cow Hollow, few open this early, and continued into the Marina district. Having started early, I arrived early, so I stood for a while gazing at the marina adjacent to the Fort and listening as small waves slapped rhythmically against the tethered boats. This part of the Bay was close enough to the ocean to smell like the sea. Expensive boats in a prestigious yacht harbor—was this what Karla wanted? She probably didn't even know it existed. Money and wealth. Wealth and power. Power and control.

"Hello," Aaron said, startling me. I hadn't noticed him until he'd gotten close. He was more casual today in a navy-blue sweater, but there was still an enviable composure to him. And something more than that. I'm not sure this describes it, but he was very present. As if his thoughts weren't off somewhere else.

We made our way to the restaurant that had high ceilings and banks of windows overlooking the marina and were shown to a table with a beautiful gray soupy view, which, if it'd been clear, would've included the Golden Gate Bridge. Breakfast here was a less intimate setting than our last encounter, and I quickly felt at ease. We talked of work, my work that is, and Aaron congratulated me for what my department had achieved with changeovers. I was pleased. When I'd described our progress to Paul last week, he'd just stared back blankly. Aaron then told me about dial-in adjusters he'd seen at a Japanese consumer products plant that did rapid changeovers. I was intrigued and made a mental note to research it. Our conversation turned to my career goals and what might be next for me.

"The thing is," I said, "to get promoted again at Appleton-Smith, I'd have to transfer to another plant."

Aaron nodded. "Corporations like yours like to move their managers around."

"Paul's moved eight times for Appleton-Smith, and he wears it like a badge, his membership in the upper management club. But moving that much, you end up having no connection to your community, or your family even, only the company."

"That's the objective. Your identity becomes wrapped up in the company, the company's needs become your needs, and then you can be trusted. Is there another location you'd like to go to? Have you put in any requests?"

"I'm not going anywhere. I didn't fight so hard to stay here just to move for Appleton-Smith."

"Then you'll have to switch companies, which may be challenging," Aaron observed. "Manufacturing in the Bay Area is seeping away to places with lower costs of living. If you're willing to work outside of manufacturing, you'll have more options." He evaluated me a moment. "Your plant's not a particularly supportive environment. You realize that, don't you?"

"You sound concerned."

He looked at me seriously. "You told me you don't have any kind of mentor or sponsor, and after meeting your boss, I'd guess he doesn't do much in the way of coaching."

I shrugged and glanced out the window at the gently bobbing masts, wishing not for the first time that Jack hadn't retired and abandoned me. "Not much I can do about it until Paul moves on."

Our waitress came by to refill our cups, and Aaron asked for the check. When he turned back, he tilted his head as if evaluating me. As if he couldn't make up his mind. But I wasn't there for a job interview. I uncomfortably stirred milk into my coffee.

"All right," Aaron said suddenly. "Here's my offer. Since you don't have anybody else, I could mentor you until you get a new boss or change jobs. Within a year one or the other is bound to happen."

I stared back. "Why would you do that? You hardly know me."

He shrugged. "Because you could and should be a star at your company. Maybe it's my contribution to improving American manufacturing. However—" He raised a finger. "This is uncomfortable to say, but I want to explicitly state that I didn't invite you here to hit on you. You're married, I'm engaged, and I find cheating both distasteful and ethically repugnant. I want to be clear about that."

I blinked and counted to three. "Are you saying that I'd naturally cheat on my husband if you weren't so morally fastidious? And with you?"

"Not at all. Ah, I see you're offended."

The waitress returned with our bill, and I nearly snatched it from her hand.

"Can we split it?" Aaron said. "Tell me how much my half is."

"No," I said, scrounging through my purse for money. "I've got it. I wouldn't want you to sully your hands."

"Sara, we're going to split the bill." He put a twenty-dollar note on the table which covered far more than his half. Though annoyed, I wanted out of the restaurant and away from him. I added ten dollars, which made a ridiculously generous tip, and we left.

I thought about going home, but since I did want to see the exhibit, I decided to make do with giving Aaron the cold shoulder. We hardly spoke as we crossed to the museum and split up once inside to peruse the thick eyebrows and dripping blood of Frida Kahlo's self-portraits. I especially liked one of her with a monkey on her shoulder. The monkey and Frida stared out of the picture in just the same way. A brochure I picked up described her crippling accident and how it affected her art.

Aaron and I wound up standing together looking at *A Few Small Nips*, a painting of a woman stabbed numerous times by her boyfriend. The boyfriend stood next to the dead body, bloody knife still in his hand.

"She doesn't shy away from the difficult, does she?" Aaron commented.

"Yet another man trying for power and control," I said and walked away.

By the time we left the museum, my anger had abated. Not saying much, we found ourselves strolling past the marina and down along the green that stretched parallel to the water. I stopped to watch two boys trying to keep their kites aloft in the faint sea breeze.

"Not really enough wind today for kites," I said, attempting conversation as we headed back towards the marina.

"No, there isn't," he agreed. "Are you waiting for me to apologize?"

"No. But you should anyway."

We walked on. "I apologize," he said a minute later, "for appearing to imply that you are any less morally fastidious than myself. Now, could you use a mentor—and a friend?"

I glanced at him as we walked. What was he really offering and what was I on the verge of accepting? I looked at my watch. "I should be getting home."

"You walked, didn't you? Would you like a ride?"

"How did you know I walked?"

"The way you looked when I first saw you. Come on, my car's parked over there."

A true consultant's car, it was quiet, expensive, and dark blue, with a lone unmarked file folder the only source of disorder. I was disappointed it didn't offer up more than just his standard business persona. Amanda's Toyota was so full of stray art supplies she got on sale that she couldn't fit anyone in the back seat, but it was a definitive statement about her life.

Aaron stopped in front of my building with the car in neutral, still running. "So tell me," he said, "do you accept my offer?"

I longed to escape without committing. I knew I wanted to be challenged and appreciated and provoked. I wanted to be treated as if I mattered. I studied Aaron a moment. His eyes were sapphire blue, his eyelashes ink black, his expression impossible to read. Yes, I could use a mentor, but . . .

"Why do you want to do this? What do you get out of it?"

"Why are you volunteering at the Domestic Violence shelter?" he asked.

Fair enough, I thought. "All right," I said. "And we will both be morally fastidious."

That afternoon I climbed to our building's flat roof with some crackers to eat and Aaron's slim volume of poetry to read. The clouds retreated from our part of the city, and I spent many minutes between each poem surveying the neighborhood and thinking. Aaron's poetry alternated between visual, physical images and interior meditations, neither of which I was sure I understood. Poetry was such unfamiliar territory. Should I be looking for theme and symbolism or for the sheer impact of how the words echoed in my mind? Both, no doubt, but I felt inadequate for either task. I should've taken less business and more literature in college. After glancing through a few more poems, I resigned myself to Aaron remaining as inscrutable as when I'd bought the book.

I crunched a cracker in my hand and tossed the crumbs near the edge of the roof as I pondered the future. Would I have to choose between leaving Appleton-Smith or leaving San Francisco to move up in my career? Should I be a good wife and go find a job in the DC area? Did Aaron really think I was star material? I had to agree that cheating was distasteful and ethically wrong; I just wished beyond anything that Mark wasn't 3000 miles away. Eventually a few small birds found the sprinkled crumbs, and I sat hugging my knees and watching them eat in the late afternoon sun.

Monday afternoon, I gave my presentation to Bob Enders, the VP of manufacturing, in Paul's celadon-teal office. Paul and his boss, also named Bob, were there as well. The three men seated themselves around Paul's conference table, all of them well-groomed in dark blue suits, white shirts, and red ties. Bob and Bob sported glasses with gold aviator frames. Standing in front of them I shuffled my papers nervously until the indulgent smiles on their faces made me realize that Paul had prepped them with what I was going to say. Annoyed, I put up my first chart. I didn't like telling old news.

My presentation was a success. The nine or ten times Paul interrupted me, I ceded the floor like the gracious underling that I was. Bob Enders smiled and nodded throughout, asked a few questions, and told me I was doing a fine job, that shorter runs and lower inventories were exactly the direction we wanted to go. The other Bob and Paul nodded in agreement.

"Thank you very much, Sara," Paul said, his tan face beaming as he glanced from Bob to Bob.

"How long have you been with us, Sara?" Bob Enders asked.

"Four and a half years," I answered, clutching my papers.

"Super. Keep up the good work. We look forward to hearing more excellent results from you." Bob and Bob rose to their feet and heartily shook my hand. As I left Paul's office, I heard Bob Enders say, "Paul, you're doing a great job developing her. Fine talent."

"I agree, Paul. Excellent," the other Bob said.

"Thanks, Bob, Bob. I've done my best." Paul went on, but someone shut the door and I couldn't hear anything more. Well, it was over; they liked it. Fine. If only I could make the changes happen in my department as easily as I could present them to management.

Paul came by my office later that afternoon, a rare occurrence.

"Where are Bob and Bob?" I asked.

"On their way to the airport. They were only here for the afternoon. Good job with your presentation, Sara, it really impressed them. You may end up giving it a few more times. Bob and Bob talked about having folks from other plants come here to learn about the concept."

"I could just send them some notes. Or there's a pretty good book about how to lower inventories. It would save money in airfare."

"Oh, no, people always have a more profound learning experience when they have to fly somewhere to get it. Besides, we'd miss all the benefits of being first. This is perfect: our plant will be in the spotlight. It'll be wonderful exposure for us. Oh, and for you, too, of course. Just tremendous." Paul stood there shaking his head as if overwhelmed by the magnitude of it all. "Another thing, Sara. Our stock price has been slipping, and there's concern about our profit picture this quarter so cost has been moved to the number one priority. We've been directed to cut all costs by ten percent."

"But Paul, lotion and cream volumes are up. We're not overspending our budget, and I can hardly cut staffing or not fix things when they break. Is it overall cost per case they want to go down? Because I think our case cost has already dropped with the volume we're running."

Paul frowned. "Bob and Bob want a list of everything we're cutting out of our budget. We can try showing case costs, but I'm not sure it'll work. Pull your figures together for a cost review Thursday. Remember Sara, it's not so important what we do, but how Chicago perceives it."

"Spin control," I suggested. Paul flashed a smile but didn't say anything, just left. Even though this was in direct opposition to Deming's points ten, eleven, and twelve, I knew I should listen to him on this one. The politics of this company were Paul's full-time concern. If he had anything to teach me, it was the wily art of how to put on the right spin. But people's jobs, their lives, were what we were talking about. I thought it irresponsible, not to mention stupid, to put somebody out of work on a whim. If the company had problems with profit, they should look at the brands that were unprofitable, not try a disruptive, last-ditch effort like this. Mark would lecture that this was the inevitable outcome of the exploitative nature of capitalism, but irrational optimist that I was, I thought there were other possibilities that could include empowerment, fairness, cooperation, and productivity. I still planned to start a quality improvement project this month, costs or no costs. Deming laid the responsibility for change at the feet of management, and it frustrated me that I hadn't made more progress. Glaciers had receded at a faster pace than my department was currently moving.

I stopped by City College for Karla's catalog, and when I got home, I found Amanda sitting in the evening twilight with the lights off, smoking. She wore a black headband around her red hair, an ominous sign. The masks on the wall above her head grinned mischievously.

"Amanda, what are you doing?" She didn't answer. "Amanda, you're smoking."

"I'd forgotten how soothing this could be."

"What's up?" I said sharply. After a stressful day I had little tolerance for cigarette smoke.

"Robert's wife found out. We're through. He told me at the cash register while he bought an eraser and a tube of cyan."

I sighed and pulled off my hurting shoes. "I told you he was a scum bucket, no doubt descended from a long line of scum buckets." I massaged my feet. Though the heels I wore were only two inches high, at the end of a long day I always wished I'd worn flat shoes.

Amanda blew out a long gray stream of smoke. "An eraser. How symbolic. He should've bought some white out, too. Too bad our store doesn't sell disappearing ink."

"Amanda, did you even like him? Honestly?"

"Don't be so plebeian, Sara. That's not remotely the point."

"So tell me, what is the point?"

Amanda tapped ash off her cigarette into a half-eaten container of blueberry yogurt. "Life. Living."

"And how are you going to live?"

"How am I going to live," Amanda repeated. "Depressed, I think. I haven't been depressed in a while. Yes, it's time for a really blue funk."

I rolled my eyes. "You're going to be a lot of fun to live with."

"Fun," Amanda said, "is not the point."

Chapter Four

True to form, Amanda sank into a nasty, slothful depression that was only part act. I cajoled, I entertained, I coaxed. I dragged her to flea markets, to used clothing stores, to Humphrey Bogart movies. She sat around the apartment wearing ugly gray sweatpants, eating ice cream, and listening to her old Bobby Sherman albums.

"Amanda, Bobby Sherman?"

"The innocence, the innocence," she said, waving a cigarette in the air as Bobby crooned: *"Julie, Julie, Julie, do you love me? Julie, Julie, Julie, do you care?"*

I rolled my eyes. "At least turn it down a little. Do you want the neighbors to know you're listening to this?"

"Like I should be ashamed? This song, I'll have you know, is part of my cultural heritage." She went over to the window, opened it, and belted out with Bobby, *"Aw, Julie, Julie, are you thinking of me? Julie, Julie, will you still be there?"*

I shook my head. "You have completely flipped out. You yell at me to get going with my life and then you revert back to pre-adolescence. Listen to that. The record's scratched and everything." I remembered when it had gotten scratched. Dad had pounded on Amanda's locked door so hard that the record player sitting on the shelf had jumped.

"You're buying me a new record," she'd yelled.

"Open this goddamned door," he'd yelled back. Amanda was the only person who could make him swear. I couldn't remember why he'd wanted to get in, probably it'd just been time for dinner. My mother hadn't tried to mediate. The only time she'd ever intervened was when she sided with Amanda about putting the lock on the door in the first place. A girl needs her privacy, she'd said. I could always tell when Dad was ready to boil over, but Amanda had a habit of pushing him over the edge that resulted in pounding, yelling, and general tension. During scenes like that one my mother receded as far into the background as possible; I went to my room to read. Things were calmer once Amanda went away to college, but two years later my parents split up. Though Mom found out about Dad's affair with Genine only a few months after it'd started, it still rendered my senior year of high school a less than halcyon experience.

As Amanda's grand depression set and jelled, I spent time with Karla who was more fun to work with because she was more interested in being helped. Karla did not have the luxury of blue funks. When I met with her the Monday after our first meeting, she'd finished three chapters of the accounting book.

"I had some time," she said. "I got me and my boys a place to live, too."

"Really? Where?"

"In the Mission. I met this woman on the bus who was moving and talked her into subletting. It's a studio, so I can afford it. She said the landlord don't like kids, but he don't live near there, and my boys are real quiet, good kids."

"When are you moving in?"

"Moved in yesterday. No time to waste. Gotta get a move on. Some of those women in the shelter, they've been there months looking for an apartment. Not me, no way. I'm out of there."

We looked through the City College catalogue. "There. You can take Intro to Accounting, seven to nine on Mondays."

"What do you mean Intro? I already did the first three chapters. I can do all the chapters before January. What comes after Intro?"

"There's Intermediate Accounting on Wednesdays, but Karla, I don't know if it's a good idea to skip the first course."

"I can do it. You'll help me. What, you don't have no confidence in me?"

I sat back a moment, considering her. "How old are your kids?"

"Five and six. Jason and Eric. Got them started at their new school today."

"You didn't work today?"

"Worked today, too." What Karla had accomplished since I'd seen her two days before was beginning to amaze me.

We went over what she'd learned in the first three chapters. In the hallway next to us hordes of children played a squealing game of tag, making it difficult to concentrate. I suggested we meet at my apartment the next time where it would be quieter. Karla appeared undecided about my offer. "You can bring your kids along if you don't have a babysitter," I said. "Or we could do it at your apartment."

"No. If it's okay, I'll bring my boys. Thanks." She held up four fingers. "I'll do four more chapters by next week. You'll see."

I ran into Meg as I was leaving the shelter and told her about my progress with Karla. Meg wore jeans and an ample yellow T-shirt. Her short blond hair was flat and rumpled. Though she looked tired and distracted, the ever-present parrots dangled cheerfully from her ears.

"You're always here at the shelter," I commented.

"Not always, just a lot," Meg said. "I come Monday and Wednesday evenings and Saturday mornings."

"And you work during the week? A full schedule—you must not have kids."

"Oh, I have a daughter. I share an apartment with a woman who has two kids. We trade babysitting."

"Where do you get the energy?"

"It's important to me. You do what you have to do." She smiled halfheartedly and then turned to another woman who was waiting for her attention.

Though it was a pleasant enough conversation, I went home feeling as if no matter how much I did at the shelter, it would never be enough, I could never compete with Meg. Why I was trying to, I didn't know. We lived in completely different spheres.

At work I launched the quality improvement project I had my heart set on, but not without trepidation. This counted to me as much as anything I'd done at Appleton-Smith, and what if I couldn't pull it off, what if my vision had me headed not at the target I intended but towards a large-scale disaster that could jeopardize my entire career? Build quality into the product, Deming's point three told me. But it was easier said than done.

On the verge of angst-induced paralysis, I made myself consider short, thick-shouldered Karla. Without whining or flinching, she took on risks far more difficult than mine. Don't be a baby, I told myself. It's a leap of faith you're going to have to make, so do it already.

"Statistics sound kind of scary," I told the group of three workers who volunteered for the project, "but the numbers really just give you a good picture of how the line is running."

Bill, Susan, and Hector stared at me blankly. They regarded statistics the way I regarded quantum physics: nice for some people but, thank God, absolutely nonessential for daily living. I wondered how Deming convinced the Japanese he knew what he was talking about. Did his enthusiasm win them over, was it his logic, or did they just not have a choice? In the videos I'd seen of him, Deming was now a crusty octogenarian whose authority came from his evident track record. I was still building mine.

"What do you think our number one quality problem is?" I asked, trying to encourage discussion.

"Bad labels."

"Bad bottles."

"Bad suppliers."

Meaning: things that are outside our control and not our fault. We looked at the last three months of quality results and added up all the different defects. Too tight caps came out the highest, surprising us all. We plowed through pages of consumer complaint reports and tallied the problems people had called in about. Too tight caps were number one there as well.

"It's a torque issue," Hector, a line mechanic, said. "How tightly we torque on the caps." We decided to have someone measure cap torques hourly. Reviewing the data a week later we discovered our capper was on average torquing a little too tightly with too much variability.

"We had to increase the torque on the capper machine last year," Hector said. "The bottles weren't lining up right underneath it. Bottles from the supplier have gotten off-centered, or something. Maybe that's our variability."

"You know, there's a part that gets out of adjustment every changeover," Susan said. "It must get bumped or something, because it's not a changeover part, it's what helps aligns the bottles."

"I know what you're talking about," Bill said. "I don't know why they just don't weld that thing down so it don't move."

"What part?" Hector said. "You never said anything about it before."

"Because we always hammer it back into place," Bill said.

We went to examine the errant piece of metal. It was out of alignment. "What do you think about welding it, Hector?" I asked.

"Let me talk to Joe." And Hector went off to find his real boss who, obviously, was not me.

It annoyed me that I couldn't get anything done without Joe, but it was the truth. One way or another, I'd have to work it through him. Twenty minutes later, Joe came to see me, his face hard and tight-lipped. One of the fluorescent lights in my office was on the verge of going out and flickering on and off. Building maintenance had promised to fix it right away, which meant they might show up some time before the next century did.

"Look. The deal is you take care of the administrative B.S., and I take care of the floor. I don't step on your toes; you don't step on mine. That's the deal."

"Have a seat, Joe." I was playing for time in the futile hope he would calm down and become reasonable.

Joe sat down and folded his thick arms across his chest. "You don't see me messing around with your computer, do you? No, I respect your property. I keep my nose where it belongs. This is yours, and that—" he pointed out my window with one stubby finger at the lines, "is mine."

"Yes, I heard you. I wasn't aware that's how you see our roles."

"You managers breeze through here every two years. You come out of college wet behind the ears, you screw around with things, and then you leave, and I stay and clean up the mess. Well, I'm sick of shoveling shit. This place is going to hell, if you want my opinion, and it's management's fault."

I narrowed my eyes and wondered how much verbal abuse I would stand before I got nasty back. "Could you tell me specifically what you're upset about?"

"You want quicker changeovers; I give you quicker changeovers. And what happens? That woman wants to renege on our deal and double the number we have to do. Is that a reward? And then you get this hare-brained idea to weld my line in place." Joe closed his eyes and rubbed the bridge of his fleshy nose. "Why don't you just take a blow torch and melt the whole thing down. Go ahead, get it over with."

I tapped my fingers against my mouth. Have some sympathy, Sara. If you were him, you'd hate this, too. The light above me buzzed and popped fully on. "Joe, I know the changeovers are hard and that it's a huge change. You've done a great job. We made a deal for ten changeovers a month, and that deal will last another six weeks. I'll make sure Althea doesn't get ahead of herself before then." I paused. Joe gave no response, not even a grunt as he cleaned grease from under his fingernails with a penknife. The man could be as stubborn as Amanda, who, of course, was ornerier than most mules. I should be good at this, I thought. All those years of living with my sister should count for something.

I tried again, my tone firmer. "Joe, you and I need to work together. I'm willing to meet you halfway, but you can't stay completely closed to change. The world doesn't stand still, even if you want it to."

"I'm open to change," Joe said. "Good change, smart change."

"Let's talk about the welding." I showed him a graph of our defects and explained that consumers were calling about too tight caps and how the welding fit in.

Joe picked up the graph and the cap torque trend chart. "All this number stuff," he said. "We've gone for thirty years without all this number stuff."

"People can't get the caps off the bottles, Joe."

"Just some of them. Two out of a hundred."

"Enough of them."

He scowled. With a careless snap of the hand, he tossed the papers on my desk. "Okay, we'll weld it. You better be right." He snorted and left.

The fluorescent light above me abruptly returned to its moth-like flickering. I called building maintenance and told them I was going to change the light myself, and I hoped I wouldn't short out the factory floor when I did it. I smiled nicely when Bud from maintenance came to replace the light fifteen minutes later.

I told Aaron about all the trials and tribulations of changeovers and caps over dinner Friday night. I'd had dinner with him again two weeks before and very much enjoyed it. Aaron knew a surprising amount about the problems I faced and made several suggestions on how to collect better statistical data on the packing lines, even pulling out pen and paper at one point to explain in detail. Just having someone listen to my ideas felt invigorating, and no indecorous stray thoughts on my part cropped up. I left the evening feeling comfortable with the boundaries of the relationship and pleased to have found an interesting dinner companion who could provide me with such useful advice.

This Friday evening we ate at a small Thai restaurant. Above our table, the elegant King and Queen of Thailand smiled benignly from their official royal portrait, their hands offering orchids to the viewer. I'd had time before dinner to change out of my work clothes into an informal shirt and skirt with a sweater thrown over. Aaron's tweed blazer looked almost worn in places, surprising me; his suits always looked so impeccable. Maybe this jacket was one of his favorites, I thought. Though Aaron was attentive as we talked, he looked tired. I was tempted to speculate why but I didn't know how to gracefully bring up the topic, and anyway, he seemed to find my dilemmas at Appleton-Smith entertaining enough.

"I worked like a demon last week putting together numbers and graphs to convince Paul not to cut our staffing," I said as a waiter served our entrees redolent of basil and lemon grass. "And then this week he has a huge meeting to inform us that Chicago says Total Reliability is now our number one priority, that we'll lower costs through greater reliability. It seems like we get a new top priority every other week."

"Management jitters," Aaron said, pouring wine into my glass. "Appleton-Smith's stock price isn't doing well."

"Why is that, do you think?"

"Too much debt. They over-leveraged themselves with their last acquisition."

"Well, that's not my department's fault. It seems crazy to manage a company with a strategy that changes daily based on stock price. Joe says that if you ignore most of the things the hierarchy comes out with, they go away. No wonder he's so resistant to the stuff I'm doing. If he stalls long enough, I'll go away, too. There's no consistency."

"Constancy of purpose, Deming's first principle."

"That's right," I said with enthusiasm. "My favorite of his principles is drive out fear."

Aaron smiled. "My favorite is remove barriers that prevent pride of workmanship."

"I can't believe you can quote Deming. I thought only manufacturing geeks like me cared about him. Do you use his stuff in your consulting work?"

"Not really. American companies love hearing about Deming, but they almost never follow his advice. It would take focusing on the long term instead of next quarter's earnings."

"It must be discouraging for him."

"Who, Deming? There must be satisfaction in being ahead of your time."

"Very long-term satisfaction," I said. "Or very internally generated."

Aaron was quiet, smiling at me with tired eyes.

"Why are you smiling?" I said.

"You're so determined. You remind me of someone I used to know."

"Someone you liked, I hope?"

He nodded—a little sadly? "Someone I liked."

"You don't remind me of anyone I've ever met." I paused and then leaned forward. "I feel ridiculous, but I have a favor to ask. My sister Amanda is depressed and to cheer her up I offered to have her meet you. Would you be interested having brunch with us?"

"How could meeting me cheer your sister up?"

"You don't know Amanda. The strangest things appeal to her. She's been wanting to meet you for a while."

"She's your older sister?"

"Yes, but we're not at all alike."

He considered the invitation. "I'd love to."

"Good." Amanda is so good at getting me to do what she wants, I thought with annoyance as I pushed rice around my plate. I glanced at Aaron, wondering who I reminded him of. "How about Elizabeth? Is she a determined person?"

Aaron picked up his glass and eyed it with the enthusiasm usually reserved for hemlock. "Determined enough. She's decided she wants to see someone else." His expression grew even more downcast.

I was deeply surprised. He didn't strike me as the kind of man anyone would jilt. "That must be hard. I'm sorry."

Aaron set his glass down. "Getting engaged was a mistake. I think we've both known it for a while but didn't want to face it. To Elizabeth's credit, she finally did." He slumped back in his chair, looking past me, not seeing me. "I'll miss her though."

We were both silent a moment. "I'd guess you don't make many mistakes," I said. "This one must be painful."

He gave a half-hearted smile. "The last couple weeks haven't been the best, but it'll pass. It always does."

"Always? Is that experience talking?"

For the last few minutes, Aaron's thoughts had seemed elsewhere. Now his attention turned back to me, and his mood appeared to shift. "Enough of my troubles. I'd rather hear more about you. You never talk about Mark. Tell me about him, this absent husband."

I glanced around to see if the waiter might be coming to clear the table and rescue me. "What do you want to know?" When Aaron didn't answer, I sighed and pushed my glass toward him. As I watched him empty the rest of the wine into my glass, it occurred to me that I'd drunk more than my share of the bottle. "Mark. What can I say? We met in college, we've been married almost four years, and he thinks he wants to go into environmental law. He's very, um, dedicated to politics."

Aaron lifted his eyebrows slightly, as if to say "indeed."

I paused. "Is that enough?"

"No. Go on."

I began lining up my silverware at precise right angles to the table edge. "He likes being an activist. His dad's a lawyer but very conservative. His mom went back to school and got her Ph.D. in history and now she teaches. She's always been a radical—marches, sit ins. It's where he gets it, which, of course, annoys his father." I watched our waiter serve rice out of a silver tureen to another couple. "Uh, he's kind of tall. He played quarterback in high school, and he has a master's in political science. I suppose he'd be considered very all-American, except he's so anti-powers-that-be. What else?"

"The most important thing. Why did you marry him?"

"That's private."

Aaron shrugged. "I'll draw my own conclusions then."

"How can you criticize him when you haven't even met him?"

"It's interesting you think I'm criticizing, but it's not true. Maybe your marriage can set an example I can use next time around."

I frowned. I hardly thought Aaron saw Mark and me as role models, but it was difficult to refuse him. "When we met, he was the teaching assistant for my political science class and every girl in the room had a crush on him. After the semester was over, he asked me out and we fell in love." I tried to shrug casually as I glanced out the restaurant window. "I like being around him, I like his being so passionate about ending injustice. We have a lot in common." I looked back. "Will that do for an answer?"

"You were young when you married, weren't you? Yes, it'll do, though on a scale of one to ten, you only get four and a half for honesty."

"You're being horrible. I thought you weren't going to criticize."

"Tell me, if you truly love Mark, why did you stay and why did he go?"

Though I'd asked myself this a hundred times before, it seared to hear it from him. My eyes began to sting, and my throat constricted. Do not cry, I ordered myself. I curled my hand into a fist and pressed it tightly against my mouth. I should just get angry, I thought. It's so much less painful than this.

Aaron looked away. "I'm sorry, Sara; I am being horrible. Because I'm feeling badly, I make you feel badly. It's inexcusable."

I met his eyes briefly. Knowledge is power, I thought, and I shouldn't have given it to him.

"How old are you?" he asked gently.

"Twenty-seven." My voice was muffled by my hand.

"And you've already been married four years. I'm thirty-five and petrified of that kind of commitment. Between the two of us, you're the more courageous. Will you accept my apology? I really do mean it."

I finished my wine feeling sore and a bit battered. I did my best to prevent even Mark from being able to hurt me, and I especially wasn't going to take it from Aaron. As Aaron waited for my answer, I remembered he'd just been dumped by the woman he wanted to marry. Maybe I could scrounge up some lenience. "Apology accepted," I said. "This time."

We paid the bill, splitting it as usual, and emerged from the restaurant still early in the evening. "You like to walk—let's go for a walk," he said. "You choose. Where would you like to go?"

"The beach," I said on impulse. It was a warm evening for late October. "I never get to walk there at night."

He suggested Ocean Beach at the far end of Golden Gate Park, but I proposed driving to Half Moon Bay so we could see some stars away from the hazy night glare of the city. Aaron glanced at me with an amused frown, but he indulged me, and we drove south down the freeway that grew dark as we left the city behind. Eventually we turned on to a winding highway that passed over the northern end of the Santa Cruz Mountains. When we reached a dark beach south of Half Moon Bay, we took off our shoes and walked across loose dunes onto wet, packed sand and ebbing surf. Breaks in the scattered clouds offered glimpses of the moon and stars overhead. I loved the beach at night, but I'd only persuaded Mark to do this with me a couple times. The sound of the waves, a few other couples passing us, the intermittent moonlight were all classically romantic, but Mark wouldn't have noticed. He probably would've told me about emission levels from coastal sewage treatment plants. Aaron and I meandered the long stretch of sand talking easily of Tchaikovsky, Tolstoy, and the current troubles in Russia. Further down the shore someone's beach campfire flickered like a lone candle in a window.

I stopped and faced the dark waves and their dancing pale froth. The grainy wet sand prickled my feet as I curled my toes against it.

"We should be going," Aaron said, his voice close, his face barely discernible. "It's getting late."

"I suppose," I said, not moving. We stood anchored, a foot apart. Suddenly the clouds cleared from the moon, and I could see the waves break a hundred yards out. A large swell raced to our feet, fell short and was drawn back to the black mass of ocean. "The other edge of this is Asia," I said. "Hong Kong, Singapore, Shanghai. I'd love to see them. Do you think there are people there right now, standing on the beach like us except facing east, wondering what's on the other side? And here we are. On the other side." I turned, knowing the question I'd asked wasn't the one I wanted answered.

Aaron's face was expressionless, almost hard. "Sara, dinner's one thing. A dark moonlit beach is another. But you know that." I waited, hardly breathing. He looked at me a long moment, then shook his head and stepped away. "I'm not getting involved with a married woman. I'm not doing it." He started to walk back to the car.

I stayed where I was, mortified. I'd crossed the moral fastidiousness line and I knew it. I could pretend he'd misunderstood me, but still he might never speak to me again. What was wrong with me? I stumbled forward in the sand.

Aaron stopped to wait for me. When I caught up to him, we walked silently a moment. Then he said quietly, "I might be free now, but you're not. If you're going to stay with your husband, you'll want to have been faithful. You need to be able to live with yourself. Without guilt. Without shame. There's nothing more important."

I put my cool hands to my face to counteract its burning. My lips tasted of salt. "You don't need to lecture me. You're right, it was a mistake to come here." Who had cheated on Aaron, I wondered? Whoever it was, he hadn't forgiven her.

"Sara—" He caught my arm and turned me toward him. We stood paralyzed at the edge of the moonlit surf. "What are you looking for—escape? Amusement? Revenge for Mark leaving you alone?"

"Don't do this," I said. "If you're not interested, you're not interested."

"Not interested? Sara, if you tried, you couldn't torture me more. Of course, at this point, what's a little more pain?" As if mesmerized, Aaron slowly reached his hand out to my face. "I'll just add it to the pile, on top of whatever shreds are left of my conscience and judgment."

I closed my eyes, overwhelmed by my body's reaction to his fingers on my skin. Slowly I turned my head until I felt the palm of his hand curved against my mouth. Aaron's hand abruptly dropped.

"I'm completely losing my mind," he said.

Looking up, I saw an unfathomable mixture of desire and anguish on his face. A string of clouds covered the moon, concealing the waves once more but leaving the ocean's rushing incantation. A siren's song.

"Let me take you home," he said.

We walked back quietly. What a mistake, I thought. What a dreadful, dreadful mistake. Of course I should stay faithful to Mark. I wouldn't ever be able to face Aaron again in the daylight.

When we got to the car, I tucked my feet up under me, closed my eyes, and pretended to sleep. Eventually I did fall asleep. It was after one when Aaron stopped his car in front of my building, and I woke up.

"Brunch?" he asked.

"What?" I said, confused.

"Your sister."

"Oh, that's right, Amanda." I'd told her enough about my platonic relationship with Aaron that it would be difficult to put her off. My groggy brain turned over slowly. I never wanted to see him again; of course, I wanted to see him again. He was dangerous; no, he had control, better control than I did. Amanda knew me too well: she'd figure all this out. Did it matter? "I'll call you."

"Will you?" Aaron said, his earlier weariness returned. "Or will you be afraid to see me?"

I opened the car door. "I'll call you."

When Karla came over to our apartment with her kids the first time, I was at a loss because I realized we had nothing for them to do. Five-years-old Jason and six-years-old Eric sat quietly in front of the television as Karla and I went over the chapters in the kitchen, but every time they made the slightest noise, Karla ran into the living room and told them to quiet down. Amanda sat on the living room couch trying to read a magazine. After twenty minutes of interruptions, she jumped up.

"Ice cream time, Jason and Eric. Get your coats, we're going."

"You don't have to do that," Karla said.

"No problem. Come on, kids. Hup, hup, hup." And they were out of the apartment for over an hour. They returned with coloring books and crayons, and then Amanda supervised a crayon colorama session, as she put it.

"Thanks, Amanda," I told her after they'd left. "You were really good with them."

"Hmm," she said. "Are they going to come every week?"

The next Monday Amanda brought watercolor sets from her store. The week after that she and the kids cut out pictures of animals from magazines and made an enormous collage the size of our kitchen table. Karla told me later the kids tacked it up on the wall in their apartment.

"You've become an Art Project Queen," I told Amanda.

"I have many talents," Amanda said. "Most of them unappreciated."

"I appreciate this one." Karla and I were almost through chapter fourteen with ten chapters left to go.

After one of my Saturday sessions at the shelter, I went to find Meg.

"Can we go out and get a cup of coffee?" I wanted to get away from the chaos of shrieking children and constant interruptions so I could talk with her seriously. We sat at a small table in a coffee house decorated with prints of Mao Tse-tung in various Day-Glo colors. I felt nervous but not sure what intimidated me. Meg was only a little older than me. Maybe it was her size or her assurance, but she seemed to fill a large quantity of space with her presence. I'd stayed away from women like her in college.

I launched my idea. "The women I'm talking to don't seem to have a clue about how to get a job. They don't know how to write up a resume, answer an ad, or do well at an interview. I could do a workshop on job-seeking, maybe four or five women at a time. What do you think?"

"It might be helpful," Meg said, but she looked skeptical to me.

"Do you think women wouldn't want to come? Or don't you think I could do it?"

"What are your motives?"

"I don't know, to help. You take someone like Karla. If the other women could just show a tenth of her initiative—"

"Karla's exceptional," Meg countered. "You have to realize that."

"But the others could do what she's doing, it just takes—"

"Perhaps it's too bad you got such an easy one so early. You can't expect everyone to take off and run by themselves like Karla has. You've got to start from where they are, not from where you wish they were."

"I've put effort into working with Karla."

"Yes, but she was at the gate ready to go. With most of the others, they've been told for so long they're worthless and inferior that first they need to be convinced going down the track is worth the effort."

"You don't think much of me, do you?" I said.

"I think you don't understand what you're dealing with. You think everything will work out fine if people just try hard enough. But it's not that easy. These women didn't deserve to be battered, and it's not just poor women that it happens to. It's no use blaming the women for a problem our society has stuck them with."

"I didn't say anyone deserves to be hit."

"You sounded like you were blaming them for not having more initiative. When women come here, we try to help them understand how the battering is controlling them and to realize there's a way out. They can hardly go out and set the world on fire if they're constantly getting death threats and bruises."

"Okay, I don't understand what these women have been through. Maybe I shouldn't be volunteering at all if I'm so ignorant. If you're not a survivor, you can't join the club." Meg didn't say anything. "I didn't make this mess, Meg; I didn't hurt these women. Why are you so angry with me?"

She surveyed me, her mouth pulled down in a tight, cheerless frown. I half expected her to get up and walk out. She drew in a deep breath and slowly let it out. "I got married young, had a kid, never finished college. You have the life I wanted to have. It's not you, it's the space you fill."

At least she admitted it, I thought. Maybe I should stop volunteering. It seemed altruism took more patience and stamina than I was prepared to spare. I'd much rather escape to Tolstoy where the only motives in question were those of the characters.

"I'm not being fair," Meg said. "I know it. I'll work on it. Truce?"

Though I still felt resentful and unsure, I nodded slowly. After leaving the café, I felt an urgent need for exercise, so I hiked the long trek to the top of Twin Peaks. There, surrounded by a mini-UN of tourists chattering and snapping pictures, I looked out over the Golden Gate Bridge, the Marin headlands, Angel Island, and Alcatraz. What interested me most, though, was the city that lay at my feet. Market Street shot out in a thick straight line ending at the Ferry Building that was newly visible now that the Embarcadero Freeway had been torn down. If you wanted to get to the Ferry Building, you took Market Street. Point A to point B. If you wanted to get to the Bay Bridge, you took the freeway. Volunteering at the Shelter should be like that —you do A and B, you get C. It should be relatively easy to do and feel rewarding. Instead, I felt unappreciated as I tried to wade through the tortuous morass it was turning out to be. I had enough conflict and stress at work. Who was Meg to judge me, and why did I let her? I'd give it another couple of weeks, and if I still felt uncomfortable, I'd stop volunteering at the shelter and just work with Karla.

I talked it over with Mark on the phone that night.

"Meg doesn't matter," he said with assurance. "The important thing is you're making a difference."

"A difference to what?"

"Class structure. Patriarchy. Capitalism. You name it, they all need work."

"I wish you were here," I said. "It'll be nice to see you at Thanksgiving."

"You're sure you want me to come out?"

"What do you mean? Of course I'm sure. Haven't you bought your ticket yet?"

"Well, I could use the time to study. Even if I come out, I'm going to have to work a lot. You know, I thought I'd hate studying law, but actually it's a great mind game. It doesn't even feel like work."

"You know, Mark, sometimes I feel it's out of sight, out of mind with you."

"What do you mean?"

"Do you think about me?"

"Of course I do. All the time."

"You think about law and the environment, that's what you think about. If I had a toxic waste site named after me, then you'd think about me."

"Sara, that's not true, but you're right, of course I'll come out for Thanksgiving. I'll get my ticket tomorrow. And I'm proud of you volunteering at the domestic violence shelter. Patricia was impressed when I told her."

Mark really knew how to score points.

Why I ever offered to let Amanda meet Aaron, I don't know. I ran out of other ideas, and Amanda depressed is a pathetic sight. I tried talking her out of it, but when she accused me of having ulterior motives for being mysterious about him, I gave in, called Aaron, and asked him to meet us Sunday morning at a restaurant in Sausalito. He was there before us with a cup of coffee and *The New York Times*. As I introduced him to Amanda, I concentrated hard on not cringing and not thinking about the beach. Aaron, in contrast, appeared composed and relaxed as he folded up his newspaper. Cringing, apparently, was not in the emotional repertoire of a good consultant.

Though it was cool, the day was clear and brilliant. We decided to sit on an outdoor patio on the water's edge, wearing sweaters for the breeze and sunglasses for the glare. Seagulls barked at us from the roof of the restaurant while sailboats careened in front of the pristine backdrop of San Francisco. Amanda appeared cheerful, the rhinestones in her sunglasses glinting as she toyed with a cigarette she couldn't light. I let her carry the conversation until she drew me into it.

"Sara," she said sotto voce. "Look at that guy's leather jacket. It's exactly like the one I used to have."

"The one you wore that summer you and Penny chased after the Skull Tones?"

"We didn't chase after them. We were dedicated fans." Amanda turned to Aaron to explain. "We followed the Skull Tones wherever they played, wherever we could get in that is. We were sixteen and always stood right in front of the stage smoking cigarettes. We must've looked like little hoodlums."

"You were little hoodlums," I said. "And you never let me come with you."

"You were thirteen. We wouldn't have been caught dead with a thirteen-year-old."

"Did they ever return the attention?" Aaron asked.

"No, they all had girlfriends. They didn't know we existed. Looking back, we were so innocent."

"I remember you innocently sneaking a fifth of Dad's gin to a concert."

Amanda shrugged. "When I say innocent, I mean innocent of soul. The world was fresh and clean, and everything was possible."

Aaron removed his sunglasses and rubbed the lenses with his napkin. "And now?" he said, squinting in the sunlight.

Amanda held her unlit cigarette a few inches from her ear. "And now, complications abound."

"But they make life interesting, don't they?" Aaron said.

"In a dreary, squalid sort of way."

Aaron smiled, amused. "You sound as though you have no control over your life, yet you strike me as very capable."

"Oh, I am capable. My loss of control is temporary."

I wondered if Aaron could get through to Amanda with more success than I'd had. It was interesting watching him turn his attention on someone besides me.

He sipped his coffee. "Sara tells me you're depressed."

Well, that's direct, I thought.

"Yes, Sara's concerned, but I think of depression as a vast ocean that cleans and purifies the soul. A bout with it now and again is healthy, don't you think?"

"Rarely. The undertows involved can be dangerous."

"Sara tells me your fiancée broke your engagement."

"Amanda," I said, shocked. I kicked her leg under the table.

After moving her body parts out of my reach, Amanda continued. "Sara's a veritable conduit of information. I didn't bring it up to be mean. I just wondered how you've reconciled yourself to it."

The subject didn't appear to bother Aaron. "I've thought about it and decided she made the right choice. She's happy, and she deserves to be."

"Philosophy and reason were your consolation," Amanda said.

"Plus some soul searching. And time."

"I don't have that kind of patience."

I wondered now why I'd spent the previous week dreading seeing him. Aaron was behaving beautifully: polite, detached, a model of decorum. That night might never have happened. Why did he still want to see me? It didn't matter. I was going to stay faithful to Mark. Leaving Mark would be equivalent to stepping into an abyss. Even gazing into the possibility sent spikes of terror through me. I've read that fear of heights is really fear that you'll give in to a desire to throw yourself off. Without Mark I'd be in free fall.

"I think he's in love with you," Amanda told me when we got home.

"Amanda, you're so annoying."

"Why's that annoying? I think it's great. He's obviously content not to rush you. He's not my type, too reserved, but he might suit you. He's attractive, in a convoluted Russian novel sort of way, and I'd guess he's good in bed, which you shouldn't underrate. If they're not good at it when you meet them, they don't get much better later."

"You're unbelievable. I know you don't like Mark, but this isn't helpful."

"Of course, you have to consider he's on the rebound. Maybe this is only a passing thing."

"Leave me out of your fantasies."

"We'll see what we'll see."

During my monthly meeting with Paul, I showed him graphs and data on the cap torque project.

"I'm not sure this is worth your time, Sara. Chicago has statistically proven that people on the West Coast complain more than other parts of the country, and they factor that in."

"They factor it into what?"

"Our plant rating."

"Still, if we can fix the problem and reduce the complaints—"

"I suppose. Just don't expect Chicago to get excited about it. Consumers aren't the big thing right now. Total Reliability is. Chicago wants us to keep those lines running. By the way, Sara, I noticed your department is only at seventy-nine percent line efficiency. How are you going to improve it? Chicago wants to see eighty-five."

"Paul, we lose ten percent on changeovers, but we're saving $400,000 a year in inventory holding costs."

"Oh. Well don't count the changeovers in your reliability numbers."

"Really? Great." I knew it was game-playing, but our reliability was fine, and I didn't want to spend time working on it. If Paul would let me calculate the numbers more to our advantage, I would, but I wondered uneasily if I'd get in trouble for it later. I knew I'd never get him to put it in writing. Paul was careful about his paper trails.

I didn't see Aaron again before Thanksgiving. I went for walks, worked with Karla and at the shelter. Tolstoy was slow going since I had less time to read these days. My bookmark seemed permanently stuck in the middle of the fat tome, a prisoner of the Russian writer's verbosity and my fluctuating interest.

Mark must've studied furiously before and after Thanksgiving, because he didn't open a book once and made an effort to pay attention to me over the vacation. We spent hours in bed talking and making love and lying contentedly next to each other. Mark's political analyses, which I didn't tend to mind except when they were excessively long or directed at me, were kept to a minimum. I'm sure we annoyed Amanda to no end. When she acerbically commented how encouraging it was that married people could still be enthusiastic about sex, not that it mattered to her, now that she had joined the ranks of the terminally celibate, we just laughed and ignored her. I couldn't remember the last time I'd enjoyed being with Mark so much, and I caught myself, as we ate breakfast or as we agreed on a Christmas present for his mother or as I caressed his cheek as we made love, thinking maybe moving wasn't such a bad idea.

Sunday I stood close to Mark at the gate entrance as we waited for his plane. "I appreciate your spending time with me. I know you have a lot to do."

He put his arms around me and hugged me close. "Sara, I love you. I know I've been busy and crazy, and this has been hard for you."

I leaned my head on his shoulder. "It is hard. I miss you."

"Christmas. We'll have two weeks at Christmas. I'll be done with finals then, and I'll forget about law and think only of you."

A few more kisses and sighs, then he was back on the plane, and I was alone but feeling better. Two and a half years left to go. That afternoon, I walked all the way down Market Street to the Ferry

Building and stood looking at the Bay. Yes, I could go from point A —here and now—to point B—successful career, happy marriage. I was sure of it. All I needed to do was concentrate. I walked home and only got panhandled twice.

Chapter Five

"Do you want to get some lunch?" Meg asked the next time I was at the shelter. I was on the verge of telling her that this would be my last time volunteering. Maybe she'd already guessed as much, and the prospect of having one less bothersome dilettante on her hands relieved her. The lunch would be a good-bye of a sort.

It was now December, and the day was cool and gray. We walked to a crowded burrito place in the Mission and waited in line while they made our bean-filled masterpieces to order. Standing next to Meg who was six inches taller than me made me feel like a munchkin. It was the same at work. Appleton-Smith liked height and both the Bobs and Paul were close to six feet. It was why I wore heels to work, but even so, I knew it was an element of the game I'd never score well on. Of course, when I thought about it, five foot four didn't exactly qualify me as a pygmy.

We unwrapped the foil from our burritos. "Sara," Meg said, "I'm wondering if you'd be willing to help out with the children's Christmas party this year. We're having it at an elementary school gymnasium with a tree, Santa Claus, the works."

A children's party, with all those kids from the shelter running around coating every visible surface with sticky candy cane. The plan sounded distinctly unappealing. "Meg, I've decided not to volunteer at the shelter anymore."

"Why? Because of what I said a few weeks ago? Don't be silly. We need you."

"I don't understand domestic violence well enough."

"Sure you do."

"You've said the exact opposite to me before."

"Sara, you're valuable to the shelter—you've got energy and a good heart. Besides, I was the problem, not you, and I think I've managed to work through my stuff."

I frowned, not knowing what to make of this profession of my worth. I no longer saw the gleam of critical judgment in her eyes that had made me so uncomfortable before, but now that she wasn't attacking me with it, I had to acknowledge that some of her earlier criticism had been justified.

"You'll help with the Christmas party, won't you?" Meg said. "And maybe after the New Year would be a good time to start the job workshop."

I looked down uncertainly. "I'll think about it and let you know."

We got to talking about her daughter, Sabrina, and her experience with public schools in San Francisco. Meg knew a surprising amount about the different schools in the area.

"Have you always lived in San Francisco?" I asked.

"No, I used to live in Portland. I came here to get away from my husband."

"Does he ever see Sabrina?" I said, thinking maybe her daughter went to Portland to visit during the summer.

"No. He wasn't a very nice husband or father. We're well rid of him."

"I'm sorry."

Meg shrugged. "What are you doing this afternoon?" she said.

I shrugged. "Not much. Going for a walk."

"I'm taking Sabrina to the Exploratorium. She's been bugging me about it for ages. Would you like to come?"

"Sure," I said, surprised that she asked me and surprised at my response.

The Exploratorium, housed at the Palace of Fine Arts, had hands-on exhibits that taught about science. Sabrina, a tiny blond ten-year-old with glasses and a serious expression, was enthralled and almost danced from magnets to bubbles to electricity. Meg and I followed along behind her talking about our jobs. She said she'd had a boss exactly like Paul once and laughed when I told her about Bob and Bob. Meg was an administrative assistant at an office downtown and said she felt completely, utterly neutral about it. She shrugged off my questions about her life before San Francisco, and soon I stopped asking. Afterwards, in the wan December sunlight, we strolled among the ocher pillars and the reflecting pools left over from a long-ago world's fair while Sabrina skipped and twirled ahead of us, her long blond hair flying in her own private dance derived from the ballet lessons she took twice a week.

Meg and I got to talking about the shelter and how city and state politics affected funding for it. She was quite well informed.

"How do you know so much when you're just a volunteer?" I asked.

Meg smiled as she watched Sabrina swing around a pillar. "I used to work for a human services agency back in Portland. It's what I love to do."

I'd taken the bus with them there but didn't accompany them back, itching instead for a walk. After only a couple miles, twilight descended darkly enough that I gave in and caught the 22 down Fillmore. Gazing out the steamy bus window, I felt satisfied with the day. Getting to know Meg had been enjoyable, even if she did hold me a little at arm's distance. I wasn't one to rush to embrace people either.

That evening, Amanda and I went out for dinner and a movie. SNO, Amanda said, Sisters' Night Out. She convinced me we both should dress completely in black, and even draped a fringed ebony shawl around my shoulders. Looking wan and gothic, her intended effect, we posed for a timed photo.

"Look severe," she said. "We can make this into Christmas cards."

"You're the one who's depressed, not me."

The camera flashed. In spite of myself, I enjoyed being pulled into Amanda's theatrics, even though it invariably meant I got cast into the roles Amanda didn't want. I'd complained once, when she was nine and I was six, about why I had to be boring Sleeping Beauty stretched out on the coffee table while she got to be both the Wicked Fairy and Prince Charming. "You're always the princess," she replied while she hacked away at imaginary briars. "And princesses don't snore," she added with a shake of her finger when I attempted a puny defiance.

"They do, too," I said petulantly. "They do anything they want." Though I stayed on that coffee table, I began to suspect being a princess wasn't all it was cracked up to be.

Arriving at the movie early, Amanda and I sat slouched in the cavernous old Castro theater amid rows of empty seats. Up front, a man in a red-sequined tuxedo played perky Christmas carols on an old-fashioned organ, the kind that raised and lowered in front of the stage. As Amanda chewed on Milk Duds and I picked at a box of unbuttered popcorn, I mentioned the children's party at the shelter.

"I want to help Meg," I said, "but I'm not very good with kids."

"Could I come, too?" Amanda asked.

"Sure, if you want. I'm beginning to think you're a closet humanitarian."

"Maybe I'm inspired by your example."

"You're the one who told me I should volunteer."

"To your credit, you actually did," she said. "It's always easier said than done."

I was pleased: a straight compliment from Amanda was rare.

"You don't seem so down these days," I said. "Are you over Robert, finally?"

"Oh, probably. He was a tedious man, even if he did drive a Porsche."

"Good. Amanda, you go on some strange detours in your life." I threw a piece of popcorn in the air and tried to catch it in my mouth.

"Detours," she said. "That implies that there's one direction you're trying to go with a specific destination in mind. Your thinking's become very linear, Sara—too much Appleton-Smith. I don't see my life that way."

"Then how do you see it?"

"Circles, cycles. Evolution and discovery. It's a journey, but whatever step I take is the next step, and there's no definitive end point. I know you don't think so, but my Robert disaster was good for me."

"Amanda, disaster and good are mutually exclusive terms."

Stretching her arms up into the air, she flexed her fingers straight. "Au contraire. I've learned just what lengths I'll go to distract myself, and that sheer ego gratification is a poor excuse for a relationship." She drew her arms back in and picked up her box of Milk Duds. "Best of all, I finally know for sure that there's something about doctors that doesn't click with me. It must be the arrogance classes they take in medical school. So the whole thing was instructive, and the sex wasn't bad either."

"You take risks I'd never take," I said, thinking about my own lack of resiliency to rejection.

"You take a different set of risks, Sara. That's why we complement each other so well."

"Amanda, how come you don't like Mark?" This had always needled me.

"Oh, Mark's Mark. I like him well enough. It's your relationship with him that aggravates me. You got married too young, before you were fully formed. Now it's stunting you, keeping you from growing. And I'm not talking about career growth—I mean your emotional growth, your spiritual growth. You keep that side of you too clamped down."

"You're talking about *my* emotional maturity? May I remind you that you were the one listening to Bobby Sherman?"

"It's a journey; it never ends. You asked me what I thought. I know you're not going to like this, but you hide behind Mark. The concept of Mark. I don't think it's healthy."

I counted rapidly to ten. Having asked for her opinion didn't make it any easier to swallow. "Look," I said as people streamed in, filling up the theater, "I'm married, I have a responsible job. You preach about maturity as if you're an expert and I know nothing."

"Poor Sara," Amanda said, but sincerely, not flippantly. "Always straight A's and good citizenship stars all over your report card. Dad shouldn't have put so much pressure on you to perform; you're still wrapped up in it. You know, usually it's the oldest child that happens to. God knows how I escaped."

The sequined man and organ were descending out of view to a sprightly refrain of *O Come All Ye Faithful*.

"So you're sorry for me for doing well in school," I said. "I should've been more on the mediocre side like you."

"The point is not to make you inferior to me or me inferior to you."

"You and your points. What is the point, Amanda?"

The theater lights dimmed. "You're my sister. I care about you. We're not competing for parental attention anymore. Oh, good, previews. I love previews."

At work, the Lotion and Cream department edged closer to my vision of great manufacturing. After Hector welded the piece in place and turned the capping machine down, the number of tight cap defects dropped dramatically, increasing my confidence in Deming's theories and my own internal sense of direction. Joe's group kept making small improvements to the changeover process, including, after some lengthy negotiations on my part, adding dial-in adjusters to the conveyor guides, to the point that our department succeeded, the second week in December, in doing a changeover in less than an hour. We were then able to increase the number of changeovers per month to eighteen, and Joe began to speak of reducing changeover time as something he'd been wanting to work on for thirty years but never got the chance.

Joe and I were standing in the hallway discussing another modification he wanted to make when Althea approached us, a stack of computer printouts tucked under her arm. "Congratulations on your changeover time," Althea told Joe. She wore a deep violet suit and towered over both of us. "Our inventories are almost cut in half, and I'd say your group deserves a lot of credit."

Joe only nodded in reply, but he turned red, even up under his crew cut, and looked pleased.

"Both you and Joe have done super work, Althea," I said. "You both deserve credit." I could hear her humming to herself as she walked away.

"She sure looks happier," Joe said. I looked at him and wondered if he had any idea how difficult he made things for her at times. The intricacies of human relationships weren't Joe's specialty. If it didn't have a solenoid or a gearbox, he wasn't interested.

Althea and Joe continued to be pleasant to each other the Friday afternoon we shut the department down for pizza and an early holiday party. I reserved the largest conference room, ordered a dozen pizzas to be delivered, and someone brought a tape player that tinkled Christmas music through the hubbub. I'd just made a speech thanking everyone for their accomplishments when Paul leaned his head and shoulders into the room. He grinned as if he were the host of the party checking to make sure we were having a good time.

"Sara, can I see you a minute?" I went out into the hallway with him. "What's going on in there?" he asked.

"A pizza celebration. I promised it to them if they got changeover times down."

"Hmm. Do you think that's a good idea with all the budget constraints? We could be sending the wrong message."

"I'm paying for it with my own money, Paul."

"Oh. Okay, then. What I wanted to talk to you about is that Bob Enders and Bob Wilson are going to be here Monday, and I've heard they're going to announce that Total Quality is now our number one priority."

"Total Quality?"

"You know, like the cap stuff you were telling me about. It's perfect. I want you to give them a presentation on it."

"Could I bring—"

"No, just you this time. See you at ten on Monday. Mind if I get a slice?" Flashing his movie star smile that contrasted so well with his tan skin, he procured himself a piece of Pork Lover's Delight, and then strode back down the hall with visions of promotion no doubt dancing in his head. Paul, the sultan of spin. At least he'd remembered my project had something to do with quality.

I stayed late to get my presentation ready for Monday, tapping away at my computer in the depressing silence of a Friday evening at work. At six-thirty I rushed home to change and then out to have dinner with Aaron. I hadn't seen him in nearly a month. I was nervous, but I told myself I would concentrate, and it would go just fine. When I dug in to be as honest with myself as possible, I knew what I wanted was Aaron's attention and company without being unfaithful to Mark. Thanksgiving had made me feel better about Mark and more confident of my ability to stay clear about the long term. Wasn't the future, after all, a function of probable events? I just had to make sure some things stayed more probable than others.

We ate at a Cambodian restaurant on Clement Street with good food, formica tables, and plastic flowers. After dinner we strolled the length of the shopping district, chatting amiably as we wandered past closed Asian grocery stores. Aaron congratulated me on my progress with the caps and changeovers, and I felt reassured I'd accomplished something substantial.

The wind blew almost icily, very cold for San Francisco, and we headed towards Brittle Books for a cup of coffee at the cafe inside. Carved out of the bottom floors of a row of old buildings, the weather-beaten shop had acres of shelving, floors of knotty yellow pine, and smelled of books and roasted coffee, a delectable combination.

"I was told you read here sometimes," I said as we settled at our table.

"Sometimes," Aaron agreed. "It's been a while since I've had anything new published."

"Are you writing?"

"I'm working on a new collection. Slowly."

"Have you been too busy working?"

"Work takes up a lot of my time, but poetry always goes slowly for me."

"Will you always do it as a hobby?"

"You think it's a hobby?"

Our conversation was interrupted by a poet who began to read from a platform at one end of the bookstore's cafe. His collection, *Wild Man Blues*, involved occasional stomping of one foot. I wondered what that looked like in the written version of the poem. Mild applause ended the reading, and then a low rumble of conversation slipped back into place throughout the cafe.

"Let me see your hand," I told Aaron. "I want to tell your fortune." I'd watched Amanda do this a hundred times, and I wanted an opportunity to try out a theory I'd been turning over in my mind the last month.

Though Aaron looked surprised, he obliged and put his hand on the table. Nervous about touching him, I didn't pick his hand up, just bent over to peer more closely.

"Okay, let's see. Lifeline here." I traced my finger above it. "Very strong. You'll live until you're eighty-seven. But a small crease here—a car accident but it won't be serious. You had a healthy childhood—you were well protected maybe?" I glanced up to see him smile but say nothing. "Now this line, your heart line. It starts out strong, a passionate affair, but it breaks here—very tragic—she must've broken your heart. After that it gets fainter and a little scattered." I glanced up again. Amanda said that usually you could guess most of what to say from a person's response, but Aaron wasn't cooperating. I turned back to his hand. "I'd guess that no one could match up to her for a while. But here, the line picks up and ends strongly so there's no need to despair. You'll find someone else, and it'll all work out." I looked up to see the effect.

"Not bad," he said.

"Is it true?"

"Truth has a way of being relative, but your intuition's pretty adept. Can I see your hand now?" It was my turn to be surprised. "I have an aunt who's an expert on hands," he said. "People in my family fight to sit next to her at the dinner table. One of my favorite memories is when I asked her to give me a lesson as a Christmas present. I was four years old, it was snowing outside, and I sat on her lap in front of the fireplace while she told me about the lines on her hand. She has wonderful hands. She gave me a lesson every Christmas after that."

"It's hard to believe you have fortune tellers in your family."

"My grandmother was Romanian. Even Jung used to read palms. You'll have to move this way or there won't be enough light." With deep misgivings I scooted my chair closer and cautiously extended my right hand. "Relax," he said, "you'll get it back in one piece." Aaron took my hand, shook it by the wrist, and then placed it palm down on the table. I wore no rings on that hand; it looked bare and defenseless to me. Turning my palm up, he drew it toward him a few more inches until I had to lean my elbow on the table for balance. "Hands can reveal a person's inner world, but they don't tell the future, they just show where the past and the present might lead. They can change over time, too." Aaron stared at my hand for a full minute, tilting it from side to side and lifting it more towards the light. "Well, that explains that."

"What explains what?"

"Just a minute. There's a lot here." He flexed my fingers back gently with his thumb, then curved them in again. "There's your lifeline, long and curved all the way down, not too close to your thumb, a good sign. Let's see, you broke your arm when you were eight."

"Nine. All kids break their arm at that age."

"Do they? And here, pneumonia, it looks like, at twelve."

I narrowed my eyes. "Did Amanda tell you that?"

"And an operation of some kind . . . when you were sixteen or seventeen. Something to do with your stomach. An ulcer, maybe? No, something else."

"Your aunt must have taught you the fine art of wild guessing."

"The way your lifeline cuts up here says you like to keep tight control over your feelings and actions and that it's worked well for you. All sorts of bars and crosses—obstacles you've had to overcome. The significant ones leave their mark. Now the other lines." His fingers traced across my palm. "Head line there, heart line there, fate line there. See how the fate line intersects the head and heart?"

"I think you're making this up." But I peered down at my hand just the same.

Aaron ignored my lack of even polite credulity. "The way your life line and fate line meet shows you sometimes give others too much control, which seems to be the opposite of what I said before. Now here, where your head line joins your life line, shows you're strong-willed and determined, but the fork at the end means you can be indecisive. Your hand's a tangle of contradictions. The interesting ones always are. You're cautious and don't like risks, but you do take them in your professional life, which makes it likely you'll succeed. You're practical, compassionate, and sensitive but sometimes selfish. What else—" He squinted. "The light in here's not very good. Now this is interesting—there are things you're both attracted to and afraid of."

"Anything specific?" I asked dryly.

He glanced at my hand a moment more before he spoke. "Power. Passion. Men in general. Some men in particular." Though his words sounded ironic, his tone did not. In silence he continued looking down in a meditative sort of way. What could he really be seeing? I tried to curl my fingers and pull away. "Not yet," Aaron said and gently opened my fingers back up. "You're afraid of emotion, but why is what I'm trying to figure out. I'm sure it's here somewhere." He cupped my palm again to make the lines show more clearly. "Mmm."

I frowned at my hand. "What?"

"A couple of nasty slashes around the same time on both your heart and life lines. Difficulties or disappointments. Painful ones." I looked up, my hand still resting in his, to see him appraise me, his expression speculative, serious. "What left those marks, Sara? Whatever it was happened before Mark came on the scene, didn't it?"

You've turned out to be a very pretty girl, Sara. No. I don't think about that anymore. How could it be imprinted on my palm?

I pulled my hand away. This time he let it go.

"Some people are tougher than they look," he observed. "But you, perhaps, are more fragile."

I pressed my lips together in annoyance. "I work in a male-dominated field, managing men twice my age. I don't think that qualifies as fragile."

"That's the outer you," Aaron agreed.

I stood and pulled on my coat. "You don't get to analyze the inner me. I'm not one to shatter, I assure you."

We left and started walking towards the other end of Clement where we'd both parked. I pulled the collar of my coat close around my neck.

"How was Thanksgiving with your husband?" Aaron asked.

"Fine," I answered cautiously.

But all he said was, "Good. Sara, can I offer some business advice?"

There were few people still out and little traffic. Even the Christmas lights in the store windows were turned off. Our footsteps echoed against the sidewalk as we made our way down the nearly deserted street. "All right," I said.

"I know you don't think Paul or the Bobs know much about manufacturing, but even so, never let your disdain show."

"But they could easily know more. They could walk into the plant and look around for a start."

"It's *your* job to know about manufacturing, and it's your job to educate them when they seem interested. Any other way of looking at it will just frustrate you and get you into trouble."

I frowned as I tried to absorb this. "But the company would be more productive and more profitable if the hierarchy knew what it was doing."

"That may be, but you've got to focus on what you can control."

I shrugged. "Don't worry, I'm well-behaved during my presentations. Well, there was that one time when I contradicted Paul, and he wasn't too happy about it."

"Let me guess, in front of his boss?"

"'Fraid so."

"When was that?"

"Back in September, before you did the audit. I did learn from it, though. I may sound outraged when we talk, but at work I'm diplomatic." I glanced at him. "It helps, actually, that I can rant and rave with you."

Aaron nodded. "That's what I'm here for."

As we walked on, he seemed lost in thought. I couldn't help wondering if mentoring truly was all he was here for. "Will you start dating again, now that you've broken up with Elizabeth?" I asked.

He glanced at me with amusement. "How do you know I haven't?"

Monday afternoon I gave my presentation about cap torque to Bob and Bob. They were delighted.

"Sara, this fits right into the Total Quality program we're implementing," one Bob said, his face beaming behind his aviator-frame glasses.

"In fact, we may just use your cap fork example when we roll the program out to the other plants," the other Bob said.

"Cap torque," I couldn't resist correcting.

"Torque," Bob said. "Yes, of course. You know, Total Quality, doing the right things right, will decrease our costs and increase consumer satisfaction."

"Yes, there's such a cost to doing the wrong things wrong," the other Bob said.

"Does the Total Quality program include any of Deming's points?" I ventured.

"Deming? Yes, exactly. All of Deming, wouldn't you say, Bob?"

"Right, Bob. Deming's wonderful. We had him in to speak to the Executive Team. Cost a pretty penny, the old goat."

"Of course at times he goes a little off the deep end," Bob put in.

"True," the other Bob said. "Our entire American way of life involves competition and what's competition without some fear? That's why we have all our plants in a friendly competition. People need to keep looking over their shoulder so they don't get complacent. Right, Paul?"

"Exactly, Bob."

"Well, Sara, you've brought up some very good points. I enjoy talking about management philosophy. Good luck with the cap fork project. By the way, do you have any data showing it'll reduce costs?"

"Not directly," I said. "But we expect to see reduced consumer complaints which should mean increased sales in the long run."

Bob looked grim behind his aviator frames. "Consumer satisfaction is all very fine, but we're hoping Total Quality will help the profit picture this quarter. Hmm. We'll have to work on a different example that shows a direct correlation to cost."

"Layoffs may be the only answer," the other Bob said.

"Or contract out the work so we don't have to pay benefits," Paul suggested.

"Now there's an idea," Bob said, raising an eyebrow. We all rose to our feet.

"By the way, Sara," Paul said. "Congratulations on your reliability numbers. Her department's efficiency has jumped ten points the last month."

"Now that's something we always like to see," Bob said.

There was no point embarrassing Paul by reminding him I'd just calculated the numbers differently. My costs are fine, I told myself. I was going to come in under budget, so I should just shut up and take the credit, although it wasn't what I wanted credit for. I was so upset after the Bob and Bob presentation that I shut my office door and called Aaron at work.

"How can they be so insane? All they think about is how they can squeeze money out of the company tomorrow. Either they're completely stupid or completely hypocritical, and I don't know which is worse."

"Both are possible," Aaron laughed. "But the real answer is they're doing what they're rewarded for."

"I don't get it. I'm not saying you shouldn't pay attention to profits, but they have to think about how to stay in business five years from now, too."

"Their bonuses are probably based on stock price or quarterly earnings or both."

"Oh." I was silent a moment, rubbing my forehead. I'd overlooked this obvious motivational tool. "I feel like I'm trying to make real improvements, and they just don't seem to care. Why should I keep caring?"

"You know the answer to that one. Because you have integrity. Keep doing what you're doing, Sara. In spite of themselves, they can't help but reward you for it."

I could tell from Aaron's voice that he was smiling on the other end of the phone. He probably thinks I'm naive and idealistic, I thought. Still, talking to him made me feel better. I looked up at my poster of Deming's Fourteen Points and sighed. "Thanks for the pep talk. Sorry to bother you at work."

"I don't mind. Appleton-Smith has a way of making me appreciate Merrisocks."

Amanda and I baked cookies, a rare activity for us, and brought them to the children's Christmas party Saturday afternoon. Amanda wore a green mini skirt, a red blouse, and a Santa hat. I wore jeans and a sweatshirt, less than glamorous but highly machine washable. Though there seemed to be hundreds of children swarming through the gym, the real number was probably closer to fifty. Meg's parrot earrings jangled as she continually turned and pointed in all directions. She assigned Amanda and me to help Santa Claus with gift distribution. Santa was on the gaunt rather than pudgy side and had large circles under his eyes, but he handed out presents, delivered the requisite ho-ho's and kidded the children. They pulled his beard, told him they could tell he was wearing pillows, and then went off with their toys and candy canes to sing carols in another part of the gym, only knocking the Christmas tree down twice in the process.

Karla was there with her kids who, as usual, were perfectly behaved. When Jason and Eric saw Amanda, they ran over and hugged her. Amanda had brought special presents for them—a set of pastels and two boxes of sixty-four crayons with their names painted on the tops.

"You're going to spoil them, Amanda," Karla said. "What do you say, boys?"

"Thank you," their little voices chimed in unison.

Amanda bent down, hands on her knees. "Bring the pastels Monday night and I'll show you how to use them."

Two hours later, after the last child had sat on Santa's lap, I collapsed with relief.

"Sara, you're being a weenie," Amanda said. She was working with Santa to box up the leftover presents. "Come help us."

"You're doing a fine job. Children exhaust me. I'm too tired to move."

Though I couldn't see his mouth hidden by his cottony white beard, Santa's eyes crinkled in a smile. "It's okay. We're just about done," he said as he handed a couple more packages to Amanda.

The gym emptied until there were just a few of us volunteers left, hands on hips, gazing around the varnished yellow wood floor for scraps of wrapping paper, tinsel, and cookie crumbs.

"At last, I can take this off." Santa's white hair and red costume disappeared, and a man in his late thirties with a short brown beard and tired, baggy eyes emerged.

"What did you say your name was?" Amanda said.

"Frank. And you're Amanda and Sara, right?"

"We're sisters," Amanda said. "Sara's married, and her husband's in law school."

She's making sure he knows which one of us is single, I thought. Typical.

Meg was waving everyone out of the gym. "All right folks, super work. Thanks a million."

Sabrina pulled Meg's arm towards the door. "Come on, Mom."

"Frank, could you drop off the leftover presents at the family homeless shelter?" Meg said. "Sabrina and I are going to see *The Nutcracker* tonight, and we still have to go home and change."

"We'll help you," Amanda promptly told Frank.

We loaded the presents into Frank's car, an ancient Volkswagen Bug. "Do you want us to come with you to unload them?" Amanda said. "You'll probably have to double-park."

Come on, Amanda, I thought. "I'm hungry," I hissed at her as I tried to wedge myself between the presents in the back seat.

"You should've eaten more cookies," Amanda said, making herself comfortable in the front.

We drove to the family homeless shelter where Frank indeed had to double-park. The woman we handed the presents to was grouchy and didn't even say thank you, but the children standing behind her gazed at the packages wide-eyed.

"Would you like to get something to eat?" Amanda said after we finished. "Verdi's isn't too far from here."

Frank looked at his watch. He'd been quiet, almost solemn in the car. "Sure."

I shrugged to myself in the cramped back seat. No one asked my opinion. Evidently I was along for the ride.

We drove to Verdi's, an Italian cafe where opera played and the waiters and waitresses occasionally broke into arias. During dinner Amanda kept her Santa hat on and put herself out to be more effervescent than usual. I consoled myself with linguine and a glass of Chianti. Frank was silent to the point of being taciturn, but he seemed interested in Amanda's chatter, gazing at her as if engrossed. Near the end of dinner he rested his chin on his hand, his eyes drooped, and I thought he might fall asleep.

"Sorry," Frank said suddenly, sitting up. "I've been up thirty-six hours so jab me if I nod off." His dark brown eyes were red around the edges, and his neck below his beard needed shaving.

"Why were you up thirty-six hours?" I asked.

"I was on call and ended up working all night."

"Where do you work?"

"SF General."

"You're a doctor," Amanda said, frowning.

"I suppose you're married," I put in dourly.

"Divorced." Frank looked down at the table and flipped a spoon over in one hand. "I work a lot. My curse and joy."

"What kind of medicine do you do?" I asked.

"Infectious diseases. I work with AIDS patients mainly these days." Frank yawned widely and then shook his head. "Sorry."

"You're exhausted," Amanda said. "We shouldn't be keeping you up. Time to go."

After Frank dropped us off, it was still early so Amanda and I walked to the video store to rent a movie. Amanda unpinned her red hat and took it off as we walked home up the hill.

"Frank seemed nice," I commented.

"Kind of quiet," Amanda said.

"You seemed interested. You going to call him?"

"I've had my fill of doctors for the year."

"He's not like Robert," I said.

"How do you know? He's divorced. He could be just like him."

"Would Robert ever have volunteered to be Santa at a kids' Christmas party?"

"Definitely not."

"So?"

"I'm not calling him," Amanda said. "Doctors are a strange breed of human. Besides, he seems happy enough. I don't need to interfere with his life."

"You had no qualms interfering this evening. You surprise me, Amanda, you really do."

"Surprises in life are good," she answered nonchalantly. "Haven't you learned anything from living with me?"

I had dinner with Aaron the Friday night before Mark came home for Christmas break.

"Will you be going to Boston for the holidays?" I asked over gumbo at a Creole restaurant.

"For a few days," Aaron said. "Then I spend a day in New York with my sister to meet her new boyfriend."

"She doesn't want to bring him home yet?"

"Paula's learned her lesson on that score. Once my mother hit sixty, she decided it was time for grandchildren. She's close to giving up on me, but with Paula she shows no mercy."

"Your mother must've been upset about your engagement ending," I observed.

"Yes, she was. Very," he said shortly.

Uh oh. Time to change the subject. "And after New York you come back here?"

"No, then I go to Paris for a week to visit friends."

"Hard life," I said. "Are your friends American or French?"

"Both. I know Monica from school. She moved to Paris and met Henri. These days both of them paint."

"That sounds romantic, run away to Paris and marry a painter. Was she an art student in school?"

"No, we met at business school. Art suits her much better, though she hasn't exactly given up on business."

"So they're not starving artists, living in the Latin Quarter in a garret with no heat?"

Aaron laughed. "That wouldn't appeal to Monica at all."

"Is she an old girlfriend?" I wondered if maybe this was the woman I'd unsuccessfully tried to get him to admit to.

Aaron sipped his wine. "Is Mark coming home for the holidays?"

"He comes back tomorrow. Now about this Monica, is she—"

"Did you know Amanda invited me to dinner Sunday?"

I blinked. "She did what?"

When I got home, I hunted Amanda down with a vengeance. "How could you?" I yelled when I found her in bed with a novel, her hair pulled back and reading glasses on, the magenta walls deepening to violet in the shadows of the room.

"Aaron told you," she said, turning a page. "Coward. He should've just shown up."

"Oh, that would've been much better. Tremendous. Just stellar. Amanda, you had no business calling him."

"I thought it might be interesting for Aaron to meet Mark. So did he."

I felt intensely annoyed. "I could invite Frank and make it even more interesting."

"Invite whomever you like." Amanda turned another page.

"You're so manipulative."

"Really, Sara, it's not as if you're sleeping with him. Why shouldn't Mark meet Aaron?"

"I should be the one to decide that. You just got it in your head to pick up the phone and call him. You amaze me, Amanda."

"Amazing Amanda, Serious Sara. Close the door when you go, would you?"

I gave the door a sharp tug and decided what the hell, I would invite Frank.

Chapter Six

When I picked Mark up from the airport Saturday evening, he was tired from studying but elated that he'd done well. He kissed me on the cheek and then put an arm around my shoulders as we walked to get his bags. He looked scrubby, his face unshaven, his thick dark brown hair overgrown. Still, women turned to look at him as we walked by. He was that good looking, though to his credit and my peace of mind, he rarely appeared to notice the attention he received.

"And Patricia did well," Mark said. "I gave her some coaching, but I knew she could do it."

"Good for her," I unenthusiastically replied.

"Most of the time, I just took Benji off her hands to give her time to study. He's a great little guy, and he loves movies. You know, Disney is coming out with some new masterpieces. Extraordinary animation."

I looked up at him. "Mark, Amanda's invited some guests over for dinner tomorrow night. You don't have to meet them. We could go out if you want."

"I don't mind, as long as they don't stay late. I have about a month's worth of sleep to catch up on. Two weeks of freedom, it feels great. Sara, let's go skiing for a couple days. There'll be a mob up there, but the skiing in the East is pathetic. Did I tell you John called before I left?

He gave me a ton of grief about skiing being bourgeois and ecologically unsound, but I lived right next to the mountains when I was a kid, I grew up skiing, and it's not like we're going to go snowmobiling. Then he accuses me of still feeling entitled because I haven't sufficiently renounced my bourgeois identity, like I'm not a good enough Marxist and he's going to disown me. The guy lives on another planet, but I told him we'd have dinner with him in Palo Alto next week anyway. Evidently his socialist coalition is falling apart. I could've told him it would: they never established their dialectic properly. Now he'll just have to start over."

In addition to the regular holidays, I planned to take a week of vacation to spend time with Mark. Though it'd been three weeks since we'd last been together, I'd been too busy to miss him much, and as we walked through the airport, I glanced at him covertly. After every gap in time I saw him now, I appraised him against my remembered conception and always felt a slight shock at the discrepancy. Physically, he appealed to me more than my memory could do justice. The reality of his smile, his shoulders, his hands—and knowing he was mine—never failed to elate me. When we were apart, though, I tended to forget just how absorbed in his own world he could be. It now crashed over me like a wave over the bridge of a ship.

With one ear I heard more about law school and his environmental student group as we stood next to the luggage carousel. He told me how there was literally an environmental war going on in our country. I thought about Tolstoy and his lengthy views about Napoleon not being a military genius, just lucky and unlucky in turn, and then about the friendly competition that the two Bobs liked to encourage between the plants. Men and war, men and politics, men and business. It was all about winners and losers and destruction and different forms of violence, and I was sick of it. Time for new metaphors, a new paradigm, one that didn't make me feel so bone-weary. I agreed with Mark that we needed to change environmental policy, but it seemed to me that in any kind of war, even a political one of rhetoric and policy, the environment always ended up a casualty. Surely recognition of mutual goals and cooperation would be more efficient and productive. I had a feeling that this attitude would be a complete failure in the military, that environmentalists wouldn't consider me of much use, and that I probably didn't even rank as a good capitalist. I sighed deeply.

"What's the matter?" Mark said, his arm around my shoulders.

I leaned my head against him. "I'm just tired." The last meeting with Bob and Bob and Paul had stayed with me, weighing me down.

I looked up Frank's number and invited him to dinner. Since he hardly knew us, it surprised me when he accepted, but maybe the Christmas season makes everyone lonely for company. Amanda planned a Tunisian couscous dish that I hardly helped her with since I considered the whole event to be her responsibility. An hour before dinner she emerged from her bedroom wearing a low-cut green silk blouse, a black calf-length skirt slit to the knee, and sheer black nylons. I tried on four different outfits while telling myself I was being ridiculous, that what I wore didn't matter in the least. I settled on a long, full skirt and a soft blue sweater. "Are you going to wear all those?" Mark said when he saw the piles of clothes I'd rejected draped over the bed. I brushed my hair furiously but it wouldn't stay back. Why did I agree to this? I should've dragged Mark out to dinner somewhere.

Ten minutes before guests were to arrive Amanda decided the evening demanded candlelight, so she turn off the lights and lit everything in the living room that possessed a wick. Frank showed up just as the fire alarm went off, causing a certain amount of confusion, but after Amanda opened a couple of windows the smoke cleared out, and when Aaron arrived, I was grateful that the dim light provided camouflage. All too soon everyone had been introduced and the five of us were installed amidst the small inferno of candle flames. Aaron seated himself next to Mark on the couch, both of them looking unnecessarily relaxed and calm. Frank, taciturn and friendly, sat in an armchair next to Amanda, the vivacious hostess and sister from hell. I pulled a dining chair into the circle but was too jumpy to sit for long, instead bringing out hors d'oeuvres or refilling people's glasses.

Gazing out the front window at the city lights, I felt a strong desire to be out walking, anything rather than listen to Aaron learn more about Mark than I wanted him to know. Aaron asked Mark about law school, and they soon moved on to environmental issues while the African masks above the couch eavesdropped with mischief in their hollow eyes. Mark spoke with animation, pleased to find a receptive listener, but even from across the room I was prone to wince, so I made myself join Amanda and Frank's conversation. Amanda had apparently decided to give Frank another chance despite his occupation. Frank looked more rested, the circles under his brown eyes having lightened to chronic fatigue rather than exhaustion. A few strands of gray ran through his shaggy brown hair and short beard.

"I can't stand doctors," Amanda was telling him with a laugh.

"She doesn't mean personally," I said.

"It's an impersonal dislike?" Frank said. He stroked his beard with the back of a bent finger.

"It depends on the person," Amanda said.

"Judging someone based on generalizations about a group is called prejudice," Frank said.

"I have many, many forms of prejudice," she replied.

"Admitting one's prejudices is the first step in getting past them."

"I'm comfortable with my prejudices. I'm not sure I want to trade them in just yet."

Frank rested the side of his face on his fist, maybe smiling a little. I couldn't tell with the beard and the candlelight.

"Be nice to him, Amanda," I said to her when we were alone in the kitchen. "I think he's lonely."

"When am I not nice?" Amanda said, pulling a dish from the oven between two potholders. "Just for you, I'll be charming." She shut the oven door with her foot, sending an aroma of clove and saffron wafting through the room.

We carried the food to the table where Amanda promptly lit six more candles. "Sara, you sit on that end, and I'll sit on this end since we're the heads of the household here."

She placed Aaron on one side of the table and Mark and Frank opposite. Her conversation with Frank quickly excluded the rest of us, which left me with Aaron and Mark, reluctant to speak for fear of what I might reveal. I knew there were flaws in my marriage that Aaron wouldn't need to see our palms to figure out. I also felt uncomfortable with Mark discovering how well I knew Aaron as I hadn't brought Aaron up much during our phone calls. This, of course, was what Amanda wanted to flush out, why she'd invited Aaron, but I didn't see how it was supposed to help my spiritual growth. Give me an ulcer, more likely. She's always had a sadistic streak, I thought as I watched her actually stoop to batting her eyelashes at Frank. It looked like she was ready to trade in her prejudices after all.

"How do you know Amanda?" Mark asked Aaron.

"It was Sara that I met first," Aaron said, smiling only a little at Mark's assumption.

"We went to the symphony together," I said. "Remember, I told you about it. It must've been September."

"Oh, right," Mark said. "Now you're not the one, no, that guy was a doctor, wasn't he?"

"A different doctor," I said, glancing at Frank who didn't appear to have heard us. "He's through, thank goodness."

"That's right, I remember now," Mark said, nodding his head as he ate. "He was married, wasn't he?"

"Yes, Amanda was very stupid," I said.

"Stupid about what, Sara? It's wonderful to have your sister insult you during dinner," Amanda said to Frank.

"Nothing. Just commenting on one of your past adventures which we are completely finished discussing. Go on with what you were saying." I waved her attention away. "Aaron, would you like some more bread?"

Aaron shook his head, his eyes meeting mine for a second before he turned away. "Mark, how did you and Sara meet?" Did he not believe my version of it, I wondered?

"I was her political science TA. I guess she wanted a good grade." This was Mark's standard joke.

"We didn't date while I took the class," I said crossly.

Mark smiled at me fondly. "No, we were very proper."

"Besides, there was always a flock of women around you. I don't think you would've noticed me except you liked one of my papers."

"Oh, I noticed you," Mark said. "Though your paper on liberation theology was pretty good. You should've kept it."

Aaron had finished his meal and sat back in his chair sipping his wine, his attention on Mark. Evaluating him, no doubt, I thought. I didn't want to know where my marriage fell on a scale of one to ten.

"Liberation theology," Aaron repeated. "And then you both moved to San Francisco after you finished school?"

"We liked living here, didn't we, Sara?"

"I still live here."

"But you know," Mark said, "San Francisco's provincial compared to the East Coast. So much more happens out there. You said you're from Boston, didn't you? Don't you agree?"

"Washington is certainly the place for politics," Aaron said.

"Definitely. Once you're there, it's a closed system. Anything beyond the Beltway hardly exists. Very corrupt and myopic, but it's where decisions get made, the big ones."

"The corridors of power," Aaron suggested.

"Exactly. Our environmental group has been able to set up forums with congressmen and the head of the Sierra Club that we'd never be able to do out here."

"What about grassroots activism, Mark?" I asked. "You used to say it was so important to get people organized on a local level."

"Grassroots is vital, and it factors in, but Washington's a whole different ball game. The contacts I'm making now will be unbelievably valuable later."

"What are your plans after you graduate?" Aaron asked.

"I'll probably work for the legal arm of an environmental non-profit. Maybe lobbying eventually."

"In Washington?" Aaron suggested.

"It'd have to be."

"I admire your commitment," Aaron said. "The temptation for most people is to do what it takes to pay back their student loans. But it doesn't sound like you're interested in corporate law."

"I'll owe a big chunk of money, it's how they try to hook you into behaving correctly later, but I'll pay it off eventually. Nothing to sell my soul for."

I blinked. So Mark wanted to stay in Washington after law school. This was news. Even though there were two and a half years left to go, and he might change his mind ten more times, it was still directly contrary to everything we'd discussed.

"This sounds like something we need to talk about," I said lightly to Mark.

"Sara loves San Francisco," Mark told Aaron. "I may never pry her out of here."

"Living here has its attractions," Aaron said.

"Right, like AIDS, crime, traffic, and the homeless," Mark said.

"It's not like Washington doesn't have those," I said. "At least this isn't the murder capital of the country."

"Sara, why don't you work on urban blight? You're spinning your wheels with hand cream when there's so much else you could be doing."

"I like my job, Mark. You go work on urban blight."

"I can't do it all. Amanda, why don't you work on urban blight?"

Amanda looked away from Frank to Mark. "I'm working on some personal blight right now. Maybe when I'm done I'll get around to urban. Would anyone like coffee?"

I helped Amanda clear the dishes into the kitchen where a lone light shone over the stove. "How's Frank?"

She shrugged her shoulders as she stacked plates. "I'm still evaluating. You seem to be handling Mark and Aaron all right."

"I could kill you, Amanda, for doing this to me."

"What, you're not having a good time?"

"Very funny. Mark's decided he wants to live in Washington forever."

"He's got bureaucracy in his blood, he just doesn't know it. Here, carry these plates out and cut up the cheesecake."

In the living room, Mark was expounding on the merits of Disney, almost evangelical after having seen so many movies with Benji.

"Take Pinocchio, for instance. One of the classics of the twentieth century. Maybe the values are more American suburb than Italian peasant, but you should really see it."

"Mark, we all saw it when we were six," I said.

"No, you've got to see it as an adult. A completely different experience."

Amanda called me into the kitchen to help her with coffee cups. "I'll go," Frank said.

I sat back down. Mark, Aaron, and I ate our cheesecake in silence for a moment, our forks clattering against our plates. Aaron looked briefly at me, then at Mark, and then down at his plate, his expression thoughtful. It reminded me of the day we first met when I'd given him my opinion of Appleton-Smith's purchasing procedures. He had listened carefully, but I hadn't been able to tell if he'd agreed with me or not.

I jumped up. "I wonder what's taking them so long? Do you two need any—" I charged into the kitchen and abruptly stopped. Frank and Amanda were embraced, kissing next to the refrigerator. Though they no doubt heard me, neither of them looked up. I quietly withdrew from the kitchen shaking my head.

"Really," I said with exasperation as I sat back down.

"What?" Mark said.

"Nothing." Amanda and Frank emerged from the kitchen with coffee that was beginning to cool.

"Well, we've got the big three covered here, don't we?" Amanda said as she sat down on the couch next to Aaron and crossed her legs. "Law, medicine, and business."

"How about art?" Frank said. "You can represent art for us."

"Me and Aaron," Amanda laughed. "Aaron does double duty in business and poetry."

"Really?" Mark said. "Have you published?"

"Oh yes," Amanda said before Aaron could answer. "Sara, you've got a copy of one his books, don't you?"

I could kill her. "Somewhere probably," I answered vaguely.

A knock sounded at the door. It was our downstairs neighbor. "Amanda, I thought I'd warn you—there's a tow truck outside ready to tow your car."

"Why?"

"You're a couple inches over someone's driveway, I guess."

"For God's sake, I'm sure they can get around me."

She tore down the stairs, Frank following, Mark close behind. When I moved towards the door Aaron caught my arm, keeping me with him in the flickering light of the dark living room. What did he want to tell me, I wondered, frowning. Aaron held my wrist, listening to the footsteps clattering down the stairs. When they'd faded, he pulled me near. I was mystified but not alarmed. What did he want? His eyes held mine a moment; then he drew me even closer and began to kiss me. Now—now I was alarmed. I thought the sexual tension between us had become manageable, a few banked embers between people who should know better. Sparks, flames, instant bonfires—this I hadn't counted on. If we'd done this on the beach, I knew I wouldn't have gone home that night.

After many more seconds than I should have, I pulled away, the cool palm of my hand held up against my burning face. The candle flames around us wavered violently in the draft from the open front door. "What are you doing?" I said wildly.

"I wish I knew. Trying to confuse things, I guess."

"Well, you've succeeded. I thought you told me to have integrity, to be able to live with myself."

"It's still good advice. The problem is I can't follow it either."

"Why now, with Mark here?"

Aaron pulled me close again, and I went as if under a spell. "Are you living the life you want?" he asked, moving the back of his fingers across my cheekbone. "Are you sure?"

"This isn't fair," I pleaded, the sensation of him touching me almost painful.

"Oh, Sara, how can you be married? And to him?"

Aaron was more deliberate as he kissed me this time, more insistent. Between the two of us, it left no room for doubt—about some things, anyway. He'd had so many other opportunities, I thought with the piece of rational mind I had left, his intent must be to torture me. I wanted to be angry, I wanted to be furious, and then, sighing, I wanted to just stop thinking.

I heard voices at the bottom of the stairs and broke away to the other side of the room. Picking up my coffee that was now dead cold, I noticed my hand holding the saucer was shaking. I knew I was in for a world of trouble.

Amanda came in and snapped on the lights. "They didn't tow it," she announced victoriously. "Crying always works."

"Women really know how to manipulate," Mark said. "That's why you make natural lawyers."

"I don't think manipulation is a gender-specific skill," I said, studiously not looking at Aaron.

"You weren't really blocking his driveway," Frank said. "I think your neighbor's hypertensive."

Amanda laughed. "Prescribe some Prozac for him, would you, Frank?"

The evening was over. Amanda took Frank's hand as she thanked him for coming, and they walked towards the front door. Mark turned on the news on the TV and put his feet up on the coffee table. Aaron followed me into the hallway. The front door was open again, and down in the dim light at the bottom of the stairs I could see Amanda and Frank with their arms around each other.

I clasped my hands awkwardly in front of me. "Have a good time in Paris," I told Aaron. "When do you leave?"

"Tomorrow."

"Oh." I reached into the closet. "Here's your coat." I handed it to him with an extended arm.

Aaron studied me a long second. "Figure out what you want."

"I thought confusing me was your goal."

"No, I want you crystal clear." But his own expression was unfathomable.

Amanda was climbing the stairs towards us.

"Send me a postcard of Notre Dame," I said nervously. "Notre Dame in the snow. It snows in Paris, doesn't it?"

"I want one of a bateau mouche with lots of people waving," Amanda said as she came in the door.

"Notre Dame and a bateau mouche," Aaron said. "I think I can manage that. Merry Christmas."

I watched him go down the stairs for a moment before I shut the door and tried to regain a semblance of composure. You're weak, Sara, I told myself. Get a grip.

"Ah, Paris," Amanda said with a sigh as we cleaned up the kitchen together. "Too bad he's not taking you with him."

"Would you keep your voice down? Mark could hear you."

"Oh, that's right, you have a husband. How could I forget?" she said, rinsing out cups in the sink.

"Probably because you were so enamored with Frank. You sure move fast. A week ago you didn't ever want to see him again."

"We got along really well."

"I guess."

"We're going out tomorrow night," she said.

"I thought he worked all the time."

"He's making an exception for me."

"Amanda, don't rush into anything. Maybe you should check him out first."

"References available on request? You're so conservative, Sara. I thought you liked him."

"I do. It's cute how he hangs on your every word."

"He doesn't hang on my every word," Amanda said, scrubbing a plate in the sink. "He's a good listener."

"I'll videotape you next time and you can see for yourself."

"How were Mark and Aaron?"

I wiped down the counter with a sponge. "What, you weren't paying attention to your little sociology experiment?"

Amanda laughed. "No."

"Fine. They were just fine."

The news ended, and Mark came into the bedroom as I was hanging up all the clothes I'd draped over the bed.

"Aaron's a nice guy," Mark said. "Amanda pretty much ignored him. Why did she invite both Frank and Aaron? Not that he seemed to mind."

"Don't know," I said, slipping a blouse over a hanger. "Mark, were you serious about working in Washington?"

"Maybe." Mark sat on the bed and took off his shoes and then his shirt. I thought for a flash of the first time Mark and I made love in his off campus apartment, the whispering, the coaxing, the nervousness. I'd known for a fact I wasn't the first girl he'd taken to that apartment, but I'd quickly made up my mind I would be the last.

"Where does that leave me?" I said.

"We need to talk about it. But not tonight. Come here." Mark kissed me and then watched as I undressed self-consciously. Climbing in bed next to him, I felt awkward and distant at first, but given how keyed up I already was, I was glad to lose myself in the tension and sensations of sex. Mark made love with an intensity I appreciated but found surprising, making me wonder if, at least subconsciously, he'd been aware of more that evening than he'd let on.

Later, when Mark was asleep, his arms around me, his breathing even and reassuring, I looked at the moonlight streaming through the window onto my white bedroom wall. Could I make the life I wanted with Mark? Once upon a time, I'd been so sure. Aaron was right about one thing: I would have to be crystal clear about what I wanted before I saw him again.

Mark and I spent Christmas with his parents in Sacramento and then went to Tahoe for a few days of skiing. Our room at a bed and breakfast was lovely with high ceilings, a patchwork quilt, and a fireplace, and the snow was unusually good for December. Mark pried me out of bed early each morning so we could hit the slopes the second the chair lifts opened, but the evenings were relaxing, going out to dinner and then making love with the quiet hiss and snap of the fire in the background. I had many internal conversations convincing myself that my marriage with Mark was fulfilling, that we suited each other well. I'd repeat them, even as I'd stop, terrified, in the middle of a double black diamond run that he'd talked me into going down. Longing to take off my skis and crawl down on my hands and knees, I'd look at Mark who'd be waving a ski pole at me from the bottom to come on, I could do it, no problem. I'd vow to kill him, but by the time I finally reached him, I'd be far too exhausted. In the chair lift back up, he'd put his arm around me, and I'd lean against him and tell myself it would all be okay. Really, it would.

It wasn't until the drive home that our major fissure resurfaced, cracking my tight vision of how I wanted things to be.

"Our anniversary is coming up," I said as we sped west, the mountains looming on either side of the freeway in the deepening twilight.

"Yep. Three years."

"Four. Maybe I could fly to Washington that weekend."

Mark looked over at me. "Can we afford it?"

"I think so. Do you want to come back here for spring break? It'll be cheaper if you get your tickets soon."

"Let me see how my classes go. I may have to study."

"Mark, let's talk about Washington. Do you really want to live there after you finish law school?"

"It's hard to describe, Sara, but I really like it there. The energy—"

"The power."

"Well, maybe the power. You know it's either revolution or reform with me, that's what I'm about. I'm not sure I believe in revolution anymore, and the best place for reform is Washington."

"What about this summer?"

"There are a couple of internships I'm looking into."

"In Washington."

"I'm sorry, what can I do? You're making me choose between you and my life."

"You don't care about being with me. You could just care less."

"I love you, Sara, of course I want to be with you. I don't think you care enough about being with me. Other wives of law students make sacrifices—"

"Only wives? Aren't there any women in your classes?"

"Okay, other spouses make sacrifices. You don't want any part of your world disrupted."

"As if it hasn't been disrupted," I said.

"You seem happy as a clam here. You've got your little job, your little apartment with your sister, your little volunteer work."

"Don't patronize me."

He paused. "I'm sorry, you're putting a lot of pressure on me. Maybe both of us aren't committed enough."

"Do you think we should end it?" I asked quietly. I felt frightened, my pulse pounding as I waited for his answer.

"Do you want to?"

"No," I said.

He took my hand, looking alternately between me and the road. "I don't want to either."

"What are we going to do?" I felt as miserable as I did in August after I dropped him off at the airport.

"Work it through a little at a time, I guess. It'll get easier. We'll figure it out."

"I don't want to be like my parents," I said.

"I know. It doesn't have to be that way."

"Mark, are you seeing Patricia?"

He appeared surprised. "Romantically? Are you worried about that?"

"Yes." I felt foolish.

"No. I just spend time with Benji, that's all. I had no idea you were jealous."

"I'm not jealous, exactly—"

"It's kind of cute. I've never seen you jealous before."

This was the time to tell him about Aaron, but of course I didn't. Mark and I would stay faithful to each other, and our marriage would last if I just concentrated hard enough.

When we got home, there was a note from Amanda on the kitchen counter.

"Look at this, Mark. She says not to worry; she's spending the night at Frank's. She's crazy. She hardly knows him."

"She's an adult, Sara. And Frank seems nice enough."

Just before the new year, Amanda and I got our requested postcards from Aaron. On both of our cards he thanked us formally for dinner and said he hoped to see us when he returned. On mine he added that he hoped Mark and I were enjoying the holidays. Very impersonal.

"That was nice," Mark said after he picked up the cards and read them. "Amanda really knows how to attract men."

New Year's Day was cool and sunny. Mark watched football and I went for a walk to contemplate the universe and my life, not necessarily in that order. Maybe I should just sleep with Aaron and get him out of my system, I told myself as I climbed a steep sidewalk. As if it would only be once, Sara. I didn't want Mark sleeping with Patricia, so how could I even consider being unfaithful? I'd spent years despising my father for his affair with Genine. If I didn't want to be tempted, I shouldn't see Aaron, however helpful a mentor he might be.

I reached the top of Liberty Street and stood hugging my arms against the breeze. Maybe just the fact that I'm tempted shows there's something wrong, that it's inevitable. No, no, no. Dad didn't have to have his affair with Genine. He made a choice. Damn him anyway—it was so awful for my mother, awful for me. Sometimes it amazed me I could still be so angry about it. Amanda might resent Dad but she didn't tend to be as bitter. There are worse things, Sara, than your parents splitting up. Worse betrayals, worse injustices, much worse suffering. Yes, I suppose there are.

You've turned out to be a very pretty girl, Sara. I'd come home from a date at two in the morning. I was seventeen and had spent fifteen minutes kissing Danny Emerson on the dark front doorstep, but I hadn't slept with him. I hadn't slept with anybody at that point and was fast becoming a minority at my high school. All the lights in the house were off. I let myself in the front door with my key, my mouth raw from so much contact with Danny's. I was gingerly creeping through the entryway when I saw there was still a light on in my father's den that faced the back of the house. Was he up? Odd. If anyone waited up for me, it was my mom, and she'd stopped doing that over a year ago. If my father was up, he'd been drinking, and I didn't want to see him.

I went to my room, changed into my nightgown and robe, and then crossed the hallway to the bathroom. When I was done washing my face and brushing my teeth—I never understood how Amanda could just flop into bed with all her make-up still on—I shut off the light and emerged from the bathroom. My father stood in the hallway. I'd worshipped him when I was little, but the last few years he'd not been so interested in me. Maybe he was too distracted by work. I hadn't even had a serious talk with him about which college I wanted to attend.

"Come here, Sara," he said quietly. He didn't want to wake my mother up. Since I rarely disobeyed my father, I did as instructed. He took my face in one hand and turned it towards the light. "You've turned out to be a very pretty girl, Sara." I could smell he'd been drinking. I stepped back impatiently.

It's human nature not to examine memories that are painful.

When my father had his affair with Genine, I wasn't surprised, somehow I knew he was capable of it, but his consequent callousness towards my mother hurt and put a huge burden of responsibility on me. I refused to talk to him for over a year. Amanda called him every obscene name a college junior can come up with, but after a couple of months she was on speaking terms and a year later even talked about forgiveness.

Once I was married, I found it easier to deal with my father, mostly because I made sure Mark was always there to act as a buffer. The arguments when my father and Mark got together, usually when my father took us out to dinner on his rare visits, were long and full of rhetoric. All I had to do was drink wine and wait until one of them ran out of steam and we could go home.

I shaded my eyes with my hand as I surveyed an unusually still city. Everyone must either have a hangover or be watching bowl games. Aaron was in Paris and not, I thought, watching television. Aaron. No, I couldn't do it to Mark. I wouldn't do it.

Mark flew back to Washington the next day, ready for another semester of school, and I made reservations to fly out the first weekend of February for our anniversary.

Chapter Seven

One Monday early in January, Karla and I finished up the last chapters of the accounting book. We sat together in the living room while Amanda instructed Jason and Eric in the kitchen on how to draw the bottom of the ocean with pastels. I could hear Eric tell Jason there weren't any clouds at the bottom of the ocean, and then Amanda say that clouds were fine if they wanted them, maybe they could color them pink to stand out against the aqua water. Jason said he wanted purple, and Amanda said that was okay, too. I looked at Karla, mother of purple and pink cloud-colorers. She seemed tired. She'd come straight from work and her Burger King uniform smelt of hamburger grease and French fries. But tired or not, her drive was unflagging.

"I think you're ready," I said and ceremoniously shut the battered accounting text. "How do you feel?"

"Ready to go, ready to fly. I signed up to see the professor next week. Since I didn't have no transcript saying I did Accounting One, they said I have to get permission to get into Accounting Two."

"You feel okay talking to him? Do you want me to write you a recommendation?"

Karla scowled and waved her hand. "No way. You don't have confidence in me?"

I smiled. "I think you can do anything you want to do, Karla. You're very impressive."

She put her fingers lightly on my arm. "You're a great teacher. I thank you. And everything Amanda's done with the boys. It's real kind. You know, that shelter, I only stayed a week, but it sure changed my life. I don't mean born again, or crap like that. I just got back on the freeway with a better map. And you gave it to me. Everybody needs a good map. I'm going to make sure my kids get one. You're a wonderful woman, Sara."

Pleased but uncomfortable, I changed the subject. "It's you that's done it, not me. Well, I guess this is our last session. I'd help you with your homework, except pretty soon you're going to pass up what I know about accounting." I was reluctant to cut my ties with her even though she soon wouldn't need me. I felt as proud of her as I did of my inventories and caps.

"There's one favor I could use. The boys, they like it here. When I go to class—"

"You want us to watch them? Sure, no problem. Amanda and I'll work it out."

"Thanks. I was thinking about asking George, but I don't want to count on him for nothing."

"Who's George?"

"My ex. He comes and gets the boys sometimes, takes them to a park, but I don't want him sitting in my apartment, waiting like some spider in a web for me to come home. It's bad enough him knowing where I live. I only do it because I want my boys to know their daddy. He don't mess with me any more, and he loves them, but I'd rather have Amanda watch them just the same."

"We'll take care of them."

After three weeks of spending every spare moment with Frank, Amanda seemed to float on a cloud. I'd seen her infatuated before and knew the signs of Amanda-in-Love Stage One: letting her hair grow long, not eating, not completing sentences, being generally cheerful and cooperative. Cloying, in my opinion, did not suit my sister. Fortunately, even in long relationships, she usually snapped back to her acerbic self by the third or fourth week. I was selfishly waiting for the snap because with Mark gone, I wanted some of her attention and company again.

"It looks like things are going well with Frank," I said one rare evening when she was home.

"Mm-hmm," Amanda said, painting her toenails, her red hair pulled into a short ponytail.

"You're more of a space cadet than usual this time. Is it serious?"

"Well, he's not married," she said.

"A major improvement."

"I think he's in love with me."

"Are you in love with him?"

She shrugged. "It's too early to tell."

This was a surprisingly practical statement for Stage One. "Why? What are his defects?"

"Initial passion is always exciting, but once that's passed, then what? Will he work constantly and take me for granted?

"You'll have to see, I guess."

"You know, he's romantic, he's considerate, he thinks I'm brilliant, and we're always laughing."

"Wow," I said. "He must really get out of his shell when he's alone with you."

"He's passionate and intelligent and treats me like I'm the best thing that ever happened to him."

"Wow," I said again.

"Doesn't it sound suspicious though? It's too perfect. It's going to fall apart."

I frowned. Pessimism never poked its head up in Stage One. "But Amanda, you seem so happy."

"Too happy. You've got to watch these things."

"Hey, you deserve a nice guy for a change."

She looked at me and burst into tears. I went and put my arms around her. "What's wrong?"

"I'm not going to see him anymore. I can't. I need to protect myself."

"Oh, Amanda." I hugged her close. I hadn't heard the I'm-too-happy one before, but if it wasn't contrary and full of turmoil, it wasn't

Amanda. "You torture yourself. He's probably not perfect, but he seems a lot less risk than most of the guys you've gone out with. You always trust your intuition. What does it say?"

"My intuition says I have to survive," she said sadly.

I thought all this would blow over by the next time Frank called, but Amanda actually told him, no, she couldn't see him anymore and hung up. Frank called back immediately. Amanda wouldn't answer the phone.

"She's flipped out," I told Frank when I answered. "I have no explanation."

"Do you mind if I come over?"

"Not at all."

"What did he say?" Amanda said.

"He's coming over."

"I'm out of here." She got her coat and purse.

"Amanda, you've got to at least talk to him. This is cruel."

"'I must be cruel only to be kind.' Hamlet." And she left.

"Just because you can quote Shakespeare doesn't mean you're right," I called after her. After going out with men who were superficial, married, egotistical, or just plain strange, maybe this was Amanda's way of sabotaging herself when she'd finally found someone who might actually work out.

When Frank showed up, I invited him in and made him a cup of tea. His eyes were at first hopeful and then a little wild once he realized she wasn't there. It must've been a pretty intense three weeks, I thought, for him to look this desperate this soon. I wanted to help him, but I wasn't quite sure of my role or loyalties.

"Amanda's a great person," I said. "But she can be erratic. She's in flight mode, you know, fight or flight, but I don't know what set her off."

Frank lightly bounced his fist against the kitchen countertop, his gaze focused on his hand. "I'm going to Uganda in March. I meant to tell her. She must've found out."

"Why are you going to Uganda?"

"I got a grant to do some research there for nine months. It's a wonderful opportunity."

"I'll talk to her," I said. "I know she likes you, and she should at least talk to you."

Amanda returned immediately after he left, making me wonder if she'd been crouching in the shadows outside. She's really frightened, I thought, shaking my head. My fearless sister.

"Uganda?" Amanda said, her voice high. "No, I didn't know. That makes it even worse. Uganda?"

"He was so sad when he was here. It was touching."

"Uganda. I knew something like this would happen. I was right to break it off."

"You've got to talk to him."

Amanda was obstinate, not unusual for her.

"I'm sorry, Frank," I said the next time he phoned. "I've done what I could. I can't be in the middle anymore. If you're still interested, you've got to figure out a way to get through to her." After I hung up, I decided I would never encourage Amanda with a guy again. I hadn't done Frank any favors, and I felt badly. My sister's paranoia mystified me because she usually flung herself headlong into relationships. I was the one who held back.

Aaron finally called the third week of January. More than a month after Amanda's dinner party.

"I'd like to see you," he said.

"I thought maybe you moved to Paris."

"How about dinner tomorrow?"

My reasons to refuse him were abundant, but nettled that he'd assumed I'd nothing better to do than wait for him to call and that, indeed, I'd spent so much time waiting, I picked my weakest. "Sorry, I have other plans."

"Sara, I know I haven't called, but it doesn't mean I haven't been thinking about you. When can I see you? I'll take any terms you offer, though I'd rather not have to do an audit at Appleton-Smith again."

The door to Amanda's room was shut. I fingered the cord of the black phone uncomfortably. Time to get serious. "Aaron, it's not so much that I'm busy, it's just, well, I shouldn't see you anymore."

"Have you made your decision then?"

"I think so."

"Will you tell me about it over dinner?"

After I hung up, I stared and stared at the violin woman in the hallway. How could I have agreed to see him when I told myself I wouldn't? Well, I would tell him in person I couldn't see him anymore. Just cutting him off like Amanda had done to Frank was too cruel. Except I wasn't kidding myself very well. I wanted to see him, and I knew it. It was irresistible. No, it was resistible. I wasn't going to sleep with him. There was Mark who I loved and was committed to spend my life with. I looked down at the ring on my finger. This was what it was for. To remind.

I met Aaron after work at a French restaurant with lace curtains, dim lighting, and intimate couples leaning across small tables. Cambodian food, formica, and fluorescent glare would've been preferable.

"How was Paris?" I started off the conversation.

"Superb," he said with a smile. "Monica took me to a Frida Kahlo exhibit."

"Was it like the one we saw?"

"Almost identical. Same paintings. They reminded me of you."

"Other than that, did you have a good time?"

"Oh, even the exhibit was worth going to. Monica kept it entertaining."

I was tired of hearing about Monica. "And her husband? Does he keep things entertaining, too?"

Aaron poured more wine into my glass. "For the most part."

"You seem to know a lot of husbands."

"Do I? I'd prefer to know fewer." He put the bottle down. "So tell me what you've decided."

"You don't like Mark, do you?"

"I'm doing my best to have no opinion about him whatsoever."

"But you don't think I should be married to him."

"That's for you to decide."

I looked down at the table. "Mark's been important in my life. You don't know what things were like for me before." Mark had been generous, easy-going, affectionate, and sincere. Transparent. He'd never probed too far. He'd been shelter, security, a safe haven. Protection. I knew why I'd married him. Glancing up, I thought I saw Aaron's eyes look anxious for a fleeting second before he lightened his expression, but I told myself I was imagining it.

"You're right," Aaron said quietly. "I don't know what things were like for you before. Is staying with him a question of obligation, then? Or is it safety?"

I made myself visualize a clear picture of Genine in my head. "My parents are divorced. I can't stand the thought of being like them."

He nodded. "Go on."

"So Mark and I are going to work things out. Which means—" I couldn't look at him. I watched another couple taste each other's hors d'oeuvres instead. "I can't see you anymore."

"Because I'm a threat to your marriage."

I looked from the couple back to him. "Yes." That was all there was to it.

He studied me contemplatively.

"What?" I said after a while, not enjoying the scrutiny.

"You know, I don't know. Have you made your decision, or are you pretending you've made it? Are you living the life you want, or are you living a life that's safe? You let out so little, your control is so tight. Why is that?"

I uncrossed and recrossed my legs and reached for the breadbasket. He caught hold of my wrist. "Don't think," he said. "Just tell me. Talk."

"There are things I'm not telling you or anybody."

"Why?"

I pulled my wrist away. "Because they're mine. It's who I am."

"You don't let anybody know you?"

"Maybe not," I said. "Maybe Amanda."

"Not even Mark," Aaron observed softly. "I'd like to know you, Sara."

"Why?" The question felt wrenched out of me.

"Because you're worth knowing."

I put my elbows on the table and cupped my hands along the sides of my face, as if creating blinders. To be known. Out of the question. It would mean risking destruction. As I stared into the abyss,

I realized the chasm was much larger than just leaving Mark. And so appealing. I would just fall and fall and fall.

"Stop thinking," he said.

"I can't sleep with you." That was my ultimatum.

Aaron shrugged his shoulders. "All right."

"No pressure?"

"No pressure," he said and then smiled. "And no beaches."

I sat back and breathed again. Something had been settled, at least temporarily, or maybe we were both playing for time.

Our entrees were served, and we consciously increased the generality of our conversation. Aaron told me about how at home his mother had worked continuously on needlepoint Christmas stockings for her as-yet-unborn grandchildren, and about how his sister Paula had held up a pair of scissors and threatened to shred each and every stocking if she heard one more word about anyone younger than eighteen. I told him how there'd been yet another priority change at work, and Total Preventative Maintenance had replaced Total Quality as the number one priority. The announcement at our plant had been more dramatic than usual. The cafeteria had been decorated with posters and streamers, and a cake saying "Total Preventative Maintenance" had been sliced and handed out. Bob and Bob had been on hand to give solemn speeches on the importance of our new priority.

"Everyone in my department ate the cake and stared at the Bobs like they were from Mars. Not that we're going to get much done this month anyway. The company president is going to visit our plant, so all we'll do is prepare for that."

"What will you have to do?"

"Besides make sure my department shines from top to bottom, I have to give a presentation, which I don't mind, except for the six rehearsals that they have scheduled."

"It might be tedious, but it's actually a great compliment."

"It's going to be a circus."

I noticed we were the last ones left in the restaurant and asked our waitress for our bill. When she brought it and put it on my side of the table, Aaron instinctively started to reach for it, but I drew the tray towards me, out of reach. Aaron stopped, hesitated, then pulled out his wallet and handed me money for his half.

"I'm glad you were free tonight," he said.

I drew an imaginary line on the tablecloth with the edge of my credit card. "Aaron, do you only call me when someone cancels on you?"

He frowned, puzzled, and then laughed. "Is that what you think I do?"

I looked away uncomfortably. "What am I supposed to think when you call at the last minute?"

"That I'm indecisive, maybe? What are you really upset about? Do you think I'm seeing other women and they get priority?"

"It's none of my business who you see. I just don't like being a substitute."

"Believe me, I like it even less. Sara, I don't call at the last minute because someone else cancels. If you didn't have dinner with me tonight, I'd be home writing, which is what I was doing last night, and which is what I'll be doing tomorrow night. Will you have dinner with me next Friday? I'm asking a week in advance, a little more considerate."

I thought about it for a moment. "What are you writing about?"

He shrugged. "The ineffable. I never talk about it until it's finished. Will you have dinner with me?"

"If I say yes," I couldn't resist saying, "can I call and cancel?"

Aaron's answer was to give me a slow, amused smile. After a second I found eye contact disturbing and was relieved to focus on calculating the tip.

As Aaron helped me on with my coat, his hand grazed my neck, and I jumped. I eyed him suspiciously.

"Unintentional," he said. "When do you see Mark next?"

"Two weeks. Why?"

"Just curious."

When Meg and I went out for lunch again after my Saturday morning session at the shelter, I told her about Aaron. I had to talk to somebody, and Amanda was too unstable at this point. Meg seemed grounded to me, solid, reassuring, and practical.

She listened and then laughed and shook her head. "He's right. If you'd made up your mind, you wouldn't see him anymore. So since you keep seeing him, he knows you haven't made up your mind."

"Why can't I just be happy with Mark?"

"That's a question you have to answer yourself."

"Living apart is driving me crazy. When Amanda was busy with Frank, I was always alone, and now all she does is read mystery novels and run out of the apartment every time the phone rings so I'm still alone. Plus, Aaron's someone I can talk to about work—there's hardly anybody that understands what I do. But here I am complaining about something you deal with all the time. Plus you're raising Sabrina by yourself. You're not seeing anybody, are you? Do you miss it?"

Meg raised her eyebrows. "Having a man around telling me what to do is the last thing I want. Sometimes I'm lonely, but overall I'm so glad to be away from Ted that all I have to do is think of him and I'm deliriously happy. It helps that Sabrina is pure joy." She tilted her head, her parrot earrings swinging. "I don't believe in romance anymore, and at this point I'm even suspicious of most forms of love, but that doesn't mean you need to be. Just remember that contrary to all the garbage we learned growing up, no man can make you happy. Good relationships can be fun and satisfying, but happiness is always an inside job."

I frowned. "Forster said, 'only connect.' Connection seems like the path of redemption in lots of literature and movies."

Meg smiled. "Another reading of Forster is that he meant connecting the head and the heart, bridging the inner world to the outer world. Individual transcendence. You integrate all the parts of yourself to be the full, authentic person you were created to be."

I stared, not really seeing her. Wasn't that the point of romance and marriage—to make you happy? I knew Buddhists would agree that transcendence was an inside job, but I didn't have the patience to sit alone on a mountain top. Worse, maybe there were parts of me I didn't want integrated.

As I continued not to speak, the silence dragged on. "All right," Meg said. "No more analysis. Do you like your job? It's something I can't tell about you."

"At times I think I'm making a contribution, and it feels great. Other times I want to leave the place screaming and never go back."

"There are other jobs that might suit you better. I'll keep my ears open. Would you be willing to take a cut in pay and fewer benefits?"

"What a deal. Maybe. What are you thinking about?"

"Nothing definite. I'll let you know."

"Thanks for listening," I said.

Meg smiled. "You're welcome," she said, nodding her head with the gentle patience of a grandmother in a rocking chair. Her parrots nodded, too.

It gradually became clear that Althea and Joe had a spat while I was on vacation over Christmas. Neither of them would give me details, but they weren't speaking to each other.

"Joe, this is childish. You've got to talk to her."

"You talk to her. You're the boss. It's what they pay you for."

And later with Althea: "The man's a pig-headed toad. Talking is useless."

"Althea, it's your job. This is getting unprofessional."

"Say what you like. I'm not wasting my breath on something so futile."

"Won't you tell me what happened?"

"No."

I wanted to scream but went to another rehearsal instead. The first two were with Paul, the next two were with Paul and Bob, and the next two were with Paul and Bob and Bob. My presentation got significantly revised each time, and I made a flurry of new charts and graphs, only to alter them again and again. One time I emphasized lowering inventories, another time reliability, another time the cap torque project. The spin of the presentation went one way and then another, until everything I'd done felt completely trivial.

"I'm not going to make it," I told Aaron over our next Friday night dinner. "I'm going to start stabbing people with felt-tipped pens."

"Their careers could ride on how well you do, you know. As could yours."

"But I'm spending all this time rehashing the past instead of doing anything productive. I should be working on our next quality issue, not playing musical chairs with Paul and the Bobs."

"You can't ignore the politics, Sara. How your hierarchy perceives you is critical."

"But they should just look at my performance. Why do I have to spend all this time on dog and pony shows?"

Aaron frowned. "You know how subjective it all is. If they like you, you'll wear a halo, and any flaws will be excused. If they don't like you, how well you do your job is almost irrelevant. It isn't something to take lightly. I've seen it go both ways with almost identical performances."

"Did it happen to you?"

"Not to me. To others."

"But it's not fair."

"I'm not talking about what's fair." His voice was almost sharp. "If you want to succeed in a large corporation, there are rules you have to follow. If you don't, then put your energy where you do want to succeed."

"If I wanted a lecture, Aaron, I'd call my father. You almost sound angry with me."

Aaron was silent a moment. Then one corner of his mouth turned up in acknowledgment. "Sorry. You're asking questions I used to ask. And I didn't like the answers, either."

"But you accepted them. And you've been rewarded for it."

He narrowed his eyes, not liking that dig at all. "How warm's your coat? Let's go for a walk."

We tersely split the bill, left the restaurant, and headed in the direction of North Beach. When I joked about North Beach not counting as a beach, Aaron didn't respond with more than a faint smile. I must've touched a nerve back at the restaurant, but I wasn't sure what it was. We walked quickly, not talking much. I wore a cotton skirt that wasn't exactly up to a chilly evening hike, but I didn't complain. At least I had on low-heeled shoes.

At the top of Nob Hill, I stopped Aaron so I'd have a chance to look at the view. With one hand I held my hair back to keep the wind from whipping it into my eyes while I stared into the distance, enchanted. Aaron watched me as he waited, how patiently, I couldn't tell, and then we continued on, descending through Chinatown and finally strolling down a side street off Columbus.

Aaron looked over at me. "Would you like to get some coffee?"

In the cafe, I kept my coat on and circled my hands around my cup as I tried to warm up.

Aaron sipped his coffee on the other side of the tiny table. "Your hands look blue. I'm sorry, Sara, I didn't mean for you to get frostbitten."

"It's all right—it was fun. I don't get to walk at night very often."

"I go out at any time and don't think about it. An unfair male privilege, I suppose."

"You're right, it's very unfair."

"I didn't create it," he said, his voice quiet. "I'd make it different if I could."

"Aaron, why were you so angry with me at the restaurant?" The question took him aback. "Talk," I said. "It's your turn."

He tapped a finger on the table. "I suppose it is my turn. All right. I used to go out with a woman who got fired because she wouldn't sleep with her boss. It was awful for her, and to watch it happen to someone I cared about—I've never felt so helpless in my life. Her boss was as despicable as they come, but there was so much she could've avoided if she'd just had a few more allies, worried a little more about spin control, as you like to put it. She was more interested in being right than surviving. All I could do was help her put her life back together when everything came crashing down."

"Are you worried the same about me?"

"I suppose not so much. You may not like the politics, but you're shrewd enough not to let them chew you up."

"What happened to her, what's she doing now?"

"She works at an investment bank in New York." The lines around Aaron's mouth relaxed into a smile. "She's figured out how to rein in her temper and she's doing fine. And things have changed, maybe not enough, but I don't think someone like her boss could get away now with what he did then."

"What happened to the two of you?"

He hesitated. "She wanted to leave San Francisco, start over."

"And you didn't want to go."

Aaron shook his head. "We wouldn't have lasted; we both knew it." His expression looked bleak for a moment; then he shook it off. "She's married now. I got a card from her at Christmas saying she's going to have a baby in April. She and her husband are ecstatic. It's all worked out for her in the end."

"You sound like you were angry with her when it wasn't her fault."

"I suppose I was. And you're right, it wasn't her fault."

"How long ago did it happen?"

Aaron considered. "Eight years."

"Were you in love with her?"

But with that question, I'd crossed the line. "Are you in love with Mark?" Aaron asked as he picked up his coffee cup.

"So that's all you're going to tell me."

"I rarely say this much."

"Because the more someone knows, the more they can hurt you? Does that mean you trust me?"

Aaron leaned his head against his fingers and seemed tired. "It means I'm willing to take a risk." He tilted his empty cup toward him. "Risk and vulnerability. They don't come easily for me either. Some things don't heal as well as they should."

I was silent. He wasn't impervious; he protected himself just like I did. I knew to be fair, the risk should be mutual, which was why he'd made it, but I shied away. I'd much rather sleep with him than do this, I thought. That kind of intimacy was much less difficult. I'm falling in love with him, I thought. This is completely out of control.

"When do you go to Washington again—next week?" he said after I didn't speak for a minute.

"Yes," I said. "It's our anniversary. Four years."

"Congratulations."

Sitting a respectable two feet apart in the dark back seat, we took a cab back to where our cars were parked. I knew I would have to stop seeing him, that was all there was to it. It was unfair to him and unfair to me. This was the last dinner, the last time.

We stood on the sidewalk next to my car, the streetlight above us cutting a chalky cone through the mist hanging in the black night. "Aaron, I can't do it anymore. I can't see you." He stood looking at me; I couldn't tell what he was thinking. "I'm sorry," I said.

"What are you protecting?"

I looked down at the keys in my hand. My ring glittered as it caught the wan light. "I'm married. You should find somebody with more potential."

"Why? It's you I want." And he drew me close. So much for our deal, I thought as he began to kiss me, but I made no move to stop him, not thinking of any moment other than the present. It was heavenly, but perhaps the forbidden always is.

When I tightened my arms around his neck, Aaron lifted his head. "Oh, Sara. All I want in the world is take you home with me, and what's worse, I think you'd go. God knows how I have any scruples left, but I won't sink to an affair with you. If you've decided, you've decided. I knew the odds weren't in my favor. You're young, married, confused. Who knows what I was thinking." He pulled my arms from around his neck. "Desire is a treacherous thing."

I stared at him, not knowing what to say.

"Go ahead and go," he said. "As of right now, I am officially out of your life."

I got in my car and left him standing in the misty cone of light.

The next Monday, Amanda received a postcard from Frank. A flower by Georgia O'Keefe decorated the front of the card; on the back it said, "Come with me."

"What's that supposed to mean?" I asked Amanda. She looked at it without much curiosity and threw the card away.

Tuesday, there was another card, this time of some African beadwork. "Come with me to Uganda," it said. Amanda looked at it and threw it away.

On Wednesday we watched Karla's kids while she was at class. Amanda tie-dyed T-shirts with them as the stereo blared Grateful Dead. Jerry Garcia was singing about a long, strange trip when Frank buzzed our intercom. I pressed the button to let him in downstairs. When he got up to our door, Amanda opened it and simply said, "Yes." He put his arms around her, and they stayed in the doorway a long time.

"Amanda," I said finally, poking at the cloth in the pots. "How long are these shirts supposed to stay in here?"

Amanda came in, rinsed out the T-shirts and got out a bottle of champagne. "We're going to Uganda," she said.

"Uganda, Uganda," Jason and Eric joyfully chanted, catching her excitement.

Frank stood in the kitchen with us.

"But you two hardly know each other," I said.

Amanda shrugged and then Frank shrugged.

"You'll have to have shots and things. You'll get sick over there."

"Frank's a doctor, he'll take care of me."

"Frank, somehow I expect this from Amanda, but how could you lead her into it?"

"Are you really upset?" Frank asked sympathetically.

"Yes. What about the rent, Amanda, how am I supposed to pay for it?"

"I have some savings. I'll give you money for my half. I'm glad you'll be here because I want to keep the apartment. It's nicer than yours, don't you think, Frank? And a better location."

"But I'll be all alone."

"I'm sorry, Sara, but it's only for nine months, not three years."

"Uganda, Uganda, Uganda." Jason and Eric were marching around the living room.

"Have some champagne with us," Amanda said.

"My intentions are the best, Sara," Frank said.

I took a glass reluctantly as I shook my head in disbelief. "When do you leave?"

"Middle of March."

I sighed.

The next day I gave my presentation for the seventh and last time. The company president was a heavy-set man with small, dark eyes behind his gold aviator frame glasses. Paul had me stand outside the conference room an hour before my presentation was scheduled in case the day's agenda progressed more quickly than expected. The four men in navy blue suits and red ties seated at the conference table were all completely silent while I talked. Bob, Bob, and Paul watched the president constantly for his reaction. At one point I made a small joke that I hadn't rehearsed, causing one of the Bob's and Paul's faces to freeze. When the president's face cracked slightly, they relaxed.

"Excellent," the president said when I'd finished. "A fine job."

"Very good, Sara," Bob said.

"Yes, very good," the other Bob said.

"We need more projects like this one," the president said.

"Exactly."

"Too true."

Paul beamed approvingly in silence, it apparently not being his place to speak on this occasion. I felt like a fat puppy being patted on the head. It was, I supposed, better than being swatted with a newspaper on the nose. I shook hands with the president, Bob, and Bob and left feeling extremely worn out. Back at my desk were notes from Joe and Althea, each one asking me to check on the other's deplorable actions. I sighed deeply. Tomorrow I'd be on a plane for a long weekend with Mark and I'd forget about this place. I'd forget about Aaron; I'd forget about Amanda. I crossly chastised Althea and Joe separately for their feud and left instructions for my absence. I hoped they'd manage not to raze the place to the ground while I was gone.

I brought Tolstoy with me on the flight. It'd been so long since I'd read it that I had to reread a few chapters to remember what was going on. One of the main characters died during the section that I read on the plane, which did not lift my spirits. I fell asleep over Ohio and didn't wake up until the plane taxied into the gate. And there at the top of the ramp waiting for me was Mark in a rumpled sweatshirt. I was getting used to these continual reunions but something in me still leapt at the sight of him after so many weeks apart. We went back to his apartment, made love, and then Mark studied and I dragged out old Tolstoy again, determined to finish the novel so I could move on to something else.

"Tomorrow morning we're taking Benji to the playground," Mark said, looking up from his text.

"You're kidding."

"No, I do it every Saturday. It gives Patricia a break."

"Are we going to go through this again?"

"Go through what?"

"I come out here and I don't see you?"

"Sara, it's a couple of hours."

"We'll spend the evening alone?"

"Completely alone. Just you and me."

I sighed. "All right."

Saturday morning, when we picked Benji up, Patricia said she'd like to come, too.

"Oh," Mark said, surprised. "I guess."

Odd, I thought. Patricia appeared serene, almost languid. Everyone wore hats and gloves except for me because I'd forgotten to bring any, and I was freezing as I sat next to Patricia on the park bench.

"Come on, Benji, I'll push you on the swing," Mark said. Benji let out a delighted yell as Mark chased him to the other side of the playground.

"It's sweet of him to spend so much time with Benji," Patricia said.

"Yeah," I said, though sweet was not how I tended to describe it.

"If you decide to let him go, I'll take him."

"Excuse me?"

"Mark. If you decide to let him go, I'll take him. But you'll have to let him go. He won't on his own."

"You want me to hand my husband over to you?"

"His life's out here now. He loves Washington."

"How much do you have to do with that?"

"Very little. It's the natural course of his life. What he wants to do, he can't do anywhere else. He'll fit in well with us."

I wanted to be angry, but it was hard to lash out because she wasn't the least bit defensive. We both stared straight ahead watching children play around us, their coats and hats a moving kaleidoscope of color in the gray morning. I felt nauseous.

"He thinks he loves you, of course," she said. "That's why you're going to have to end it."

"And why would I do that?"

"Because you don't want him."

"This is a ridiculous conversation."

"Because it would be best for him."

"Best for you, maybe."

"He'd be good for me, and I'd be good to him. I understand men like him. His passion isn't for people, it's for ideas, and I can accept that."

"You don't feel guilty, trying to break up my marriage? You've already had one fall apart."

Patricia pushed her blond hair behind her shoulder. "No, I'm being honest with you. It's your decision. If you decide to keep him, then you keep him. I won't be able to touch him."

I had a Twilight Zone feeling of being transferred to a parallel planet where everyone looked the same but acted in very alien ways.

"I do want him," I said. "We've been married four years. I'm not going to throw it away because it'd be convenient for you."

Patricia rose from the bench. "I'm going home. Nice to see you again." And she left. I stayed on the bench another five minutes before crossing over to the jungle gym.

"Mark, I'm cold. Could we go somewhere to warm up?"

"Sure. Where's Patricia?"

"She went back to her apartment."

"Oh. Come on, Benji, let's go get some hot chocolate. Can you hop on one foot all the way to that fence? Let me see."

I followed slowly behind.

I made dinner that evening in Mark's apartment while he studied. As we ate, we were both pensive and didn't say much. I began to feel sick, my stomach in knots. I stopped eating.

"What are you thinking about?" I asked.

"The next election and how much of Congress will turn over."

"Why?" Congress was far from my thoughts.

"It could make a huge difference on environmental votes."

I felt the little I'd eaten turn over in my stomach. There was a huge, suffocating wall I had to push through, and when I was finished, I would be on one side and Mark on the other. Would there be a ledge on the other side, or would I just fall and fall?

"It's no good, is it?" I said.

"What's no good?"

"Us this way. You here and me out there. It's like we're different people now."

"Sara, we go over and over this. You know this is important to me."

"Mark, I'm not blaming you. Maybe we shouldn't be holding on so hard to each other if it just doesn't fit." Tears brimmed out of my eyes.

Mark got out of his chair and pulled me up into his arms. "Sara, I love you. Come on, don't cry. We'll work through this."

I pulled back and stood apart from him, wiping my nose with a napkin. "I'm letting you go. If you want to. Think about it. Think about what's best for you and best for me."

Mark stared at me.

"We've had a good time," I said. "Maybe now we're holding each other back."

"I don't get it, Sara. You're the one who wanted to get married in the first place. Now you've changed your mind? Don't my feelings count in here somewhere?"

"Mark, if you met me for the first time today, you'd say nice to meet you, and that'd be it, because you'd know what I want doesn't fit with what you want."

"What do you want, Sara, besides me to move back to San Francisco? Are you serious about this, or is this a threat, or some kind of retaliation?"

"I'm serious and I'm not trying to threaten you. I want you to stay here and do everything you want to do."

"Alone," he said.

"I doubt for long."

"What's that supposed to mean? I know we've had problems, but I love you and I thought you loved me. Isn't that the most important thing?"

"I don't think it is. It's important, but it's not the only thing. I want you to be happy, and how can you be if I'm always tugging on you to do something different? Because I wouldn't be happy here, I guarantee that, and you're not going to be happy anywhere else, at least not for quite a while."

Mark closed his eyes, his hands on his hips, and took a breath. "Sara, I thought you didn't want to be like your parents."

"I don't." At this, I broke down and sobbed. Mark hugged and kissed me, wiping my eyes and pushing my hair out of my face, telling me it would be all right, everything would work out. We made love, sadly, gently. I went to wash my face and when I returned, Mark was sitting in bed crying, as handsome in his all-American way as ever. I've hurt him, I thought, my throat tightening. You've started it, Sara, you've got to see it through. There's another life for him after all this, you already know what it is. At that moment, I let him go.

I slept in his arms that night, and in the morning we started to talk about how to do the paperwork and avoid lawyers if we could. Though the discussion started off well, Mark grew more and more reluctant to talk until we got to the point he was just staring silently at me from across the table. He abruptly told me he needed to study, and I said okay.

"You're serious," he said, standing at the door ready to go to the library, his backpack over one shoulder.

I nodded.

He looked down at his feet. "I was so head over heels with you when we first started going out, I didn't even consider what might happen in five or six years. I guess no one ever does. We seemed compatible enough, but maybe not as much as I thought." He looked up at me. "I don't regret it though, not for a minute. Apparently you do." Mark blinked a couple of times and then opened the door and left. As the door clicked shut, I put my hands over my eyes and told myself to breathe, this would all pass, that eventually I'd stop feeling as if the marrow were being sucked out of my bones.

That afternoon I walked to the Mall by myself under a light snowfall that melted when it hit the ground. I thought about the good memories over the years since that first political science class, cried, and then remembered that today was our anniversary and cried some more. For a few minutes, I put energy into hating Georgetown and Patricia but then stopped, considering how useless it was. I found myself standing in front of the Freer Gallery but didn't have the heart to go in, not even for Whistler's Peacock Room. I looked off at the Capitol Building, hard to see through the murky snow that filled the late afternoon sky. The corridors of power. I supposed Mark did belong here. I headed back, darkness falling early with the snow. From a street vendor on a corner, I bought a soft white knit hat and wore it as I trudged back to Mark's basement, my raw hands deep in my pockets.

Monday morning, both of us exhausted, Mark took the Metro with me to the airport. We stood swaying, holding on to the handrails, surrounded by commuters wearing suits and clutching briefcases. Is this what Mark will look like in ten years, I wondered? I hoped not, but he'd still be the best looking one on the train. He and Patricia will make a striking couple, I thought dully. We didn't talk much until we got to the gate.

"Sara, I love you, I'll always—"

"Mark, don't say it."

"Call me if you change your mind."

I met his eyes. "Tell me now if you don't think it's the right thing to do."

He started to speak, then closed his mouth and looked sad, almost angry.

"See?" I said gently. "I love you, too, but it doesn't matter. Not as much as other things. I want the best for you, Mark, I just can't be part of it."

He took me in his arms. "I'll always love you," he whispered. I got on the plane and opened Tolstoy but didn't read a word.

Chapter Eight

"I feel like I'm bleeding," I told Amanda as she drove me home from the airport in her black Toyota overflowing with boxes and sacks and flyers from work announcing sales. It'd taken the two of us a couple minutes to empty the passenger seat enough so I could sit down without crushing something.

Amanda watched me with concern, only glancing occasionally at the road. "When you say over, do you mean big fight over?"

"I mean divorce over."

"Well, that's a surprise. Did he just spring it on you?"

"I sprang it on him."

"You did? You didn't tell me you were going to do that."

I closed my eyes. "I didn't know. It was awful."

"Poor Sara, you've got a painful road ahead of you. But your timing." Amanda sighed. "I've waited for years for you to do this, and you pick now, when I'm traveling to the other side of the planet. It couldn't be much worse." She pressed down on the accelerator and swung around a car crawling along at the speed limit. "Damn this traffic. I have an appointment to get a typhoid shot."

"It's okay," I said listlessly. "Dying in a car accident sounds appealing." She'd waited for years and hadn't told me. Great. Am I in free fall? No, this felt more like drifting through a polar sea on a huge floe of ice. Everything around me looks white. Funny, I thought, it doesn't snow here. It doesn't even freeze.

"Sara, I absolutely hate to do this to you, but I promised to meet Frank and his sister for dinner after the shots. Would you like to come with us? She's only in town for today, and I wouldn't go except she's Frank's only living relative, literally."

"No, I'll be all right. I'm going to go to bed early."

"Come with us. A bottle of wine would do you good."

"I don't want to be around people right now. You don't need to babysit me, Amanda."

With a quick hug she dropped me off and raced to her shot appointment. I trudged up the stairs thinking about how nice Mark's visit over Christmas had been. Inside, I took off my coat, sat down on my bed and rubbed my fingers over the nubby pattern on my white bedspread. Wandering into the kitchen, I opened and closed a few cupboards with no idea what I was looking for. I went into the bathroom, opened the medicine cabinet, and stared for a long time until I realized what I was doing. Shaken, I called Meg. There was no answer. I thought everyone had answering machines these days. I made myself a cup of tea and read the newspaper. The mayor and the police chief were quarreling; a woman had been killed by her stalker. I folded up the paper before I got to page two. Amanda called.

"You doing okay? You can still come to dinner."

"I'm okay. Have a good time."

I put down the phone, stared at the photo of the violin woman, and thought a long time about calling Mark. Was he perched by the phone, anxiously waiting for me to call? More likely he was seeing *101 Dalmatians* with Benji. Let him be, Sara. Why had Amanda painted the hallway white? The hallway in the house I grew up in had been white. My mother had washed the walls once a month when we were little to clean off the childish smudges of fingerprints.

You've turned out to be a very pretty girl, Sara. Is that what the boys tell you? Sara, are you still a good girl?

I knew I shouldn't be married because I wasn't the kind of person someone should be married to. Too cold, too afraid of intimacy. In fact, I felt cold. I looked at the thermostat. With her impending trip, Amanda had become cost conscious and must've turned the heat down before she left to get me at the airport. I turned it back up and then went to my bedroom for a sweater. Once there, I fell face down on my bed, listening to the springs complain as I let myself bounce against them. He's better off without you, you know. You used him from beginning to end. No, I loved him, I did. I do. Hardly, Sara. You're not capable of it.

I turned my face to the side and could feel the patterned bumps on my bedspread push into my skin. I'm in free fall. How far would I go? I tried to picture what had been in the medicine cabinet. Though I'd stared at it for at least a minute, I could only remember the toothpaste. I'm a horrible person, I thought. Cold, heartless, and cruel. Amanda wouldn't have anything around anyway. Pretty far, I could fall pretty far. I'm already close to bottom. There was the oven, the roof, even. Or you could call him. Maybe he's your ledge. Like Genine. My dad and Genine. No, thank you. You'd rather hit bottom? I'd rather float along by myself on my iceberg and freeze to death if necessary.

Don't be a self-destructive fool. You know better now. You need someone. Call him.

"I did it," I told Aaron on the phone.

"You did what?" he said.

"I made my decision. Actually, I think Patricia decided."

"Who's Patricia?"

"Can I come see you?" I said, my voice no doubt forlorn.

"Sure, Sara. Are you okay?"

"I don't know where you live." The thought almost made me cry. He gave me an address in the Duboce Triangle, only a mile from my own. I have no business seeing him the day after I've broken up with Mark, I told myself and then promptly ignored my advice. Though it was dark, I decided to walk, a fierce glare my weapon of choice against anyone who looked threatening. I felt frozen and mean, only occasionally blinking back tears. Aaron's building was three stories with one flat occupying each floor. He lived on the second.

"Are you all right?" Aaron asked as he let me in. He looked like he'd just gotten home from work, his jacket and tie off, but his long-sleeved white shirt still on.

I didn't answer, just took off my coat and looked around.

A woven Persian carpet covered the living room floor, bookshelves lined one wall, and a sofa and two chairs filled the middle of the room. Near the window stood an old walnut rolltop desk; over the couch were a trio of prints in rich, translucent hues. There wasn't an item out of place anywhere, not even a stray piece of junk mail, the kind that seemed to float around our apartment for weeks. Still the perfect consultant, I thought. But though nice enough, his neighborhood wasn't all that fashionable, and the flat wasn't all that large. Not an extravagant man. Maybe he's saving his money, I thought with a mental shrug.

"Who's Patricia?" Aaron asked again.

"A woman in Washington who wants Mark."

He gave me an odd look.

"I let him go," I said.

"You let him? It's not mutual?"

I closed my eyes. Aaron didn't seem to matter; I was still falling. My chest felt constricted to the point it was becoming hard to breathe.

"Sara?"

I didn't think I was crying, but my face felt wet. I knew I shouldn't have come. People decorate with white far too often, I thought as I glumly surveyed his walls. My room at home had been white. Amanda, on the other hand, had contrived to paint her walls deep purple. For a couple years she'd had a poster of Bobby Sherman above her bed, his tan neck surrounded by white puka shells. He was later replaced by Johnny Rotten, a more appropriately rebellious idol. At twelve my mother had given me posters of Monet's water lilies to decorate my room. "A nice peaceful room," she'd said. I'd wanted to paint my room blue, but my father wouldn't hear of it. He'd lost the battle with Amanda and didn't intend to with me. I grew up with white.

Aaron stood patiently waiting for my lead.

"I should go," I said.

"But you're here. Why did you come?"

To have you rescue me, I thought, but I don't want to be rescued. I'm content to float on my iceberg. I'm fond of it. I felt mute.

Aaron shook his head slowly. "Sara, you don't have to be so alone."

"Yes, I do," I said. With a sigh he put his arms around me and held me while I cried and cried and cried.

He stroked my hair as I leaned into him and let me cry as long as I needed to. At last I stopped, drawing in my breath with a small shudder. When I wiped the tears away, I noticed I'd gotten mascara on his otherwise immaculate shirt.

"Sorry," I said, dabbing at it with a tissue.

"It doesn't matter." He smiled and pushed my hair away from my face. "You need someone to take care of you, but given the circumstances, I'm not sure I'm the best person. Where's Amanda?"

"Frank's sister is in town, and she wanted to meet her. I told her it was okay. Did I tell you? Amanda's decided to go to Uganda with Frank."

"Uganda? I guess I'll have to do then. Have you eaten?"

"No."

He got me a drink and made us some dinner. While he cooked, I lay down on his couch and stared blankly into space until I eventually fell asleep. He woke me when the food was ready and we ate.

"How are you feeling now?" Aaron said, appraising me. "You're not going to jump off any bridges, are you?"

"No bridges," I said. The Golden Gate bridge was far too tall; I'd never have had the nerve. I noticed Aaron had changed his shirt while I slept. I wondered if the blotch of mascara would come out, or if he'd just have to throw it away.

"You're still not in very good shape. You walked here, didn't you? I'll take you home, and you should get some more sleep."

"Oh."

"What's the matter?"

"You don't want me to stay." Sleeping with him was the only thing I knew for sure would keep me from thinking and feeling.

"It wouldn't be a good idea. This is a huge transition for you, and you're fragile. Besides, you need to make sure your decision's going to stick."

"How come you get to decide this, and I don't get any say?"

"That sounds more like you. You know, you had me worried when I first saw you." Aaron surveyed me with concern, no doubt taking in my red eyes, smudged mascara, rumpled hair. "I wish there were a way to make this easier for you. I just don't think there is." Amanda was there when he took me home. She put her arm protectively around me, and I felt like a child handed from one adult to another.

I went to work the next day but was only good for deleting email messages I didn't want to read. I called in sick the next day and spent hours walking in Golden Gate Park trying to clear my head. I paid the admission for the Asian Art Museum, stood for a few minutes in front of a gilded Buddha, and then abruptly left. I walked through the botanical garden, only a few flowers in bloom this time of year, and then gazed for a while at the patient, sullen bison in the west end of the park. I continued on, heading past the broken windmill all the way to the ocean where gray sky met slate-colored water. At least it was warmer here than in Washington, though chilly enough I wore the soft, white hat I'd bought there. Had I made the right decision? I watched the waves slap against the sand. Probably, but not definitively. That was the best I could come up with, a resounding maybe. I felt like I was dying and by my own hand. I took the N-line back home, leaned my head against the window, and watched Outer and Inner Sunset pass by under a leaden sky.

Mark didn't call. He had Patricia. I didn't want the life he did, and we both knew it. Mark wasn't right for me, and I knew it.

"I'm never going to be happy again," I told Amanda.

"You're going to be okay," she said, hugging me. Amanda watched Karla's kids with me Wednesday evening and told Frank she couldn't see him until I was better.

"You can see him Friday," I said as I watched Amanda fold and cut sheets of white paper into snowflakes with Jason and Eric. "I'm seeing Aaron."

"Do you know what you're doing?" Amanda said.

"No. But I don't want any advice."

"Now unfold it, Eric." Amanda helped him pull the notched edges of the paper apart. "See, it looks like lace, doesn't it?"

Paul came by my office when I went back to work Thursday. He must have a sun lamp at home to keep his face so tan, I thought.

It would probably give him melanoma eventually, but it was his skin. Cigarettes, alcohol, sun lamps—we all go somehow.

"I didn't get a chance to catch you before you left on vacation," Paul said. "You did an impressive job with your presentation. It makes this plant look very good."

"Thanks," I said with little enthusiasm. It seemed a complete lifetime ago.

"Have you thought about your next career move?"

I paused. This was new from him. "I've thought about it some."

"We should talk." Paul pulled out his pocket appointment calendar. "I'm in Chicago Monday and Tuesday. Can you meet next Wednesday, say ten o'clock?"

"Sure." Career moves. Ostensibly I'd broken with Mark to further my career. The whole idea seemed like a distant, not too funny joke.

Friday evening I called Aaron.

"Can I come see you?"

"Are you sure you want to so soon?"

"I don't want to be second-guessed."

"All right," he said. "You know where I live."

I drove to his apartment feeling numb and detached. Well, maybe this was the way it was going to be from now on. It didn't feel too bad, as long as I never thawed.

"You look better," he said. "How are you feeling?"

"Alive." I walked past him and sat down on the couch.

Aaron sat down as well and evaluated me with an expression more cautious than I found flattering. What did I expect—him to be at my feet? Well, yes, after all that had happened.

"Have you thought this over?" he asked. "Leaving Mark's a serious step."

"Fine time to mention it now. Maybe you should've thought about that a few months ago."

Aaron sighed. "Somehow I thought this was coming. Sara, you need to be clear this is your decision."

"As if you didn't pressure me to—"

"If you're not absolutely sure you're doing the right thing, go home and think about it some more. In the end this is your responsibility. It has to be."

"It's all very amusing for you, isn't it, Aaron? You're entertained, and I reap the consequences."

"I'm less entertained than you think. Blaming me won't make it easier, it'll just postpone what eventually you have to face."

"But I hurt him."

Aaron looked down at the venetian red carpet. "I'm sorry endings are painful. God knows I've been through enough myself to know."

"If it weren't for how scheming you and Patricia—"

"Careful," he warned.

"Of what? Hurting your feelings? Since you don't have any, that would be impossible."

Aaron crossed over to the window and looked down at the street. "The armor's back up in full force. Sara, I refuse to be a dartboard for your guilt."

"Go to hell." I picked up my coat and started towards the door.

He caught my arm. Standing close, he looked at my mouth and then my eyes. "What are you doing here? You know it's too soon. You're not ready."

"Why not? Are there prerequisites I have to pass first? Let's see, should I sign up for Beginning Adultery or Infidelity 101? Lucky I have a mentor to give me pointers on the subject."

He let go of my arm. "I'm not playing this game. You need to grieve and face your pain."

I stood paralyzed, coat in hand, unable to move. I knew he was right. Though I'd never consciously thought about it being his fault, blaming him would've made me feel better, and if he'd been Mark, I would've succeeded. I was not my father's daughter for nothing.

"I know you're hurting," Aaron said, his expression softening. "But you want me to magically make everything better, and I can't promise that. I can't promise much of anything, actually. I should never have gotten tangled up with you, Sara, but whenever I tried to stay away, I couldn't. Even now I know what I should do is send you home." He raised his hand to my face. I closed my eyes and turned my head until I felt his palm against my mouth. "But I can't. Ah, Sara, I've waited so long for this." And he began to kiss me. My coat dropped to the floor. As Aaron kissed my neck, my ears, my eyes, he whispered that I was beautiful, that he was glad I'd come, that he wanted me—things that were exquisite to hear after all the pain and doubt.

Then he paused and pulled back. "Do you want to stay?" The passion was still there but joined by restraint. I reached up to continue kissing him. Wasn't that admission enough? But he held me back. "You need to answer. I don't want you not speaking to me tomorrow."

I gave in reluctantly. "Yes. Do you want me to sign a consent form? You could keep it on file."

His arms drew me close again. "I'll take your word."

We gradually made our way to the bedroom, any further issues of consent shifting from the verbal to the physical, our clothing on the floor before I knew it. In bed, I reached to pull the sheet up.

"No," he said, pushing it back down. "Now that you're finally here, I want to see you." His hand ran down my stomach, my hip, my thigh. "How you like to hide. And how little you need to."

He seemed to take pleasure in just looking at me, but as I watched his eyes travel down my body, I felt tense and exposed. What am I doing, I thought, am I crazy to be in bed with this man? Completely crazy, Sara. I shivered and wished he hadn't given me time to think.

"Are you cold?" he asked.

"Your apartment's not incredibly warm."

"Sorry. If you're still cold a minute from now, tell me."

He pulled me close until I felt his warm skin along the length of my body, and soon I didn't care whether there'd ever been any sheets on the bed, forgetting my anxiety, forgetting about everything, just absorbing and reacting. He was much better at knowing what I wanted than Mark had ever been. Or maybe he was just more experienced, a small portion of my brain suggested cynically. My body didn't care which.

"Aaron, stop . . . no, yes . . ." With a soft moan, I pushed against his chest. "You're doing this on purpose," I accused.

"Of course I am," he murmured. "Shhh."

At one point he drew my hands towards my shoulders and gently pinned my wrists against the bed. Taken by surprise, I wanted to resist but found myself willing to be overwhelmed. He bent his head down to kiss me and in another moment he'd let go, but not before a flash in his eyes made me suspect it gave him considerable satisfaction to finally be in control of me. It made me wonder if control wasn't more important to him than he let on, but I decided to think about it later, much later, when his mouth wasn't biting into where my shoulder met my neck, the pleasure so sharp I cried out.

Startled, Aaron lifted his head with concern. Then, satisfied with what he saw, he relaxed. As I reached up to glide my hand across his mouth, he kissed my fingers. "All the waiting," he said, "was absolutely worth it."

I don't think we ever did get around to eating dinner that night.

I woke the next morning to find him already awake. I nestled closer, shielding my face with my hand. "Don't look. It's too early in the morning."

"You know you're beautiful even when you squint."

I peered through my fingers. "You're still staring."

"Mmm." He picked up my hand and drew it away from my face.

"What are you thinking about?" I said.

He smiled. "You, of course. Last night was the first time I've seen you forget to hide. Maybe a little amnesia suits you."

I turned my face into his chest. "Don't tease me." I'd spent years with Mark learning how to concentrate enough to forget.

"I don't mean to tease. It's wonderful. Every inch of you is wonderful." He ran his hand down the side of my body. I closed my eyes with a sigh. "It's an escape for you, isn't it?"

I opened my eyes. "Isn't it for everyone?"

Aaron didn't answer, his sapphire eyes enigmatic.

"You know, I've never seen you really over the edge," I said. "I'd like to see you intensely passionate about something, really angry, maybe."

"No, you wouldn't," he said matter-of-factly. Sitting up, he pushed the covers aside, took my foot in his hand, and then thoughtfully observed my leg as he slowly bent and straightened it. "You have nice knees. Yes, I like your knees." He glanced over at my face. "How much more passion do you need, Sara?"

The night before had been more than adequate, and he knew it. "How many women have you slept with?" I countered.

Aaron laughed. "I'm hardly going to tell you that."

"How many married women have you slept with?" I actually wanted to know the answer to this one. Had women left their husbands for him before?

"That's right, you're still actually married, aren't you?"

Aaron didn't look pleased I'd reminded him, and I saw I wasn't going to get any further on the subject. "Let's both forget a while longer," I said, putting one of my hands against the wiry black hair on his chest.

He shook his head slowly. "No wonder I can't think straight. I've almost forgotten whether I seduced you or you seduced me. Do you remember?"

I sat up to kiss him. "I'm still speaking to you, at any rate."

"Among other things."

With my head resting back on the pillow, my body claiming his attention, his mouth and hands demanding mine, I gave an inward sigh, glad not to talk, willing just to give him pleasure and experience what he wanted me to feel.

When, a bit later, I lay folded in his arms, sleepy and content, his breath warm against my ear, I asked him what time it was.

He turned to look at a clock on a table next to the bed. "Nine-fifteen."

I sat up with a jolt. "Yikes, it's Saturday. I've got my first job workshop at the shelter. I told Meg weeks ago that I'd do it today."

Aaron smiled. "Go take a shower. I'll make you a cup of coffee. You want some toast to go with it?"

After finding him so inscrutable for so many months, I liked knowing what kind of shampoo he used, the texture of his sheets, how he looked in the morning when he woke up. After my shower, I hurriedly dressed and emerged from the bathroom. Aaron sat in an armchair wearing a robe, sipping his coffee, and reading the newspaper, his legs hairy, his feet bare. I took my toast and coffee from the table where they were waiting for me and wolfed them both down.

"I have tickets to a play tonight," he said. "Would you like to go?"

"You've waited until the last minute to ask me again. How could you be sure I'd come over last night?"

"I'm never sure of anything to do with you, Sara. Can I pick you up at six?"

I spent the rest of the morning with five women going over how to answer an ad and fill out job applications, as well as had them do mock interviews. It went well. Afterwards, I went to lunch with Meg. I enjoyed her company more and more.

"At least today I don't feel like crying all the time," I said.

"How do you feel?" she asked.

"Sad and elated both. It sounds like it should be impossible."

"An ending closely followed by a beginning. Not so impossible."

I set my burrito down. "Am I doing the right thing?"

"That's not for me to say," Meg said. "Besides, I'm not much of a believer in right and wrong anymore."

"You think violence against women is wrong."

"I think abuse of power is wrong. But not in a good versus evil sort of way. It's because it creates closed, unhealthy systems that limit the human race from reaching its potential. Domestic violence harms not just the women who suffer from it, but also the men that inflict it. And then there's the children who witness it. Stopping it helps everybody."

"You don't think these guys should be arrested? What about justice?"

"Society should do whatever it takes to interrupt the cycle and to protect victims from their abusers. But I'm not so sure I believe in human justice anymore. We can punish when people don't follow laws, but that doesn't equate to real justice. Besides, look how relative moral frameworks are. In some cultures, leaving your husband and sleeping with another man would get you stoned to death."

"Thanks for reminding me."

"But in my frame of reference, you owe it to yourself to do what's right for your growth and your survival."

"As long as you don't hurt others."

"Sometimes you may even have to hurt others. You have to weigh it out. What you've done is okay with me, if that helps any."

"Now you seem sad," I said.

"I guess I've seen a lot of hurt, a lot of suffering. A lot of pain in this world."

"Do you want to talk about it?"

Meg shook her head, her parrots jangling, her face weary. "Sometimes it's better to let sleeping dogs lie."

"You don't think I'd understand?"

"It's not that. It's nothing to do with you at all. Please don't push me on this."

"All right," I said, not understanding in the least.

I saw Amanda at home before Aaron picked me up. She was in the living room watering her plants and pulling off dead leaves. The hollow eyes of the African masks on the wall seemed to follow her from plant to plant.

"Was he what you expected?" she asked.

"What do you mean?"

"Aaron. I assume you slept with him because you didn't come home last night."

"Amanda, I'm not going to give you details. Come on."

She smiled and reached up to one of the hanging plants. "Not that I blame you. I would've a long time ago, if I'd been you. I guessed right about him being good in bed, didn't I?"

"Don't tell me what Frank's like in bed, please."

"He's wonderful." Amanda snipped off a greenish brown leaf with a tiny pair of scissors. "When are you going to see him again?"

"Tonight."

"Sara, make sure he's nice to you. You're in a very fragile phase."

People keep telling me I'm fragile, I thought, annoyed. "I don't think I can make Aaron do anything, least of all be nice."

"Tell him I said he'd better be. Or else."

Aaron smiled when I told him this over dinner. "She's worried about you," he said, "which is natural. But I wonder what qualifies as nice in her mind."

"I wouldn't pay too much attention. I don't think she's ever liked anyone I've gone out with. She's worse than my father."

I found myself squarely in Stage One that evening, somewhat incredulous because I knew I should still be distraught over Mark. I would pay for this, I expected with certainty. I'd been in love this way with Mark once, delirious to catch sight of him across campus, to have him come by my dorm room when he had an hour between classes, to go to his apartment the first time and see the poster of Trotsky and Diego Rivera on the wall over his bed. It'd been magical.

Watching the play in the dark theater, I was intensely aware of Aaron's presence next to me. He wasn't a man to turn heads like Mark, but I'd started to notice that when women did give him a second look, they kept on looking. I wondered about his other relationships, what the women had been like, how they'd ended, what the future for me could possibly hold. I knew none of this could be discussed with Aaron, at least not for months and months. The word love couldn't even be mentioned until he said it first. He was thirty-five and wary of commitment. I would have to be careful and patient and it still might fall apart. I yearned to know the real reason why he and Elizabeth had broken their engagement.

At one point during the first act, I let my hand lie on the armrest between us. Aaron lightly glided his fingers down mine, stopping at my ring. I'd put it on in a hurry that morning, not thinking, like I had every morning for four years. He pulled my hand a few inches toward him, tilted the ring on my finger and then put my hand back down on the armrest. I looked over at him. He appeared to watch the stage.

The small theater was hot. During intermission we stood outside on the sidewalk for some air.

"It bothers you, doesn't it?" I said.

"What does?"

"My ring."

Aaron said nothing just turned to watch a cab pass by. I looked down at my hand, took my ring off and slipped it into my purse. I felt sick, but it was the choice I'd made. He still didn't look particularly pleased.

He took a breath and let it out. "Thank god you don't have children. That would be much worse."

"Why are you feeling bad? As you've said multiple times, it was my decision."

"I still feel responsible."

"But you wanted me to leave him."

Aaron stared at me, his hands in his coat pockets, his shoulders hunched in a little. He looked like he wanted something he couldn't have, but surely he'd gotten what he wanted? Most likely he always did, I thought.

"Yes, I wanted you to leave him."

"Are you sorry now?"

Slowly, he shook his head and started to smile. "No. Not at all."

Though the play wasn't bad, we left that intermission and ended up again at his apartment talking and making love. Around midnight I asked him if he'd give me a lesson in reading palms. I could tell I'd caught him off guard but at the right moment because he looked for an instant as if he might indulge me in anything. He turned a reading lamp on, tilted it up, and we angled our hands toward the light as he showed me some of the differences and similarities between our palms.

"So what does your fate line say?" I said.

"Compared to yours?"

"Okay, compared to mine."

Aaron lined my hand up parallel to his. "Hmm. Well, it looks like both of us may have multiple careers, and that you'll be more successful than I will. See, look at the way my line ends up here and yours ends up more over there. My achievements will be modest but satisfying, whereas yours will be remarkable but troubling, gratifying your biographer enormously when she goes to write the chapters on your middle years."

I laughed. "You're going to lose your reputation for fortune telling if you go around predicting things like that."

"You're the only one I have a reputation with. I told you, I don't read palms very often. Maybe I'm slipping."

"What about your aunt? Does she still give you lessons?"

"She tells me these days I'm an unmotivated student, though I did break down and let her look at my hand at Christmas."

"What did she tell you?"

"A lot of things I didn't want to hear. She knows me far too well."

"Better than anyone else?"

"Maybe. We were close while I was growing up. She used to drag me to church with her—Eastern Orthodox, quite a counterpoint to my atheist father and Presbyterian mother. It's funny, Elena's been a social worker in Boston nearly thirty years, she's a devout liberal, but when it comes to religion, she says the mysterious is the mysterious. It's probably why she's so amazing with hands, dangerous even. I'm not fond of my soul being pulled inside out for inspection."

"Maybe it was good for you," I said. "Like a spring cleaning."

"What a depressing thought. The spring cleaning, by the way, was why I didn't call you for so long after I got back from Paris."

"Your aunt told you not to call me? You told her about me?"

"I didn't have to tell her. I told you, she's amazing. She didn't tell me not to see you; she's not prescriptive that way. In fact, she was so cryptic, I'm still trying to figure out what she did say."

I turned more towards Aaron in bed. "But you did call me. What changed your mind?"

"I debated with myself for a month, but in the end I couldn't resist." He seemed abashed, surprising me. "I'm pretty sure punishment comes in this life, not the next, so when you told me you didn't want to see me anymore, I knew I'd gotten what I deserved."

I traced my finger along the line on the side of his mouth. "You were really upset?"

It took him a moment. "Yes."

"And now?"

"Now?" Aaron said, pulling me close. "I still can't resist. Fortunately, I don't have to."

The next morning Aaron brought me bagels and the Sunday paper in bed.

"What service." I pushed a pillow behind my back as I sat up.

"I didn't want you to get dressed. I like seeing you in my bed with no clothes on."

"We could just stay here the whole day."

"We could."

The phone next to the bed rang, and Aaron picked it up. "Hello? . . . No . . . This isn't a good time . . . No . . . Let me put it this way, it's an extremely bad time." There was a pause during which Aaron did not look amused. "Yes . . . À bientôt," he finished tersely before hanging up.

I raised my eyebrows, but he just shook his head, implying it was insignificant. "I should've let my answering machine catch it. Sorry."

We were able to share sections of the newspaper, a reasonable test of compatibility. We got up eventually and spent a lazy afternoon visiting the Museum of Modern Art.

"A week ago I was looking at the Capitol Building in despair," I said as we toured a photography exhibit.

"You're not done with it yet, you know," Aaron said.

"What do you mean?"

"Being with me is diverting your attention, but it's just a postponement. Grief is patient and merciless."

"You don't think I should be spending time with you?"

Aaron considered his answer with even more care than usual. "At this point, I think it's a physical impossibility. But no, I should've given you much longer to work things out."

He looked troubled, even a little sad. Then, gently telling me he had work to do, he drove me home. Though I felt deflated, I knew I couldn't spend every minute with him. We were establishing ground rules for the relationship, and I had a feeling he would insist on quite a few involving his space and my ability to make demands on him.

I called Mark when I got home because I knew I should. I still cared about him, and I didn't know what kind of pain he was in.

"How are you doing?" I asked.

"Studying," he said.

"How are you feeling?"

"Sara, I can't talk to you." Suddenly there was a dial tone.

160 · In the Land of Porcelain

I drew in a breath and hung up my end. Mark had often been inconsiderate, but never in the time I'd known him had he been rude to me. Well, what did I expect, I'd done damage. He loved you, Sara, he trusted you. You're appalling. I looked down, expecting to see a knife hilt sticking out from my chest. I don't want to grieve, I told myself. If I started, there would be so much of it. I sat on my bed in the dark, hugging my knees, rocking back and forth.

You've turned out to be a very pretty girl.
I turned off the bathroom light wearing my nightgown and robe. "Come here, Sara." I went because I never disobeyed. "You've turned out to be a very pretty girl," my father said as he held my face in his hand and turned it towards the light. I stepped back impatiently. I could smell the alcohol on his breath. I hated it when he'd been drinking. When I was little I'd been proud of my handsome father, but to a teenager anyone over forty looks more pathetic than attractive. He poured himself some scotch into a glass and picked it up. "Is that what the boys tell you, they tell you that you're pretty?"
I said nothing, unsure what to do.
He downed his drink. "I'm sure they do, all of them. Tell me, Sara, are you still a good girl?"
"Dad, you shouldn't ask things like that," I said with annoyance. "I'm tired. I'll see you in the morning."
He grabbed my arm. "Answer me, young lady."
"Ow. I haven't had sex with anyone if that's what you mean."
"Keep your voice down. Your mother's asleep." The grip on my arm loosened. "I'm sorry, Sara. I worry about you." He pulled me towards him and kissed my forehead. I'd always been his favorite. All right, I thought, just let me go to bed. He pulled me closer and kissed the side of my face. I stiffened. He held both my arms. I turned my face away and closed my eyes tightly. "You're a beautiful girl, Sara." Letting go of one of my arms, he turned my face toward him and kissed my mouth, his hand lightly caressing my neck. It's my fault, I thought, my eyes still tightly shut. I kissed Danny too long on the front porch. It's my fault. I felt a tug loosen the tie of my robe.
"No," I cried and wrenched away.

I flew into Amanda's room, the room with the lock. With shaking hands, I pulled the small piece of metal across and down into place, and then leaned back against the door, my heart pounding. My mother was asleep in the next room. I could yell and wake her. I was terrified to, terrified of what she might guess.

"Sara," my father whispered. He was only inches away from me on the other side of the door. "It's all right. Open the door." The hair rose on the back of my neck.

This is not happening, I thought. I tried to breathe but my lungs refused to expand. I could see Johnny Rotten's sneer in the asphyxiating dark.

"Sara, I won't hurt you."

I'm going to wake up, I thought. Breathe. Concentrate.

"Sara."

I heard a key turn in the lock as Amanda came home.

"Sara?" she called. She pushed my door open and flipped on the light switch. "What are you doing?"

I looked over at her and shrugged my shoulders. "I called Mark," was all I could manage to say.

With a sigh she sat behind me on the bed and circled her arms around me, her head leaning against my back. "My poor sweetie."

"Could I paint this room?"

"Any color you want."

Wednesday at ten, I knocked on Paul's door and entered his celadon-teal enclave.

"Sara," he said, after we'd passed polite preliminaries, "what you're going to need next is a bigger plant so you can get a larger department."

"There are larger department's here, Paul. I was thinking of Shampoos and Foaming Baths."

"Nope, Tom won't be ready to move for a while yet. No can do. And Bob and Bob would like to see you at a plant in Chicago. I will say, you've really impressed them. You could get a nice promotion and your career would just take off. Seven or eight years and you could be a plant manager. They're scrambling for women at my level. Now your husband's in Washington, right?"

"Yes." I didn't want to get into the whole thing with Paul. I still wore my ring to work.

"Well, then he won't mind if you move to Chicago."

"If I don't want to move right away, what are my options?"

"You could stay where you are six months, tops. Your position's a great developmental role for a manager, and we don't want to plug up the plumbing with someone who hangs around forever. Cheer up. Things are looking good for you. By the way, I need to officially reprimand you for using the company car without permission."

"What? But that was last fall."

"It just came to my attention. You must always get my permission first."

"I'm sorry I didn't, Paul. It's hard to remember, but I think you were out. It saved us from being down half a day."

"I admire your initiative, Sara, I really do. It's one of your best qualities, but I'm still going to write this up. It'll be in your file for the next thirty-six months and copies will get sent to Chicago. But if you keep doing as well as you have been, it shouldn't have any effect. I wouldn't worry about it."

I'd never gotten an official reprimand before. It was a long form I had to sign in two places. We shook hands and then I left, walking down the corridor shaking my head in disbelief. Time to get my resume together. At least I had six months. When I got back to my office, Joe waved me over to him. He stood by Althea's door.

"Could you tell her that Wednesday's far too late to be changing the schedule? And that she's worked in this department for over a year so when's she going to figure it out?"

Althea came to her doorway. "Could you please tell him that we got a last-minute order that represents a hundred thousand dollars worth of business, and I'm doing my job so would he just butt out?"

"That's it," I said. "The two of you. In my office. Now."

They stared blankly back at me. "I said NOW."

They filed into my office.

"What wrong with you two? It's like I'm a human telephone, and I'm sick of it. We're going to sit here until we work this out."

Joe and Althea sat grim and silent, their chairs angled away from each other, their arms folded across their chests.

I sighed. "Look, I want to hear both of you, and I want you to hear each other. We can make each other miserable indefinitely, or we can work through this. Will you please try?"

"He doesn't like me," Althea said.

"That's it?" I asked.

"I don't know what's wrong with him," she said with a small shrug. "Unlike some people, I just do my job."

"I ain't working with no nigger bitch no longer," Joe said, one hand karate chopping through the air for emphasis.

"Joe," I said, appalled.

The three of us sat frozen. I glanced sideways at Althea, almost afraid to look at her. She flipped a pen slowly around her fingers, a deeply angry frown on her face. Her eyes focused on the factory floor out my window. "If that's what he thinks," she said, "I'd rather have him say it. That's better than him just thinking it and making cracks about fried chicken and watermelon. Show his true colors for everyone to see, however ugly and disgusting they are."

Joe's face got redder, if that was possible. "You frigging women and blacks come in here and piss and moan and get handed everything without lifting a finger. Well, my ma was a wetback—when I was kid you had to hide that sort of thing. Nothing to be proud of, nothing to gain with a big sob story. You don't see me saying, gimme, gimme because I'm a minority."

Oh my goodness, I thought. Breathe. Have compassion.

"I didn't know, Joe," I said.

"Of course you didn't. I didn't tell you. I didn't tell anyone. And now you'll probably go blabbing it all over the plant."

"I'm sorry," I said. "It must've hurt to hide that as a kid."

"Hurt, schmurt. I called myself Joe soon as I got to school. Spic name like José wasn't gonna do me no good. My skin's light; my last name's gringo. I joined the Marines."

The three of us were stone still.

"Joe, I can't hide that I'm black," Althea said at last.

Resentfully, he looked over at her. "No, I don't s'pose you can." Joe closed his eyes and shook his head. "Aw, what's the use. I'm old; I didn't go to college. I'm going nowhere. When I retire, this company's going to spit me out like a wad of stale gum." He leaned forward and put his face in his hands. He was right, I thought sadly. He wouldn't get promoted again. The company wanted him to keep putting out hand cream, day in and day out, so that young managers like me could move up the corporate ladder.

Althea leaned forward, her expression ironic. "I can't believe I'm going to say this, but I've got a deal for you, Joe. Let's cross train. I'll train you for a week, and then you train me for a week. If you see any way for me to do my job better, once you understand it, I'll listen."

Joe sat with his hands together over his nose and mouth, his eyes blank. "Sara'd have to cover for me," he said abruptly. "Don't know if you know enough to cover."

"You went on vacation for two weeks last summer and I managed somehow," I reminded him.

"And you can't be wearing those purple suits on the floor," he told Althea.

Althea actually smiled. "I'll wear jeans."

We decided they'd start the next week. I left work drained but, except for the reprimand and the threat of transfer, relatively pleased at the turn of events.

At home I started to work on my resume while Amanda melted crayon shavings between wax paper with Jason and Eric.

"The kids tell me Amanda's going to Africa," Karla said to me when she came to pick them up.

"Can you believe it? My sister is Miss Spontaneity."

"Guess I'll have to look for another babysitter."

"I'll still watch them, Karla."

"I thought you didn't like kids."

"I'll do it, don't worry. How's your class going?"

"Just fine." She waved a hand. "Sometimes when I have a problem there's another black woman in the class I call. And guess what? I got a new job."

"Really? Where?"

"Accounts payable at Oracle Office Supplies. My professor told me about it. He said he thought I could do it. It pays better, and they'll give me insurance, even if it costs extra for the boys. I'm done with emergency rooms. I'm going to get us a real doctor now."

"Congratulations, Karla, that's wonderful. Amanda, did you hear?"

Friday evening over dinner at an Italian restaurant, I told Aaron about Paul wanting to transfer me.

"He's moving fast; that's quicker than I expected," Aaron said. "Will you go?"

I was annoyed, even hurt that he'd asked in a tone so matter of fact. "You think I should move to Chicago?"

"I think you should do what's best for you. Do you want to stay in San Francisco?"

"I've gone to some lengths to stay so far. What if you were offered a transfer?"

"I'd consider it."

"So you're telling me not to stay for you because you wouldn't stay for me."

"Sara, you and I are just starting out. You can't possibly know yet if I'm worth passing up a promotion for. Besides, you're jumping to conclusions. I said I'd consider a transfer, I didn't say I'd take it. You're not the only one who's made sacrifices to stay in San Francisco."

"What sacrifices have you made? Besides the investment bank woman."

Aaron's expression hardened; he asked the waitress for the check. "Tell me about Amanda and Frank. When do they leave for Uganda?"

"You're changing the subject."

"Very astute. I'd prefer it stay changed." He pulled a credit card from his wallet. "Please," he added, trying to soften the order.

I evaluated him icily, wondering if what I could see in his eyes was a trace of pain he hadn't been able to camouflage. Another nerve touched maybe, but it didn't excuse dictatorial commands. I pulled my purse off the floor and sifted through it for money.

"You still won't let me pay for you? Sara, I make a great deal more than you do. Please let me."

I held a twenty-dollar bill in my hand. My salary at Appleton-Smith was decent, far higher than Mark's had ever been as a community organizer. Even so, I suspected Aaron made triple, maybe quadruple what I did. And who knew what lay ahead? Maybe I should be saving up. "No, I like it this way," I said, setting my twenty down between us.

Aaron glared at the green note on the white tablecloth. "I hate taking money from you. I almost despise it."

"Good."

"Will you at least tell me why it matters? I understood before, but now I'm mystified."

I thought of my mother's grocery allowance and the tuition checks reluctantly written. "It just does."

Later, I lay curled up sleepily next to him in bed, my hand on his chest, my bent knee crossed over his leg. "Aaron, what sacrifices?"

"You've got a one-track mind." He stroked my hair, his voice amused. "It's late. Get some sleep."

"You won't let me near you."

"You're lying right next to me."

I could feel the rhythm of his heart under my hand. "Emotionally."

"Sara," he whispered, picking up my hand and kissing the palm. "We both have locked doors we don't let the other through. If you're not willing to open yours, I'm not sure you have the right to ask me to open mine."

I was quiet after this, wondering sadly if I'd just received another official reprimand. No signatures had been required this time, but a little slash would probably show up on my palm as a permanent record.

Chapter Nine

At Amanda's suggestion, the day before Valentine's Day Aaron and I met her and Frank for dinner at Zuni Cafe on Market Street. Our table on the second level felt like a box seat beholding from on high the drama of the main floor and the double-story windows facing the busy street. With a clientele that was eclectic and San Franciscan, not a tourist in sight, the Zuni ranked as one of my favorite restaurants, though too expensive to go there often.

"Fancy this turn of events," Amanda said as we sat down. "Frank and me, Aaron and Sara. At my little dinner party before Christmas, who would've guessed?" With two fingers she drew a cigarette from her purse.

"Amanda, you can't smoke in here," I said.

"I know, I know. I'm quitting. I won't light it."

Frank had been studying the wine list and ordered a bottle from our waiter. "No, let's get this one," Amanda said, pointing to one on the sheet twice as expensive. After the waiter departed, Aaron asked Frank about his research project in Uganda.

"You'd better take it easy on the luxury items," I hissed at Amanda as the other two talked. "Remember, you need to leave me money for rent."

Amanda laughed. "Oh, I expect Aaron'll pick up the tab tonight. I'll be dirt broke by the time I get back, and Frank about gives away half his salary every month. You'd think he's taken a vow of poverty or something. You know, Sara, you're still too paranoid about money. I think Dad being so stingy with you in college warped you. Was he punishing you, do you think, for being angry with him?"

I thought of the loans, the jobs, the money I'd had to borrow from Mark to get through my last year of school. The stock market had fallen, my father had written me. The check he was sending was the best he could do. "You worked when you were in college, Amanda. I remember you having a bunch of different jobs."

"Not because I had to. Sometimes the mood to work just hit me. Now, of course, things are different, but money always seems to appear when I need it. Tonight, it's from your well-to-do paramour."

"You're in a wicked mood."

"Just wait."

I wasn't looking forward to how we'd tackle splitting the bill. Perhaps I should let Aaron pay for it and write him a check later.

"Frank," I said, turning away from my pugnacious sibling, "do you have to get all the shots Amanda has to?"

"No, I was just over there for a short trip last fall. I'm caught up, but shots don't bother me anymore, anyway."

"Aaron," Amanda said, tapping her cigarette on the table. "May I inquire what your intentions are for my little sister?"

"That's the sort of question fathers used to ask," Aaron answered evenly.

"Dear papa isn't around, for which we are all very grateful. I'm his surrogate."

"Surely it's a little early for the third degree."

"I'm leaving soon. I have to rush."

Aaron leaned back, still affable but now cautious. "Are you serious?"

The waiter brought our wine and poured some for Amanda to taste. She said it was excellent. He filled our glasses and left, and then Amanda picked up the bottle to examine the label more closely.

"You know, Aaron, I heard something about you," she said. "From a friend of a friend of someone who knows you. You know how it is." She put the bottle down.

"What did you hear?" Aaron said quietly, his attention intent.

"Echoes from your past."

"Could you be more specific?"

I pivoted my head back and forth between Amanda and Aaron as if I were watching a high stakes tennis match, even though I had no way of telling when points had been scored.

"It's my trump," Amanda said, sipping her wine. "Don't worry, I'm not going to play it unless I have to."

Aaron narrowed his eyes. "One could say vague accusations with no substantiation are irresponsible, Amanda."

"Let's talk about irresponsibility, Aaron," Amanda snapped.

Frank and I looked at each other, both of us clueless. Aaron now appeared visibly annoyed, unusual for him, and Amanda scowled. Escalation into armed conflict did not appear out of the realm of possibility.

"Do you two want to go outside and have it out?" I asked. "Frank and I'll have a nice dinner here."

Amanda ignored me. "I think you should know, if you don't treat her well, I'll kill you."

Aaron drank some wine before speaking. "Coming from you, that's not an idle threat. Do you really think being over-protective is helping her?"

"I can't believe this," I said. "Hey, what am I, invisible?"

"I'm not over-protective, but given how vulnerable she is right now—"

"Well, you'll be in Africa and not much help, won't you?"

"I'll send a poison dart in the mail."

"That's enough," I said firmly, looking incredulously between the two of them. "I thought you two liked each other."

"It appears we have some differences to work out," Aaron said. "Had we but world enough and time, Amanda."

"It rains into the sea," Amanda said, "and still the sea is salt."

Aaron gave a short, amused, if irritated, laugh.

"Do the two of you have some sort of secret code?" I asked.

"'The toil of all that be helps not the primal fault,'" Aaron said. "'It rains into the sea, and still the sea is salt.' Houseman, a fairly obscure poet these days."

"I thought if I spoke your language, you'd understand me better."

Aaron's face was serious again. "I understand what you're saying. And I don't like being judged without a trial."

Frank and I talked a while, Amanda joined in soon, and not too much later even Aaron was laughing at Amanda's jokes again, but his eyes were cold when I caught him scrutinizing her from across the table.

"I'm sorry about Amanda," I said as we drove back to his apartment, interrupting a fairly intense silence. After the scene at the restaurant, I hadn't made a peep about offering him money for the meal.

Aaron glanced at me as if he'd forgotten I was in the car with him. He said nothing.

"Why were you so furious with each other?"

He watched the traffic. "I wasn't furious. I can't answer for Amanda."

"I know she's crazy sometimes, but I love her, so I hope you don't stay angry."

"I know she's important to you." Aaron shook his head, his annoyance relenting. "You Whitfield women are ornery as hell. Don't worry, Amanda and I'll manage to get along somehow. You know, I never asked you how the job workshop you gave went. Are you planning on doing another?"

"Why?" I said, smiling even though he'd yet again changed the subject. "Do you need help with your resume?"

He looked in the mirror before he changed lanes. "I haven't had to write one in so long, I've probably forgotten how. It's nice to know I have an expert around if I need it."

When we got inside the doorway of his apartment, Aaron held me close and kissed me, but later, as we began to make love in the bedroom, he seemed distant. "What hurts?" I asked, my fingers touching his cheek, then gliding along the tense muscles in his shoulders.

His eyes softened, and I could feel his body relax as he looked and looked at me. I gave him time, wistfully wondering what he was thinking. That he had the blackest eyelashes I'd ever seen was all I knew for sure.

At last he sighed. "She's right, of course."

"Who's right—Amanda? About what?" I sat up a little. "You want to talk about it? I'd love to listen."

His marvelous sapphire eyes smiled back at me with affection. It was a look worth passing up a promotion for, whether he thought so or not. "Just having you with me is enough. I'm unspeakably lucky, and I know it. At least I've got that figured out."

I tried to probe Amanda later about her argument with Aaron.

"I just wanted to give him a hard time," Amanda said.

"Why? You know, I do like him. I wish you'd be civil."

"I want him to think twice. Measure twice, cut once."

"Amanda, what are you talking about?"

"I said I wouldn't say anything, and I won't. I keep my word."

During the next several weeks Amanda raced around the city like a wild woman to get shots, visas, plane tickets, and to see all her friends before she left. We managed to squeeze a couple of conversations into her departure countdown. One evening when Frank was at the hospital, I made her a cup of tea as she gave me instructions about her plants.

"Water them Wednesday nights and Sunday mornings, except the tree next to the living room window. He only gets it on Sundays."

"Is the day so important?"

"They're used to it. It'll hurt their little psyches to change."

"I'll do my best to keep them green, that's all I promise. They may need psychotherapy when you get back."

"Pinch off dead leaves, but don't prune them. They'd be terrified to see you with scissors."

"Fine."

"Lightly fertilize them every other month."

"Amanda, I'm not a botanist."

"It's not that hard. Here, I've written it down for you." She smoothed the sheet of instructions flat against the counter. "Sara, I'm agonized that I'm not going to be here with you through all this."

"Worry about your plants, not me."

"Divorce is always messy, and you're just starting to wade through it. Look, you're still wearing your ring."

I looked down at my hand. "I don't want to explain things yet at work. Amanda, you're thinking of Mom and Dad's divorce. Mark and I couldn't be more different."

"Dad's still not through the divorce. He's spent ten years hiding behind Genine."

"I'm not hiding behind Aaron." We stood side by side leaning against the kitchen counter, steaming cups of tea in hand. "Amanda, what are you going to do all day in Uganda? Won't Frank be working?"

"I haven't the faintest idea. Learn to cope with poverty and death, I suppose. Half the people there have AIDS." She turned to me. "I'll be fine. It's you I worry about so much it makes me sick."

"Nothing's going to happen, Amanda. Promise."

"I won't even be able to call, except in an emergency." She frowned at me intently. "What if Aaron dumps you? Could you survive that?"

"Do you think he's going to?" Was this part of her secret stash of information?

"I have no idea. But you should be prepared for anything."

"Quit worrying," I said with exasperation. "I'm resilient."

"Come to Africa with us."

"Right, Amanda. I'll just pack up and go."

"It's what I'm doing."

I laughed and hugged her. "Amazing Amanda."

"Serious Sara," she whispered, her arms tight around me. "How am I going to take care of you?"

I leaned against her, my point of safety, a second longer and then went back to my tea. Even after Dad moved in with Genine, I still used to sleep in Amanda's room sometimes. Seeing Johnny Rotten sneering from purple walls reassured me, her rebellion an emotional blanket I could pull up to my chin. "Amanda, why did you put that lock on your door?"

"You mean in my room at home? Mostly because I knew it would make Dad mad, but it was also a big help later on when I sneaked boys into my room."

I was incredulous. "Really? Who? How'd they get in?"

"Through the window, of course. Sam Goldsmith once and Dave Owing twice."

I shook my head, but I had to laugh. "And Dad never found out? He would've killed you."

Amanda smiled. "Oh, I don't know. By high school, I think I'd won the battle with him. He didn't find out, but I don't think he wanted to know. He wasn't as jealous with me as he was with you. You, he would've killed." She paused, looking at me. "And you came close enough during the divorce, didn't you? I know you don't like talking about it, but I still have nightmares sometimes."

I studied the black and white tile on the floor. "It was a long time ago."

"I've never understood why the two of you didn't speak to each other for so long. You were always his little princess. You've still never told him, have you?"

"No." There are things, Amanda, I can't even tell you.

I saw Aaron on the weekends. During the week he often traveled for work or worked late, and he wanted time to write, so we hardly even spoke Monday through Thursday.

"Sara, you're a resourceful person. You don't need to see me all the time," he said when I called him one evening, having spent the previous hour watching TV and flipping channels so fast I got motion sickness.

I stared at Man Ray's violin woman in the hallway. "No, but with Amanda at Frank's so much—couldn't I come over and just read? I wouldn't bother you."

He laughed. "That wouldn't work. You'd sigh, and I'd look up and want to head to the bedroom with you. I'd never get anything done. Remember you told me once about the interior life? I need it. I kind of have to insist on it."

"It's like I'm this little compartment of your life labeled 'diversion.'"

"You're much more than that."

"Do you care about me?" I asked impetuously.

"Is that what you need to hear?"

I was silent.

"Yes, Sara, I care about you. Very, very much. I can't always be with you."

I was satisfied and unsatisfied. After I hung up, I went into the bathroom and stared at the mirror on the front of the medicine cabinet. He said he cared, Sara—it should do for now. Yes, but what did it mean? It means you should concentrate. Go finish Tolstoy.

Home alone another evening, I made a second attempt at calling Mark.

"Hi," I said when Mark answered. "Are you going to hang up on me?"

"No. Sorry about that. This hasn't been easy."

"Are you doing better now?"

"I'm okay. Studying most of the time. This is a brutal semester. How are you doing?"

I twisted the telephone cord idly around my hand. "I'm okay, too. It's nice to hear your voice."

"Any second thoughts?"

"About 3000 of them," I said sadly. "Same conclusion, though."

"You know, I've known you, what, six years? But I've just realized you have more courage than I do. I couldn't have done it, but it had to happen."

I wrapped the black telephone cord another time around my hand and pulled on it. What had I wanted him to say? That he was frantic, distraught, that he'd mourn forever? I realized my hand hurt and unwrapped the cord. "How's Patricia?" I said, surprised at myself. Maybe I wanted to feel the edge of the pain like a seven-year-old wiggling a loose tooth.

Mark took a moment to respond. "I'm seeing her. I guess you figured that out. Are you upset?"

No, he couldn't be. It'd been only three weeks. Abruptly, unexpectedly, the tooth had been yanked out leaving a crater gaping behind. Well, I'd gone to Aaron the very next day—you're such a hypocrite, Sara. "I want you to be happy, Mark." I closed my eyes and struggled to keep my voice even. "Maybe we should get things going with the divorce."

"Let me do the work. I'll find out what we have to do."

"Okay. You've got millions of lawyers around to ask, I guess."

"I can't help missing you, Sara."

I opened my eyes, the violin woman in front of me. Oh, Mark, what have I done? "Can we still talk sometimes?"

"Sure."

I hung up, took a deep breath, and walked over to turn up the thermostat. Amanda was always turning it down. I wondered if Mark slept with Patricia at his apartment or hers. Hers, of course. There was Benji to consider. The bed in Mark's apartment was too small for two people anyway.

I came back to stare at the pictures in the hallway, the past too painful to think about, the future too frightening, certain motifs resonating persistently. It's my trump, I heard Amanda say. Irresponsibility. Measure twice, cut once. I'm seeing her, Mark's voice said, I guess you figured that out. Very astute, Aaron's voice cut in. I'm not sure you have the right. Yes, I care about you, Aaron's voice was softer now, I can't always be with you. I'm unspeakably lucky and I know it.

What did it add up to?

Concentrate, Sara.

The violin woman was in front of me. She must have froze posing for that picture, I thought. She sat up straight, poised, her arms pulled forward out of sight, her beautiful back bare except for the scroll-like marks of the *f*-holes. She wore a turban with her head turned to the side enough to reveal a silhouette of her face. Had she minded when he put the black scrolls on her back, had she known what he was doing? Her name was Kiki. She'd been Man Ray's lover in Paris during the Twenties, Amanda told me. "Man Ray was a manipulative bastard with women but I love him anyway," Amanda had said laughing as we looked at the photograph together. I peered now even more closely. The entire print, the background, her elegant body, was composed of grainy shades of a beautiful pearl gray. What was behind my back that Amanda could see but I couldn't?

During the two weeks Joe and Althea cross trained, I worked late each evening in order to cover for them and still do the rest of my job. Joe and Althea huddled for hours in front of her computer as she showed him how she figured out the schedule. The week after, I noticed Althea squatting on the floor beside Joe looking underneath a piece of machinery. I was pleased with their progress and decided now was the time to start on our next quality problem: small black specs that appeared sporadically in the hand cream. I recruited another group of workers, and we got off to an animated start. Despite Paul and the Bobs, I could still get enthusiastic about Deming, and it didn't even faze me when they announced at a large banquet luncheon for all the managers at a posh downtown hotel that our new number one priority was Total Cost Control. It would be easy enough to ignore, though I'd have to offer up to Paul some charts and graphs to placate him. It was a demanding period, but I enjoyed it until Paul requested my presence one Friday afternoon for further career discussions.

"It's final. They've offered me a promotion if I transfer to Chicago," I told Aaron over dinner at my apartment that evening. An hour earlier I'd opened my door to see Aaron, straight from work and still formal in a dark suit and tie, his black hair ruffled from the wind. In his arms he held twenty rose-colored lilies and a bottle of wine. My heart leapt, and I helplessly realized I was being knocked back into the middle of Stage One, just when I thought I was climbing out of it. But when Aaron kissed me all too briefly, he seemed tired, worn out, unusual for him.

"Is it an interesting position?" he said picking at his salad. He'd not eaten much, mostly just drunk a few glasses of wine. I wasn't the world's most amazing cook, but I thought the food had turned out okay.

"A department twice the size of mine that makes toothpaste," I said. "Paul called it a plum. You don't like the pasta?"

"What? No, Sara, it's very good. I'm just not hungry. And if you don't go to Chicago? What did he threaten?"

"He said nothing else this good would come my way for a while, although something in Georgia might open up in June."

"When do they want you in Chicago?"

I rolled my eyes. "Three weeks, which is the other thing: they expect me to just drop everything and go."

Aaron sipped his wine. "I wonder if Paul feels he's competing with you for attention. He may want you out of the way."

That hadn't occurred to me. "Lately he's seemed pretty supportive." Except for the reprimand. I hadn't told Aaron about that because I was still embarrassed by it.

He shrugged. "Just a hunch. He's an ambitious man."

"Do you always look for ulterior motives?"

Aaron smiled but his face looked weary. "Yes, I look for motives and intentions, dreams and desires. They're always there pulling the strings, consciously or subconsciously. Business isn't particularly rational, but it is predictable."

"How can the irrational be predictable?"

"People tend to be irrational in the same way," he said. "Or maybe I should say people are motivated by their perceived self-interest. You made Paul look good for a while, so you were an asset, but maybe you look too good now, so you're making him nervous. If he thought you were necessary to his success, plum assignments in other plants would come and go without you ever being considered for them."

"You know all that from what I've told you?"

"I met Paul, remember? And I've listened to what you're trying to do, and I know how corporations work."

There was an unamused edge to his voice, but I didn't think it was me who'd provoked him this time. "Aaron, do you like your job?" We always talked about my job, never about his.

"No," he said simply, almost seeming depressed. He poured himself another glass of wine. I shook my head when he offered me some.

"I guess I always thought you did. Why do you do it then?"

"It pays well. I'm good at it. Not the best of reasons, but they'll do."

"You look worn out. Aaron, if you don't like it, can the money be worth it?"

"Why, do you think I should quit?"

"Well, yes, if you want to."

He smiled halfheartedly. "If it were only that easy."

"You have some savings, don't you? You could write for a while, get another job later. You've worked at Merrisocks a long time. Maybe you need a change." He looked less than enthusiastic. I tilted my head. "Why not?"

Aaron closed his eyes. "Sara, look, it's been a God-awful week in more ways than one. This isn't a good time to push."

I went over to him. He did look beat. "Come here," I said, pulling him to his feet. He had loosened his tie. I disentangled the knot, pulled it off, led him to the couch and pushed him into it. "Relax. Would you like a cup of tea?"

He leaned his head back. "The healing powers of a cup of tea. Yes, I'd love one."

I cleared the dishes, and when I returned with his tea, he was asleep, the masks above watching over him like guardian angels. Sitting down next to him, I carefully let my head rest against his arm stretched out over the back of the couch. With a deep sigh I wondered if he would ever let me into his interior life. Such a private man with his own private world, and my passport only held a visa for one country in it. He smelled of cotton and paper and of Aaron, I thought. Everyone has their own smell, if you get close enough. I liked his. What a week. I'd stayed at work the previous night until nearly nine working on a cost control memo for Paul. I'd had to stay so late because I'd spent most of the day covering for Althea, ordering supplies and figuring out next week's schedule. I knew the hectic pace at work was only temporary. It would pass.

I woke to find my head leaning against Aaron's chest, his hand stroking my hair.

"What time is it?"

Aaron pulled his cuff back from his wrist. "Nine-thirty. Do you still want to see a movie?"

"No, I don't want to move." But actually I wasn't that comfortable. I sat up and looked at him, savoring him, noting each line, the angle of his nose, the midnight blue of his eyes, building up my memory for the days I wouldn't see him. "How's your poetry doing?" I hoped he was at least getting satisfaction from that.

"Not so well. Poetry and celibacy seem to go hand in hand for me."

"You mean you write better when you're not sleeping with anyone?" I said with surprise. "How often have you been celibate?"

"Often enough."

"So I'm keeping you from writing?" I didn't know what to make of this.

"Sara, it's not you, it just happens. It's a curse." He rubbed his eyes and yawned. "Only a temporary one. I have to work through it, that's all."

I stared at him, more than a little perturbed.

"Don't be upset," Aaron said with a smile. "I shouldn't have said anything. Writing's important to me, but any difficulty I'm having is worth it. More than worth it." He took my hand and gently massaged each of my fingers. I'd remembered to take off my ring before he got there. "I'm glad you're not going to Chicago," he said.

"Are you?" A wave of longing surged painfully through my chest up to the top of my throat. There was so much I wanted to hear from him.

"I don't think Appleton-Smith deserves you or knows what to do with you. When I first met you there, you stood out so clearly. There are other companies that might be a better fit."

"They're probably all alike." I sighed and pushed my hair away from my face. "Maybe I should just stay at Appleton-Smith. Maybe if I refuse to be transferred, they'll give me something decent here." Aaron studied me intently, his expression pained. I looked back curiously. "What?"

His hand tightened around mine. "There's something you need to know. What I said about Paul earlier was based on more than a hunch."

"What do you mean?"

"The audit I did at Appleton-Smith—Paul was trying to set you up. The whole thing was trivial, but it makes me believe that if he wants you gone, staying will be difficult."

"What do you mean, he set me up?"

"I went through three times the number of records in your department as I did in any other. His directions."

I frowned. Did it fit with what I knew about Paul? Unfortunately, yes, it did. "Why didn't you tell me about it before?"

"At first, I didn't know how you'd take it. Once I knew you better, you were handling things so well, you seemed safely past it. I didn't want to shake your confidence. To tell you the truth, I was worried if I told you, you'd get angry and confront Paul. If anything had gotten back to Merrisocks, it might've made things difficult for me. Especially since I was seeing you."

"What would've gotten back . . . Aaron, what did you find on that audit? I was right in the room with you. I thought there weren't any major problems."

"Your purchasing system was byzantine: I found enough in every department to hang all of you. But punishing you or anybody else wasn't going to solve anything; the whole system needed to be overhauled. I reported a couple deviations from every department, yours included, to illustrate the problems and support my recommendations. Your department was better than most, but since I went through so many more records, of course I found more deviations. Since my report was going to go to your hierarchy in Chicago, my guess is Paul wanted to embarrass you, knock your credibility down a notch."

I was astounded. "You protected me. Why, because you liked me?"

"It was more that I didn't like Paul. He tried to justify the extra records by telling me you were too independent, verging on out of control, which made me guess he saw you as a threat. I was actually intrigued to meet you. I wasn't sure what to expect, certainly not what

I found. The fact that I liked you made it easier, but you weren't the only one whose deviations got underreported. I did what I thought was best. God, I despise audits."

I was floored. My boss had told a complete stranger I was out of control—what else did he go around saying about me? It occurred to me that Aaron needn't have bothered about the audit: Paul managed to nail me with the company car anyway. Who knew what else he had up his sleeve.

I sighed, disgusted and depressed. "And I thought things were going so well there. Well, I have to find another job anyway, what does it matter."

"Sara, you've done fine at Appleton-Smith, even with a weasel for a boss. You're good at your job. You'll do well anywhere you go. Power games like these are just an ugly part of business that you have to maneuver through."

I smoothed my skirt down over my knees. "These games, were they a special case, or are they standard fare for you?"

"I usually help companies set strategy, not clean up botched procedures, so the politics I'm involved in are on a much different level. Most of the time I just observe. Most of the time I don't particularly care."

"But sometimes you intervene. How often do you decide to rescue people?"

"Ah, Sara." He smiled. "How often do I come across someone who is bright, ornery, and so enchanting they turn my life inside out? Rarely. How often do I invite them to symphonies, let them lure me onto beaches, and then find I can't concentrate five minutes straight without thinking about them? Almost never. You've always been exceptional."

I looked down. That answer was nearly on a par with the twenty rose-colored lilies. "I didn't lure you," I said, starting to smile. "I suppose I should be thanking you, not chastising you."

"Maybe I deserve some chastising. I was playing my own power games with Paul. Did I ever tell you he roped me into having lunch with him while I was at your plant? Someone in my office told him I'd done a project for your Executive Committee in Chicago, and he wanted to know all about it. It was excruciating. At least it gave me the chance to put it into his head he'd get more credit for your success than your failure. It's amazing how the obvious escapes people."

And I'd given my first presentation to the Bobs shortly thereafter. My wonder bordered on incomprehension. There were so many unknowns with Aaron, I thought, so much he held back. What was the difference between reticence and secrecy? I didn't have an answer. But you do, Sara, what does your instinct tell you?

Instinct says when it gets down to it, it's a leap of faith. And sometimes you fall, and sometimes you make it across.

Aaron was watching me, waiting for my response. I stretched up off the couch to kiss him. At first he was motionless as my lips touched his; then he pulled me close and kissed me more like he should have after not seeing me all week. With an internal sigh of relief I relaxed because I knew, poetry or no poetry, he still wanted me.

"So my scum bucket boss brought us together," I said a minute or two later.

"In a way. It was probably the last thing he intended."

I touched the side of his face. "Do you want to stay the night here?"

He smiled, still tired but now content. "In your room?"

My little white room, I thought.

Chapter Ten

I visited Paul's plush office the next week and told him that while I appreciated the offer of a promotion, I didn't want to move just yet. Attempting to look crushed with disappointment, Paul sighed sadly and shook his head. "It's the best I can do for you, Sara. I worked hard on this one."

"Sorry, Paul. Maybe this summer."

He brightened and flashed me his movie star smile. "I'll tell Bob and Bob."

I hated to lie, even to Paul, but I needed more time. No, I take it back: lying to Paul didn't trouble me at all. I tilted my head. Something was different about the old scum bucket.

"Paul, you got glasses."

He grinned, took off the gold aviator frames, and wiped them in a large linen handkerchief.

"Yep, the old eyes are giving out. Just got them checked."

"You must be working too hard. It's funny how glasses always make a person look older. Are those bifocals?"

Paul frowned at the frames in his hand.

Walking down the hallway back to my office, I smiled a little. It was inevitable ambition would get the upper hand on Paul's vanity, though I hadn't expected it to happen so soon. At home I finished my resume and sent it to ten companies in the area that looked interesting.

Late Friday night I lay next to Aaron, the two of us cocooned by a circle of yellow lamplight while rain pattered against the window. I geared up my nerve. Aaron had seemed more pliable lately, ever since enlightening me about the audit. I decided to risk it.

"Tell me about Elizabeth?" I asked softly.

Aaron sighed. "You don't give up, do you?"

"Is it still so painful you can't talk about it?"

"All right," he said. "If it'll make you happy. What do you want to know?"

"How did you meet?"

"Elizabeth's mother knew mine. They engineered for us to meet at a party. Neither of us wanted to go; then it turned out we liked each other. Suddenly I found myself coming up with reasons to fly to Boston every other week. At times it felt like I spent half my life on the plane." He stopped and stared off into space. "It seemed worth it."

"You got engaged," I prompted, wanting to cut to the chase. "What made you want to marry her?"

"We had a lot in common. Her family was similar to mine, we'd gone to the same sort of schools. My mother thought she was perfect."

"You don't marry people just because your mother likes them."

Aaron smiled a little. "You haven't met my mother. No, when I met Elizabeth, she'd just gotten out of a disastrous relationship with a guy who was abusive. She was hurt and lonely and needed to be taken care of. What I liked about her most was she loved theology and philosophy; she could face religion without flinching. She never agonized about her integrity because she didn't have to—she never deviated from it. She's one of the least deceptive people I've ever known."

It occurred to me that this wasn't a category I'd score clean marks in, and I began to doubt the wisdom of this line of inquiry. Fools rush in, however. "Why did she break it off?"

"She met someone else that suited her better."

"That's what you said before." Still, I couldn't quite believe it. "You didn't like, have a big fight, she threw your ring at you, you wanted to rip the other guy's face off?"

Aaron laughed with surprise. "Sara—no, it wasn't like that at all."

"Are you still in love with her?"

He frowned. "No."

"You look so sad when you talk about her."

"It wasn't a happy event in my life, but it's over. I'm glad things have turned out the way they have."

"Really?"

"Really." Aaron kissed me and turned off the light.

Nestling into my pillow, I wondered more about Elizabeth, what he'd been like with her. Then I heard his voice in the dark. "Sara, do you want to rip Patricia's face off by any chance?"

I cringed. I knew I'd shown too many cards. "Maybe."

Aaron laughed and tightened his arms around me. After a few seconds passed I relaxed, relieved the subject had closed so easily.

"Sara, does Mark know you're seeing me?"

Not so easily. And I was unlikely to get away with changing the subject. "I doubt it," I admitted.

Aaron didn't respond.

"I didn't want to tell him until he was feeling better. He's getting things started with our divorce though." Still he said nothing. "Are you upset?"

"No." He actually didn't sound upset. "I suppose some ambivalence is natural."

"Ambivalence? Just because I'd like Patricia to drop off the face of the earth doesn't mean I'm ambivalent about getting divorced."

"You're right, murderous intentions generally indicate complete disinterest." He sounded amused.

"Fine, don't believe me then." I punched my pillow and turned onto my side.

Aaron ran his hand over my waist and began to kiss my shoulder. "Lucky for Patricia," his mouth was in the vicinity of my spine, "she's well out of the reach of any bloodthirsty Whitfield women, otherwise I might warn her. I'm grateful to her for coming on the scene when she did."

His hand pushed my hair away from my neck, and I closed my eyes. It's so unfair, I thought. All he has to do is kiss me, and he wins every argument.

Amanda held a bon voyage party on the Ides of March, the evening before her flight overseas. I convinced Aaron to come to it with me, telling him Amanda would be so busy she wouldn't have time to bug him. He said not to worry about it, that he'd like to see Amanda again before she left.

"Wait a minute," I said as we were on the verge of leaving his apartment. "We need something that starts with the letter U."

"Why?"

"It's a Ubiquitous Uganda party. Knowing Amanda, if we show up U-less she won't let us in."

Aaron shook his head. "Nine months in the middle of Africa with your sister. I hope Frank knows what he's doing."

We arrived around nine, Aaron with a copy of *Ulysses*, me with a little paper cocktail umbrella that I dug out from the bottom of my purse. Inside the apartment the Ramones predominated on the stereo with their non-stop machine gun beat, and each room except mine was so crowded we could hardly make it down the hallway. Amanda had invited an assortment of fledgling artists, musicians, actors, and others who worked at close-to-minimum-wage jobs to support the imaginative portions of their lives. There were unicorns, a utility pole, an umpire, more umbrellas, an udder or two, a cup of urine, and maps of Uzbekistan and upstate New York. One guy wore a tie, carried a briefcase and a PDA, and told everyone he had an ulcer. I believed him until Amanda pointed out the PDA was fake. Another of Amanda's singularly insane friends came as an upholstered armchair. Frank had rolled up one sleeve and written "ulna" on his arm. I left Aaron talking to Frank, the only person he knew, and helped Amanda put out more chips and salsa.

"*DDT did a job on me, now I am a real sickie,*" Amanda sang, bobbing up and down as she tried to pry open a tough plastic bag. Frank had suggested she serve U hors d'oeuvres, but Amanda didn't care to push a theme too far, especially when the only food she could think of was sea urchin. For the occasion she wore a drawstring cotton skirt tie-dyed in red, green, and yellow, and she'd wrapped a black and green scarf borrowed from my collection around her hair in a turban. Two eyeliner dots of an umlaut decorated her forehead.

"I'm playing the Ramones because they're all so ugly, they qualify," Amanda said. "I can't believe my adolescence is becoming golden oldie. Next thing you know, there'll be a muzak version of *Cretin Hop*. Hey, did I tell you I called Dad this morning? I felt bad about going to another continent without letting him know."

"What did he say?"

"You know him. Not much. Have a good time, don't get malaria. He wouldn't even let on he was surprised, as if it would kill him to show any emotion. Who knows, he's been repressing it so long, it just might."

"Well, it's good you told him, I guess." Better than him calling here and me having to explain it, I thought. I'd told my mom, but I hadn't told my father about Mark and me splitting up. I should've figured out an ingenious way to get Amanda to tell him, but too late now, she was leaving tomorrow. Amanda drifted away, her turban disappearing behind a clump of people. I went out into the living room with a refilled bowl of tortilla chips.

"TWENTY, TWENTY, TWENTY-FOUR HOURS TO GO, I WANNA BE SEDATED," the stereo blasted.

Someone grabbed my arm. I looked over and saw Jake, an old boyfriend of Amanda's who'd shaved his golden-brown hair extremely short. He wore round, tinted-green glasses, camouflage army fatigues and a pair of underwear on his head. He was eager to hear all the details of my life since he'd last seen me, but not wanting to get into my life, I asked him questions about his. He still played in a band, still lived in the Haight, still had a friendly engaging grin. He said he'd joined the Green Party, but that he thought they'd already sold out and that San Francisco was becoming a bastion of liberal pretenders. We'd eventually choke on our tapas bars and lattes, not that he had anything intrinsically against either. A good cup of coffee was important to the proletariat, too. He sounded too much like Mark. I tried to think of a polite way to disengage. The true radicals were all moving to Oakland where they could afford the rent, Jake said. There was going to be class warfare between the East Bay and the Peninsula. When it happened, Marin would sniff, put up more security fences and ignore the whole thing. I told him he was overlooking the posh neighborhoods along the East Bay hills. Jake grinned and said one more fire and they're goners anyway. I raised my eyebrows. No, he wasn't that much like Mark, but I still wanted to get away.

We were jostled by the crowd in the living room until we stood next to a vibrating stereo speaker. Joey Ramone was telling us that Sheena was a punk rocker.

"I used to have such a crush on you," Jake shouted in my ear. "It made Amanda furious. I would've gone out with you, but weren't you married?"

He was standing too close. I edged away.

"Yeah. I still am." Kind of, I thought.

"Is he here? I'd like to meet him."

"No," I shouted. "He's not here."

"I thought I saw you with a guy a while ago."

"Yeah," I said, looking away, wondering where Aaron was now.

"I think I still have a crush on you."

"Jake," I said, shaking my head, "you don't know me. I'm not like Amanda."

"All the better."

I searched back in my memory for what Amanda's time with Jake had been like. Oh, that's right. He'd been very, very intense. He'd moved in with her after two weeks of dating and stayed for months. A crush on me was not a good idea, a source of stress I didn't need. Amanda had ended up shaking him off, but she was good at that sort of thing. She'd said that even though she'd had to pry him loose, she'd always liked him, which is why she'd invited him tonight.

"Jake, I've got to go. Nice talking to you."

"Can I see you next week?"

"No. I'm not interested." A brutal thing to say, especially when I had to scream it at the top of my lungs to be heard, but I wanted to be clear.

"I'll call you," he shouted, grinning.

I fled. I bumped into Frank as I searched the crowded kitchen.

"Have you seen Aaron?" I asked.

"I think he went with Amanda to get some more ice."

"He did what?"

"I thought it was odd." Frank smiled, looking satisfied and untroubled. Though he was clearly out of place with Amanda's bizarre conglomeration, he didn't seem to mind. "I don't think they'll kill each other."

"No, they'll probably stop with maiming. Maybe I should go after them."

"I think they're back. I can hear Amanda." Frank left the room in the direction of her voice that was barely discernible over the din.

Aaron entered the kitchen with a bag of ice and set it on the counter. "Where were you?" I said.

"I got an invitation from your sister I couldn't refuse. Her tactics resemble the Mafia's sometimes."

"And?"

"We talked. And came to an understanding."

I raised my eyebrows expectantly.

Aaron pulled me into his arms. "I know you want a report, but not talking about it was part of the understanding."

"You're so exasperating." I laid my head on his shoulder, and we stood together, a self-contained island in the noisy, bobbing sea.

Amanda entered the kitchen, bantering and laughing with each group of people she passed. When she got to Aaron and me, she smiled and reached around us to open the refrigerator and pull out a beer.

"Don't forget," she said, tapping Aaron on the shoulder with the neck of her bottle. "If you mess up, I'll still kill you."

"I rarely forget threats on my life," he answered dryly.

"Great party, isn't it? If I die in Africa, you can regard this as my wake."

"Hey Amanda," Jake yelled from the kitchen doorway. "There's some old dude at the door. Says he's your dad. Should I let him up? He doesn't have a U."

Then my father, wearing a dark blue suit and red tie, his hair almost silver now, pushed Jake aside and entered the kitchen as if it were a corporate boardroom.

I stiffened and withdrew from Aaron's arms. Jake came over and stood by us, leaning against the refrigerator with his arms folded.

"Holy shit," Amanda said. "Dad, what are you doing here?"

He had an audience, even if they were unknown to him, which must've made him decide to play the affectionate father. "Sorry to barge in, Amanda. I know I'm crashing your party, but I wanted to see you before you left."

"So you just popped right up. The wonders of modern transportation. Do you want to stay here tonight? I suppose you could have Sara's room."

"No, I'm taking a midnight flight back. I don't want to impose."

Amanda looked up to the ceiling as if praying to the saints. "Right. As if you're not imposing. Well, I guess you should meet Frank. Let me go get him."

As she left the kitchen, my father turned towards me, his focus seeming to narrow. "Sara," he said, nodding in salutation.

I winced. "Hi, Dad."

He looked at Aaron and then at me again. "How's Mark?" he said.

"Fine," I answered nervously. "This is Aaron Lambert. Aaron, my father, John Whitfield."

They shook hands, Aaron curious but wary, my father looking for faults. Joey Ramone sang about fun, fun, fun, fun, fun in the warm California sun. This is without a doubt one of the worst moments in my life, I thought. And there were far too many witnesses.

"I'm Jake," Jake said, still sporting BVD's on his head as he stuck out his hand. "Nice to meet you, sir. I used to live with Amanda. She told me all about you." My father frowned as he reluctantly shook the proffered hand.

Amanda returned with Frank and introduced him. Then the six of us stood in a circle next to the refrigerator. "This is ridiculous," Amanda said. "Let's go somewhere we can talk. Jake, you stay here and host the party."

Jake bowed. "A privilege, madam."

"I'd like to talk to just Amanda and Sara," my father said, looking at Frank and Aaron. "If you don't mind. Get your coats, girls." Lifting her eyes and palms in helpless resignation, Amanda left the kitchen, my father behind her.

"God, I don't want to go," I said. "I wish I could drop off the face of the earth." I felt like a bug stuck through with a pin and still squirming as it's added to the collection. Serves me right for not telling him sooner, I told myself. Unlike Amanda, I would always get caught.

"You haven't told him about leaving Mark, have you?" Aaron said.

"No. I never talk to him."

"You go with them. I'll wait."

"You don't have to."

"I want to. You look like you're going to face a firing squad. How bad can it be?"

"You don't know him."

In a booth in an all-night diner, I sat next to Amanda across from my father, all of us drinking decaffeinated coffee. When had he gotten so spontaneous? I wouldn't have guessed in a million years he'd fly up to see Amanda off. He looked extraordinarily out of place here surrounded by wild-looking young people taking a break between parties. A couple, one in a wedding dress and veil and the other in a ragged tuxedo, sat in the booth behind us.

"Aren't both of them men?" my father said, frowning as he surreptitiously glanced over his shoulder.

"Half of San Francisco's gay, Dad," Amanda said. "Calm down."

He was still an attractive man, my handsome father who I'd been so proud of as a little girl. He'd always got what he wanted, or at least he had since he cast himself off from us. He had a young wife—Genine wasn't too much older than Amanda—a sailboat for cruising around San Diego, and membership at an exclusive golf club. Recently promoted to vice-president, he probably wouldn't go much higher at the insurance company, but he'd done well enough to be very comfortable, especially in the years since he'd finished paying for our college. I could hardly bear to look at him.

"I want to know, Sara, what the hell's wrong with you?" he began his tirade. I hadn't heard him chew me out since high school. "You have a perfectly fine husband, and here you are running around like a tart. Has it just been since Mark went to law school, or have you been doing it all along?"

I closed my eyes. "Dad, Mark and I are splitting up."

"Splitting up? You haven't been married that long. What's wrong with you?" The look on his face seemed very near to genuine pain.

"Lay off her," Amanda said. "You're a great one to talk."

"Oh, so this is my fault."

"I'm sorry I didn't tell you," I said.

"Don't be sorry, Sara," Amanda said. "She's doing what's best for her."

"And you've been giving her advice, no doubt. You're a great one, picking up and running off to Africa on a whim. I thought I brought the two of you up to be responsible. Responsible and productive. If I've said it once, I've said it a thousand times."

I clenched my teeth but didn't say anything. This'll be over soon, I thought, and snuck a glance at my watch.

He turned back to me. "You, Sara, you break my heart. What a disappointment. This is the last thing I expected to find. I thought you were happy."

"Any heart breaking has been more than mutual, Dad," Amanda said. "You've done your share, you know. You said you came here to see me, not yell at Sara. So here I am. What do you want to say? You've got twenty minutes before you need to leave for the airport."

"I just wanted to see you one more time, that's all. I've gotten sentimental in my old age, much good it does me. I have a present for you." He reached into the bag he carried.

"Oh, Dad," Amanda said, exasperated. "You didn't have to." She unwrapped newspaper and tape to unveil a five-inch bronze statuette of a water buffalo with little birds perched on its back.

"They said it was African," he said.

"It is," Amanda said, examining it with a smile. "Burkina Faso."

"That's not where you're going," he said, disappointed.

"No, but it's very nice. I like it."

"Have you had all your shots? I've heard you should take your own supply of needles so you can be sure they're clean if you need any."

"Dad, Frank's a doctor. He's got all that figured out."

"A doctor? Really? Did you tell me that?"

"I can't remember," Amanda said. "I know you're impressed. Don't try to hide it." The diner's bright lighting made all three of us look jaundiced at such a late hour. Amanda had adeptly deflected his criticism from me. She was never afraid to face up to him. I could take on Paul and the Bobs and even the company president, but with my father I couldn't speak for fear of exploding and fatally wounding us all. Ten minutes later my father kissed Amanda's cheek and then mine, his aftershave still the same brand after all these years. After he hailed a late-night taxi cruising the Castro, Amanda and I returned to the apartment to find Frank and Aaron sitting outside on the front steps.

"Jake started playing Uriah Heap and we couldn't take it," Frank said. "Getting old, I guess."

"You sure are," Amanda said, putting her arm around him as she sat down on the steps beside him. "You're lucky I like old men."

"I'm sorry," I said to Aaron. "I didn't think you'd end up waiting out here."

Aaron smiled as he got to his feet. "It's been a musical education."

We walked to his apartment under a light mist, the brake lights of the few cars that passed us reflecting red off the glossy asphalt.

"How was it with your father? I don't see any bullet holes."

"Bad."

"Why don't you get along with him?"

"I just don't. I don't want to talk about it."

"Okay."

Aaron put his arm around me, and I leaned my head against him as we walked. Aaron didn't wear aftershave. Neither did Mark. I hated aftershave.

Aaron glanced at me as if he might say something but then didn't. We walked along. He looked over at me again. "Sara, I know this is an odd time to ask, but would you like to meet my mother? She's going to be out here in a few weeks."

"You told her about me?" I said, surprised. "Or is she psychic like your aunt?"

"I happened to mention I was seeing somebody. A week later one of the charities she's on the board of is suddenly planning a function out here. It's unlike her to be so transparent."

"She sounds formidable."

"A lot of people find her terrifying." Aaron shrugged, amused. "She's my mother. She adored Elizabeth, so meeting you's going to be hard for her, but eventually she'll come around. That is, if you want to deal with her. You don't have to. She can easily go back to Boston as curious as when she came."

We stood waiting for the light to change so we could cross Market Street. The picture he'd painted was daunting, but he was offering up a part of his life I very much wanted to see. "I'd like to meet her. Will she absolutely hate me? You've never said anything about your mother being terrifying before."

Aaron pushed a strand of hair away from my face. "She won't terrify you, Sara. I've never seen anyone intimidate you, except maybe your father. Besides, she can't help but like you. I certainly do, and that counts for a lot."

He'd said what I wanted to hear, or at least a rough equivalent of it. The light changed and we crossed the street.

Half an hour later, I lay next to him in bed, his hand like velvet as it caressed my skin. With his mouth against mine, I pulled my fingers through his thick black hair, enjoying the texture of it. Unexpectedly, he stopped kissing me and lifted his head.

"Sara, what happened between you and your father?"

I rolled my eyes and looked away. "Nothing. He just yelled at me. Called me a tart. What an archaic word."

"Not tonight. I mean when you were growing up, what happened?"

Alarmed, I shook my head. Gently taking one of my hands, Aaron kissed my palm and then my wrist. "You can tell me."

I pulled my hand away. "Don't."

"What are you hiding, Sara? What has you so frightened?"

I turned my head away. The tears falling down my face surprised me: I hadn't realized they were so close to the surface. I knew Aaron would draw his own conclusions, he probably already had, but I didn't care. "Don't make me tell you. Please, don't make me."

He sighed and drew me close. "Shh. It's all right. You don't have to tell me anything you don't want to." I said nothing, just let him hold me. He stroked my hair until I relaxed and fell asleep in his arms.

Early the next morning I drove Frank and Amanda to the airport, all three of us the worse for the late night before. Amanda let Frank sit in the front.

"You've got money?" Amanda asked him, her face peering forward between the seats.

"Yes."

"Tickets?"

"Yes."

"Passport?"

Frank turned slowly to look at her. "Amanda, I've traveled overseas at least a dozen times."

"That's fine for you, but I've never been to Africa. It's these vicious vaccines boiling in my blood. I feel so wretched I can hardly think."

I looked at her in the rear-view mirror. "Staying up half the night probably doesn't help. I don't envy you, Frank. It would drive me crazy to sit next to her for the next thirty hours."

"She'll do fine," Frank said placidly. He closed his eyes and appeared to try to sleep.

"How do you know you're doing the right thing?" I said to her, my eyes catching hers in the mirror.

Amanda flopped back in the seat. "How do you ever know? What got into Dad, do you think? Maybe his conscience is finally working again after all these years. His coming up here must've really pissed off Genine."

"What did you talk to Aaron about last night when you went to get ice?"

"I just finished up my fight with him in private so you wouldn't have to hear it."

"You don't need to protect me."

"You're my little sister. It's my job."

I stood at the gate with them as the last call was announced.

"See you," Amanda said, tears streaming down her face. "Serious Sara, you take care of yourself."

I nodded. "Write, okay?" Amanda hugged me and told me she loved me. I watched her pass through the door with Frank to the plane, my solar plexus tightening into a hard walnut of misery. I was so sick of airports. I could only equate them with leaving and loss.

When Karla dropped Jason and Eric off the first time after Amanda left, the two boys anxiously stood together in the hall, obviously not knowing what to expect. Am I that monstrous with kids, I asked myself? "I don't bite," I told them. Their little round eyes regarded me even more nervously. I took them to the library and invited Meg to bring Sabrina and come with us. Jason and Eric checked out three books each, both beaming with pride over their new library cards. We went for ice cream afterwards.

"Here, give me your books so you don't spill on them," I told Jason and Eric as we sat around a small white table in the shop.

Sabrina had checked out *Little Women* and was already engrossed in it, twirling her blond hair around one finger. Meg looked over at her and smiled. "That was one of my favorite books when I was her age."

"Mine, too. I was so sad when Jo didn't want to marry Laurie."

"And when Beth died," Meg said.

"I cried buckets," I said.

"But it ends up so domestic. The women get their husbands and have children and stay in their place."

"And live happily ever after. I never wanted Jo to leave New York."

"I need to find some good feminist literature for girls," Meg said. "But she'd probably refuse to read it."

Jason tugged on my sleeve. "Where's Amanda?"

"She's in Africa, Jason. Can you lick your cone there? It's dripping."

"Is she coming back?"

"Yes, but not for a while. She'll be back after Christmas which is a long time away." What would my life be like by next Christmas, I wondered?

"Will she bring me a present?"

I smiled. "I'm sure she will."

Jake called me three times the week after Amanda left, leaving messages twice and catching me on the phone once.

"Jake, I'm involved with someone. I'm not interested in going out with you."

"Yeah, I met him at Amanda's party. Interesting guy. I heard him read once at Brittle Books. But hey, you have one lover; you could have two. I don't mind sharing."

As if I need this, I thought. "Bye, Jake." And I hung up.

I got a postcard almost immediately from Amanda from London where they'd stopped over before continuing to Uganda. The front of the card was a reproduction of an old poster for George Bernard Shaw's play, *Pygmalion*.

"She said I'm to be sure and show it to you," I told Aaron when I brought it to his apartment Friday evening to fulfill Amanda's request. We had tickets to the symphony, and Aaron was making me dinner, one way, I suspected, of ensuring he didn't have to take money from me. "I don't know why, except for the little dart she drew on it down here in the corner. Her poison dart, I suppose."

Aaron looked at it briefly and set it on the counter with a smile.

"You're glad she's gone, aren't you?" I said.

"No, I like Amanda. She just has a blind spot where you're concerned. A very big one."

"I miss her."

He put his arms around me. "I know you do."

"I think the vegetables are burning."

The phone rang. Aaron stepped away and picked up an extension located on the counter separating the kitchen from the dining room. I went over to sauté the vegetables so he could talk, though periodically I looked his way, curious.

"Congratulations, Kate," he was saying, "that's wonderful." He glanced reflexively at his watch. "But I thought you weren't due for a couple more weeks."

I turned down the heat on the stove and searched his cupboards for some more olive oil. Aaron started to turn away from the kitchen, but then he stopped and leaned back against the counter instead, not facing me, but not facing away. On purpose. He didn't mind if I overheard, or at least he was trying not to.

"It sounds horrendous, but I'm glad she's all right. And how are you doing, are you okay?" He smiled as he listened. He looked younger and more carefree than any time I'd seen him in the past few months. "I'm sure she's beautiful, just like her mother. How much time are you going to take off work? . . . Of course you should, it can wait . . . No, Kate, out this way I hear only good things about UUB . . . That's right, Paula said she ran into you last month . . . Oh, he was nice enough for a banker." Aaron listened and then laughed. "Nothing's wrong with bankers . . . I don't know, I can never tell when Paula's serious anymore. How's Dave doing? . . . He is? Good for him . . . Kate, you must be tired . . . I'd love to see her, too. I'll call you."

He hung up. I turned the burner off under the pan.

"Thanks for covering for me."

"You're welcome. Who's Kate?"

Aaron smiled. "The investment banker."

"Oh," I said. "She had her baby."

"This morning. She's thrilled."

"She's friends with your sister?"

He nodded. "They see each other occasionally in New York."

I prodded the vegetables. "Are you going to send Kate flowers? It's still early. If you call right now, they'll get there first thing tomorrow."

Aaron looked at me curiously. "You should send her flowers," I said. "I'll start on the salad."

"Start on the salad in a minute." He kissed me, and I really did forget about salad and banks and babies for sixty seconds.

Tuesday morning at work, I received a phone call, a double ring from an outside line. This better not be Jake, I thought.

"Is this Sara Whitfield?" a woman's voice asked.

"Yes."

"My name's Monica Girard. I'm a friend of Aaron's. I wonder if you'd like to have lunch with me?" The Monica from Paris? It must be. All these women from Aaron's past were popping up. How much were they still in the present? Reining in my curiosity, I accepted her invitation, no questions asked. I wondered why Aaron hadn't told me she was here, unless he didn't know, but I wanted to hear what she had to say before I asked him about it. I didn't call him at work. Mark always said women had a way of closing ranks.

We met at an upscale Mexican restaurant not far from my work. Monica was an attractive, self-confident woman in her thirties with thick, long strawberry blond hair, a throaty voice, pale skin, and green eyes framed with mascara. She wore an above-the-knee forest green knit dress with long sleeves and a deep V neckline. She seemed sophisticated and sensual, and as she sat down and crossed her legs, I felt a quick surge of jealousy. Get a grip, Sara, I told myself. Find out about this woman.

"You may find me presumptuous," she said, flipping her hair behind her shoulders after we ordered, "but I've known Aaron ten years, so I'm going to take some liberties. I hope I'm not shocking you terribly."

"I'm curious, not shocked. I suppose that was what you were counting on." She smiled. "You live in Paris," I went on. "Your husband's name is Henri and you met Aaron in business school."

"I'm impressed. He wouldn't even tell me your name."

"How did you get my number, then?"

"There was a postcard in his apartment addressed to you. And at Christmas, Aaron mentioned he knew someone who worked for Appleton-Smith. So I took a chance and called. Here I am."

"You went to a lot of trouble."

"I did. I'm rather pleased with my detective work."

"I take it Aaron doesn't know you're talking to me."

Monica smiled. "He'd be furious."

"But you're friends."

"Very much so." Monica leaned her cheekbone against her fingertips, her red fingernails striking against her fair skin. She noticed my hand. "Are you married?"

"Separated," I said uncomfortably. Of course I'd forgotten to take my ring off.

"Well, that's unlike him." She stirred her iced tea with a long spoon. "He must've been quite captivated by you."

"How long are you in San Francisco? Is your husband here, too?"

"I got here yesterday; I go to LA tomorrow. Henri's back in Paris with our children."

"I didn't know you had kids. Where are you staying?"

"With Aaron. He's sleeping on the couch. Just to put your mind at rest."

I narrowed my eyes. I didn't want to hear about Aaron's couch. "You said you had a reason for asking me to lunch?"

Monica scrutinized me. "Yes, I think you're up to this. Elizabeth wasn't at all."

"You met her?"

She nodded. "She's a very gentle person, and I wasn't sure she'd have the stamina. You, though, strike me differently. I wanted to see you before things went too far. I think you might suit Aaron well, and since he's obviously enamored, you have a reasonable chance."

"I'm not following."

"Your friend who sent the postcard, Amanda—"

"My sister."

"Ah, your sister. She's very perceptive. Or was *Pygmalion* just a coincidence?"

I closed my eyes and rubbed my temple for a moment. "Okay, you're an old girlfriend of Aaron's, and you're here, what, to warn me about something?" I thought of the scrolls on Kiki's back.

"I was the first one," Monica said, amused. "Not his first affair, I'm sure he'd had many, but his first little project. I was desperately unhappy, he helped me figure out what I wanted, and away I went to Paris. I've been very happy with Henri, teaching and painting, ever since. Aaron knew what he was doing. After me there was Kate, and then one I never did find out the name of, and then Suzanne and Elizabeth. All women he met, turned their lives around and then stepped out of the way when they flew."

"And now me." I felt nauseated. It all fit.

"And now you. Don't get me wrong. He was very good for these women's lives, but he's thirty-five now. He can't go on playing Henry Higgins forever. It's time he hung up his hat. I'd like to see him married but look at what happened with Elizabeth."

"Why are you telling me this?"

"I'm giving you a leg up. It's taken me ten years to figure this out. It'll be wonderful for a while, he'll open doors in your mind for you, and then he'll put it in your head you need to move on. He deserves more, he's just too perverse and obstinate to let it happen. He'd rather start over from scratch every two years. Poor Elizabeth, she got cut loose without ever understanding what had happened."

"Two years," I said. "So that's how long it lasts." I blinked my eyes a few times to keep them from filling with tears.

Monica frowned with concern. "Did you leave your husband for him? He'd better not have done that."

"Maybe this isn't about me. Maybe you can't let go of him."

She shrugged a shoulder. "I can see why you might not trust me. I don't know you at all, but I care about him. He needs someone to be persistent, to get past the ramparts. My intent is to help, but it's completely up to you, of course." She sighed. "The thing is, he's getting worse as he gets older. It's annoying how he tries to have everything under control these days. God knows what it's doing to his poetry." She smiled at me, her eyes showing faint traces of future lines, the neckline of her dress revealing far more of her breasts than I would've dared. The watch and rings she wore were expensive, especially the marquise diamond glittering on her left hand. I didn't know what to make of her. We appeared to have opposing interests, yet she seemed like a woman who didn't bother competing with other women anymore. "You can tell him you've had lunch with me if you want, just let me get out of town first. It'll probably be a year before he speaks to me again." Monica laughed, and I wondered about her life in Paris. She did seem happy.

We walked to the parking lot together.

"You have Aaron's car," I said, surprised.

"I told him I wanted to go to Half Moon Bay, which is where I'm headed next. I enjoyed meeting you, Sara. Maybe you can convince Aaron to bring you to Paris and visit us."

Monica waved cheerfully as she drove away. I spent the rest of the afternoon turning the conversation around and around in my head, her strawberry-blonde hair and dark green dress always present like a troubling Trojan horse outside the gates.

Chapter Eleven

Meg had invited me to dinner that evening, so I set out in the buoyant spring evening light to walk the half mile to her apartment.

"You should be careful about walking alone at night."

I jumped. "Jake, you startled me. What are you doing here?" Today he wore an Iron Butterfly T-shirt, a cheap nylon windbreaker, jeans with holes in them and black high top basketball shoes, untied. He was medium height, medium build, a plain and basic body type, a plain and basic face, even if his smile showed a slightly chipped front tooth. With different haircuts he could've been someone who worked on a farm, taught high school, or traded stocks on Wall Street. Now that he wore clear lenses in his round glasses and I saw him in the daylight, I could see his eyes had the-world-is-my-oyster-even-if-I-haven't-figured-out-how-to-shuck-it-yet look Amanda had complained about. "It's his optimism," she'd said at the time. "I can't bear to be the one to crush it." Jake was a little younger than Amanda, a little older than me, and seemed as innocent as Jason and Eric.

Hands in his pockets, Jake shrugged his shoulders. "Going where you're going."

I started to walk. "I'm going to dinner at a friend's."

"Your boyfriend?"

"No. But you can't come with me."

"I'll just walk with you. Be your bodyguard."

I need a bodyguard from you, I thought. "Jake, did you know there are laws against stalking?"

"I'm stalking you?" He grinned. "Well, I guess I am in a way, though it's a very unfeminist thing to do. I should be ashamed of myself."

I picked up the pace. "As if you care about feminism."

"I'm a feminist. I'm a card-carrying NOW member. Look, I'll show you." With difficulty, as I didn't slow down, Jake sorted through his wallet to find his documentation and handed the little piece of paper to me.

Curious, I stopped to look at it and then handed it back to him. "You use this to pick up women?" I asked skeptically, walking again.

"Works every time. No, I'm committed, I really am. Oppression of women is immoral and has got to end. You don't believe me? I've marched for pro-choice, ERA, comparable worth, and Take Back the Night. I subscribe to Ms. magazine, even after they raised the price to go non-commercial." I kept walking. "I've read *Backlash*, and I can quote Gloria Steinem at will."

I shook my head.

"I'm hurt, Sara, hurt that you doubt my sincerity."

"You're completely crazy. How did Amanda put up with you for six months?"

We'd reached Meg's address. "Six and a half. My innate charm and sexual prowess."

I knocked. "Jake, go away."

Meg opened the door. "Well, hi Meg," Jake said, standing behind me. "This is a nice surprise."

Meg looked at me as I rubbed my fingers across my forehead. Then she looked at Jake.

"Do I know you?" she said.

"Yeah. I helped you fix up that woman's apartment."

Meg smiled. "That's right. I remember."

"Something smells good. What are you making for dinner?"

"Jake, go home," I said.

"I haven't got paid in a while. There's nothing to eat at home."

"You're pathetic."

"Come on in," Meg said. "We've got plenty."

I rolled my eyes wondering when this was going to end.

We entered the dingy first-floor flat. The woman and two kids Meg and Sabrina shared the place with were watching TV in the living room. Although the plaster walls were cracked and scuffed, and five people sharing a two-bedroom apartment seemed crowded, the rooms were well organized, children's art hung on the walls, and old furniture had been slipcovered with bright cotton fabric.

"Cool, *Star Trek*," Jake said. "I've seen this episode six times."

Apparently entranced, he sat down to watch TV with the others. With a sigh of relief, I followed Meg into the kitchen. Sabrina helped her mother make spaghetti while I sat on a bar stool sipping wine and talking about Monica, glad I had someone to confide in with Amanda gone.

"What do you think?" I said after I described my problematic lunch.

"Ditch him," Sabrina said, draining the noodles with huge potholders on her small hands. "Guys that play games with your mind aren't worth it. It's emotional fascism."

"How would you know?" Meg said. "And where'd you hear about fascism?"

Sabrina struck a ballet pose, one arm circled over her head. "I read. I'm going on eleven." She hopped onto a stool next to me and picked up her library book.

"Going on twenty is more like it," Meg muttered, stirring the sauce. She shook her head, her parrot earrings shaking with her. "This Monica sounds like a piece of work. Maybe her story's true, maybe it's not. Maybe only parts are true. Just be careful not to let others control you—Aaron, Monica, or anybody. The narrative someone feeds you can be just as much a form of control as physical abuse."

"Yep, let's get out the control theory," Sabrina said, not looking up from *Little Women*.

"What do you mean?" I asked Meg.

"When I was married to Ted, he did amazing things to make me believe I couldn't live without him. I was insecure when I married him, but with all the mind games he played, my self-worth went to zero. He kept all our money because he said I was incompetent. If I saw friends or family, he got jealous, so to make him happy I got to the point I was totally isolated. When he went into his destructive rages—yelling, punching holes in the wall—it was always my fault. For the longest time, I thought if I were just a better wife, a better mother, if I were prettier, if I were smarter, he'd love me more, he wouldn't get so angry. He didn't hit me every time, just often enough I never knew when he would. He broke two sets of dishes while we were married until I finally bought plastic. But I had options besides buying plastic. Once I got up the courage to admit what was going on, there were women who helped me leave that prison behind."

"Meg, I'm so sorry," I said. "It sounds like a living hell. You must've really transformed. I can't imagine that happening to you now."

"It can't happen to me now," Meg agreed. "I had to rebuild myself almost from scratch, but I cleared out all the poison he fed me and purged every bit of resentment, shame, and guilt that were keeping me in chains."

I blinked. "How'd you get rid of it?"

"By facing my toxic thoughts and beliefs. Resentment is the easiest once you realize it punishes you way more than the other person."

I thought about my father. "Are you saying you have to forgive whatever anyone does to you, no matter what?"

"You don't have to forgive, just let it go. Think of each resentment as a huge boulder you're hauling around, weighing you down. Then visualize tossing it down a hill so you're not carrying it anymore. Even if you have to visualize it a hundred times before it doesn't come back, it's worth it. It doesn't mean you let people push you around or hurt you, but resentment doesn't protect you from that anyway. Having boundaries does."

"How about guilt?" My guilt around my impending divorce seemed pretty unshakeable.

"Guilt's harder, especially if it's for an actual mistake that hurt someone. First thing to remember about mistakes is that everyone makes them, without exception. It's part of how we grow and learn.

With the littler mistakes, you acknowledge what you learned and promise yourself you won't repeat them. A really big mistake you might have to atone for, but in the end you've got to forgive yourself, or the guilt will squawk and circle and peck at you to death."

"Do rocks peck?"

"I see guilt as birds that torment you until you let go of self-blame. Then they fly off until they're just little specks on the horizon."

"You're a secret poet," I said, doubtful my guilt wanted to fly off anywhere. "And shame?"

"Shame's the hardest because it's so unconscious. It's the stuff that makes us squirm, that we don't want to acknowledge or even think about. It's also society's most powerful form of control. If you can see that any shame you carry originally came from the outside, that whatever you've done doesn't make you inherently bad or unworthy, that it was just a bunch of mud someone smeared on you to curb your behavior, then you can imagine a warm shower washing brown ooze off you until you're clear and clean."

I frowned. What she was talking about seemed like a strenuous amount of inner work. And yet how much was resentment, guilt, and shame shaping my life? And how did this fit into my current dilemma? The more I thought about Monica, the more I distrusted her, but even so my intuition said there was something hidden in Aaron's past that needed to be unearthed and rooted out. "Even if Monica's story is true, I don't think Aaron's abusive. He might not let me into his inner world, but he never shames or guilt-trips me, he never attacks my self-worth. Although I can see that the secrecy is a form of control in a way."

Meg checked the vegetables, a white-gray cloud of steam escaping. "All relationships have their issues of power, but I agree, yours doesn't sound abusive. What you're struggling with is if it's meeting your needs. Whether Monica's telling the truth or not, it sounds like Aaron owes you an explanation."

I finished my glass of wine. It was inexpensive and bitter and made my tongue stick to the roof of my mouth. "Aaron being short-term in his relationships must be what Amanda heard about, and why she threatened him. She doesn't want me to get hurt. It's funny, I tried to kill myself once when a boyfriend left me."

Meg looked up from the stove. "I don't think it's funny at all."

I put my elbow on the counter and leaned my head on my hand. "My parents were getting a divorce. His name was Danny Emerson, and he dumped me so he could date a cheerleader. I took a bunch of my mother's sleeping pills and Amanda found me. That's why she's still so paranoid about me now. But I'm not seventeen anymore."

"I wouldn't have guessed that about you, Sara."

I thought of Joe's mother and even, for an instant, of myself leaning with my back against the locked door. "What you said about shame, I've been so ashamed of it, I've never told anyone before. We all have things we hide, I guess."

Sabrina looked up from her book at her mother. Meg smiled at her, and Sabrina looked back down. I never had that kind of relationship with my mother, I thought as I watched them. But I did have Amanda.

Meg left the stove and came over to envelop me in a big hug. "Congratulations then, Sara. You've just taken a big step." I accepted the hug and then wiped my eyes that were unaccountably tearing up.

"How do you know Jake?" I said, wanting to change the subject.

Meg handed me a tissue. "Some people trashed an apartment a few houses down. I convinced the landlord that if we cleaned it up, he'd let one of the women in the shelter rent it without having to put down a deposit. We were working on the place when Jake passed by and offered to pitch in. He stayed half that day and came back and worked all the next. He's got a good heart."

"My ears are burning," Jake said, walking into the room. "Dinner ready yet?"

After dinner Jake walked me home because I couldn't convince him not to.

"You're a nice guy," I said at the bottom of my steps, "but I'm not interested. I don't know how else to make you understand."

"Yeah, I know you're in love with that guy."

"Then why are you bugging me?"

He shrugged. "With Amanda gone, you need me."

"Let me decide who and what I need." I turned my key in the door and went inside. I'm not sure how long he stayed on the steps.

Some women gave bonus points for tenacity. Jake needed to find himself one of them.

Aaron was on the phone when I came over Friday evening. We'd planned on dinner, maybe a movie. He let me in the door, kissed me, and went back to his conversation. Glancing around his apartment I saw no sign of Monica or the postcard. Lamb chops were already in the oven, and rice was cooking on the stove, so I started on the salad.

"Sorry, Jeremy, now tell me again? . . . Alison? You're not serious, are you? . . . I know that, but . . . Yes, I'm sure she is, but you've only . . ." Aaron closed his eyes as if hearing something painful. "Sounds like you've made up your mind. Well congratulations . . . Jeremy, how about dinner next week? . . . Then how about lunch? . . . That works for me. See you then." He hung up the phone shaking his head.

"Who was that?" I said casually, though I was quite curious.

"A friend of mine who's gone completely insane."

"Why? What's he done?"

Aaron poured me a glass of wine. "He's getting married to someone he's only been seeing three months."

I chopped green onions noncommittally. "Pretty stupid."

"Alison, of all people. Maybe I can talk some sense into him next week. No, this is the kind of mistake you can't talk someone out of. It's hopeless. God."

If it hadn't been for my lunch with Monica, I might've found his vexation entertaining. Everything was finished except the lamb chops, so we went into the living room to wait. I patted the couch a second as I sank into it. I couldn't imagine sleeping on it had been very comfortable, if, indeed, he had.

"Aaron, you don't trust me very much, do you?"

He still looked distracted by his conversation with his friend. "Why do you say that?"

I crossed my legs, my top foot kicking restlessly back and forth. "If you trusted me, you'd be more open." He frowned but didn't answer. "So you admit it?" I said impatiently.

"Are you trying to pick a fight? Play fair, Sara, and tell me what you're upset about. If you make me guess, it may take all night."

"How come you didn't tell me Monica was visiting you?" I tried to keep my voice calm and low, away from the shrillness of my mother's accusations.

Aaron squinted, all humor and some color leaving his face. "Monica. That's what this is about." He stood and walked to the window. "I should've guessed. No one else has such a talent for blighting my life. What happened, did you call here, and she answer the phone?"

"She called me. We had lunch."

"Lunch?" He turned, incredulous. "When did you have lunch?"

"Tuesday."

"Tuesday—" He frowned, remembering. "Which is why she wanted the car. How did she . . . the postcard. Sara, she had no business talking to you."

"She thought she did."

"She thinks a lot of things. But this. She's outdone herself this time. What did she say? She's not the most reliable source of information."

"Reliable or not, you didn't tell me she was here, staying with you. That you can't dispute. You lied to me, a lie of omission. She must be important to you that you're willing to lie about her."

"Monica and I were over a long time ago." Aaron's face looked strained, and the slump of his shoulders made him appear burdened, hounded even. "You don't need to be jealous; I just didn't want her to meet you. What did she say? You're upset with more than just her being here."

"Why didn't you want me to meet her? She's an old friend, you saw her at Christmas. I'm not allowed to meet your friends? Aaron, there's no symmetry between us. I'm not on an equal footing. You make all the decisions, and you don't even tell me you're making them."

"Sara, that's hardly true."

"For instance, what did you and Amanda talk about when you went out for the ice?"

It took him a moment to answer. Hands in his pockets, his mouth grew grim. "She told me about the sleeping pills when you were in high school."

No. Amanda, how could you? "She shouldn't have."

"She was worried about you. She thought I should know."

"I'm not a child. It wasn't hers to tell."

His eyes were pained. "You could've trusted me with that, Sara. I wish I'd known even sooner."

"You said you came to an understanding with Amanda," I said sharply. "What was it?"

"You want the truth." He glanced out the window and back again. "The truth is I promised her I wouldn't abandon you while she was gone in Uganda. She was satisfied."

"You made a deal."

"Of a sort. She was insistent, and I knew I could promise it. God, this is an awful conversation. Are you angry that I committed to being with you?"

"Tell me, Aaron, did my two years with you begin last fall, or when we first started sleeping together?"

"Is that what Monica told you?" He was speechless for a moment; then he crossed over to the couch and pulled me into his arms. "You're going to have to decide whether to believe her or me. I know she's persuasive, but Sara—" He kissed me, and I didn't fight. "I want to be with you, only you, more than I know how to say. Don't make both of us miserable. Don't let her come between us. Please."

I leaned my head back and turned it to the side as he kissed my neck, my ears, my mouth. He whispered that no one else mattered, he wanted me more than he'd ever wanted anything. I let him pull me into the bedroom, my senses overwhelmed as the tension between us turned into an attraction I'd found irresistible from the very first time we'd met. A few minutes later our clothes were on the floor, my arms were wrapped around his neck, my tongue drawn into his mouth. Yes, I wanted him—how much had he counted on it?—but that wasn't the point.

Half an hour later I sat across the table from him wearing his robe, picking at over-done lamb chops and cold rice.

"Monica said you probably wouldn't speak to her for a year."

"I'd say never again. I suppose I'll save on phone bills."

"She said the way you're living is bad for your poetry." I knew I was pushing it. "She didn't mention celibacy."

"What's the point of this? Hasn't she done enough damage?"

"You wanted to know what she said. She wants me not to abandon you."

"How very generous of her."

"She said you're getting too old to play Henry Higgins, that it's time you hung up your hat."

Aaron looked appalled for a moment. Then he just shook his head and started eating again. "Henry Higgins. That's a new one. Jesus."

"I'm supposed to have patience and break through with you. But she's wrong; I'm not up to it. I'm not going to spend every day wondering when you're going to persuade me to leave."

He put down his fork. "Sara, I don't want you to leave. How can I convince you?"

Both of us worn out, we went to bed early. "I can't do this anymore," I whispered as we lay sleepily on our sides, my back against his stomach, his arm over my waist.

"You can't do what anymore?"

"Let you control me."

"Shhh," he said, stroking my hair.

"You don't believe me, do you?"

Aaron kissed my shoulder. "I don't control you, Sara. You'll feel better in the morning. We both will." He sighed. "Goddamn woman. Ten years and she can still do this," he said, or at least I thought he said.

You've turned out to be a very pretty girl.

I looked at Johnny Rotten's sneering mouth framed by deep purple in the moonlight.

"Sara," my father whispered, inches away. The hairs rose on the back of my neck.

Concentrate, I told myself. I could still smell his aftershave on my skin.

"I'm not going to hurt you. Open the door."

I woke up early the next morning and made Amanda's bed, wanting to creep into my own before my mother noticed. I waited until I heard my father leave for golf; then I pulled the lock back and stepped into the hallway. I heard my mother sniffing, and I could smell coffee from the kitchen. I decided to go see if she was all right but froze when I reached the entryway. My father was still there, getting some golf balls from the inventory he kept in the hall closet. He looked up, as startled as I was. My heart pounded as I nervously tugged my robe closed. *My father*, a voice in my head said with curious surprise. *I'm terrified of my own father.*

His tan throat showed through the open collar of his white golf shirt. He slipped a package of golf balls in his jacket pocket as he looked me over. "Lock your door all you want," he said. "Pretty girls aren't hard to come by." And he opened the door and left.

You haven't been drinking, I thought. *There's no excuse.* But somehow I'd tempted him. Maybe I was to blame.

Numb, I continued down the hallway and found my mother, head in her hands, at the kitchen table. Her hair wasn't graying as nicely as my father's. Amanda had been encouraging her to color it.

"What's wrong, Mom?" I said, not wanting to know.

"Things between your father and me—" She gave a weak sigh. "They're not good." She started to cry with long shuddering sobs. I put my arms around her, but I had no words of consolation.

I figured out ingenious ways to protect myself, pushing my dresser in front of my door while I slept, spending the night at friends' houses, unobtrusively locking myself in Amanda's room. Gradually I saw that my efforts were unnecessary. The rare times when we were both at home my father ignored me as if I'd ceased to exist.

When Danny called two days before Christmas—a week after we'd found out about Genine and six days after Dad had moved out—he was apologetic and confused but determined. "At least I'm telling you," he said. "Other guys would've just done it behind your back."

"Is it because I won't sleep with you?" It almost killed me to ask.

"Sara, I really like you. I gotta go."

I hung up and wandered into my parents' bathroom while the hall clock chimed six. My mother was out with some friends who were trying to cheer her up. Amanda had gone Christmas shopping. I stared and stared at the contents of the open white medicine cabinet. If I weren't here, I thought, there'd be no reason for Genine. My father could come back, everyone would be happy. Even Danny wouldn't have to feel bad about his cheerleader. If I weren't here. I felt a nonentity as it was. As I stared, the solution grew obvious.

I don't remember much past the medicine cabinet. Amanda said when she came home, her arms full of shopping bags, and found me limp on the floor, it was the most hideous moment of her life. She raced me to the hospital and got me in and out of the emergency room without my parents ever finding out, I have no idea how. We both agreed it'd be better for Mom not to know, and neither of us at that point were speaking to Dad. I concentrated the rest of Christmas break on filling out applications for college. Amanda didn't let me out of her sight and called me once a day when she went back to school.

I got up early the next morning and was dressing when Aaron woke.

"What are you doing?" he said, sitting up.

"Leaving."

"Why?"

"Did you hear anything I said last night?"

Aaron pulled on his robe. "Sara, what the hell is going on with you?"

I paused as I buttoned my blouse. "Some things aren't negotiable. Maybe I've figured out what they are."

"So you're going to leave. Just like that."

"You know where I live—if you're interested in talking to me, that is, not just entertainment in bed." Aaron's mouth pressed into a grim line. I wondered how much further I could push him. Behind the self-control, he was in there somewhere. "What, no comment, no persuasive argument? You're at least as persuasive as Monica is. Do they teach it at business school, Manipulation 101?" I was possessed by demons. I wanted him to bleed so I could see what color his blood was.

"Sara, I'm so angry, I can hardly speak."

"There's something between you and Monica that you're not telling me. I don't know what it is, but I'm not a fragile doll, Aaron; I can handle the truth. I won't break. But maybe dolls are all you like to play with. Most of them don't talk back."

A muscle played in his jaw. His glare was intense. "You're right. Right now, you should go."

I let myself out the door, feeling sick. I would stand my ground, but I had a feeling the price I'd pay would be high.

I arrived at the shelter to give my weekly financial advising just as a woman with three children got out of a taxi. We all stood together on the doorstep with their luggage, waiting for the door to open. One of the children wiped her runny nose on her coat sleeve. Her mother didn't notice. After the session, I ate lunch at the burrito place with Meg feeling dazed and lackluster as I was nudged along by the others in line. Meg was in an energetic, good mood.

"I've got a job possibility for you," she said. "The food bank's looking for an Incoming Operations Coordinator. The position reports to the director there, a friend of mine."

"Should I send my resume?"

"Call her up for an interview. I told her about you, and she's interested."

"Thanks, I appreciate it. But wait, why don't you apply for it?"

"It doesn't have the family benefits the job I'm at has. And she's looking for someone with a business background. I don't fit the bill."

"But you know so much about this city, and how human services work."

"Don't worry about me. You go for it."

I didn't tell her about Aaron. Though resolved, I was unsure what was going to happen. I walked to the food bank after lunch, wanting to see and get a feel for it. It was housed in an ancient warehouse south of Market. As I approached, I could see a line of people stretching around the block, most waiting patiently, some morose and unenthusiastic. Could I deal with that much wanting and not having?

I walked home concentrating on the rhythm of my feet and the hardness of the concrete underneath them. Clear out all hope, all desire, I told myself. Focus on the here and now, the light, the wind, the flowers in pots perched on steps. I felt an ache and knew I wanted something, but I told myself it was better not to want. After all, I had a job, enough to eat, and a safe place to live. I didn't need Aaron, and I didn't need Mark. My father didn't matter; in fact, all men didn't matter. I could even manage without Amanda. I hated the thought of Aaron treating me differently because of the sleeping pills. If I took them, it was because at seventeen I thought life would never get better. Now I knew that the low points, hard as they were, didn't last forever.

Look around, I told myself. The light, the color, the hills. They still took my breath away. As I gazed at the heart-breaking robin's egg-blue sky, I told myself at this moment San Francisco surrounds me and that's enough. I believed it while I walked, but eventually I climbed the last hill home.

When I saw the unblinking light on my answering machine, I ignored my disappointment and continued into the kitchen. Mocking me from the refrigerator door were childish violet and magenta peacocks drawn by Jason and Eric the Wednesday before when I'd been desperate for ideas. I hadn't been able to give them much guidance— they knew more about pastels than I did—but they'd captured the general idea. The boys had proudly showed the peacocks to Karla when she came to get them. They'd be disappointed if I took them down. Besides, what reasons did I have besides sorrow, disillusionment, anger, and longing?

Around six I left to rent a video, returning with *Casablanca* and Chinese food. Look at Bogart, I told myself as I watched the movie and ate with chopsticks out of a small white container. Men are trained to be uncommunicative. Oh, but you could tell Ingrid broke his heart. I couldn't tell anything with Aaron.

At nine, Aaron rang the downstairs buzzer. I let him into the living room where the masks on the wall formed a tribunal that would surely decide in my favor. We stood awkwardly apart, Aaron calm, if stiff. He must be feeling something, I thought, but what? I still had a terrible desire to see him over the edge, even if it meant he took me with him.

"I'm sorry it's so late," he said. "I've spent most of the day thinking, and you're right, I wasn't listening very well last night. I owe you an apology."

I lifted a corner of my mouth. "I was pretty hideous to you."

"I suppose that's what it took to get my attention."

"I'm sorry." I knew, however, that if being angry and mean were my last defense, I might resort to it again.

"We're even, I guess. I want to know, Sara, what are your terms, what's nonnegotiable?"

I took a breath, my heart racing. This was it, one way or another. "I don't want to be one of a string of women who come and go out of your life because you never let any of them close. It's not enough." I turned and walked to the window, staring out at the lights of the city without seeing them. *Sara, you're in love with him, why are you doing this? Monica or no Monica, all you want is to feel his mouth on your skin.*

"One of a string—" Aaron let out his breath in exasperation. "Sara, I'm thirty-five. Yes, I've had other relationships, but women don't just come and go in my life. Whatever Monica told you—"

"This isn't about Monica," I said, "this is about you and me." I glanced out the window again but saw only the two of us caught in the mirror of the black night.

"Maybe you're wrong about that," he said softly.

I turned. "All right, tell me about her. What was she like, and why did it end? And was the damage permanent—because you're still in love with her, aren't you?"

"This is crazy. Monica's not important to me; you are. I'm not going to talk about her."

"Why not?" It was almost a cry.

He stared at me, his eyes pained. *He is still in love with her,* I thought. *That's what's tormenting him. This is hopeless.* "You've never gotten over her," I said flatly.

He took a breath as if trying to recover his patience. "That is completely untrue. I don't want to be with her; I want to be with you. There's no one else I care about, but you refuse to believe me. Why are you torturing both of us like this? You want to get closer to me—I'm trying, I truly am, but you ask for parts of me I can't offer up."

"It's not that you can't, it's that you won't. You don't share your life with me, Aaron; you allow me into pieces of it when it suits you. It's a form of control, and it's not good for me. It ends up hurting."

Aaron put his hands in his pockets and appeared to survey the masks. They grinned and howled at the altar, waiting for a sacrifice. "You seem intent on hurting yourself. Maybe it's a pattern with you."

I froze. Of course he knew where to cut to make me bleed the most, but I wasn't defenseless. "Were all of us necessary for your ego? Little puppets to manipulate, pat on the head, and send off when you wanted something new?"

"Are you going back to Mark? Is that what this is about, you want an excuse?"

"This has nothing to do Mark. It has to do with you being manipulative."

"Who manipulates whom, Sara? Mark never did figure out who was in control of your relationship, did he?"

"Don't you talk to me about him," I snapped. "Are you listening to a thing I'm saying?"

"Yes, I'm listening," Aaron said, his teeth nearly clenched. "I don't agree." He closed his eyes and took a breath. "Arguing with you is driving me crazy. I don't want this."

I pointed. "There's the door. Go find another project to amuse you. Maybe the next one will be more appropriately grateful."

Aaron put his hand up to the side of my face, his thumb lightly gliding over my lips. "God, you push me. You want to hurt me, is this the power you want? Okay, you've have it. I hurt. I'm telling myself you can't help it, it's because of all you're going through, and I know I have only myself to blame, but I was never going to let anyone do this to me again. Ah Sara, hurt me as much as you have to, but don't push me away."

Looking up at his eyes, I hesitated. I could smell the cotton of his shirt, felt his fingers on my face, my lips. It was so hard when he was touching me. A slight motion on my part and I could be embraced by his arms, let him restructure my life according to his vision—the scrolls unseen behind my back. All I'd have to do was submit. It was almost irresistible.

"You can't keep all your doors locked to me," I said sadly. "Not the ones that lead to your heart."

"There are doors, and there are doors," he answered enigmatically, his eyes tight and dark with distress. "Do you want me to beg? If that's what it takes, I will."

If he tells me he loves me, I thought, it's all over; I'll be trapped, in love forever with a stone wall. "Tell me about your past. Tell me about Monica."

"You're not my project, Sara. She fed you a fairy tale."

"So contradict her, tell me your side of it. Share your life with me, Aaron; treat me as if I really do mean something to you."

"Do you want me to marry you, is that what you want?"

I drew a breath and spoke slowly. "All I want is for you to talk."

He shook his head. "It would only make it worse." The sapphire of his eyes had become almost entirely black. "Sara, have I really made you so unhappy? You're the best part of my life. I need you."

I swallowed. I wished I were strong enough, wise enough, to do this another way. "I'm sorry that endings are painful, Aaron. I've been through enough myself to know."

He winced as if I'd struck him. He looked at my mouth and then my eyes, nodding his head almost imperceptibly. "You win." He picked his coat off the back of a chair and shut the apartment door quietly behind him.

I sat down on the couch, clutched my arms to my stomach and doubled over until my forehead touched my knees. Twenty minutes later, when I could bear to open my eyes, I made myself a cup of tea and watched *Casablanca* again, fast forwarding to where Ingrid first walks into Bogart's bar, falling in love with Bogart when he talks of all the gin joints in all the world, refusing to cry like I usually did when she walks away from him in the fog. I'd seen this movie so many times, but I finally realized I didn't want to be Ingrid being told what was right to do at the last minute. That wasn't why I watched the movie. I wanted to be the one struggling with my conscience, making decisions, outwitting Nazis. The one in control. I wanted to be Bogart.

My first thought the next morning was whether Amanda had come home that night. Of course not, I thought, turning over in bed with a sigh. It still seemed strange not to have her around painting her toenails and lugging art supplies up the stairs. Alone in my bed, the apartment felt like a vast, empty cavern. I got up and took the peacocks down off the refrigerator. It's time, Sara. I drove to a paint store and bought a gallon of flat latex.

"What color did you want?" the clerk said. "Or did you just want white?"

"Aqua," I said. The color of underwater kingdoms.

I pushed all the furniture in my room into an island in the center and covered them with old sheets. Then I washed the walls and started painting. I'd got one coat on and was working on the second late in the afternoon when the phone rang.

Maybe it's Aaron, I thought. No, it's probably Jake. I picked up the receiver, expecting to be disappointed.

"Sara? It's Karla. I need a favor." Her voice sounded strange, muffled.

"Sure. What's up?"

She was calling from the hospital. Her husband had shown up at her apartment that afternoon angry because a friend had told him she had another man.

"He had a gun," Karla said. "He didn't shoot anything; just hit me with it. I got some bruises and my shoulder's all out of place—got this sling thing on. He didn't go away looking too good either, let me tell ya. But Jason and Eric, they saw everything. My little boys. He said I was seeing someone. What a goddamn joke. I ain't seeing no man. I'm done with men for good."

She told me that after he left, she'd called the shelter, and Meg had come. After dropping the kids off at the shelter, Meg had taken her to the hospital. Their next stop was the police station to file a report and start the process of getting a no-contact order.

"Could the kids stay the night with you? I hate asking, but they like it there, and I want them safe. That shelter's busting at the seams with people; I'd rather have them with you. After the police, I'm going to clean up the apartment and do me some thinking. I'll pick up the boys tomorrow before you take off for work."

I was stunned; I'd do anything she wanted. "I'll go get them. You can stay here, too, if you want."

"No, if he comes back tonight, I'm going to kill him. I'm gonna be there ready."

I knew without a doubt this was a super bad idea, but I also knew Karla was with Meg. Meg was wise. Meg would calm Karla down and make sure she was safe.

I picked up the boys and buckled them into the back seat of my car, trying to be calm even if I couldn't manage cheerful. We went to the grocery store and stopped to get a video; then I made them macaroni and cheese and carrot sticks, things I liked when I was a kid. They ate on the other side of the table from me, watching me with their little round eyes. What those little eyes have seen, I thought, resting my face against my hand, not eating the salad in front of me.

"Do you want to color or watch *Pinocchio*?" I asked after dinner.

"*Pinocchio*," Eric said quietly.

I sat on the couch with one of them on each side of me, my arms around them loosely protecting. I wondered if the tale of a puppet turning into a boy could possibly comfort them.

Jason looked up at me. "Sara?"

"What honey?"

"Our daddy hurt our mommy."

"Yeah, I know." I squeezed him against me. "She's safe now. It's going to be all right."

Jason snuggled closer until he was sitting on my lap. How do I know she's safe, I thought? Was it really going to be all right? Hugging them close, I kissed both boys on the tops of their heads. When the movie was over, I tucked them into Amanda's queen bed and left the door cracked so they could see the hallway light. They fell asleep holding each other's hand. I finished painting my room and then made a bed for myself on the living room couch so I didn't spend the night breathing paint fumes.

Karla's face the next morning was puffy and purple in places. She seemed very low. Meg had convinced her to spend the night at the shelter.

"How are you doing?" I asked.

She waved a hand. "Oh, I look worse than I feel. Don't know how I'm going to explain this at work though." She sighed. "You know what they say—when it rains. The neighbors called the landlord about the noise, and when I got home from the police, he told me I had two days to get out. Said he had the right. Meg says he does, legal-wise."

"Karla, I'm sorry."

"Well, I have to move anyway so George can't find us. Like a no-contact order'll mean anything to that man. I'm getting a divorce, and I'm getting custody. Meg's going to help me."

"You never divorced him?"

"It wasn't worth the trouble, but he ain't doing this again. I got rights, too. I wanted the boys to know their daddy, but this isn't any good for them."

"Why don't you move in with me? You can stay until Amanda gets back in December. It'll save you money."

Karla frowned. "You crazy or what?"

"I'm serious. Stay here until you find somewhere else to live at least."

After work I helped her bring her stuff over, minimal as it was. Karla couldn't do much besides supervise Jason and Eric so I did all the lifting. In front of my apartment, I leaned over the trunk of my car and pulled out a box.

"I'll get that."

"Jake," I said, sighing. By the time I stood up to scold him, he'd already taken the box and was heading up the stairs. I shook my head.

"Who's that?" Karla said after she'd passed him on her way down.

"A friend. Kind of."

Jake helped us carry everything into Amanda's room. Karla would have to share Amanda's bed with the boys. "It's a little crowded," I said, gazing around the magenta room at the boxes and suitcases on the floor.

"It's no problem," Karla said. "About as much space as we had."

"Sara, can we put this up?" Eric said. He held the collage of magazine pictures that he and Jason and Amanda had made together months ago. I took down one of Amanda's surrealist pictures and put up theirs, thinking I'd have to write Amanda and tell her who was living in her room. I was sure she wouldn't mind at all.

Jake was making himself at home watching a *Star Trek* rerun in the living room. "You know, Sara, after all that work, pizza sounds really good. You going to order one?"

"Are we going to live here, Mom?" Eric asked.

"For a while, pumpkin, for a while. And you boys are going to have to be good and mind and not touch anything, you hear?"

I ordered a pizza to be delivered, and the five of us ate sitting around the kitchen table—almost like family, I thought.

"You can go home anytime, Jake," I said as Karla put Jason and Eric to bed. I picked up the watering can. Since I'd forgotten to water on Sunday, should I give the plants extra today? I'd forgotten last Wednesday and drenched them Friday.

"You're going to drown them," Jake said. "Look, the leaves are turning yellow." It was true they didn't look especially healthy. He took the can from me and started sticking his finger in the pots to feel the dirt. "Why Amanda would make you responsible for her plants when I've always been devoted to them, I'll never know. You'll kill them in under a month." He checked a few more and then wiped the dirt on his fingers off on his jeans. "None of them need water." He turned towards me with as serious an expression on his face as I'd seen. "Aren't you afraid he'll find her again?"

I pressed my lips together and looked towards the window. "I hope he won't." I pulled the living room curtains closed.

Jake slouched back onto the couch, his feet up, his hands behind his head. His glasses shone as they reflected the light of the lamp next to him. "Let me stay here tonight. I'll be your bodyguard, no charge. And I don't even hog much of the bed."

"Get out of my face, Jake." I shut off the TV with a jab.

"Ooh, I love it when you're mean."

"Hey you," Karla said, standing in the doorway. "She told you to go home. We don't need no man." Even in a sling, Karla looked like someone not to mess with.

Jake grinned. "Yeah, yeah, all men are scum. I've heard it before. I'm in love with Sara, but you, Karla, you I really like. What a woman."

"OUT," I said, pointing at the door.

The door buzzer rang. Who would it be this late at night? "Who is it?" I said into the intercom.

There was no answer.

"Let me go look," Jake said. He went down the stairs and came back up shrugging his shoulders. "Nobody there."

I looked at Karla, my heart pounding. Her husband had had a gun last time. Should we call the police? For what, a door buzzer? It was probably just a mistake. It probably wasn't her husband.

"I know you can do it on your own," Jake said apologetically. "The last thing I want to do is use fear of this guy to pressure you. Take pity on a poor guy who hasn't paid his gas bill so his apartment's cold: let me sleep on your couch. I won't bug you, I'll just dream of you."

I looked at him and sighed. "Just for tonight."

Aaron wasn't going to call. I should get used to it, I thought as I tried to open the drawers of my dresser without knocking over my bookshelf since all the furniture in my room was still jammed together. After what I'd said, what did I expect? Men didn't change. He was who he was, and if it didn't fit, it didn't fit. Some things weren't negotiable. I thought of the dark moonlit beach, the waves reaching and falling back, Aaron staring at the water with his hands clasped behind him. I knew I didn't have the whole story, I didn't understand him, but if he wanted to renegotiate and reconnect, he'd have to initiate, he'd have to call, and I knew it was unlikely he would. That was the way he was.

Not having the energy to move everything back against the wall, I climbed over my desk to get to my bed. As I pulled my blankets up to my chin, I felt afraid and unsure of the future but happy with the strange new glow of my room.

Chapter Twelve

As I trudged up the stairs coming home from work the next day, I could hear Jake playing one of Amanda's old albums full blast. I opened the front door into a wall of sound, the intensity peaking in the living room where the windows vibrated with each drumbeat.

"*YOU START WEARING BLUE AND BROWN,*" Jake was yelling at the top of his lungs, "*AND WORKING FOR THE CLAMP DOWN.*" His eyes were closed, his arms flying in the center of the living room.

I walked past him and abruptly lifted the needle from the record. He opened his eyes. "Sara. I didn't hear you come in."

"Why are you still here?"

"I don't have a key. If I left, I might not get back inside."

"Listen, Jake—"

The phone rang. We both started towards the hallway. "It's my phone. I'm answering it," I said as boss-like as I'd learned how to be. Jake gave me a quick bow and let me pass. "And keep the music off."

It was Mark, calling to tell me what forms I needed to pick up, sign, and send out to him. I told him I would, sighing as I hung up the phone. Soon I'd be unmarried, unattached, unwanted, and completely alone, all due to the irreversible forces I'd set in motion. My choices.

"So you're divorcing him?" Jake said. "Are you going to marry Aaron? That would work. Then Aaron would be your husband, and I could be your lover."

Marrying or not marrying Aaron was too painful to think about. "I hate people who eavesdrop. I want you out of here."

"Where's your sense of humor, Sara? I always fall in love with women with no sense of humor."

Karla came in the front door with Jason and Eric. I'd given her a key. "Come on, come on," she said crossly, shooing the boys with her good arm, her sling obviously annoying her. "Go hang your coats up."

"Bad day?" I said.

Karla looked as if I'd spoken a foreign language. She leaned back against the door, hung her head down, and pressed her good hand against her face. "It's my fault. It's because she went with me to the police. I knew I should've had the guts to go alone."

"What's your fault, Karla? What are you talking about?"

"Meg's been arrested for kidnapping." Karla looked up, lost. "Kidnapping her own daughter. That girl loves her mother, don't they know that?"

"Holy Toledo," Jake said, his hands in his pockets.

"She's out on bail," Karla said to me. "She wants to see you."

I practically ran the blocks to Meg's apartment. Out of breath, I knocked and waited anxiously. Meg opened the door. Solid, wise, reassuring Meg.

"I'm going back to Idaho tomorrow," Meg told me as she let me in. "If I didn't, they'd extradite me. I'm making some tea—you want some?"

Dazed, I followed her down the hall. Four women from the shelter were in the living room packing her things in boxes. As I walked past they glanced up mournfully, resentfully, as if I'd been the one to serve the warrant.

I sat down uneasily on a bar stool in the kitchen. "Idaho? Kidnapping?"

"Idaho and kidnapping," Meg repeated. "What a combination. It won't even make the paper here, but it's probably on the front page in Boise tonight."

I looked around. I had to ask, dreading the answer. "Where's Sabrina?"

Meg closed her eyes. "They took her with them this morning when they arrested me. He's probably already got her on a plane back."

"Meg, I don't understand. What's this all about?"

"It's about Ted's revenge, and the end of this stage of my life. Sara, I'm not from Portland, I'm from Boise, and my name's not Meg, not legally, anyway. I left Ted, took Sabrina with me, and never looked back. After I left, he got a divorce, and he got a judge, a friend of his, to give him custody. Then he spent a lot of money tracking us down. I've been in that police station a hundred times, but the guy Ted hired had just been through passing out pictures. Someone recognized me when I went with Karla. Tell Karla it's not her fault. Bad luck or fate or something, but not her fault. I suppose I never expected to hide forever, but it would've been nice."

"How long ago did you leave?"

"Five years. We went to Portland first where a cousin of mine lives and changed our names. Then we came here. It's why I couldn't tell you about my past. I couldn't tell anybody. Even volunteering at the shelter was a risk."

"What's your real name?"

"Amy. Or it was. I stayed with *Little Women*. You know, Meg, Jo, Beth and Amy."

"And Sabrina?"

Meg smiled tiredly. "She chose that name for herself. As long as we were going through all this, I thought I'd let her have some fun. I named her Lisa when she was born." The corners of her mouth pulled down, and she sipped her tea. I thought of the little blond girl, the secrets, the comradeship with her mother. Now she was with a father she hadn't seen in years and had every reason to fear.

"Why didn't you stay and fight him for custody?"

"Ted's a doctor. He knows judges; he belongs to the country club. When fathers sue for custody, they get it seventy percent of the time, even when the judges aren't personal friends."

"But if he was violent—"

"Two years after we were married I put too much milk in the mashed potatoes and ended up in the emergency room with a broken arm. Ted was with me. I told them I slipped on the stairs. Later, when I went to the police black and blue, their advice was to stop talking back to my husband. I finally started working with the shelter in Boise to document the incidents and make sure I had a case—that's when Ted threatened to kill me and Sabrina if I ever left."

She wearily ran her hand through her short hair. "I think he thought it would keep me in line for good, but it did just the opposite. It freed me. I stopped worrying about how I'd make it on my own; I stopped caring whether anyone else would ever love me. It's crazy, but back then I really believed the hitting and shouting was proof Ted cared about me. But it was something about himself, his own life that he was trying to punish and control and couldn't. Transferring it onto me gave him a solid object to kick and torment. And now he has the government doing his persecuting for him. I knew disappearing would drive him crazy, but I thought after a certain point, he'd let go, he'd give up. He didn't.

"They're charging me with breaking laws in three states, mostly false identity stuff, but I spent seven years with Ted in a prison worse than any they can send me to now. I know it's hard to understand, but when people don't believe you, ask you what you're doing to provoke it, tell you you're paranoid one minute, masochistic the next . . . At the time I didn't know what Ted was capable of, I only knew we were in danger. Relying on the legal system seemed like a joke. I picked up and left everything behind but Sabrina." Meg slowly circled her spoon in her cup. "It's been hard on her, hard on both of us, but the last five years have been the best of my life."

I looked down at my own cup feeling overwhelmed and inadequate. "What will you do now, Meg? I mean Amy. Is that what I should call you?"

"Meg's fine. I'm going forward, not backward. There's not much choice, is there? Go back to Boise. Fight. Besides the criminal stuff, he says he's going to sue me for all the money he's spent trying to find us, but the director of the shelter here is giving me some help, and there are a few new judges up there. Maybe I'll get lucky."

"You leave tomorrow?"

She smiled weakly. "I'm abandoning you, just like your sister."

"Oh, Meg. I've learned so much from you. If there's anything I can do—" But there wasn't. It was a time for lawyers and people with far different skills than I had.

Meg closed her eyes. Her hair was flat and unwashed, and she looked like she hadn't slept for a week, but it had all just happened that morning. The parrots perched smugly on her ears. "The pain's extraordinary," she said, her eyes still shut. "It radiates from my chest; I feel it in my face and my back and through the bones in my hands." She opened her eyes. "But I'm not afraid to go back. I'm going back clear; I'm going back strong. If I go to prison, I go to prison. My love for my daughter is unbreakable. We'll both make it through." She reached up and touched her earrings. "The day Sabrina and I left we stopped in eastern Oregon to get gas. There was a jewelry stand inside the station on the counter, and even though Sabrina was just this tiny little thing back then, she asked me for money and told me to turn around. When we got in the car she handed me a little paper sack and told me we were birds of a feather, and we'd flock together. I've worn them every day since."

On the counter was the copy of *Little Women* that Sabrina had checked out from the library.

I pointed to it. "Did she finish it?"

Meg shook her head. "No. Jo was in New York."

"I'll take it back to the library. Can I come visit you in Boise?"

"Maybe later. I'll call you. I've enjoyed being your friend, Sara. You should go home now and take care of Karla and her kids." She hugged me good-bye. "You'll call Madeline at the food bank?"

I nodded, trying not to cry. I walked home in fading twilight, my arms folding the book tightly to my chest. The whole way I saw Sabrina dancing in front of me, her arms extended, her blond hair flying in an endless, slow-motion pirouette.

When I got back, I dug into the hall closet, searching for a blue plastic box that Amanda kept her acrylic paints in.

"Sara?" Eric's little musical voice came from behind me. I glanced over my shoulder. "Jake says dinner's ready, and do you want some?"

"I'll be there in a minute."

I squeezed several bright colors out on a palette having almost no idea what I was doing. In the center of one aqua wall I painted a small purple fish. I liked it. I gave it green dots. I painted a bigger one, gold and red, next to it. Then a black, yellow, and magenta one. I cracked the window open for air.

"You going to eat?" Jake said, standing at my door. Eric and Jason stood on either side of him with little questioning eyes. "We're already finished."

"I'm not hungry," I said.

"What are you doing?" Eric said.

"Painting fish." I was in the middle of a fat blue and pink striped one.

"Can we help?" Jason said.

I looked over at them. "Okay."

"Cool," Jake said and went for the box of paints.

"You get that wall," I said, pointing. "The other three are mine."

Jason and Eric argued about clouds at the bottom of the ocean again. Jake let them paint two small ones, pink and purple, and then got them to work on a sunken treasure ship. Late that night, I climbed over my desk into my island bed. This is going to take a while to finish, I thought, managing not to think about anything else for an entire minute. Then I cried myself to sleep, afraid for Meg and Sabrina, afraid for myself. Why hadn't Aaron called? He wasn't going to. Oh, Meg. I dreamed of airports and loss.

The next morning, Paul popped his head into my office and flashed his white teeth at me. "Guess what? We've got folks from three plants out here Friday to hear about lower inventories. Can you pull together a presentation?"

I had an inspiration. I was fearless. "I'll have Joe and Althea prepare one."

"No, Sara, just you this time."

"Joe and Althea have done most of the work and deserve credit."

Paul took off his glasses and wiped them with a handkerchief. "Sara, I know how much you like to support your people, but not this time. I want you to do it."

I was suddenly, colossally sick of him and his games. "You know, Paul, I'm sure Bob and Bob wouldn't like us taking credit for what others have done. Even bringing it to their attention would be unpleasant." Paul's eyes narrowed and his jaw tightened. I'd never flat out gone against his wishes or threatened to go around him. And he thought I was dangerous before. "They'll do fine," I continued. "They'll make you look good. I'll make sure of it."

Paul sucked in his cheeks and appeared to consider my proposal, although the hand he was clenching and unclenching was a good sign he'd rather knock me out of the room. "They need to make the plant look good, Sara, and you'd better make damn sure they do." He put on his glasses and strode quickly out of my office. I knew to win this battle I'd have to be willing to lose the war because he wouldn't forgive this. I loved Deming, but if war was what it took, I wasn't interested anymore. Too much of my energy was wrapped up in battle tactics—what had happened to my mass transit system? The potholes had turned into foxholes. Improve constantly and forever, Deming's point five said. Well, there were other things that needed to be improved, too.

I shut my door and called Madeline at the food bank. I was the last person she had left to interview; she'd like me to come as soon as possible. I agreed to meet her at noon the next day. After I put down the phone, I stared at my computer screen and wondered if Paul would cancel the presentation or figure out another way to sabotage me. The visitors' travel arrangements had probably already been made. Paul would lose face if he canceled now. Whatever it took, I'd make sure Joe and Althea gave the presentation, just like Bogart made sure the plane left to Lisbon. Meg's plane is probably reaching Boise about now, I thought. I went to find Joe and Althea and get them started.

When I got home from work, the apartment was empty, an unusual occurrence lately, and the phone was ringing. I picked it up and my heart skipped a beat when I recognized my father's voice. He never called me.

He cleared his throat. "Sara, I've decided you shouldn't divorce Mark. You should never have stayed behind, but what you need to do now is move to Washington and be with him. You've got a good job, and I understand why you don't want to give it up, but you'll have to sacrifice it."

"Dad, this is none of your business."

"You're destroying your chances for happiness. For once you should follow my advice."

Hundreds of vindictive things to say bounced through my mind, but I just pursed my mouth and stared at the violin woman's back as the silence stretched.

"You're not going to listen to me, then. Sara, I know about these things."

"I'm doing what's best for me."

"Maybe Mark will have more sense. Or how about the man you're seeing, what's his name?"

I was alarmed. "Dad, no. You don't have my permission to interfere like this."

"I'm your father. I'm not going to sit back while you destroy your life."

The conversation was intolerable. "You don't have much choice, do you? Now, sorry, I've got to go." Shaking, I put down the phone. He wouldn't really call Mark, would he? I was fairly sure he wouldn't remember Aaron's name. I dialed Mark's number.

"I thought I'd warn you," I said when Mark answered. "My father's gone lunar."

"What do you mean?"

"He objects to our splitting up. He's demanding I move to Washington."

Mark laughed. "Kind of ironic, given his track record. Do you want me to talk to him? Maybe I can calm him down."

"No," I said. "I can deal with it. I just wanted to warn you in case he called." Which he still might. Tell him, Sara. I took a breath.

"Mark, I know you're seeing Patricia—well, I was seeing someone for a while, too."

"Oh," Mark said. "Is it rude to ask who?"

"Aaron, the guy at Amanda's dinner party. Do you remember him?"

"Yeah." Mark paused for a moment. "Sara, were you faithful to me? Not that it matters much now."

I closed my eyes. "I didn't sleep with him until after we broke up." Small victory. It hadn't been easily won. "But we went out to dinner some last fall."

"You said were seeing him—you're not anymore?"

"No," I said, my chest tightening. Yes, it feels terrible, but Sara, just breathe. One breath at a time. It'll get better.

"I still miss you, Sara. I feel bad thinking of you all alone with Amanda gone."

"I'm not so alone. Karla and her kids moved in." I didn't feel up to explaining Jake. "And I'm thinking of quitting my job."

"Really? I thought you loved it."

"They want to transfer me, and I'm sick of the craziness. I'm looking around now."

"Good for you. I never did like Appleton-Smith. I should tell you, when my lease is up, I'm planning on moving in with Patricia and Benji. If you're going to change your mind, you'd better do it soon."

Am I going to change my mind, I thought? "Would you take me back?"

"I don't know. Do you want to come back?"

I thought of Washington, of Mark's scrubby, handsome face, of being connected and wanted and safe and not a failure. In a way, I still loved him. Maybe if I concentrated hard enough, I'd believe I could be happy. I used to be good at concentrating. Face it, Sara, you married Mark for the wrong reasons. You know he can't offer what you want, and all the concentrating in the world wouldn't change that, it'd just repress and obscure it.

"Be happy with Patricia, Mark. You have my complete permission, not that you need it." My words sounded like scissors snipping the last threads between us. "Doesn't it feel strange to already be through your first marriage?"

"Yeah, it does." Mark gave a short laugh. "We shared our first marriage together. I guess we'll always have that in common."

I blinked, my eyes smarting. The violin woman seemed to gaze off in the distance at something she wanted but wasn't allowed to reach for. After I hung up, I changed into my long blue walking skirt and was putting on my coat when Jake buzzed downstairs.

His voice was distorted over the intercom. "Sara, fair maiden, Juliet of my dreams, could you let me in? I bought stuff for dinner."

I thought about it. I couldn't very well leave him standing on the steps with groceries in his arms. Impatiently I buzzed him in.

"Where are you going?" he said as I finished buttoning my coat.

"For a walk."

"Sara, it's getting dark. I can't be a proper bodyguard if you walk around at night without me."

"I'm not looking for protection, Jake. See you."

The light from the cloudy evening sky was already dimming. I put my hands in my pockets as I climbed to the top of the hill. People were coming home from work, their faces tired and hassled as they searched for parking. As the wind picked up, I wished I'd worn a warmer coat, but I was glad to be out of the apartment for a while. My room was still chaotic, and soon Karla and the kids would return and things would feel crowded. Though I considered our neighborhood safe, Jake's parting comment had made me edgy. Cars were turning their headlights on; maybe I shouldn't be out this late. I decided to turn back.

Aaron hadn't called. He'd done all the begging he was going to do. I told him I didn't want him on his terms; he obviously didn't want me on mine. I didn't want Mark on Mark's terms. I would be alone until the end of time. Look at Meg, I told myself. She was alone in Boise now, fighting for her freedom and her child. I had a sudden aching wish that when I got home, Aaron would be there, he would take me in his arms, and I could tell him about Meg, the latest things with Paul, my father, my job interview, and he would listen and tell me I was doing the right thing. You're being a baby, Sara, you can do this on your own. Face it, it wasn't the end of the world. Well, just kind of. Was I wrong to want to be with him? Was I wrong to want intimacy and respect? It seemed a clear trade-off, but I knew we hadn't unmasked all the issues. We'd both kept so many doors locked. How long would it be, I wondered, before Aaron found someone else to mentor, console, and encourage? Monica said he left all his other women on good terms. I imagined he'd hold a grudge against me a long time for not letting him end it properly. I wondered if I'd made any difference to his life at all.

As I stepped up over a curb I stumbled and fell. When I sat up, clutching my stinging knee, I saw that I'd ripped my skirt and my knee was bleeding. It hurt, but really, it was all too much. My life was a catastrophe. I felt like I had cuts, scrapes, and scars all over my body from events, some under my control, some not. Pick yourself up, Sara. Pick yourself up and go on. What else was there?

Buddha-Mind walking was no longer even a remote goal. I'd be lucky to make it home in one piece. Limping back to the apartment, I didn't attract much attention. In a city where a man in a wedding dress doesn't get a second look, a woman with a torn skirt hardly rates a twitch of the eye.

"What happened to you?" Karla said as I came in the door.

"Nothing. Tripped over a curb."

She shook her head. "You're worse than my kids. Come here, let me look at it."

"Just a second."

I went to my bedroom to take off my skirt, not sure if I could repair it, suspecting the blood would probably stain it anyway. After I put on my robe, I let Karla wash my knee with her good arm and put biting disinfectant on it. As I wiped grit off my palm left over from its contact with the concrete, I examined the lines on my hand. I wondered what they showed now, but it was unlikely I'd find someone who could tell me.

After dinner we painted more fish: gaunt fish, fat fish, happy fish, angry fish, punk fish, surreal fish, Malcolm X fish, Emma Goldman fish, Joey Ramone fish, kite fish, snowflake fish, violin fish, aardvark fish, iguana fish, Pinocchio fish, fish with belly buttons, fish with umbrellas. Fish swam around my room in laps, sharks chased schools of fish on bikes wearing helmets. Standing on chairs, Eric and I together created a giant iridescent whale that ended up with an enigmatic expression very near to Amanda's as it floated at the top of the room, calmly surveying the scene. I let Jake, Eric, and Jason stray from their original wall in a fish painting free-for-all. Jake, resident gentleman of leisure, had no doubt painted fish all day while the rest of us were at school or work. Fish shimmered, careened, and caroused through a jungle of drifting, weaving seaweed. A few glowed when the lights were off, phosphorescent.

"It's like living in an aquarium," Jake said.

"It's like the bottom of the ocean," Eric said.

Jake trundled Eric and Jason off to have a bath. I wanted to put glitter on one fish, and I thought I remembered Amanda having some in the hall closet, but when I opened the door, I yelled for Jake.

"What's this?" I said, pointing. Our jumbled closet had been neatly reorganized, which was fine, but it now also held a suitcase, two boxes labeled 'Jake Dellingham,' and an electric guitar.

"This was a mess. I cleaned it up."

"Jake, I didn't say you could bring your stuff over."

He scrunched up his face, knowing I wouldn't like his answer. "A friend of mine came into town, and I offered to sublet my apartment to him the rest of the month. Otherwise, I couldn't pay the rent."

"Jake, why don't you get a job?"

"I have a job. Our band's got a gig Saturday night. Which reminds me, could I have a key so I don't have to wake you up when I come home?"

I gave a shriek of exasperation and even shook a fist at him. "You have so much gall. There are already four people living here and you want me to take care of you, too. It's too much. I can't do it." I pressed my lips together, trying not to cry. "What has happened to my life?" I mumbled.

Jake put his hand on my shoulder. "Sara, look." He pushed me into the living room where Karla sat studying. She looked up momentarily and then ignored us. "Do you see my stuff anywhere? No. The living room is clean and neat. There's plenty of space. Notice the plants—already they look better. Okay, now the kitchen." Unwillingly I shuffled along with him. "I made dinner, right?"

"Yeah," I said. It'd been nice to have dinner on the table when I came home from my walk.

"And now the kitchen's clean and organized. Better than your and Amanda's chaos." He pulled me back into the hall and knocked on the bathroom door. "Jason and Eric—almost done with your bath? Time to get out and then I'll read you a story." Jake turned to me. "See, I'm a great nanny, too. You're getting a bargain. You're not taking care of me, you're subsidizing my rent which is only fair because you make considerably more than I do, and I'm taking care of all of you, which you need right now."

I sighed and put my hands in the pockets of my robe, conscious of my bare feet and the bandage on my knee. "You've descended on me like a plague."

Jake's glasses glinted as he tossed his head back and laughed. "I think I'm a gift from God. Which is what the plagues were, in a way. You know, I always liked this place. It feels good to be living here again."

"This is temporary, Jake."

"Isn't everything?"

I wondered what it would take for me to get annoyed enough to throw him out. The violin woman caught my eye. I went to look at it a moment before returning to my fish.

Jake stood behind me. "Did you know I helped Amanda put these up? Your sister cannot line things up to save her soul."

"How did he put those marks on that woman's back, do you think?"

"*Le Violon d'Ingres*, one of Man Ray's most famous photographs. Woman transformed into object. The f holes were superimposed after the photo was printed. The title's kind of a joke. Ingres used to play the violin as a hobby, and Man Ray was saying photography was only his hobby, even if it did pay the bills. His true love was painting."

I glanced over my shoulder at Jake with surprise. He was staring at the photograph with the same intensity I always did. "Every time I look at her, I think she looks cold sitting there," I said.

"An occupational hazard of modeling, I'd say. Her nickname was Kiki, the beauty of Montparnasse. That's where Man Ray's buried, Montparnasse. There's a great story of when he met her she didn't want him to photograph her because she didn't have any pubic hair. But he convinced her, and they were together six years. Before they went out at night, he used to put on her make up, paint her eyes with kohl, draw on her eyebrows in different shapes. Her face was his. Or I should say her image was his. He liked masks."

"You and your stories," I said. Pubic hair, indeed.

Jake leaned over me and blew on the photograph, sending dust flying. "You'd think it would kill you or Amanda to clean a couple times a year. It's Windex city tomorrow." He traced a finger down the side of Kiki's body. "Man Ray said she left him, but others say he was jealous of her success as a singer, and he pushed her away. He liked independent women but hated it when they got so independent they left his control. He was into control, into taking pictures of women in handcuffs and leather masks with no eyeholes. Amanda didn't want any of those up on her wall."

I considered the nude woman differently than I had before. Maybe she had participated, collaborated with Man Ray to make this image. "What happened to them later in life?"

"Her real name was Alice Prin. Her heydays were the Twenties. She even wrote an autobiography that was banned in the US. Later, she got poor, sick, and died when she was fifty. Man Ray had a series of lovers, did portraits and fashion photography to make money and left for Hollywood when the Nazis occupied Paris—he was Jewish. I don't know why he went to Hollywood, since he refused to go commercial there. Eventually he returned to Paris but was always disappointed he was acclaimed for photography and not painting. Maybe by the end he got reconciled to it."

"How do you know so much about Man Ray?" I asked.

"I majored in art history and did my honor's thesis on him. It was tough to dig out the truth because he hated to expose himself, and his friends did a great job of protecting him. Even his biographers were infatuated with him. You've got to be willing to see both the dark and the light if you really want to know someone. Man Ray knew that. He spent his whole career on dark and light. Anyway, that's why Amanda let me move in with her—I knew more about surrealists than she did."

"I thought it was because you were a guitarist."

"Nah, there's lots of guitarists around. Of course, it doesn't take long to learn about surrealists, either. About six and a half months."

"It still hurts?" I asked gently.

Jake shrugged and grinned. "You're better than drugs, Sara. When I look in your eyes, nothing hurts. Do you think you could get a key made for me?"

"What have you been doing until now?" I said with a scowl. "You've obviously been going out."

"Leaving the door unlocked."

"Great," I said. "Just great." Why didn't he pass out flyers on the street with a list of our easy-to-steal possessions, too? Throwing on shoes, I scrambled outside in my robe to get him the extra key I kept in my car. Then I returned to my fish.

My interview with Madeline, an Asian woman with a booming voice and black hair striped with gray, was more interesting than I expected. I'd surreptitiously left work early at lunch to arrive on time at her large, chaotic office, and now I sat in a worn armchair eating a sandwich that she offered me while I talked about my work experience and future goals. Every once in a while, I looked around at tired but cheerful turn-of-the-century toys scattered everywhere, on bookshelves, on filing cabinets, all over her massive old desk. A large doll with clothes of satin and lace and a painted china face gazed at me with a permanent expression of wonder.

"Aren't these great?" Madeline said when she caught me looking at the toys. "My grandmother collected them. She had an indulgent father. Her family was upper crust Chinatown in those days."

"They're wonderful."

"It's terrible about Meg," Madeline said as our conversation came to a close.

"Yes," I said.

She folded her hands on her desk. "Some of us have taken up a collection to pay legal expenses for her. We've already raised $3000. Would you like to contribute?"

I realized I hadn't offered Meg any money, and she probably needed it. She hadn't said anything. She'd told me to go take care of Karla. "Yes, I'd like to."

Madeline considered me a moment. "Sara, I've already interviewed seven other candidates, and I probably should think about this a little more, but I'm going to offer you the job here and now. You're what we want. But we need whoever we hire to start as soon as possible."

I was surprised. "Can you tell me what the salary would be?" The figure she mentioned was exactly half of what I was making at Appleton-Smith.

"I know it's not enough," she said, "especially for living in San Francisco, but it's one of the higher paid positions here."

Even though I already had an interview lined up with a cereal manufacturer, I agreed to let her know my decision by Monday. Then I wrote out as large a check for Meg's legal expense fund as my bank account could handle.

"I've enjoyed talking with you." Madeline looked at her watch. "Got to go. United Way meeting. It's always something."

I'd coached Joe and Althea and made them rehearse with me, telling Joe when he complained that this was in his best interest. That afternoon, Althea and Joe gave their presentation as scheduled to thirty visitors from four other plants. Wearing a long skirt to cover my wounded knee, I stood in the back of the room near Paul, who looked at me only once, though with as malevolent a glare as I'd ever seen from him. Quite unexpectedly, Bob and Bob were present. Tall Althea, striking in her purple suit, and crew cut Joe, uncomfortable in his polyester blue one, made a wonderful pair. What we'd accomplished had obviously arisen out of both their strengths. I was proud of them and, in a way, deeply satisfied. When the presentation was through, Paul made a point of shaking both Althea and Joe's hands. I could tell Joe was surprised.

Bob and Bob stood up and the crowd grew silent. "Excellent work, Joe and Althea. Just tremendous."

"Wonderful results. And from such a diverse pair. We're touched by what we can do when we work together."

"It's a lesson for all of us. We want to announce, while we have so many of you here, that Paul, the man behind it all, is going to have a chance to inspire a whole new set of people. He's being promoted to Chicago in a special assignment to improve quality and lower inventories throughout the company."

Everyone clapped. The aviator frames had evidently worked. I raised my eyebrows thinking that Paul's understanding of both quality and inventories was minimal, but maybe he'd find someone like me again to do it for him.

"Sara, can I see you a minute?" Paul said. "In my office."

I followed behind him, gearing up my nerve, wondering how much he was going to yell. Paul sat down at his desk, tugging at his cuffs. I remained standing.

"Okay," he said. "You were right. They did fine. But let's get this straight—you will never do that to me again."

"You're right, Paul. I'm leaving Appleton-Smith."

He turned his head slightly. "You're what?"

"I have another job."

Paul stood and walked towards me holding up his palms, smiling his boyish grin. "Wait a minute, slow down. I'm sorry I yelled. Sara, I want you to come to Chicago and work for me. Think about it. You can do what you've been doing here except on a larger scale and without the hassle. No Joe to manage, no lines breaking down. I'm counting on you to help me improve quality in every plant in the country, maybe even internationally. Think of the impact you could have, the exposure it would give you."

I smiled just slightly. "Last week I was clogging up the plumbing, this week I'm indispensable. Sorry, Paul, you'll have to find someone else to make you look good."

"Is it the money? We can fix that."

"No, it's the integrity, and that you're unlikely to fix. First you'd have to be familiar with the concept."

Paul's eyes narrowed. "I thought we understood each other, Sara; I thought we got along. Yes, I wanted to transfer you because you're so headstrong, but you're bright, you're talented, and Bob and Bob love you, God knows why. A little more polish, a little more political savvy—I would've made your career."

As long as I made yours, I thought, twisting my ring that I still ridiculously wore to work. But further antagonizing Paul was pointless. I didn't want to get even: I just wanted to get out. "I've learned a lot working here, but I don't want to live in Chicago, and I don't want to work for a big corporation anymore. Sorry."

He sighed and sat down. "What am I going to tell Bob and Bob?"

Though I'd enjoy seeing him in trouble, I thought I might as well set the situation up as best I could for the people I cared about. "I'd suggest replacing me here with Joe or Althea."

Paul sat hunched over, chin on fist. "Hmm. Joe's out of the question, no education. Chicago would never tolerate clogging the . . ." He glanced at me and didn't finish his sentence. "But Althea, now that's a possibility. A smart black woman rising in the ranks—it'd look good, very good. I'll check with Bob and Bob right away."

As I let myself out of the celadon-teal office, I wondered idly what color it would be after the next plant manager redecorated it.

"You were so in with the hierarchy," Althea said when I got her and Joe together to tell them I was quitting. "I thought you were going straight to the top."

I shrugged. "It's an ugly tune you have to dance to sometimes."

Joe scowled. "I just got you trained. Now we'll have more fool ideas. Next thing you know, they'll want us to make glow-in-the-dark lotion packed in light bulbs. I wish they'd think up a policy called Total Leave People Alone."

"They were trying to transfer me. I'd be leaving anyway."

"We'll miss you," Althea said.

Joe rubbed the back of his fuzzy head. "I hate to say it, but you're not so bad. Kind of pushy maybe, but not so bad."

I smiled tiredly. "Thanks, Joe." It was the nicest thing he'd ever said to me.

The Bobs appeared in my office doorway. "Can we see you a minute, Sara?" Althea and Joe hurriedly cleared out. Bob and Bob pulled up on the thighs of their navy-blue pants as they sat down in my cramped office.

"Paul says you're thinking of leaving us."

"I'm going to take a job at a food bank in the city."

"That sounds worthwhile, but it's a little dead end, isn't it? Did Paul tell you about the opportunity working with him in Chicago?"

"Yes. I'm not interested in moving to Chicago."

"Actually, there's so much travel with the position, you could be based anywhere, even here. And Paul says your husband's in Washington. You could easily pop out from Chicago or Atlanta on the weekends to see him."

"And then when would I be in San Francisco?"

"I see your point. Well, we're disappointed. We had great faith in Paul's ability to develop talent."

"Such high hopes. You're thinking of Althea to follow you? Excellent choice."

"It shows you have an intuitive feel for the corporate world, Sara. We'd like you to reconsider."

"Thanks, Bob, Bob. I appreciate it, but I've made my decision."

"If you change your mind, give either of us a call."

"Well, not me, actually," the junior Bob said.

"That's right," the senior Bob said. "We're spinning off one of our subsidiaries into its own division. Bob's going to head it up. A promotion for him."

"Congratulations," I said. The world was being promoted; I was cutting my salary in half. What was money, anyway, I told myself. So I had Karla, Jason, Eric, and even Jake as dependents now. Not working at Appleton-Smith, I'd save a fortune on dry cleaning alone. My throat felt dry as I swallowed and surveyed the two wealthy, well-manicured men in front of me. It was only money. If I told my father what I was doing, he'd probably go lunar about this, too. Yet another good reason to quit.

Chapter Thirteen

When I got home that evening, tired to my bones from events of the day, my blinking answering machine held messages from two more companies wanting to set up interviews with me. I listened with a tinge of pleasure and curiosity, but after my confrontation with Paul I had zero desire to hop off one merry-go-round onto another. I'd call them back Monday and tell them I wasn't interested, as well as cancel my other interview. I went into the living room and gazed at the crisp skyline framed by the window like a giant postcard. Urban blight—it was hard to see from here. I smiled remembering Mark's admonition to me so long ago. He'd been right about me spinning my wheels with hand cream. Though I was sure it would be full of problems and irritations and challenges I couldn't conceive of at this point, the food bank would be a good place to invest my energy for a while. I flopped down on the couch, took off my shoes, and rubbed my feet. Time to buy some flat shoes for work. Madeline, my future boss, was shorter than me. It would be a new experience to work for a woman.

I noticed the stereo was completely turned off, an unusual occurrence lately, and Jake didn't appear to be around. Now that I'd given him a key, maybe he felt more secure about leaving the apartment. As I stood gazing out the window again, Karla came into the room, her face looking much better, her impatience with her sling evident.

"I'm taking the kids to a movie," she said. "Get them out of your hair, but you can come with us if you want."

"No, thanks. I've had enough drama for one day at work. I want to finish organizing my room and go to bed early."

"Sara, I thought you had a boyfriend. How come he's not around?"

The skyline in the slanted late afternoon sun looked perfect and unreal, the angles too sharp, the shadows too black, like a diorama trying to fool a skeptical eye. "I'm not seeing him anymore."

"And you're still splitting with your husband?"

I nodded.

"And now you've got Jake on your case? You sure run through men." Karla looked away a moment and twisted her mouth. "Sara, I've got something to tell you. Can we sit?" Her dark brown eyes were full of concern. My stomach sank as I prepared for more disappointment. "I want to thank you very, very much for all the help you've given us. You've been a true friend, and I don't want you thinking I'm ungrateful, but I found another place to live."

It surprised me how much her announcement hurt. "You don't like it here?" I asked softly.

"We like this place fine, but we're guests, and guests get in trouble if they stay too long. The other black woman in my class, she and I are going to share an apartment we found. We'll have more space, and maybe we can live there a long time. I need to get my boys stable, back on track. You and Jake took care of us when we needed it." She tugged on her sling and smiled. "I'll always remember. I feel real lucky."

"When are you going?"

"Not till the end of the month. Two more weeks, if you can stand us that long."

I gazed at her, the forces of gravity tugging on the corners of my mouth. "You're right. It is best for you, but I'll be sad when you leave. Jason and Eric paint wicked fish."

Karla gingerly hugged me with one arm. "You've got a good heart, girl. Don't let anyone tell you different."

Jason and Eric stood in the doorway with their coats on. "Sara, are you coming to the movie with us?"

"No, Jason, but thanks for asking. You have a good time."

After they left, I was in my room changing my clothes when I heard Jake come home. I'd just finished tugging a sweater over my head when he walked into my room.

"Don't you knock?" I said, hurriedly pulling the sweater down over my stomach.

"The door was open. Don't be mad. I've brought you a present." He held a child's pail towards me.

"What is it?"

"Beach. I took the N-line all the way out to get you some." He emptied the pail in a corner of my room.

"Jake, you're pouring sand on my floor."

"Can't have a beach without sand." He reached into his pocket. "And look, shells. All we need now are the sound of waves and a whiff of decaying marine life. I'll work on it."

I smiled in spite of myself. My own little beach. I nudged the sand with my toes. "I guess I should say thanks. I've never had my own beach before."

He shrugged. "And I fixed your skirt."

On a corner of the bed my skirt lay washed and ironed, the rip neatly sewn.

"You didn't have to do that." But I was pleased. I would've botched it terribly.

"I told you, I'm a godlike housekeeper. Do you need help pushing your furniture back?"

As we disassembled my furniture island, something I hadn't noticed before caught my eye. "Jake, what's this?" I pointed at corner down near the floor.

"A peacock. I know it's not very fish-like, but while you were out walking yesterday, Jason really wanted one, so I had an inspiration and made it gold like Whistler's. Have you ever seen his Peacock Room in Washington?"

My shoulders sank in unexpected defeat as I stared at the peacock's golden plumes fanning across the aqua wall. There was something subdued but brilliant about it—glittering, even. Serves me right for taking Jason and Eric's down, I told myself. It was Friday night, and I was alone, well, almost alone. He hadn't called; he wouldn't call. He would have to be the one to call.

Jake tilted his head, trying to read my silence. "You got a big date planned? You don't look like it. You know, if you're so in love with Aaron, why isn't he ever around? I mean, you talk to Mark more than you do him. Of course, you talk to me more than either of them. Where does that rank me? Do you talk least to the people you like most? But that would mean you're head over heels with complete strangers you've never—"

I sank to the floor and put my head in my hands. My knee stung, still raw under its bandage. I want the world to go away, I thought, just completely go away. I was so sick of crying, but tears flowed anyway. I felt Jake put his arm across my shoulders as he sat down on the floor next to me.

"Who are you crying for? I know you've got a lot of options."

I sniffed morosely and didn't answer.

"Option A, Mark. The reality of the divorce is setting in. Option B, Meg. She's screwed and there's nothing you can do to help her. Or option C, Aaron. Hmm. What's happened with you and Aaron, anyway?"

"I'm not seeing him anymore," I said, wiping my face with my sleeve. I noticed Jake had a big rip in his jeans baring one knee.

"But you want to. Why not?"

I shook my head. "I don't know. Power and respect and symmetry. Because he's still in love with somebody else."

"That's hard," Jake said. "It's hard loving somebody who loves somebody else. And symmetry, that's important, but a tough one. Ah, love. We all want someone whose aim is true, but what we usually get are tears and souvenirs."

I looked over at him. "You're not really in love with me," I said.

He looked up at the fish swimming in aqua paint. "'I should have been a pair of ragged claws scuttling across the floors of silent seas.'" He looked back over at me, his eyes smiling behind his round glasses. "No, I'm not. It's a good thing, too, because you'd break my heart. But I sure like you."

I closed my eyes and leaned my head against his shoulder. I could finally relax with him. "So why are you here?"

"Well, at first I didn't have anything better to do, but then I saw you had a family, and I need a family right now."

"What do you mean I have a family? My parents are divorced, and Amanda's in Africa."

"Karla and Jason and Eric. They're your family right now and my family, too."

"They're going to move out in two weeks. Karla just told me."

Jake paused, considering the news. "It's okay. It's wonderful while it lasts. Like I said before, everything's temporary when you get down to it, although you'll find me much more of a challenge to get rid of."

I stretched my hand out to the sand, pinched a little between my fingers, then let it drop, grain by grain, onto the palm of my other hand. "I don't get it. People help each other, people hurt each other. We damage and we repair the damage. What's the point? Just endless cycles of pain and conflict."

"And joy and transcendence. It's all mixed up. You know how Amanda talks about being on a journey? With any luck we help each other along more than we set up ambushes and roadblocks. I think as a species we're managing to go forward, but I've always been an optimist."

"Sometimes people think they're helping, and maybe they're really blocking." Even Amanda's help had gone too far at times, I thought.

"Mistakes get made. I make them all the time, and if you see me do it, tell me. But intent is important, too. If I make a mistake because I was thinking of myself more than the other person, I deserve to get chewed out. But if my heart's in the right place, then maybe what I need is some teaching."

"Meg thinks you've got a good heart."

"I'm a nice guy, generally. A little pushy, maybe."

"Only a little?" I poured the sand in my hand onto his bare knee. "So are you going to call Aaron?"

"If I do, we'll just argue, or I'll give in. Nothing will change."

"I don't know, he might be more teachable than you think. I was reading his poems, and I was thinking, wow, this is a really intense guy. It's great stuff, but so acid. You wouldn't know it to meet him, but I suppose that's the way art works—you suppress and subvert your passions, and they get squeezed out as art, but at least they get out. Most of the rest of us lock up tight. Hey, did I tell you I ran into Aaron Tuesday?"

"You what?"

"At Brittle Books. He was with his mother."

"His mother?" My heart sank. That's right, I was supposed to meet her. With Monica and our fight, I'd forgotten all about it.

"Yeah, I was standing behind them in line at the cash register, and I was about to say hi, but then I realized that all this murmuring back and forth between them was actually a nasty argument, and I was in a perfect position to eavesdrop. His mother's this tiny bone-china kind of woman, but tough, very tough, and she was laying into him like you wouldn't believe. He took it for a while and then he stuck out his arm and said he felt awful enough as it was, if she wanted to see him bleed, why didn't she just open a vein. A great line—I'll have to try it with my mom sometime. So she gave him this icy drop-dead look, you could see where he gets it, and told him he wasn't feeling nearly badly enough. Kind of mean, but when he looked away, her expression changed, and you could tell she adores him. Moms are nice that way. That's when I introduced myself."

I felt as if I were listening to the play-by-play of a disaster movie. "And?"

"I kind of startled him, but he remembered me and introduced me to his mom, and since I was buying one of his books, I think I scored a couple points. With her, anyway."

"You didn't say anything about me, did you?"

"Well, sure, I mentioned I'd moved in with you. I was surprised he didn't know."

I cringed. "In front of his mother? You said you were living with me in front of his mother?"

"Yeah, Aaron wasn't too thrilled. He just sort of stared at me—no, I'd say glare would be a better word—but his mom said how lovely it was to meet me, that the book I was getting was Aaron's best. And then she dragged him out of the store. That's when it occurred to me the two of you might've had a fight."

"Oh my God. Why didn't you just say I'm a drug addict and sell children into slavery?"

Jake raised an eyebrow. "Like that's an equivalent? Geez, Sara, I may be unemployed, but I'm not a total degenerate." He shrugged his shoulders good-naturedly. "Anyway, it's not as if it matters. Since you're never going to see him again."

I put my hand over my eyes and groaned.

"Now you're mad at me, right? You going to yell? Throw me out? Give all my clothes to Goodwill? Tell you what, I'll let you break my guitar, but you'll have to buy me a new one afterwards."

I sighed. "Jake, I'm not going to give away your clothes or break your guitar." I glanced at him. "Have women done that to you?" He shrugged. I leaned back against the bed and stared up at Amanda-the-whale. So Aaron probably thinks I'm sleeping with Jake. What a perfect way to top off an absolutely stellar week. I closed my eyes, inexpressibly weary. "You're right, it doesn't matter."

"Yeah, I can see it doesn't matter to you at all. What a relief, I'm really getting to like your couch. By the way, you got any extra pillows? I searched this morning, but—"

"Jake, why did you wait until today to tell me all this?"

He grinned. "Sara, in love and comedy, timing's everything. Plus, I needed a couple more days to grow on you. People don't always appreciate me right away." He got to his feet and offered me a hand. "You want to get something to eat? You'll have to treat. I'm broke."

I took his hand and pulled myself up. "As if I didn't know. Okay, but we're going somewhere cheap. I'm not going to have much money soon—I'm quitting my job."

"You are? How extraordinary. It reminds me of something. Job, job, something about a job."

"Like maybe you're getting one?"

Jake frowned and then snapped his fingers. "That's right. Someone called this morning, she said from Paris, and left a strange phone number. She said to call her back, that she was worried about quitting a job."

Monica? "Jake, that doesn't make any sense. She wouldn't call to tell me about her job."

"Well, I don't know what she was talking about. I was in the shower when the phone rang, and dripping pools of water, I had to simultaneously listen to her, hold my towel and write down the message. It was heroic. You need to put some decent pens by the phone. By the way, do you think you could buy a couple bars of Lifeguard next time you go shopping? Not that I mind smelling like hyacinth. And while you're at it, get some chocolate sauce; it goes great with Cherry Garcia. Oh, and don't forget Cheerios. Here, I'll make list."

Though all I wanted in the world was to curl up early in bed in my nice, organized room, because of the time difference I waited until eleven-thirty before calling Monica, wondering as I dialed how much this would cost me a minute. It'd better be worth it.

The connection was good. Her throaty voice sounded unnervingly close.

"Sara, I want you to go check on Aaron."

"What?" She'd caught me off guard. "What does this have to do with you quitting your job?"

"I'm not quitting my job. Aaron's quit his, and I'm worried about him."

As I let this sink in, I wondered if it could possibly be true, or if she were playing games with me. "Monica, did you tell me the truth when we had lunch?"

"The truth. What would you have done with the truth? You've botched it up enough as it is. You weren't supposed to leave Aaron, Sara, you were supposed to make him happy, or at least content."

"How do you know he quit, did he tell you?"

"I heard from a friend of a friend who works with him. Aaron wouldn't talk to me except to say my lunch with you didn't work."

"What really happened between the two of you? Why are you still trying to control him?"

"Oh, no one controls Aaron. You should've figured that out by now. What I will tell you is that when I left him, it wasn't his idea. He didn't want me to go like he did the others, and sometimes I think he's still not over it. I feel responsible in a way—he needs to get past me. Maybe I was wrong about you being the one to do it, but I'd still like you to go check on him."

"Monica, I'm not your lackey. Check on him yourself."

I heard children's voices in the background. Monica said a few words to them in French, and then I received her full annoyed attention again. "I can hardly do that from here, can I? You don't know him like I do. This is rash, very unlike him. Who knows what else he might do? You've set this in motion, Sara; I hold you responsible. Don't you care about him at all?"

"I can't promise you anything."

"Sara, I thought I could count on you."

Her voice had the same edge to it as Paul's today. I had to laugh. "Monica, you're very good. You'd hang on to him forever if you could, but it won't be through me."

After I hung up, I got out my one volume of Aaron's poetry and read until quite late. The poems weren't impenetrable this time, they were fascinating. Strings of words flew across the page creating images that were urban, colorful, and intense. Others enshrined memories of nature, stillness, and love. One or two were mystic, almost religious, and a few poems were full of blistering anger. What was it he was so angry about, I wondered? Was it that he wanted Monica and couldn't have her? Or was it some other aspect of his private world he had never let me see? I'll probably never know, I thought sadly. I shut the book and turned off my bedside light.

I was sailing in a boat with Amanda on a lake so large it was an ocean. She was fishing, though as far as I knew Amanda had never fished in her life. She'd catch a fish, it'd flop on the boat and then disappear. "You're supposed to tie them down," she told me. "We'll never get there this way." But the fish kept coming and disappearing and the only ropes were those attached to the sails. "I'm disappointed in you, Sara," she said. She was wearing turquoise stretch pants with white polka dots. A huge boat behind us sounded its horn. We have the right of way, I thought, disgruntled. The horn sounded again.

It was the door buzzer. I stumbled out of bed and pulled on my robe.

In the hallway, I saw Jake in boxer shorts and a T-shirt. "Oh," he said, "you going to get it?"

I ran my hand through my hair and yawned. "Yeah." I pushed the intercom button. "Who is it?"

"Sara, it's your father."

"Where are you?"

"Outside the door."

That's right, I thought, this isn't the phone, this is a nightmare. I buzzed him in and opened the door when he got to the top of the stairs.

"What are you doing here?"

"That's what I get? No 'hi Dad, it's nice to see you?'"

"Hi Dad, it's nice to see you. What are you doing here?"

He wore a casual shirt and pants straight out of a catalog, the well-dressed executive relaxing on the weekend. "I wanted to talk to you. I have a flight back at noon."

I stared in disbelief, not wanting to comprehend, not wanting to have to deal with him. He must've taken a six a.m. flight to get here this early. I tugged my robe closed. "Okay, we'll go out to breakfast. Let me get ready. Here, you can wait in the living room."

I led him down the hall to where Jake, Eric, and Jason were all eating bowls of cereal watching Saturday morning cartoons, Jake sitting amid his pillow and blankets still on the couch.

"Who are these people?" my father asked.

"They're staying here right now. That's Jason and Eric, and Jake you've met."

Jake grinned and waved a hand. "Nice to see you again, Mr. Whitfield."

My father abruptly turned. "I'll sit in the kitchen."

I got him the newspaper to read and then took a shower. I let the water fall on my back as hot as I could stand it, trying to scorch my overwhelming feeling of dread. My father absolutely had to stop showing up on my doorstep, I thought. It was bad for my nerves.

As I dressed, I heard Karla ask Jake to watch the kids while she went to the shelter. I leaned my head out my bedroom door and asked her to come talk to me a minute.

"Why are you going to the shelter?" I said as I slipped on a pair of walking shoes.

"Somebody's got to cover Meg."

I smiled. She was right, someone should, and Karla was very capable. I could envision her pointing and directing and counseling and consoling. "I think I've got two women signed up," I said. "Could you apologize for me and tell them I can't be there? I've got to go to breakfast with my dad."

"A surprise visit, huh? Well at least he comes to see you. My folks are back in Detroit. Haven't seen hide nor hair of them in five years."

My father and I walked to the diner we'd been to with Amanda before. It felt odd to be walking the streets of San Francisco with him. It was my territory.

As we stood at a corner waiting for the light to change, a bus roared by, causing me to step back and brush his arm. I stiffened. "Are you sleeping with that guy?" he asked as the noise faded. "What happened to the other one?"

"It's absolutely none of your business."

"Looks like he spent last night on the couch. What happened, you have a fight?"

Gritting my teeth, I didn't answer. The light turned green, and we started across.

"I thought Amanda was bad, but at least she wasn't running a youth hostel in her apartment. Does she know you're doing this?"

I counted to ten. Amanda wasn't here this time. I'd have to deal with him myself. "Stop bullying me."

"I'm bullying you. Right. Is anything you don't want to hear bullying? I know we haven't gotten along lately, Sara, but I'm still your father. I care about you, and I can't stand to see you doing this to yourself."

I stopped and turned towards him. "I don't believe that. You don't care about me. You care about yourself."

"Maybe you think I deserve that. I don't think I do."

We stared at each other for a moment, and then I started walking again. I'm shaking, I thought, stuffing my hands in my pockets. When we reached the diner, we were seated in a booth.

My father scowled. "Why are those women winking at me?"

In the booth across from us were two women with fluffy streaked blond hair wearing jumpsuits and a little too heavy make-up. "They're transvestites, Dad."

He put on his reading glasses and raised his eyebrows as he opened the menu. "They're very good. You need a guidebook to survive in this city."

We ordered and my dread increased. He didn't fly up here for just the few barbs he'd already let fly.

"I talked to Mark," he said.

I gave a short laugh of exasperation. The nerve of the man.

My father cleared his throat. "He said he's involved with someone else, and he thinks this is for the best."

"And?"

"I told him he was wrong, that he had obligations to you, commitments. You both do."

"And?"

He grimaced. "Let's see, how did he put it? He said I've confused the oppression of patriarchy and capitalism with the responsibilities of the father, but he admitted in the end it was up to you. That it was your decision. You know, Mark's father is a very sane man. He should never have let Mark get anywhere near a political science class. Still, he's your husband."

"Why do you want me to stay married to him? You got divorced; you seem happy enough. And I'm not abandoning two kids and trading in my spouse for a younger model. Your hypocrisy astounds me."

He narrowed his eyes. One look like that used to be enough to enforce instant obedience. "One thing about all this, Sara, it proves you're not any better than me. No, not better than me at all."

I searched for my trump, the most critical point of vulnerability. Adrenaline pumped through my arteries as I set my sights and steadied myself. "Did you know I tried to kill myself after you left? Did you know?"

He stared at me, and I knew my aim had been true. He said nothing, just stared, clouds of pain casting shadows on his face. The waitress brought us cups of coffee. I thought about getting up and walking out.

"I never meant to hurt you, Sara."

"You did." I felt like a heartless judge and jury. I had to be heartless to deal with him.

The silence stretched. He drummed his fingers on the table. "I think maybe you've got some things confused."

I couldn't believe it. Was he going to pretend the whole thing never happened? I shrugged desolately. "Go ahead and deny it. How could I ever prove it?" I leaned my face into my hands, my entire body feeling like an open wound. Was there ever really a time when I felt safe and loved? "Just go away and stay out of my life. Stay out for good this time. If you show up again, I'm not going to see you."

He didn't answer for a long moment. "You were just a child, weren't you?" I glanced up. His eyes were closed, and he looked like an old man. "My child. I don't know why I lost sight of it, but I did."

My eyes filled with tears. A woman at another table was wiping off her child's face. "I'm still afraid to be around you," I said, blinking, not able to look at him. Our food was served. We both just stared at our plates.

He picked his fork up and abruptly put it down. "Some things you do in life—" He paused, his eyes on a corner of the table. "If you think about them, they're almost unbearable, so you blindly hope they'll be forgotten. But they aren't forgotten. Instead, you end up with a child who hates you."

He might sound contrite, but there was no way I was going to forgive him. My father was right: I hated him, there wasn't a cell of forgiveness in my body. Some things weren't negotiable. From his favorite daughter he'd transformed me into someone he could blame and punish for the confusion of his life. How many of my choices, I wondered, had truly been my choices, and how many had been just reactions to his choices? Yes, when I leaned against that locked door in fear, I'd still been a child, so vulnerable, so few defenses. Painfully, instantaneously, I'd also lost a father, someone I could trust, a pivotal safe harbor for my life. It still hurt. I'd been angry and silent for so long—so silent, I didn't know how ashamed.

I pushed my plate away, unable to eat. He asked the waitress for the check.

We stood outside blinking, our eyes adjusting to another brilliant San Francisco day. I expected him to walk to Market Street to get a cab but instead he accompanied me back toward my apartment.

"I don't suppose you have any intention of forgiving me," he said.

"No."

He nodded his head. "Genine and I are splitting up."

Well, that was a surprise. I wanted to ask questions but refused to be curious.

He sighed in a long, tired exhale. "Sara, I've made a lot of mistakes that I don't want to admit, but none of them compare to the one I made with you. I know being sorry isn't enough, and to tell you the truth, I'm having a hard time remembering how, it's been so long since I let myself. I do remember what pain feels like though."

We walked along. "Will you stay in San Diego?" I asked.

"I expect so. Genine's moving to LA."

"Do you already have a replacement for her?" I couldn't resist being cruel.

"No. She's leaving me. I bet you're thinking it serves me right. Perhaps it does. Perhaps it does."

My father was close to sixty, still an attractive man with a good income. He won't be lonely long, I thought, trying to harden my heart, but I realized he'd probably come to see me because Amanda and I were the only people he felt connected to in the world, and we were tenuous. Concern for my divorce was a smoke screen. He looked more alone to me than anyone I'd ever seen.

"You've got a lot to learn, Dad."

We walked quietly side-by-side to my apartment, our backs to the crystalline skyline.

"Do you need a ride to the airport?" I offered.

"I'll call a cab."

The apartment was empty when we returned. Jake must have taken Eric and Jason out. I stood with my father in the hall as we waited for the cab he ordered over the phone. In the awkward silence he examined the Man Ray photographs.

"I think I've seen this one before," he said, pointing to the violin woman. "Did someone draw those marks on her back, or are they pasted?"

I couldn't help but smile. "Jake says they're superimposed." Even though it was a photograph and pretended to represent reality, the image had never actually existed in three-dimensional space. It was a creation of the artist's mind and the skill of his technique. How often I'd been locked in by a reality that I'd accepted as truth but was actually a fiction structured for someone else's benefit, not mine.

You have to look out for yourself, your own growth, Meg had said, and I agreed self-interest was legitimate until it was taken too far. Exactly where self-interest turns into selfishness is hard to define, but it was clear my father, Paul, and, I suspected, Monica, had crossed well over the line. And Aaron? To really know someone, Sara, be willing to look at both the dark and the light. I had my own share of selfishness to own up to.

I watched this man, my father, continue to evaluate Kiki's nude, odalisque back. He'd helped me with my homework growing up, taught me how to ride a bike, dug a grave in the backyard for my dead rabbit, carried me at Disneyland when I couldn't stay awake through the fireworks. In the end, inside all the onion layers of rage and resentment, I wanted to be connected to him.

"This is going to take years."

He turned, his face serious, trying to understand me. "I've got time."

When his cab arrived, he didn't kiss me good-bye, just looked at me a moment before he left. My handsome father who'd turned the adoration into fear. I'd struggled so long, but the worst was over. I went out for a walk.

Chapter Fourteen

City Buddha-Mind walking always took a few blocks to get going, to drop into the rhythm, to absorb the mood of the light and the weather. Today, the light was exquisite, the weather sublime. After a two-mile loop, I crested Liberty Street and stood exhilarated with the porcelain city spread in front of me. A landslide of resentment boulders had bounced down a cliff, a flock of guilt birds had taken wing, and pounds of mud shame had washed off me into a sewer where it belonged. Whatever the past and future might hold, today it was excruciatingly perfect to be alive. Though it galled me to do anything Monica suggested, I felt clear, and I felt strong. I set off for my next stop.

Aaron stared at me for what seemed like forever when he opened his door. "I didn't expect to see you," he said at last.

"Can I come in?"

His apartment was a mess, mostly from books cast about on the furniture and strewn in piles across the floor, some open, face down. Aaron didn't look good either, tired and unshaven in a rumpled shirt rolled up at the sleeves. He eyed me dourly.

"I heard you quit your job," I said.

"How did you hear?"

"Three guesses."

He picked up a book from a side table and glanced at its spine. "Monica, the great communicator. She should run her own talk show."

"She wanted me to check on you. But that's not why I'm here." I pushed a stack of books aside and sat on the couch. "Why did you leave your job?"

Aaron didn't seem inclined to speak, so I folded my hands in my lap and waited until at last he sighed and sank down into a chair. "Ten years ago, when I left business school, I made a deal with myself to work until I saved enough money; then I'd quit and write, maybe not forever, but for a while anyway. I reached my financial goal last summer, and I've spent the last nine months disgusted with myself for being too afraid to follow through. I suppose I needed a catalyst, but no, I'm not losing my mind, I'm not being rash or foolish, or a host of other adjectives I've heard the last three days from just about everybody I know. Have you come to lecture me, too?"

Monica doesn't know him as well as she thinks, I thought with pleasure. Of course, I hadn't known either. His private world. But he wasn't incapable of change. "No, no new adjectives from me. So you've been writing?"

"I wish. Reading mostly. It's been a difficult week."

I stood and held out my hand. "Come with me."

He shook his head. "Sara, almost everything you said last week is true. I've tried to control you more than I want to admit. I certainly haven't treated you like I should have. I don't want to do any more damage."

"Do you still care about me?"

"Too much to go on hurting you. You can tell Monica I'm fine. I appreciate your checking on me."

I didn't move. He closed his eyes. "I can hardly bear to see you. Please go."

I put out my hand again. "I'm not telling Monica anything. Come with me."

He didn't budge, just kept his eyes on the carpet. His black hair hadn't seen a comb recently, and though I had an urge to smooth it down, I didn't dare.

I cleared my throat. "Jake said he ran into you and your mother. I'm sorry if she ended up disappointed, coming all the way out here. What did you tell her?"

Aaron twisted his mouth briefly, unhappily. "I told her she couldn't meet you because you didn't want to see me anymore. I got a whole series of lectures about my singular inability to maintain relationships. She thought Jake was charming."

"He's moved into my apartment."

"So he said."

"There's a story that goes with it."

He looked away, across the room. "You don't have to explain. It's none of my business. Though I thought you'd go back to Mark, not move on to someone else."

"Jake's helping take care of Jason and Eric," I said with a smile. "They've moved with Karla into Amanda's room, and Jake's sleeping on the couch. It seems to be a common practice these days. I haven't moved on. Now come with me," I insisted.

"Karla and her kids are living with you, too?" he said, puzzled.

"It's a long story. Come with me and I'll tell you about it."

He tapped his foot against a pile of books on the floor. "Where do you want to go?"

"To see my beach."

Though he glanced at me sharply, he put on his worn tweed jacket that must've been his favorite, and we made our way outside to join a stream of people enjoying the bright afternoon. After we crossed Market and progressed onto quieter side streets, I told him that I'd quit my job, too, and that I was going to work at the food bank. The news startled him, but he told me it was Appleton-Smith's loss, that the food bank was lucky. Then he abruptly stopped on the sidewalk.

"Where's your beach, Sara? Why do you want me to go to your apartment?"

"It's a surprise," I said. "You're going to have to trust me. And you don't like trusting anyone, do you? We've covered this ground."

He stood facing me, his hands in his jacket pockets. "You don't know how hard it was not to call you this week."

"Why didn't you?"

He was having trouble meeting my eyes today. "My mother spending two days telling me I'm a worthless excuse for a human being was part of it. That, and I thought Jake might be the one to answer the phone."

I tilted my head. "Did you really think I was seeing him?"

He shrugged uncomfortably. "It doesn't matter. You were right to end things with me; I just didn't want to believe it. Once you convinced me, the best thing for me to do was disappear from your life."

"Aaron, I love you. I don't want you to disappear. How much more convincing do you need?"

He closed his eyes. "Sara, being in love with me isn't a good idea."

It hurt. He wouldn't look at me again after he opened his eyes, but then I remembered his angry, bitter poems. We had a trek ahead of us, one we both needed to take. I took Aaron's hand and pulled. "Do I have to drag you? I will, you know."

Aaron smiled reluctantly. "That's always been my problem. You're impossible to resist."

When I put my key in the upstairs door, I heard a giggle and a little voice say, "She's home, she's home," followed by small running footsteps. What was going on? I drew Aaron towards my bedroom. When I opened my door, I heard the sound of waves and smelt a distinct odor of the sea. I smiled. On my desk a tape deck played the sound of waves crashing, and a piece of slimy green seaweed now crowned a much larger pile of sand on the floor. As beaches went, it was one of the best.

When Aaron stepped into my room after me, he stopped, transfixed as he took in the blue walls shimmering with marine life.

"What do you think?" I asked.

"It's wonderful," he said, gazing around. "I don't see you a week, and you transform your life. You should've sent me packing sooner."

"I had help. Come here." I pulled him down on the floor next to me. We sat with our backs against my bed, sand and ocean at our feet, the golden peacock in the periphery of my vision. I'd finally figured out that glittering peacocks had little to do with Aaron and a lot to do with me, but it'd been a long journey I might not have made without him. I could return the favor.

Aaron rested his arms on his bent knees. "Sara, you're generous to share your beach with me, but I don't deserve it."

I took his hand and turned it palm up. "You told me once hands can change over time, but how could they unless their owners were capable of change, too?" I traced my finger down his lifeline. "Your life isn't over, Aaron. You're not beyond redemption yet." I put his hand between the two of mine and held it in my lap. "I'd like to tell you about my father."

He looked as if I'd just started carving a pound of flesh out of him, but he said, "I'd like to hear."

I told him about what had happened when I was in high school and about breakfast this morning.

"Of course you didn't cause your parents' divorce," he said gently. "You weren't responsible for what your father did."

"It might be obvious to you, but I was so ashamed, I never told anyone, not even Amanda. I resented him, and he punished me for it as best he could. I was no match when I tried to punish him back. It's crazy, we've spent all these years acting like it never happened. I told myself not to think about it, that it wouldn't matter if I didn't let it. But it always did. You guessed, didn't you?"

"Pretty close, anyway." Taking his hand from mine, Aaron brushed a strand of my hair back from my face. "But you dealt with it on your own, which is what you had to do, I guess." His sapphire eyes, tired and red around the edges, searched my face. "Oh, Sara, what I'd give—"

The tape ended with a click. He rested his arm on top of the bed.

I waited but he shook his head. "I've spent the week trying to let go of you," he said. "You know I don't even have a picture of you? I've looked and looked."

"Will you tell me about Monica?"

His face fell. "So that's why I'm here. I suppose I owe it to you. Having you hate me is hard to face, but maybe it'll make it easier for both of us in the end."

Would I really hate him, I wondered? How awful could it be? Aaron folded his hands in front of him and appeared to study three fish halfway up the wall drawn to look like characters from Star Trek—

Vulcans or Romulans, I couldn't tell. Of course, I hadn't seen each episode six times. Aaron seemed off in another world.

"I'm listening," I prompted.

He sighed. "I thought things couldn't get any worse, but here goes. I met Monica at business school. She was sophisticated, clever, amusing. We had an affair. After graduation she wanted to move to Europe, and she wanted me to go with her. Though I was fascinated by her, I knew she wasn't right for me, and I didn't want to tie my life to hers. She was furious when I took the job here. She went to Paris where she promptly met and married Henri. She wasn't one to waste time.

"I was lonely at first in San Francisco, and like a fool, I wrote to her. Come to Paris to visit, she wrote back. When I got there, it was like she and I had never broken off. When I got back here, I started seeing Kate, but I told myself I hadn't made any commitments, and when an opportunity came up at work to go to Europe, I went again. Henri didn't seem to care. After that, things got more serious with Kate, and she moved in with me, but I took another trip to Paris, and Monica came out here once. She even met Kate who never suspected anything.

"When Kate got fired and found a new job in New York, I made plans to transfer to Merrisock's New York office. Kate would go first and get us an apartment. Monica thought I was getting too serious about Kate, so just as Kate was set to leave, Monica called and let something slip about our affair. When I got home that night, Kate was gone, no note, nothing. I found out she was staying at a friend's. Finally she agreed to see me. She was furious. She accused me of two-timing her, which I had. I admitted everything, apologized, and told her I loved her. Which I did."

"She wouldn't forgive you?"

"I knew I had to give Monica up, no question, but when Kate asked if I was going to, I hesitated. Not long, not even a second, but enough for her to catch on that it felt like a sacrifice. And at that point, she'd already been through so much. She didn't speak to me for two years. I pleaded, sent flowers, even showed up at her New York apartment, everything I could think of. After a while I realized if I were her, I wouldn't forgive me either. The friend Kate stayed with, Mindy, despises me to this day. That's who Amanda talked to, by the way. Amanda wanted me to guarantee I'd changed my ways."

"Monica said all your women left on good terms."

Aaron gave me a chiding look. "Monica is an amazing liar."

She certainly is, I thought. "All right, what happened after Kate?"

"I went on with Monica. I told her if she ever did that to me again, it was over, so she put up with whoever I was seeing out here, but I was also more careful about keeping my distance. I never lived with anybody again."

"Then there was Elizabeth."

Aaron kept his voice flat and matter of fact. "Then there was Elizabeth. I suppose I thought she could fix me and my vices. Divinity school was absolutely right for her, even if I wasn't."

"You kept seeing Monica?"

"By that time our affair had been going on eight years. I talked to her once a week on the phone. It was almost like I was married to her. She was upset about Elizabeth until she met her and figured out she could wrap her around her finger because it never occurred to Elizabeth not to trust me. Eventually it got too painful. Rather than go on lying, I withdrew. Elizabeth got the hint and found someone else."

"Why didn't you drop Monica? Just because Kate didn't forgive you didn't mean Elizabeth wouldn't."

He shook his head. "I couldn't tell Elizabeth; I couldn't do that to her. The guy she'd been involved with before me, when I said he was abusive, that included being sexually abusive. It took forever before she trusted me enough to have any kind of physical relationship. Betraying her sexually was one of the worst things I could've done."

I could imagine Aaron with Elizabeth—patient, gentle, perceptive, but always keeping part of himself back. Ultimately refusing to be vulnerable. Ultimately manipulative. "Freezing her out was better?"

He looked sad and didn't answer.

"Are you still in love with her?" I'd asked him this before but figured I had a better chance at the truth this time.

Aaron looked down at his hands resting on his knees. "I don't think I ever was. I cared about Elizabeth, I thought with time it would happen, but it never did. That was probably the real problem."

I took a breath. I wasn't sure I wanted to go any further. "And then there was me. Or were there others after Elizabeth?"

"No others, and you weren't supposed to happen. When I first met you, you seemed so on your own at work, I thought maybe I could help you. But after the night on the beach, I couldn't get you out of my head. I'd tell myself I was a fool, I was torturing us both, I should leave you alone. And then I'd call. What I didn't want was another affair like I had with Monica or, worse, turn you into another Monica. That's why I was devastated when you wouldn't leave Mark. And then, miraculously, you showed up at my apartment, and you were mine. For a while, anyway."

This was all very interesting, but there were other things I wanted to know. "When you went to Paris at Christmas, you slept with Monica, didn't you?"

"Yes."

His answer was like a stab. I pictured Monica smiling at me in her low-cut green dress. "And a week and half ago?" I asked. "Did you both lie to me about that?"

Aaron shook his head. "No. Not that I expect you to believe me."

"Why not? You had opportunity, motive."

Aaron paused, his expression pained. "I was sick of the guilt, and I actually didn't want her anymore. I had you. Of course, I didn't realize ending things with Monica meant sacrificing you. If I had, I wonder what my choice would've been. When I called to tell her it was over, Monica accused me of being sentimental and idiotic, asking me what had changed, my tie to her was greater than it'd ever be to anyone else. Which is my greatest fear. She showed up without being invited, but it let me make it clear that she and I were through."

"If you broke with her, why didn't you just tell me? It wasn't like Kate and Elizabeth."

"Sara." He closed his eyes. "This is what I've dreaded you finding out. This is what I couldn't admit to. Monica was here in February, too."

I looked over at my beach. The seaweed had started to ooze off the sand onto the floor. "When in February?"

"After you left Mark. After we started sleeping together." He looked towards the window, anywhere but at me. "She called the end of January when I thought you were out of my life, and I said, sure, come visit. And when she got here, I didn't tell her no. Even after all you and I had been through. Even though I almost couldn't work because you were all I thought about. Monica was good at making me feel impervious, detached, like the world couldn't get at me. With you I felt all sorts of other things that, to be honest, I had a hard time facing. Looking back, maybe I believed Monica was all I deserved. And then later, when I allowed myself to want more, I'd already done damage."

He'd cheated on me that very first week? This was a blow I hadn't expected. I'd given myself to him. I'd trusted him. No wonder he'd so steadfastly refused to discuss Monica. I narrowed my eyes. "So all your talk about cheating being distasteful and ethically repugnant—"

"I absolutely deserve to have those words thrown in my face. The thing is, I do think cheating is ethically repugnant, not to mention despicable and unforgiveable."

I was noncommittal. "What exactly happened two weeks ago?"

"Letting Monica stay at my apartment was incredibly stupid, I should've packed her off to a hotel, but I did sleep on the couch. I thought I could protect you, protect myself. I was an idiot. When you told me you'd seen her, you can't imagine what went through my head, but I don't think she intended to split us up. She wanted to show me she could manipulate you so I'd keep the affair going and you'd never know. You'd like and trust her like Elizabeth did."

I realized if Aaron had decided to go along with Monica's story, the two of them could've played me for a fool for quite a while. But Aaron hadn't chosen that option. It pleased me to picture Monica fuming right now in Paris. "You didn't tell Monica about wanting to quit your job."

"There's a lot about me she doesn't know."

"Are you still in love with her?" Tears filled my eyes as I looked at the floor, waiting for his answer.

"Oh, Sara. What I feel for Monica is fury mixed with self-loathing. Elizabeth only trusted Monica because she trusted me. I was the one who betrayed her. I was the one who betrayed Kate; I was the one who betrayed you. I can be angry with Monica, but I have only myself to blame."

For a moment I almost felt sorry for Monica because I saw now that she was in love with Aaron, and that he'd never really loved her back. It was why she'd been so desperate to keep her sexual hold on him.

"You said once I reminded you of somebody. Was it Kate?"

After a second, Aaron nodded.

"You've never forgiven her, have you?"

"What, for getting fired? That's long past."

"No, I mean for her not forgiving you about Monica. You expected her to. Maybe you even counted on it."

He shut his eyes. "Sara, just tell me you hate me and never want to see me again."

"Are you still in love with her?"

He lifted his hands, exasperated. "You keep asking about love, but I'm not sure I'm capable of it."

"Negative two and a half for honesty. Let's try again. Are you still in love with her?"

Aaron looked up at the ceiling. "I've lost track. Who am I supposed to be in love with?"

I suppressed a smile. "Kate."

"It was such a long time ago."

"Answer."

"I used to think I was. And then there was you. I should be going."

He started to get up, but I grabbed his arm and pulled him back down. "No. You owe me this, every last detail."

"Sara, have some pity. It's been an awful, painful, humiliating week."

"Too bad," I said cheerfully. "So you had some people yell at you. It's not the end of the world."

"If it were only that. I've had to admit I've become someone I don't respect. When I let my aunt look at my hand last Christmas, she told me I had a thousand deaths ahead of me. Ego deaths I can survive, but not being able to write—" He paused. "I used to think it took pain to write poetry, but this has been about as painful as anything I can imagine." He lifted a palm. "You've heard all the sordid details. Besides I'm sorry, there's not much more to say. Sara, let me go. I'm so tired I can hardly think."

The floor beneath me was beginning to feel hard. I shifted.

"Aaron, I'm not Kate."

He frowned.

"So you hesitated," I said. "You should've broken free earlier, but you finally did it."

He shook his head, suspicious. "How could you possibly trust me again?"

I looked at his hands. Instinct, intuition, or blind faith, there were some things I knew for sure, like Deming's Fourteen Points. "Okay, you've lied to me and betrayed me, and at times you were pretty rotten to Kate and Elizabeth. And you've also coached me and encouraged me and taken care of me when I needed it. I know you're capable of caring about other people, Aaron. You really did care about Kate and Elizabeth, and I think you care about me. You should've told me the truth from the beginning, but you deserve some credit for finally dumping Monica. In my mind, clemency's not out of the question."

There was a second of silence. "Amanda accused me of irresponsibility with you," he said slowly, "and she was right. You're better off without me."

"I thought you made a deal with Amanda."

"We underestimated you. You'll do fine on your own."

I saw that we'd gone as far with the beach as we could. I rose and offered Aaron my hand. "Come on, next stop. Don't bother arguing. You don't get to go home until I say so."

Aaron reluctantly let me pull him up and lead him down the hallway past the violin woman forever frozen on one side of the camera. I loved being able to move through three-dimensional space. So many more possibilities. As we passed the living room, I heard Jake talking to Karla, but it wasn't the time to stop. We took the back staircase to the roof, our feet crunching the rock and tar paper surface as we stepped on it. The sun, much lower now in the western china blue sky, cast a heartbreaking amber glaze on the city. The wind blew coolly enough to make me wish I'd worn a sweater. Though the view was superb, I crossed my arms in front of my chest and kept my eyes on Aaron. I was counting on the power of topography. After all, it'd always worked with me.

"You know, except that we're so screwed up, we're two pretty capable people," I said. "The damage hasn't gone so far that we can't repair it. If not me, Aaron, who is it you're going to trust, who will you let close? Give me names."

He paused, weighing his words. "Maybe there's too much darkness in me, Sara. I'm not a risk you should take."

I shivered and folded my arms more tightly. "We all have shadow, Aaron. We all make mistakes. What you've done doesn't disqualify you from all future happiness."

Aaron took off his worn jacket and put it around me. "Here. You don't have to freeze to death on my account."

"You are so stubborn." I held out my hand. "Tell me you want to be alone, Aaron Lambert. Tell me that's what you really want."

The wind whipped around us as I held my breath. The years of distrust and distance were evident in his eyes as he struggled with wanting again what he'd resigned himself to do without. You can do it, Aaron, I thought. Step through this miasma of doubt and self-blame. There's a ledge on the other side.

He stared at the hand I offered and at last spoke with difficulty.

"It's not what I want at all." As his hand tentatively wrapped around mine on that windy rooftop, I knew I'd finally finished the journey I'd begun when Mark left for Georgetown. When Aaron pulled me close, I was surprised at how long and how tightly he held me, but I suppose I shouldn't have been. He really had had a wretched time of it.

At last his arms loosened and he looked at me with wonder. "I was so convinced I'd lost you."

I brushed a few grains of sand off his scratchy jaw. "Do you know you look like hell? Not that I mind. It's nice to know you're human."

Bemused but happy, Aaron started to speak, faltered, and then laughed. "Why is this so hard to say? Because I'm terrified, probably. I love you, Sara, absolutely and completely. You're not locked out of my heart; you exist right in its very center. There's no one in the world I'd rather share my life with."

As I kissed Aaron that glittering late afternoon, it was April, T. S. Eliot's cruelest month, mixing memory and desire, but that was the appropriate business of life. Pain and joy, conflict and transcendence—inevitably they all get mixed up together, sometimes to the point it's hard to tell which is which.

I pulled back. "Does this mean I have to like Patricia?"

Aaron laughed. "You know the guy Elizabeth started seeing after me? I can't stand him."

Good, I thought with satisfaction.

I heard voices from below call my name. Holding Aaron's hand, I cautiously crept to the edge of the roof to see Jake, Karla, Jason, and Eric on the sidewalk below, their heads craned up, Jason and Eric in their tie-dyed shirts jumping up and down with excitement. Jake cupped his hands around his mouth. "We're going to the park. Family outing. See you later."

As I waved at the temporary family, I wondered if Amanda would mind Jake living in her room until she got back. Aaron and I stayed on the roof talking of poetry and food banks and love until stars showed above the city in the blue-violet evening sky. ATBW, Amanda later told me. Appropriately terrified but willing. Usually shows up around stage six or seven.

More Books by Karen Lynn Allen

Beaufort 1849

When Jasper Wainwright returns to Beaufort after a long absence, he meets his cousin's beautiful niece, Cara. Jasper is an abolitionist and Cara will inherit hundreds of slaves one day, so it's fortunate Cara wants nothing to do with him. Jasper's cousin, Henry, wants Jasper to settle in Beaufort. Jasper's former slave, now friend, Spit Jim, wants Jasper to leave Beaufort as soon as possible. Even though Beaufort is full of beauty, culture and charm, Jasper knows he needs to leave. He can no longer drink, and drinking and dueling are the predominant pastimes of men in Beaufort. And yet the writings of a certain Eustace Woods gives Jasper hope that Beaufort and the rest of the South could gradually evolve away from slavery with the right encouragement. Maybe that's the reason why he stays and stays . . .

Universal Time

Cait doesn't have time to flit about the Universe with Atraxis. As the divorced mother of two girls, she's fully busy with her job, her children, and even babysitting her ex-husband's new baby. Yes, she might find visiting alien planets interesting, but she's just an ordinary human and can't understand why Atraxis is so set on wooing her to be his wife. Her ex-sister-in-law, Nancy, tells her to give Atraxis a chance, but Nancy has no idea what she's talking about. Blue-skinned aliens, goggle-eyed space journalists, and saving far-flung planets from destruction, all before breakfast, are not Cait's cup of tea. If only she could make Atraxis understand . . .

www.ingramcontent.com/pod-product-compliance
Lightning Source LLC
Chambersburg PA
CBHW072357110726
47909CB00003B/727

* 9 7 8 0 9 6 7 1 7 8 4 4 8 *